BLOOD MOON

Heather Graham *and* Jon Land

TOR

A TOM DOHERTY ASSOCIATES BOOK

NEW YORK

BLOOD MOON

Copyright © 2022 by Heather Graham and Jon Land

A Tor Book
Published by Tom Doherty Associates
120 Broadway
New York, NY 10271

www.tor-forge.com

Tor® is a registered trademark of Macmillan Publishing Group, LLC.

The Library of Congress Cataloging-in-Publication Data is available upon request.

ISBN 978-0-7653-8971-8 (hardcover)
ISBN 978-0-7653-8972-5 (ebook)

Our books may be purchased in bulk for promotional, educational, or business use. Please contact your local bookseller or the Macmillan Corporate and Premium Sales Department at 1-800-221-7945, extension 5442, or by email at MacmillanSpecialMarkets@macmillan.com.

First Edition: 2022

Printed in the United States of America

0 9 8 7 6 5 4 3 2 1

BLOOD MOON

BY HEATHER GRAHAM AND JON LAND

The Rising

OTHER BOOKS BY HEATHER GRAHAM

Flawless
The Hidden
The Forgotten
The Silenced
The Dead Play On
The Betrayed
The Hexed
The Cursed
Waking the Dead
The Night Is Forever
The Night Is Alive
The Night Is Watching
Let the Dead Sleep
The Uninvited
The Unspoken
The Unholy
The Unseen
An Angel for Christmas
The Evil Inside
Sacred Evil
Heart of Evil
Phantom Evil

Night of the Vampires
The Keepers
Ghost Moon
Ghost Night
Ghost Shadow
The Killing Edge
Night of the Wolves
*Home in Time for
  Christmas*
Unhallowed Ground
Dust to Dust
Nightwalker
Deadly Gift
Deadly Harvest
Deadly Night
The Death Dealer
The Last Noel
The Séance
Blood Red
The Dead Room
Kiss of Darkness
The Vision

The Island
Ghost Walk
Killing Kelly
The Presence
Dead on the Dance Floor
Picture Me Dead
Haunted
Hurricane Bay
A Season of Miracles
Night of the Blackbird
Never Sleep with Strangers
Eyes of Fire
Slow Burn
Night Heat
Haunted Destiny
The Unforgiven
*The Forbidden and the
  Unknown*
Sound of Darkness
Aura of Night
Voice of Fear

OTHER BOOKS BY JON LAND

The Alpha Deception
*Betrayal (nonfiction)
**Black Scorpion: The Tyrant
  Reborn*
*Blood Diamonds
*The Blue Widows
The Council of Ten
*Day of the Delphi
*Dead Simple
*Dolphin Key
The Doomsday Spiral
The Eighth Trumpet
*The Fires of Midnight
The Gamma Option
*Hope Mountain
*Keepers of the Gate
*Kingdom of the Seven

Labyrinth
*The Last Prophecy
The Lucifer Directive
**Margaret Truman's Murder
  at the CDC*
**Margaret Truman's Murder
  on the Metro*
The Ninth Dominion
The Omega Command
The Omicron Legion
Pandora's Temple
*The Pillars of Solomon
**The Seven Sins: The Tyrant
  Ascending*
*Strong as Steel
*Strong at the Break
*Strong Cold Dead

*Strong Darkness
*Strong Enough to Die
*Strong from the Heart
*Strong Justice
*Strong Light of Day
*Strong Rain Falling
*Strong to the Bone
*Strong Vengeance
*Takedown (nonfiction)
The Tenth Circle
The Valhalla Testament
The Vengeance of the Tau
Vortex
*A Walk in the Darkness
*The Walls of Jericho

*Published by Forge Books

BLOOD
MOON

BLOOD MOON

Heather Graham *and* Jon Land

TOR

A TOM DOHERTY ASSOCIATES BOOK

NEW YORK

BLOOD MOON

Copyright © 2022 by Heather Graham and Jon Land

A Tor Book
Published by Tom Doherty Associates
120 Broadway
New York, NY 10271

www.tor-forge.com

Tor® is a registered trademark of Macmillan Publishing Group, LLC.

The Library of Congress Cataloging-in-Publication Data is available upon request.

ISBN 978-0-7653-8971-8 (hardcover)
ISBN 978-0-7653-8972-5 (ebook)

Our books may be purchased in bulk for promotional, educational, or business use. Please contact your local bookseller or the Macmillan Corporate and Premium Sales Department at 1-800-221-7945, extension 5442, or by email at MacmillanSpecialMarkets@macmillan.com.

First Edition: 2022

Printed in the United States of America

0 9 8 7 6 5 4 3 2 1

For Tom Doherty and Bob Gleason,
who walk among giants
And the amazing folks at the Goddard Space Center,
who reach for the stars

There is a certain enthusiasm in liberty, that makes human nature rise above itself, in acts of bravery and heroism.
—Alexander Hamilton

BLOOD MOON

FROM SAMANTHA DIXON'S JOURNAL

"I HAVE TO GO," Alex said, beneath the crystalline sky dotted with what looked like a massive display of the Northern Lights, residue from what we'd unleashed on Alcatraz Island.

The soldiers who'd come in the Zodiac rafts were all dead and Raiff, our enigmatic protector, was prepping one of the Zodiacs for a quick departure.

"I'm not coming?" I asked, fearing the answer.

"You can't," Alex said, his voice cracking.

I should have been relieved, glad to resume my normal life. Except it could never be normal again, not after what I'd experienced, what I knew now. Alex had been my life for three whirlwind days, and I couldn't bear the thought of parting like this.

I didn't know what to do or say, so I just hugged him as tight as I'd ever hugged anyone. And I wouldn't let go, no matter how many seconds passed. Because as long as I was holding him, Alex couldn't go off somewhere without me, to continue fighting this war. As long as I was holding him, I'd know we were both safe.

Alex let go first and eased me away.

"I'm never going to see you again, am I?" I managed, through the thick clog that had formed in my throat, not afraid to cry, because I saw tears welling in his eyes too.

"We don't know that. We don't know anything really. That's one thing I've learned from all this."

I tapped the side of my head. "What about . . ."

"We'll figure something out."

"It'll kill you, Alex."

He forced a smile. "I'm tough, remember?" The smile faded from his expression and he took my shoulders in his grasp, squeezing lightly. "I don't want to leave you either."

"Then don't."

Alex looked back toward Raiff, who was waiting for him in the Zodiac, as patiently as he could manage. "There's nothing left for me here. You still have a life, a family."

I turned and looked back toward my parents, who were shaking from the chill breeze and all they'd just been through, barely managing to survive. They were speaking with Dr. Donati, but kept looking toward Alex and me.

"I can take care of myself, in case you've forgotten."

"No," Alex said, smiling tightly. "I haven't forgotten."

"What about the state championship?" I asked him, failing to muster even that much of a smile. "Who am I going to watch play now?"

"Friday night was the first game you ever went to."

"Guess I got bitten by the football bug."

Our eyes met, neither wanting to move.

"We'll see each other again," Alex said, his words barely audible. "I promise."

And then we were hugging again, and I waited for Alex to let go first again, because I never would have.

We take so much for granted, simple things mostly, like our routines, our dreams, our goals. Until that football game Friday night, when it had all started, I was focused on graduating as senior class valedictorian. I had applied early to CalTech, the California Institute for Technology, to study space science to pursue a career at NASA.

My dream, my goal.

But no more, not after I answered Alex's call on Saturday night when he had no one else to turn to. I'd been there for him then and I knew I couldn't refuse him now.

We were hugging, and then we weren't. Alex was standing before me, and then he wasn't. His raft left first, Raiff doing the piloting, and I glued my eyes to Alex until the fog swallowed the small craft, and it was time for me to go too.

I was naive to think I could just walk back into my life, after all that had happened. Naive to believe it was over, when it had only begun. Naive to believe I could erase the last three days and just walk back into my old world.

Maybe if I had known what was to come, I wouldn't have answered the phone. But if I hadn't, no one's dreams would've had a chance to come true anyway, including mine. If I hadn't answered that call Saturday night, there would've been no college to go to, no graduation to attend, no valedictorian speech to give.

We thought we had stopped the rising of an enemy committed to destroying civilization, as it was known today. What we didn't know was how many generations, how many centuries and eons ago, that rising had been set into motion. Nor, as I watched Alex disappear into the fog over San Francisco Bay, did I have any notion that the next battle to stop the rising would be fought not in the light of day, but beneath the shadow of a blood moon.

PROLOGUE

THE MONK

Admont, Austria; April 27, 1865

May God have mercy on my soul.

The monk knew he was going to die; he'd known it ever since he'd undertaken this mission.

The smoke rising from the fires that were consuming the abbey itself and the vast monastic archives dating back to Admont's founding in 1074 turned the monk's lungs raw. Embers left flecks of char across his thick woolen robes. Yet he remained comfortable in the darkness, because darkness was his life. Other than a few glances at his reflection in the abbey windows, he had no sense of his own appearance, beyond the long hair normally tucked under his hood and the thick beard that stretched past his throat. Those few times he'd caught his reflection had revealed a pale and sallow visage, from too much time spent in silent prayer and not enough exposure to the sun.

But that didn't matter, *he* didn't matter.

Only the book did. The book that had been handed down to him to safeguard for the rest of his life. Eventually, when he grew feeble and infirm, a successor would be chosen and sent in his wake to join the monastic order here at Admont Abbey and take up the same mission until the inevitability of age found that man too. It would continue that way until the book was needed, until the time came when the Resistance of which he was a part could figure out how to use its contents to save this world.

The monk clutched the book tighter against his chest, the way a mother might hold a newborn, certain whoever had set the abbey ablaze was coming. He'd glimpsed only shadows in the course of his flight, sprawling dark specters rendered absurdly large by the splash of flames.

The book needed to be protected at all costs. Written in the language of his world that no one native to this one could ever decipher, it contained the means to fight back against the enemies of freedom, hope, of life itself. An insidious, unstoppable evil force committed to stamping out resistance at all costs, both here and back home in a world he would never see again.

The monk had made his escape from the abbey via the cobweb-stricken and rat-infested catacombs thought sealed centuries before and, thus, long forgotten. In addition to the book, his predecessor had passed on the location of the secret entrance and a map to guide him through the many warrens of the mazelike confines he had long ago committed to memory.

The earthen ground and walls smelled of stale, rancid dirt, moist and especially rank in areas where groundwater had leeched in and pooled. This spring had been especially rainy in the region, and the monk feared the ancient integrity of the catacombs might be compromised enough to result in collapse, entombing him for eternity along with the book that provided the only hope for the survival of not one, but two worlds.

He had only the flame of a single lantern by which to guide him and, suddenly, that flame flickered in the face of a cold breeze that chilled the monk to his very bones. The route he was following through the catacombs lay beneath a vast library with the largest assemblage of man's accumulated knowledge anywhere in the world, amounting to over seventy thousand volumes displayed and nearly twice that number held in storage. The most valuable items in the vast collection included more than 1,400 original manuscripts, the oldest dating back to the eighth century, and the 530 incunabula, books printed before 1500.

The monk had always been struck by the beauty of the abbey sculptor Josef Stammel's creations, especially his "Four Last Things," which consisted of the oversized figures of Death, Judgment, Heaven, and Hell that adorned the library's great hall. The monk found those to be particularly appropriate, given the nature of his mission.

He was thinking specifically of the figure of Death, when he spotted another of the shadows he recalled being splayed against the walls of the burning abbey above. It loomed before him, out of the reach of the meager flame lighting his way. The monk squeezed himself into a depression in the earthen wall to hide within the darkness, extinguishing the flame between two fingers. He heard footsteps that squished into the sodden floor of the catacombs and a guttural retch that sounded like labored breathing.

Whatever the hulking dark shape was, it was no shadow. Its steps grew louder, a dull red glow brightening as the shape advanced.

Its eyes, the monk thought, certain he was facing some otherworldly creature he'd been warned about. He sucked in his breath and held it as the thing neared his hiding place, drawing even.

From the dark recesses of his hideaway, the monk could make out no features other than a pair of blazing eyes the color of blood. Those eyes burned through the darkness, silhouetting the massive shape of a creature that seemed to slither more than walk, making the monk think of a snake with arms and legs.

He began taking soft, shallow breaths again only when the red glow had passed, the tunnel still and quiet again. He had no way to relight the flame of his lantern and left it behind, only the book to carry as he felt his way blindly to the secret exit that, according to the map, would spill out onto the banks of the Enns River. The monk had long kept a small boat hidden there. Not big enough to get him very far, but at the very least away from whatever monsters had come to the monastery on his trail.

Why now? What was happening?

Having spent thirty years in this world, he'd lulled himself into believing he was safe, that the guise of a monk performing his penance in an isolated monastery had served him well in this regard. Believing that he would safeguard the precious book until the time came to pass on that responsibility to his successor. Now the monk knew otherwise, knew enemies from his native world had tracked him down. He couldn't fail in his mission, couldn't let the book end up in their possession at all costs, not with the future of two worlds at stake.

The monk followed the bends and curves of the tunnel to reach a wooden door, camouflaged by dried, layered mud. Open that door and the night was his, just a few hundred meters from the shores of the Enns, where his small boat was camouflaged by brush and stray branches he'd made look random.

Only the door wouldn't open, not even budge. The dread realization that the route beyond back to the surface had indeed collapsed, his greatest fear realized. Either from this wet season or another, it mattered not.

The monk cradled the book in both arms across his chest. If he buried it down here amid the muck and mire, the book would likely never be found. Keep it, and the hope it promised might die with him. The monk found neither of those alternatives acceptable.

Think!

The monk had not come here to fail, hadn't spent thirty years planning for this very moment only to accept death and defeat. He was a warrior whose monk's sash concealed the scars of battle and whose hands that now held a book had once wielded all manner of weapon.

Think!

And then the answer came to him, absurd in its obviousness. The book could be salvaged, preserved against all odds. His life was forfeit in any case; survival meant capture and capture risked him revealing the hiding place for the book he'd settled upon at last, where no one would ever think to look or succeed in finding it if they tried.

The monk started on again, energized by a fresh resolve. His pace quickened, the map long committed to memory guiding him to the point where it was almost as if he could see through the dark.

And then he could.

Because red eyes were glowing behind him, not just one pair but several, having picked up his trail from the burning abbey above. The monk had presided over enough funerals to know the rancid stench of death, realizing it wasn't dirt these creatures smelled like at all, but rot and decay. As if, somehow, they'd been fashioned of the earth in which the dead were buried.

The monk ran, trusting in the map and his memory, the book pressed against his thudding heart. The heavy thump of his footsteps drowned out that sound and all others, except for the scratchy breathing of the things giving chase through the tight confines of the tunnel.

He kept running, maintaining the distance between him and the red glow. A second secret passageway lay somewhere just ahead, and the monk pressed his shoulder against the wall to feel for it. He tapped about its earthen mold, until he struck something solid. Heaved his shoulder forward with all his strength.

The wood didn't give. Then a faint reddish glow broke though the darkness behind him, catching him in its spray. He thrust out with his shoulder again, felt something splinter down by the latch as heavy, sloshing footsteps pounded the ground in his wake.

The monk slammed into the door once, twice, three more times, the rank death smell flooding his nostrils. The door finally gave, and he surged through and charged up a set of stairs through the darkness, the door that would take him into the library gaining shape, almost there . . .

Then the monk felt something grasp his ankle. He thought at first it must be a hand, only it didn't feel like a hand, at least not one he'd ever felt the touch of before. Whatever grasped him seemed to compress itself, while it squeezed. In spite of that, its grasp was stronger than any he'd ever felt, the pain giving way to numbness, before a second rubbery grip fastened on his other leg.

His stomach turned at the grave stench. The familiar reddish glow dully illuminated the door at the top of the earthen-covered wood stairs, brightening as more of the creatures descended upon him.

The monk tried desperately to kick free of the twin grasps wrapped tight around his ankles. He felt them pulling, his maintaining a stalemate the best he could do when a tremor shook the world. The earthen ceiling of the catacombs began to rain dirt downward. First in fissures, then in blankets, and finally waves.

The walls of the burning abbey above must have given way, the entire building crumpling in upon itself and collapsing the secret underground tunnels. The monk held his breath against the dirt threatening to choke his nose and mouth, the red glow swallowed by the walls tumbling inward. He felt the wet grasp on his ankles slacken and then slip off, creating the brief opening he needed to lurch the rest of the way up the stairs, finding the door just as the creatures flailed for fresh purchase of him, dark clawlike hands that looked as if formed of mud protruding from the piles of dirt entombing them.

He held the book, the means to save this world, with one hand and worked the latch with the other, bursting through the door into a drainage culvert. The culvert had been designed and positioned to keep moisture from destroying the contents of the floors above him. The monk knew he was in the right place, that his memory had not betrayed him, just steps from the means to stash the book in the best possible place, where its secrets might be preserved.

He pressed himself against a wall that was moist and soft as clay. His hand nearly sank in when he ran it along the mushy contours for guidance, finding the second set of stairs leading to the library.

The heavy door at the top burst open, spraying shards of wood through the air, more of the dark creatures revealed pushing their way through in the deepening reddish hue. He couldn't go forward, couldn't go back, hope now and forever lost, the creatures coming for him from above. Then the monk remembered the object in his pocket, designed to provide a brief burst of light when its magnesium wick was ignited by a spark. For emergencies, though not at all like the one he faced now.

Clutching the book tightly against him in one hand, the monk used the other to yank the object from a pocket sewn into his robe as the rancid, stench-riddled things closed around him, choking his breath. He lowered the thick round husk of wood to the contours of his shoe and struck it to create friction and the spark he needed.

Nothing.

Hands dripping with rancid mud closed around the monk, his breath a memory as he felt their grips tighten and pull, intent on tearing him apart. He managed to strike the head of the wood husk against his shoe again.

Still nothing.

The pain was everywhere, his grasp on the wood and life itself slackening when he struck it against his shoe a third time. A burst of light blinded him but sent the creatures lurching away, uttering a collective high-pitched squeal that made the monk's ears ache.

He realized he was free and clutched the book again in both arms. He pushed himself up through the opening from which they had descended on him. The monk slammed and bolted what remained of the door behind him to buy the last bit of time he needed to preserve the book and save this world, as well as his own.

He was fifty feet from the door, smelling the rich vellum and paper comprising the shelves and shelves of volumes miraculously spared by the flames, when he heard the wood shatter. Almost instantly, the putrid stench of the creatures replaced the pleasant aroma he had known so well for thirty years.

He knew he was theirs, but not before he managed to save the book, and the hope it provided, for whoever came after him. His own fate was sealed but a much greater fate was about to be pre-served, as the monk disappeared into the sprawling stacks of the library.

ONE

BEFORE

Eighteen years ago . . .

Let us sacrifice our today so that our children can have a better tomorrow.

A.P.J. ABDUL KALAM

1

WASTELAND

"STAY WITH US!" SKYE, the leader of the fighters, ordered Raiff. "We can't protect you if you stray!"

The route they needed to cover would take them across an urban landscape dominated by collapsed or crumbling buildings. The machines, massive steel-tentacled monsters as big as buildings themselves, swept through the area, slicing away at anything that moved. The initial flank of Resistance fighters had emerged from their hiding spots to draw the machines' attention away from the small group using the rubble for camouflage, sacrifices to a higher purpose.

Raiff smelled death in the air. It rose from the bodies strewn amid the wreckage of a landscape once dominated by towers of gleaming glass and steel, now riddled with blight. Only eighteen years old, he had no recollection of anything but death and destruction. His earliest memories from childhood were of hiding from the machines, the tentacled monsters and fighter drones programmed to kill anything that moved.

Raiff drew even with Skye behind the remnant of a building's foundation.

"They're looking for us, aren't they?" he said to the woman he knew to be one of the Resistance's best fighters, having led missions that had taken down murderous machines comparable to these.

Skye almost managed a smile. "You figure that out all by yourself?"

Raiff looked at her, sharing enough in common with her physically so they appeared as brother and sister. Same dark hair, same soulful eyes somewhere between black and brown, same smile on those rare occasions when one came.

They both watched as a fighter drone descended from the gray, smoky sky toward a phalanx of fighters trying to draw the machines away from them. A silent burst of plasma fire blew the machines apart and spewed pieces of them in all directions.

"You must be awfully important," Skye said to him, easing herself back from the concealed position.

"I wish I knew why. It's not like I've ever done anything."

"Well, kid, you're about to."

Skye led the fighters enclosing Raiff through a gap in the rubble, seizing on a moment when the attention of all the machines looking for them was trained on their decoys. They covered the next hundred yards without incident, starting to believe they were actually going to make it when the fighter bringing up the rear stepped on a land mine.

"Oh, shit," he managed before he was vaporized into a red mist.

Raiff watched the rolling monsters and the fighter drones swing in their direction.

"Come on!" Skye roared, breaking into an all-out run down a rubble-strewn road that once had been the main artery for this city.

She managed to steady and fire her plasma grenade launcher as she ran, knocking out the hardware of one of the tentacled machines, jolting it to a halt in mid-stride. Raiff couldn't believe his eyes, never having witnessed one of the monsters stopped by a single shot.

Skye and other fighters trained their fire on two more of the towering things, never seeing the fighter drone hovering just behind them. Raiff screamed a warning just as it opened fire and felt Skye tackle him, using her body as cover amid the refuse.

"Stay down!" she blared into his ear.

Raiff felt a wash of heat and something wet soaking through his clothes. He heard Skye gasp and realized she'd been hit, as he eased himself out from under her and tried to drag her along with him after the drone had passed over them.

"No," Skye managed, "go!" Adding, when Raiff resisted, "Save yourself, save the mission . . ."

"Mission?"

"Go!"

Raiff jetted off, trying to find speed as he zigzagged through the obstacles in his path. No idea where he was going or what he would find if he got there. If only Elaina were here . . . Elaina would know what to do.

He heard the hum of another drone and dropped low, freezing too late to avert its motion sensors.

"Hey! Hey!"

He turned to find Skye on her knees, waving one arm while the other hung bloody and useless by her side.

"Hey, asshole, come get me!"

When the drone turned to do just that, Raiff sprinted off again, all caution thrown to the wind. Darting, leaping, and tearing along, all efforts aimed at concealment abandoned. He heard the sizzling hiss of the drone's fire and didn't bother looking back at the sound of Skye's final scream. Just kept running.

Toward where? For what?

Raiff cut between the splintered shapes of twin towers that had been snapped like matchsticks. His feet pounded atop a debris field, crunching over a combination of glass shards and human bones. Nothing before him that looked anything like the rendezvous point Skye and her fighters had been leading him to. Nothing before him at all.

He heard the familiar whine of a fighter drone settling into position and swung to find it frozen in the air, hovering fifty feet before him, a distance that made it look like they were face-to-face. Raiff squeezed his eyes closed, wondered what the next moment would feel like.

Boom!

Raiff opened his eyes to see the fighter drone explode. He dropped low to avoid the blast debris, turning as he rose to find a woman staring at him. She held a plasma grenade rifle in one arm, the other clutching a crying baby to her breast.

"Took you long enough to get here, kid," Elaina said to him.

2

CONVERGENCE

THOMAS DONATI CAUGHT UP with his NASA supervisor inside the elevator just before the door slid closed within the secret facility constructed in San Ramon, California. "You need to take a look at these figures."

"I have," Orson Wilder told him.

Wilder inserted a square, flat key into a slot tailored for it and turned it all the way to the right.

As the cab began its descent, Donati reached out and turned the pages Wilder was still holding around. "Right side up this time."

Wilder sneered, then nodded grudgingly. "What am I looking for?"

"Signs."

"Signs?"

"Of a potential cosmic celestial convergence of unprecedented proportions. Here, let me show you . . ."

The elevator whirred further downward.

"This earthquake in Tibet," Donati continued, "a rogue wave wiping out an entire island in the South China Sea, the inexplicable malfunction of our interstellar monitors located in the northeast Pacific Ocean." When Wilder failed to respond, Donati whipped a marker from his pocket and drew a circle on the elevator wall. "Picture this as the Earth. Here are the locations of the stimuli I just mentioned." Donati drew X's to accompany his continued narration. "Tibet, the South China Sea, the northeast Pacific Ocean. A neat line," he finished, drawing his marker across the elevator wall to connect them, "perfectly following the curvature of the Earth. We're talking about extreme seismic levels of quantum disruption, accompanied by radical spikes in the discharge of electromagnetic radiation. You see what I'm getting at here?"

"No, not really," Wilder said impatiently.

"Our lab exists on the same plane as these apparently random events. Our work could be causing disruptions leading to ripples in the time-space continuum. Or . . ."

The cab settled to a halt twenty stories underground between a million tons of steel and reinforced concrete.

"Or what?"

"The pattern could indicate contact from the other side of the doorway we're trying to open."

3

THE BRIDGE

SHE WAS A MOTHER, and one thing was imperative.

Saving her son.

"Take him, Raiff!" Elaina said, handing the infant over, once they had descended into one of the many underground bases used by the Resistance.

This one was different, though, Raiff realized. It hummed with electricity, far more than that normally provided by the limited power of the portable generators. It wasn't just the hum either; he felt something, like a constant vibration, at his very core.

"But—"

"No buts! We've been betrayed! They knew we were here, which means they know about our plan!"

"What *plan*?"

"Take him!" Elaina ordered, pushing the infant into Raiff's arms.

It was the first time he'd ever held a baby and he struggled for the right grasp. "You're the one who should go."

"You're the warrior, Raiff. Far better suited to protect him once you get there. And he'll need protection—both of us know that. It's only a matter of time before they come. They always come."

Raiff held the infant stiffly in his arms. *I'm just a boy myself,* he wanted to say. But he knew what Elaina would say in return because he'd heard the story so often of the time his own parents had been killed trying to do the same thing they were doing now.

Escape.

The Overlords were determined to seize absolute control and they placed

little value on life in general and certainly not when their rule was threat-
ened or questioned in any way.

But this was about more than escape. This was about survival.

"I don't know enough about the plan," Raiff said, holding his ground.

"Keep the boy safe—that's the plan. The others will find you when you get there."

Back down the tubular-shaped steel hall, the small-arms fire had become more sporadic, the last of their party falling to the enemy's vastly superior numbers and firepower.

"Go," Elaina said, her voice soft but emphatic. "There's no more time."

Her tone reassured him, made him feel there was still hope. Raiff wanted to ask her *why him?* Of all the fighters she could have chosen for this mission, why choose one who was no more than a kid? Raiff knew the infant was the key, the reason so many had given their lives to get him this far. Something about the infant was important enough to make a mother relinquish her own child.

"He knows the way," Elaina said, stroking the baby's head and watching his eyes widen as he looked at her, smiling at the loving touch.

"The way to what?"

Elaina backed off stiffly, the infant suddenly feeling unsteady in Raiff's grasp. "Trust me. This is our only chance. We can help them win, help them preserve their world and save ours in the process. The child is the key."

"You've got to come too, please!" Raiff implored. "I can't do this alone!"

Elaina wiped the tears that had started to spill from her eyes. "Somebody has to operate the controls from this end, and you don't know how. And someone needs to destroy the bridge once you're through so they can't follow. Take this," Elaina said, pressing a cylindrical object into his free hand.

"What is it?"

"You'll know when the time comes. It's the only weapon that can destroy . . ."

"Destroy *what*?" Raiff managed, pocketing the ball-sized object.

"Let's hope you never have to find out. Call it a precaution."

Elaina entered a sequence into an unmarked keypad, fingers dancing up, down, then up again. The heavy door before them spiraled open, disappearing into the walls contoured to its shape.

"Go!" she ordered. "You need to go *now*!"

4

SIGNS

THEY REMAINED INSIDE THE cab, even after the elevator door had slid open.

"All right," said Wilder, "what would you recommend?"

Donati hesitated before responding. "Shutter the lab."

Wilder thrust the pages out between them. "I couldn't shutter the lab even if I wanted to."

"Why?"

"You know full well why."

"I guess I don't."

"You think we're the ones in charge here, making the decisions, pulling the strings?" Wilder shook his head slowly. "Not even close. It's the people pulling *our* strings who call the shots from behind a curtain that would make the Wizard of Oz proud."

Wilder started to step from the elevator, but Donati latched a hand onto his forearm. "They don't know what we're dealing with here, *we* don't know what we're dealing with here."

"Are you trying to scare me, Doctor?"

"Inform you."

"And now you have." Wilder looked down at the hand still clamped to his suit jacket. "So if you don't mind . . ."

But Donati left it in place. "Shut the lab down, Orson. There's one more indicator I left out."

"And what's that?"

"The last energy readings for the quantum field displacement grids registered at an eight-point-five on the eigenstate of the wave function."

"So?"

Donati's eyes bore into Wilder's. "So our generators are only capable of producing slightly over seven."

He released Wilder's arm but the facility's director made no effort to leave, holding a hand before the door so it wouldn't close again. Wavering for sure, until his expression steeled anew.

"I'll take this under advisement, review your findings in more detail, Doctor."

"Then keep this in mind." Donati had his marker back out and ready by the time Wilder turned, adding a fourth X to the neat, symmetrical line around the Earth. "This is us, right here. We're next. I can't explain what's happening any better or clearer than that. I just know you need to shutter the lab until we understand this phenomenon better. Beyond that—"

The shrill screech of the emergency alarm blaring throughout the facility cut off his words before Donati could continue.

5

THE VOID

THE TUNNEL HUMMED AMID a strange yellow glow, alive with motion and sound. Raiff held the infant close, hoping he wasn't hurting it.

The tunnel was black; no, more than black. It was empty, a void like a gap carved out of the world. Which, he supposed, was essentially what it was. Tubular in design, yet without true form. Or form that could bend and stretch and re-form itself from moment to moment to manage crossing the contours of inner space when folded over, to allow passage between dimensions.

It felt as if they were floating more than walking. But Raiff couldn't walk fast. Every time he tried to pick up the pace, to reach the unseen end of the tunnel faster, he ran up against what felt like a buckling headwind. So he kept his pace to what the electromagnetic fields generated by the centrifuge allowed. Blended with its flow, finding the seams.

The tunnel shook suddenly, blotches of air seeming visible before him. It could be what he heard scientists refer to as a disruption, a minor ripple in what they called the space-time continuum. It was a term unchanged through time and, in this case, referred to the fact that this journey which would feel like mere minutes to him was actually unfolding over a significantly longer period in the world he was about to enter. The opening of the wormhole forming the spacebridge would trigger electromagnetic disturbances for thousands of miles, inevitable ripples and disruptions that posed the greatest danger when traversing the inter-dimensional space between worlds.

Raiff knew the source of the ripple originated back at the tunnel's start, coming moments after Elaina had closed the door. True to her word, she must have blown the chamber so Raiff and the baby couldn't be followed, sacrificing herself to buy them the time they needed. He looked back that way, covering the baby's eyes for some reason as he did.

He felt another ripple, like melting ice dragged down his spine, leaving a slick residue behind through his shirt. The chamber seemed full of air bubbles colliding with each other that passed straight through Raiff as he continued on, clutching the child tighter.

6

THE CREATURE

DONATI FELT THE WORLD quake, after he burst from the elevator against Wilder's protestations that he return to the surface with him. They couldn't save themselves from whatever had arrived from there, might not be able to save the facility from anywhere.

He felt the rumble in the pit of his stomach. He continued along the long hallway that curved to conform with the shale and limestone formations around this secret level containing Laboratory Z. He had the same sensation in his ears that he got when a plane was landing or taking off, a pressure building in his head. He tried to quicken his pace, but it was like pushing against the wind.

Then the walls began to bleed—not red, but black. Mercury-like droplets emerged through jagged cracks and fissures that ran from floor to ceiling, pooling and seeming to coagulate.

This can't be happening!

His whole life had been about pursing what many deemed impossible, yet this was the first time he had directly experienced it, as the black droplets continued to leak outward. *The wiring,* Donati realized, *the wires were melting!* The corridor lighting took on a strobe effect in the instant before he felt something scratching at his spine, leading him to swing back around.

Something was forming. A light, misty cloud that darkened as it absorbed the black pools of the mercury-like substance he thought to be melted wiring. And then Donati saw a shape congealing within the cloud, one that kept shifting from one moment to the next. Growing, expanding, at times resembling something vaguely humanoid.

It's looking at me! It knows I'm here!

Donati formed those thoughts, more of the impossible, as he

began to backpedal as fast as he could to maintain distance from the shifting cloud of what appeared to be a form of pure energy. Could this be an actual life-form from some world they'd built a bridge to and then, inadvertently, opened a doorway? Donati watched the dark shape within the gaseous cloud forming and re-forming, seeming to reconstitute itself from millisecond to millisecond.

Donati felt and heard a heavy rush of footsteps pounding at his rear, technicians fleeing Laboratory Z at the alarm's sounding. A few wearing lab coats, along with protective visors and goggles, jostled him as they rushed past. Their flight took them straight into the path of the still-darkening cloud that was coming their way.

They vanished into the cloud and their awful screams bubbled in Donati's ears. Blood, gore, and bone matter spewed outward as more technicians were absorbed into the shifting mass of energy. He turned and found the resolve to make himself run through the heaviness the air had taken on.

"No! No! No! Stop! Go back!"

His warnings to the next wave of technicians fleeing the lab went unheeded, their horrible, high-pitched screams enough to alert him to their fate. He sped on, reaching the entrance to Laboratory Z just after the last stream of the lab techs had poured through the reinforced steel door: twelve inches thick and built to keep anything from getting out of the lab.

Or in, *as the case may be,* Donati thought, as he pulled the door closed behind him and slammed back against the wall.

Watching the impregnable steel begin to buckle and bend.

7

LOST

RAIFF FOUND HIMSELF TOTALLY disoriented, all sense of place and direction lost. The tunnel seemed to have no shape, no beginning or end. Trudging on felt like passing through one of those infinity mirrors that stretch on forever.

Raiff had heard stories of those who'd entered chambers like this, only to never reach the other side, disappearing forever. Where had they gone? Raiff was struck by the dread fear it was nowhere at all, that they were stuck in these confines in a kind of scientific purgatory, doomed to exist only in a celestial ether for eternity.

Suddenly the air bubbles, pockets, or whatever they were began pounding him harder. Raiff realized he could no longer feel the floor beneath his feet, felt as if he was everywhere and nowhere at the same time.

Raiff didn't think he was going anywhere, pushing up against some kind of invisible, impenetrable wall, the air so heavy it was suddenly difficult to breathe. And just as he sucked harder to quench his lungs' thirst for air, the baby struggled to cry.

Something was wrong.

Then the world was shaking—not just the chamber, but the entire cosmos around it, a tear being ripped in the space-time continuum through which the others who'd disappeared must have slipped.

Others?

No, he couldn't let himself join them. The child was too important. The child was the only hope for not one, but two civilizations, thanks to whatever secret he possessed.

Raiff pressed on, but didn't feel as if he was moving. The ether darkened, the feeling that of entering storm clouds rife with electricity and static. He felt minor shocks, one after the other, the baby's wails indicating he was feeling them too. Raiff's ears detected rapid hisses with each strike. And then he was shaking along with the concentrated world around him, as if he'd been trapped in the most powerful earthquake ever experienced, the sense of it all reaching him at his very core.

The baby was screaming now.

Raiff wished he could go back. Had no idea how much distance he'd actually covered, but it didn't matter, since there was no *back* to return to. Elaina had blown the control room and Raiff feared the integrity of this chamber had been compromised as a result. The space-bridge closing up on both sides, closing up and closing in, capable of compressing him and the baby to absolute zero, like they'd never existed at all. He had to move fast, keep pushing forward, even if it felt as if he wasn't moving at all.

The air thickened to a wall Raiff bounced off, nearly losing hold of the infant. The entire world before him was a collection of vast swirling storm clouds that seemed to be building substance as they darkened, closing off his only exit from the tunnel before the entire chamber became no more than a pinprick in the vast galaxy.

Residue . . .

Something had crossed the bridge ahead of him through another entrance, leaving behind these disruptions in the energy fields. Only something of incredible force and power could create chaos in the void between worlds, something that was chaos itself. Raiff had heard tales of such creatures but believed them to be the stuff of legends culled to strike fear.

Then he remembered the object Elaina had pressed into his hands and their final exchange.

"*You'll know when the time comes. It's the only weapon that can destroy* . . ."

"*Destroy* what?"

"*Let's hope you never have to find out. Call it a precaution.*"

It was more than a precaution, Raiff realized now. Elaina had known something had preceded him and her baby across the bridge through space and time.

Something that was waiting for him.

8

CLOUDS

DONATI SLUMPED TO THE floor, paralyzed with fear. The heavy steel composing the door before him continued to buckle inward. One rivet popped out and embedded itself into the wall just over his head.

The rivets kept popping, the heavy steel starting to show fissures, the door ready to give.

What have we done?

Donati somehow maintained the presence of mind to pose that question to himself. They had built a bridge in Laboratory Z having no idea where it might take them, or what awaited on the other side. Never once had they even considered that the door could be opened from that other side as well, that they had served up an invitation to whatever loomed not on another planet, but from another dimension entirely.

It was what made the work conducted at Laboratory Z so controversial, the mere thought that worlds could exist all around ours instead of just light-years away. In Donati's mind it had never been a question of if, just how to find passage to those other dimensions that promised untold scientific riches on a level beyond even Einstein's greatest discoveries.

And, now, something else. Something that didn't operate on the rules of this world, because it was from a place that might as well have been a zentillion miles away.

The final rivets popped free. The two-ton door rocketed inward on an angle that obliterated the wall to Donati's right, barely missing him. He gasped for breath, unable to will his limbs to move, when he felt the cold emptiness of the cloud-thing re-forming before him.

Donati couldn't breathe, because the air around him was . . . gone. He had the sensation of floating in a vacuum, feeling nothing at all until he caught a glimpse of the shape of a figure barreling into the cloud.

9

LOST AND FOUND

AN CHIN WAS PERFORMING her maintenance chores outside an emergency exit of the facility known only as Laboratory Z, twenty levels beneath the surface, when a shrill emergency alarm sounded. The heavy door burst open and a peculiar smell emerged. It made her nose feel hot, actually hot, when it reached her. Metallic and coppery, a combination of something left burning on a stove and spilled blood. Amid the steady flash of the emergency lighting, she heard cries and screams, plaintive wails coming from inside the laboratory.

Instinct took over and she dashed inside into a noxious white mist that burned her eyes. An took it to be some sort of fire suppressant at first, doubting that assessment as quickly as she'd formed it.

Then she heard a baby crying.

The noxious odor grew thicker the deeper into Laboratory Z she ventured, intensified the more she drew into a white, dewy mist that felt hot and cold at the same time. Sparks flared, illuminating the semblance of a path for her. Cries and screams sounded, seeming to come from beyond a wall of super-thick glass that was fracturing into a spiderweb pattern even as she neared it. She caught glimpses of motion beyond that glass where the mist thickened the air to a soup-like consistency that formed a curtain over the world beyond.

An sucked in mouthfuls of the stench-riddled mist, expecting it to be like smoke when it turned out to be nothing but stained air. The sustained cries drove her deeper inside whatever the mist contained. Following the line of fracturing glass when the thick blanket finally stole her vision, tracing it to the sound of the baby.

The swirling clouds of energy, electromagnetic radiation, left what felt like alternating pockets of searing heat and biting cold. Raiff knew these were illusions, coping mechanisms of the body to manage the effects of cross-dimensional travel on the metabolism. He knew this journey was effectively unfolding between beats of his heart and ticks of a clock. Knew that he had the sense he couldn't breathe because the moment was captured between breaths. That explained why the baby wasn't crying anymore and when he heard that sound again he'd know he'd reached the other side.

Unless he never reached the other side. Unless there was no other side. Unless the other side had already been destroyed by whatever had preceded him across the spacebridge.

Raiff had become one with the emptiness around him and feared this would be his eternity if the spacebridge's hold on the other side was lost. Retracing his steps would do no more than spin the void around him. He felt the infant pressed against him, thought he detected the slightest shadow of breath, of warmth, enough to remind him of his mission and purpose. Raiff felt he was dancing through blips of nothingness where there was no sound, no light, no feeling, the world reduced to an airless vacuum. He schooled himself to hold his breath, aware the baby could hardly do the same, and was suddenly left gasping, which meant, which meant . . .

Which meant *what*?

Finally, he came to a white wall of mist that dissipated as it climbed higher, only to recharge itself by building the wall anew in a constant repetitive cycle. This too held an airless void, Raiff left with no choice but to enter with no sense at all of how big the void was.

How long exactly could he hold his breath? How long could the baby survive in panic with no air?

Raiff felt a change in temperature, the swirling clouds brightening to a clear white before him. He could see color beyond, not shapes or objects, just color, which was enough to tell him he'd reached the opposite side of the bridge, now collapsing in on itself. Afraid he'd be unable to get through in time, Raiff thrust the infant forward, more watching than feeling his arms penetrate the cloud wall, as the baby disappeared from his line of vision.

———

An Chin saw a disembodied shape emerge, a pair of arms with the rest of whoever they belonged to hidden by the mist. Those arms were holding a baby, extending him out toward her.

"Take him!" a voice screeched. "Get him out of here!"

Then the arms were gone and the shape beyond them was gone too, pulled back inside the thicker portion of the mist. An looked down to see an infant in her arms.

The final rumble swept Raiff off his feet, swirled him around, and sent him forward, free of the limitations of time and space. He was suspended between breaths, suspended between life itself and death. And then he landed hard on a floor moist and slick with the residue of the mist that had seemed to sweep him forward. He could breathe again, but the misty air was hot, revealing that the chamber had finally ruptured behind him.

Raiff felt its electromagnetic residue pinging everywhere, destroying the molecular integrity of whatever lay on the other side of the bridge. He smelled burned wires and charred metal, could sense as well as feel something between cold and heat, the clashes of energy extending the void further out from the remnants of the chamber.

Raiff clawed back to his feet, taking huge gulps of stale but welcome air, before sprinting off with white-hot flames nipping at his heels, remembering the cylindrical weapon Elaina had tucked into his pocket.

She knew! She knew it would be here!

And she had given him the means to destroy it. Just follow the path of fire and ice, the residue left in the thing's cosmic wake wherever it had emerged from the spacebridge.

Destroy the creature.

Then find the child.

An Chin fled Laboratory Z through the same emergency exit as she'd entered it with the infant tucked protectively against her chest to shield him from whatever the mist might be carrying. Climbing the steep stairwell, spiraling twenty stories upward, was like being trapped inside a steam oven. She had the sense she was pushing against the wind or, more accurately, a vacuum trying to suck her back down into some airless void.

The motions of the baby's mouth and eyes, its bubbling tears, told her he was crying, but she couldn't hear his sobs. She realized she felt better when holding her breath and sucked in as much as she could, pushing against the efforts of something to pull her back down.

Donati caught a flash of long black hair, eyes as determined as they were fearful.

A boy, it's a boy!

The boy vanished into the cloud, rendered invisible within the shifting and re-forming meld of the blackness sprouting branch-like limbs in all directions. He heard a buzzing. A flash blinded him, then his vision cleared to the sight of the last of the cloud dissipating and the boy disappearing through the mangled doorway, as an object clattered to the floor at his feet.

An Chin was holding her breath again when she burst outside through another emergency exit into the cool, clean air of the parking lot.

Halfway across the asphalt, she was struck by a shock wave that seemed to swallow her up and then cough her out. An felt airborne, but when she looked down, her feet had never actually left the concrete, which had cracked underfoot like thin glass. Everyone around her was rushing, the wail of sirens sounding intermittently in her head as if someone were turning them off and then on again.

An charged through the parking lot strewn with cars missing all their window and windshield glass. Hers was parked in a lot reserved for lower-level employees, explaining why it was still intact when she reached it, gasping for air with the burned-wire stench stuck in her nostrils.

She got her door open and climbed inside with the baby nestled

in her lap. He'd stopped crying, seemed to be smiling, his eyes looking up to meet hers.

Donati pushed himself up the wall, back pressed against it. On the
floor before him rested a perfectly spherical, slightly opaque, crystalline object. It was maybe twelve inches in diameter and featured
spiky, symmetrical extensions that reminded him of a microbe or
virus.

Not about to touch the object, Donati nonetheless stooped to
examine the crystal sphere closer. Nothing otherwise remarkable
stood out, except for the fact...

It's alive ...

Donati couldn't explain how he knew that and didn't care. The
realization that his life's work in building Laboratory Z was gone
struck him hard and fast, along with something else:

This was just the beginning.

TWO

HOME INVASION

The Present

Not all those who wander are lost.
J.R.R. TOLKIEN, *THE FELLOWSHIP OF THE RING*

10

THE DAY AFTER

"I'M HEADED BACK THERE now. There's still time."

"Time for what?"

"Same thing, Sam, to save the world. But we need to save you first."

Samantha Dixon continued to stare at the cell phone, as if willing Alex to call back to flesh out his cryptic message. He was on his way here now, something she greeted with relief, excitement, but also trepidation.

Because she was still in danger.

"You hungry, Sam?" her mother called from the bottom of the stairs. "I can fix you something."

Sam looked away from the throwaway cell phone long enough to poke her head out her bedroom door to answer her mother. It was Monday morning and she should have been in school. But she had barely slept the night before and figured she could take a day off.

After all, last night she might well have, along with Alex, saved the world. Well, almost. Literally.

"I'll be right down, Mom."

Her mother was putting on a brave face, doing her best to ignore the events she and Sam's father had witnessed on Alcatraz Island, how they'd been taken hostage to use as leverage against her and Alex, especially Alex. Even now pondering all of it, it made no sense. But it happened and the memories weren't going anywhere no matter how much her parents wished they would.

———

THE NIGHT BEFORE . . .

"We're going to the police," her father had said adamantly, after the taxi dropped the three of them back at home.

"And tell them what?" Sam asked him.

"What happened, what we saw."

"That Alcatraz prison vanished into a black hole."

"We don't know that's what happened."

"But it's gone. And Alex saved your lives. Mine too."

"What's that got to do with anything?"

"The police will want to know what happened to him too, Dad."

"And what did happen to him?"

Sam had taken a deep breath. "It's better if you heard the whole story. From the beginning."

And that's what she had done over several hours that stretched into the early morning. Neither of her parents said much through the course of the tale, not wanting to believe what they were hearing but knowing it was the only explanation for what they had seen. They had questions Sam did her best to answer, except those pertaining to Alex. She couldn't bear to think of Alex out of the dread fear that she'd never see him again.

"You feeling better?" Sam heard her mother continue from the foot of the stairs.

"Much."

"We need to talk about all this. Your father's down here too. We're still processing everything. We have more questions, Sam, starting with what happens now."

"I'll be right down," Sam said, because she could think of nothing else.

She stuck the phone back into the back pocket of her jeans. It was of the old-fashioned flip variety and didn't feel comfortable tucked in there at all. She and Alex had purchased matching ones the day before. And she had thought, at least hoped, that what transpired on Alcatraz Island last night would have marked the end of this, which it clearly hadn't.

You're not safe, Alex just said.

She was so grateful to hear from him, given that she'd come to fear he'd left her life forever after they'd parted the night before, even if it meant she was still in danger. It had been foolish for Sam to think that she could just pick up her life again. Go back to school Monday morning, and resume her senior year in high school as if the world hadn't almost ended Sunday night. As if the frantic battle beneath the bowels of Alcatraz had never happened.

And what about Alex? He was still carrying around a computer chip in his skull, dangerously close to his brain, the contents of which might be the only thing capable of saving the world in the battle that remained ahead, if it didn't kill him first. That wasn't something you could just walk away from and pretend never happened, no matter how much her parents wished that were the case.

Speaking of which, both television news and the internet were strangely quiet about what had transpired the night before. The fact that Alcatraz prison itself had literally vanished from the face of the Earth was being blamed on a sub-sea earthquake, the collapse of the island's brittle integrity, and numerous other factors. Conspiracy theorists were already weighing in with their explanatory versions, some of which were far closer to the truth than the so-called science experts cable news kept trotting out. But no one was able to confirm anything since the island had been cordoned off to all other than official personnel, the Coast Guard strictly enforcing a one-mile perimeter blockade that included the air space over the island, currently closed to all aircraft.

In her capacity as an intern at NASA's Ames Research Center for astrobiology, Sam had learned plenty about the oddities and contradictions of space science, and imagined the electromagnet radiation around Alcatraz was still reading off the charts. Scientists, like her own boss, Dr. Donati, had likely determined that the general area around the island itself remained atmospherically unstable, due to the residue of whatever had sucked the prison structure into oblivion. Last night, Donati had called it a black hole or, at least, the semblance of one.

And to think just Friday night she'd been sitting in the stands of St. Ignatius Prep, watching Alex Chin lead the Wildcats to a victory over the Granite Bay Grizzlies to win the Central Coast Section Championship. That, though, was before he was injured and rushed to the hospital in the fourth quarter, setting the stage for the unraveling of both their lives.

Sam's father knew his way around boats and had been able to steer a Zodiac raft, left behind by commandos who had never emerged from the remnants of the former prison's structure, back to the pier. They docked not far from where she'd set out with Alex in a tour boat that had been attacked.

Sam had kept nodding off from exhaustion during the ride home, but had trouble falling asleep after doing her best to lay everything out for her parents. Memories of the past three days unspooled like videos in her mind, like . . .

Her and Alex sharing a room at the Monterrey Motor Inn, then forced to camp out in the woods just off the Pacific Coast Highway, where they'd drifted off to sleep in each other's arms.

She had feared he was gone forever, but now he was on his way to her house.

Because she was in danger.

Sam's throwaway phone rang again and she yanked it from her back pocket, knowing it must be him.

"Where are you?" she asked.

Static.

"Alex?"

More garble, followed by a sizzling sound.

Sam felt a surge of heat sear her palm and dropped the phone to the floor. It bounced lightly atop the throw rug that covered this side of the room all the way to her desk.

And exploded.

Metallic fragments and thin shards of glass coughed into the air. She felt one or the other, maybe both, prick the skin of her face, feeling like ice crystals that left her cheeks numb. A mini-fireball swallowed the phone's housing, what remained of its inner works popping and fizzling.

You're not safe, Alex had warned.

"What was that, Sam?" her mother's voice called from downstairs. "Are you coming down?"

Sam rushed from her room, certain her parents weren't safe either.

Not even close.

11

REVEREND BILLY

"SHE'S NOT ANSWERING," ALEX said to the man driving the beat-up old van, throwaway cell phone feeling useless in his grasp. "I think her phone died. Or was killed," he added, without knowing why.

"We'll be at your girlfriend's in a few minutes," the man he knew only as Reverend Billy said, trying to get more speed from the van's engine.

"She's not my," Alex started. "At least, she wasn't. I think, well . . ."

Reverend Billy waited for Alex to continue, didn't bother coaxing him on.

"It's like she's more than that," he finished finally.

"Do you love her?" Reverend Billy asked.

He had pinkish, sunburned skin that was mottled and patchy dark in spots. His hair was a splotchy mess of gray spikes and waves. His eyes were bloodshot in spidery lines that circled the tired blue irises, which looked as if someone had bleached the color out of them. The van smelled of old weed and cheap aftershave baked together into the fabric, thinly disguising the musty odor of stale sweat and unwashed clothes. It had once contained more seats, but they'd been removed behind this single row to make room for a grungy, coffee-stained mattress and boxes overflowing with books that looked like Bibles.

Reverend Billy, as he'd introduced himself the day before, tightened his fingers around the steering wheel, Alex's eyes again drawn to the single letter that had been tattooed on each finger just below the knuckle:

T-H-E-N-D-C-O-M-E-S

Reverend Billy didn't have enough fingers on his left hand to spell "the end" out all the way, so he must have improvised.

Alex, in his mind anyway, didn't look much better. Staring straight ahead through the windshield had revealed occasional glimpses of a face he barely recognized, his expression seeming worn and tired, the very life bled from it. His long, sandy blond hair was an oily, tangled mess that looked like it did after being confined by a helmet for a whole football game. Come to think of it, he hadn't washed it since Friday night, when he'd ended up in the hospital instead of the shower. His eyes looked laggard and jittery, shifting with uncertainty. He knew that expression from anxious freshmen on the first practice of summer two-a-days, having little idea of what awaited or was expected of them.

Football . . .

He didn't want to think about it in the rearview mirror of his life, but what choice did he have? St. Ignatius would be playing their opening round game for the California state championship next weekend without him. Conceding that to himself drove home the finality that life as he knew it, pretty much everything he'd known as of Friday night, had been stripped from him. His parents, football, college, the NFL . . .

His future.

Whatever future he had was no longer his; it belonged instead to others, higher powers and higher causes. Things that threatened to overwhelm him and still left Alex with a sense that this was some awful, concussion-induced nightmare he'd eventually wake from.

But he wouldn't.

Because it wasn't.

No, he told himself dryly. It was a nightmare—just one he was really living.

And one into which he had inadvertently pulled Sam.

All he had was Sam. They'd known each other peripherally since first grade, but Alex hadn't even realized that until she was assigned to be his academic tutor to help him keep his grades high enough to stay on the field. He had Sam, but he didn't want her if it meant she'd have to sacrifice her future too. It wasn't fair to let her lose her dreams, and become captive to someone else's instead. Specifically, a dream lived out by the refugees from his native world who believed they could save this world, even if they couldn't save their own.

"Why'd you ask me that, if I, er, love her?"

"It's just a question," Reverend Billy said. "Seems obvious."

"What does?"

"The answer. The way you talk about her, care about her. That's the something more you're talking about. Where I come from, we call that love."

Alex didn't bother arguing the point. "Something's wrong," he said, dialing the number of Sam's matching phone again and, again, the call went straight to voicemail.

"I thought we'd established that much," Reverend Billy said, as if trying to sound light and flippant. "There's plenty wrong."

Alex got his bearings, realized exactly where they were. "Take the next right."

Reverend Billy had already eased the van in that direction.

"Five minutes," he said.

12

GHOST IN THE MACHINE

SAM CHARGED DOWN THE stairs, taking the last three in a single leap and almost twisting her ankle when she landed alongside her mother.

"I guess you *are* hungry," said Allison Dixon.

"Where's Dad?" Sam asked breathlessly.

"In the kitchen. He's—"

Sam burst that way, trailed by the rest of her mother's words without processing what she said. Sam found her father at work at the kitchen table boxing up bags of various strains of marijuana her parents grew out of their backyard greenhouse as licensed cultivators for a number of local dispensaries. The weed had been packaged into large ziplock bags that could not hide the pervasive skunk-like smell, each stickered with the appropriate label. The printed names and descriptions reminded Sam of the assortment of specialty coffees at Starbucks.

"Dad!"

"I was just making some toast. Want some?"

"Toast," Sam echoed, steering for the toaster, only to have her mother block her path.

"We need to finish our talk, Sam. You need to tell us everything about what's going on. No more secrets, no more leaving anything out. You could have been killed."

"*We* could have been killed," her father added. "That means we're involved now, like it or not."

"I need to unplug the toaster," Sam said, instead of responding.

"What?"

"We need to unplug everything!"

"This has to stop," her father chimed in, coming around the kitchen table while wiping his hands with a rag. "Whatever's going on here, whatever you and Alex have gotten yourselves into."

"That's what we're here for," her mother added. "We just want you to be safe."

Sam finally pushed her way past her mother toward the toaster set back on the counter. "Then let me unplug the goddamn—"

But the toaster exploded before she could finish her thought.

A pair of toast slices jetted into the air and stuck to the ceiling. Sam managed to swing round in time to shield her mother and shove her backward, something blistering hot smacking her in the spine and sticking there. She imagined one of the toaster filaments burning through her shirt to her skin, still glowing orange.

Allison Dixon's shoulders smacked into the refrigerator just as ice began spewing from the ice maker. It flew everywhere, her father's legs taken out from beneath him when several cubes pelted him in the forehead.

"David!" her mother cried out.

She tore free of Sam's grasp and rushed toward his downed form on the floor, just as the door blew off the oven and crashed through a window, leaving behind a curtain of flames that Sam dove to the floor to avoid. She staggered back to her feet and whirled toward her mother.

Beep-beep-beep-beep-beep-beep . . .

The squealing sound was coming from the microwave, currently flashing nonsensical images on its LED message readout. Sam crashed into her mother and took her to the floor, an instant before the microwave's door blew open and a torrent of scalding-hot coffee flooded outward and soared past where the two of them had just been standing, splashing against the wallpaper. It burned through it all the way down to the wood, leaving a smoking, impressionistic design behind.

Still perched over her mother, alongside her father on the floor, Sam heard something explode in the backyard. A staccato burst that reminded her of movie machine-gun fire.

The greenhouse! Sam realized, picturing the high-output fluorescent bulbs that supplied light for the various strains of weed David Dixon often boasted had won awards at conferences.

The glass walls of the greenhouse went next, breaking apart into a million pieces as Sam watched through the window. Impact shattered that and every other window facing the rear of the house and rained jagged shards of glass in a massive wave, shredding everything they touched. Smoke flooded in next, blown outward from the flames consuming the plantings and filling the house with that awful skunk stench.

"What's happening?" Sam's father managed, dazed but conscious. "What's happening?"

His eyes were glassy, seeming to have trouble focusing. His words aimed at Sam, as if he somehow knew she could tell him. But what could she say? Sam thought, recalling the moments following the rupturing of the particle accelerator the night before. An entirely different experience, yes, but somehow the air felt the same. Prickly and supercharged with electricity Sam reasoned could only be due to a massive discharge of electromagnetic radiation that was somehow behind this . . .

Attack.

That's what it was—an attack. Sam's house under siege from the beings she'd almost let herself believe she and Alex had defeated the night before. But this was much bigger than a single battle or a single night. This was about the future of civilization, and mankind's enemies weren't going down without a fight—make that a war.

Alex, where are you?

Sam knew he was coming, knew he would save her family, even though he hadn't been able to save his own. Sam had been there when An and Li Chin had died, killed by those from whom they'd hidden and protected Alex for eighteen years. All for naught, after a CT scan had sent his longtime pursuers converging upon him.

Alex! she wanted to cry out, huddled on the floor with her parents, safe for the moment anyway.

Until every electrical cord in the kitchen twisted into the air, unfurling like snakes and flailing above Sam in crisscrossing patterns. As if feeling for her, seeking her out.

"The table, Mom!" she cried out. "The table!"

The two of them took hold of her father and dragged him with them under the kitchen table.

"What's happening?" her father asked again, in even more of a dazed fashion.

The electrical cords were slicing across the walls and ceiling like whips, leaving chips and divots in their wake and plaster showering the air. Picking up speed as they dipped and darted through air riddled with static, fizzling so much Sam thought she could see miniature starbursts flashing in and out of her vision.

She was picturing Alex racing to their rescue, when one of the cords twisted tight around her throat and yanked her out from beneath the kitchen table.

13

GREEN IS FOR *GO*

"RAIFF SENT YOU," ALEX said, as the old van thumped along the road toward Sam's home in Moss Beach, the landscape dotted with houses that looked remarkably similar. "After he told me it was too dangerous for us to stay together, that he had something else he needed to do."

Raiff was Alex's self-described "Guardian," who'd brought him to this world from his own in a mission gone horribly wrong. A mission that somehow involved the deadly chip implanted within Alex's brain that was on the verge of killing him even now. According to Raiff, that chip held the means to defeat the highly advanced civilization determined to conquer Earth. But he didn't know what it contained and removing it would almost certainly kill him. So to save the world, he might have to die.

"But you're not like Raiff," Alex heard himself resume, when Reverend Billy didn't respond. "You didn't come from the same world he and I did."

Reverend Billy squeezed the steering wheel tighter still. "No, sir, I did not."

"I'm not a sir."

Reverend Billy flashed him a longer, pointed look. "Really?" He grinned, but there was nothing happy about the expression. "Could've fooled me."

"You found Raiff."

"More like he found me. Quite random really."

"How's that?"

Reverend Billy swallowed hard. "Remember what I told you when I picked you up the first time?"

I've seen things, things I wouldn't wish on another human being. Things that make you question the very nature of man and humanity. See, before I came to be what I am, I served as a military chaplain in war zones. You know when you see all the truth of the world laid bare? When you look into the eyes of a dying man. I was the last thing far too many of them saw and I do believe a little of me died each time.

"Yes," Alex said, remembering, "I do."

"In the wake of all that, I found myself giving away Bibles, as many as this old van here could carry. So many sometimes that the worn-out springs couldn't keep its ass end from dragging on the pavement when I hit a bump. I'd look in the rearview mirror and see a shower of sparks."

Alex thought of the previous night, all that had transpired inside and beneath Alcatraz. "I can relate to that."

"I entered a diner, lugging a duffel bag full of the Good Book, hoping to spread God's word to anyone who'd hear it. Raiff was sitting at the counter. I gave a Bible to him, our eyes met, and I knew."

"Knew what?"

"I'm not sure exactly. Only that he was different from anyone I'd ever met before. Something about him sent a chill up my spine. I thought he was an angel at first, here in the earthly world, walking among us."

"You're kidding, right?"

"Is that really any harder to believe than the truth?"

Reverend Billy had a point. "I guess not," Alex told him.

"Well, I *know* not. 'It's Armageddon, isn't it?' I said to him.

"'Not yet,' Raiff said. Then he asked me to take a seat and bought me the best meal I'd had in weeks. But I stopped eating when my plate was still half full, because he told me the story. About who he was, where he was from, how it was only a matter of time and how some crazy man was committed to wiping out all his kind. How he could use my help, because I couldn't be tracked. That's what he said."

"Go straight at that traffic light coming up," Alex told him.

Reverend Billy kept his gaze focused on the road ahead. "I'm not saying I believed all of Raiff's story from the get-go, but I believed enough of it. Figured he, and whatever he was a part of, might be just what I was looking for. Figured maybe I was supposed to be giving away all these Bibles, if for no other reason than to bring us together."

"And now you're with me."

"Like I was saying."

Alex swallowed hard. "It is the end, isn't it? The Four Horsemen of the Apocalypse and all that shit?"

Reverend Billy nodded, as if to measure his thoughts. "I've seen the true depths of depravity to which man can sink, and in the eyes of dying men I saw the world's fate as only they could show it to me. But in the last light in their gazes, I also saw hope, as if they'd been given a glimpse of where they were headed."

The van sailed toward the still-green traffic signal, Sam's house just a few blocks beyond the light, which had stayed green for too long. The cars headed east and west had the red, but they kept coming toward the intersection without slowing. And, as Reverend Billy's rusted-out husk of a van drew closer, Alex realized that the light was glowing green in both directions.

"Stop!" he cried out.

Too late.

Reverend Billy never saw the car going west as he went south, the two converging in the intersection at virtually the same moment. The showroom-new SUV slammed into the van's rear quarter panel and sent it whirling across the road, spinning like a propeller.

Alex was thrown one way, and then another. But, miraculously, other vehicles managed to avoid the van's churning menace. He heard the ear-wrenching sounds of squealing brakes and the crunch of metal against metal. Then, just as fast as it had whipsawed into motion, the van slowed to a stop like a timed-out amusement park ride.

"Oh, boy," he heard Reverend Billy rasp.

Alex was halfway out of the van by then, sprinting off to cover the final blocks toward Sam's house, the door left open behind him.

14

THE NICK OF TIME

SAM MANAGED TO GET her hands curled under the electrical cord before it tightened all the way, heaving for whatever air she could take in. She realized, absurdly, it was the cord attached to the iron her father used to vacuum seal the bags of weed. She could hear the thud of the heavy Proctor Silex banging up against the tile floor as she battled the ever-tightening cord, feeling it gradually pinching in on the fingers desperately trying to hold their ground. It was getting harder and harder for her to steal some breath, any breath, the intervals between success growing longer and longer.

"Sam!"

Her mother started to crawl out from beneath the table to help her, but the whiplike cords chased her back, seeming to work in concert, possessed by whatever electromagnetic energy was running the show.

Until Saturday, Sam would have laughed off such a scene, even in a movie, but that was before she and Alex had done battle with the entity they called the Ash Man. An astral projection with grit for substance beamed here from another dimension, a whole different plane of existence. If a being like that could exist, then so could an energy force capable of controlling anything powered by electricity.

She felt her consciousness ebbing, her eyelids gone fluttery. Snapping alert again to heave in a desperate breath she feared might be her last.

Alex! she screamed in her mind, her head feeling like it was going to burst. *Alex!*

I'm coming, Sam, I'm coming!

Alex had no idea what made him form that thought in his head. He thought for a moment he'd heard Sam's voice and repeated her words in his mind, even after he realized he'd heard nothing at all.

He'd never run faster. Not in his timed forty-yard dash, not when he was showing off for college scouts, not even on the football field while speeding toward the end zone. There were three blocks to cover from the broken traffic light to Sam's house, but time moved at such a crawl that it felt like three miles.

And there was more.

It wasn't just that single traffic light. By the look of things, the whole area was affected. Alex glimpsed a much larger pileup at an intersection just before the turnoff for Sam's street in Moss Beach, announced by a stubbornly blaring horn. And, as he rounded the corner for the final stretch to her house, a transformer crackled, sparked, and blew out in a wash of flames.

Whether connected to that or not, the bulbs on the LED street-lights overhead began flashing on and off, growing to flashbulb brilliance before exploding in a rolling crescendo as Alex passed beneath them.

Is it me? Am I doing this?

He didn't think so, but with a computer chip lodged in his head, he couldn't be sure. Yet the sight of garage doors going up and down in a neat row all the way to Sam's house was cause to believe whatever was happening had nothing to do with him or the chip at all.

Alex ran past a house where a man was dousing a car engine fire. A few houses down from that one, and two short of Sam's, a driver-less go-cart seemed to be chasing a boy around his yard, rumbling up the front steps after him as he hammered on the door.

Machines seemed to be going crazy, electricity turning against this neighborhood stretching all the way back to that first traffic light. After all that had happened these last three days, Alex didn't even bother questioning that, not in the wake of doing battle with androids and astral projections. But now it looked like it wasn't just him and Sam who were being targeted.

Not even close.

Alex neared Sam's house, leaped over the curb onto her lawn, homing in on the blown-out windows, wafting stench-riddled smoke, as he took in the crazy sounds coming from inside. He thought of all the machines he'd passed on his way here, seemingly waging war on man. And to fight a war, you needed a weapon, Alex thought, gaze fastening on something affixed to the side of Sam's house.

Sam felt herself sliding down the wall, black floating shapes starting to congeal before her eyes as the world darkened around her. She remembered staying underwater too long once while swimming in the ocean. What it felt like those final moments before she clawed her way to the surface.

It felt like this.

She tried to use her hands to loosen the electrical cord still tightening around her throat, but realized she couldn't feel them anymore. They flapped and twitched, numb and useless, by her sides as more cords that looked like flying snakes swirled through the air in the kitchen before her. She could see her mother's lips moving, while Allison Dixon did battle with the electrical cords, flailing away while desperately trying to reach her.

Sam! Sam!

She made out the shape of her name on her mother's lips, but the sound reached her as little more than a whisper.

"Sam! . . . Sam!"

Louder now, coming from another voice.

Alex's voice, Sam realized, just before a torrent of water hit her.

15

SHORT CIRCUIT

BACK OUTSIDE, ALEX HAD twisted the nozzle and rushed to the front door with the thick garden hose unspooling in his wake. He heard the soft squeal of its churn and squeezed the grip on the sprayer pistol screwed into the hose's end. A concentrated stream of water burst outward, much more powerful than he'd been expecting.

A good thing.

Alex shouldered through to the kitchen, hose blowing out water in a thick straight plume, before he had anything at which to aim it. Then he spotted the shards of glass littered about the floor, table, and counters, the wash of thick, foul-smelling smoke blowing in through the shattered windows, the room lit in large part by a starburst of flames in the backyard where the Dixons' hydroponic greenhouse had once stood.

Sam was sitting on the floor, her eyes going glassy, being strangled by what looked like a disembodied electrical cord attached to an iron that rested by her side. Alex hit it with the hose from bottom to top, hit it hard and kept spraying until he heard a hissing sound, the cord-thing twirling in a way that made it look like it was tightening around air.

Alex rushed toward the now-soaked Sam, as the cord flopped to the floor like no more than the rubber that it was. Its grip had slackened around her throat, allowing him to yank the cord off and toss it to the side, kicking it farther away when the distance didn't suit him.

"Breathe, Sam, breathe!" he urged, spraying the electric cords still swirling about the air and the entire kitchen with waves of water, trying to short-circuit them.

"Alex!" a new voice cried out.

He realized it was Sam's mother, emerging from beneath the kitchen table and crawling over the downed cords, which continued to flap about.

"That's it, Sam, that's it," Alex soothed, when Sam started taking in great heaves of breath, still gasping as he held her against him.

She had taken in too much smoke and had to cough plumes of it out, as heavier clouds bearing the skunk-like weed odor flooded the air.

"My head," Alex heard, and looked again toward the kitchen table to see Sam's father clawing out from beneath it as well. "Where's all that smoke coming from?" he wondered, his hands scraping against the glass shards scattered over the tile floor.

"We need to get out of here," Alex said, easing Sam from his grasp and to her feet by his side.

He could feel her heart hammering, but Sam's still-rapid breathing had somewhat quieted. Alex kept his left arm around her, steering her toward the door. He was still clutching the sprayer pistol in his right hand—in case.

Sam's mother fell into place alongside him, supporting Sam's father in similar fashion.

"This isn't happening," she mumbled. "This *can't* be happening! Tell me this isn't happening!"

Before Alex could respond, something crackled overhead and he looked up to see the ceiling fissuring along lines of wide cracks, fragments dropping into the smoke-filled air. A smoke alarm was wailing too. Maybe it had just started, or maybe Alex just hadn't noticed it.

Then he felt a wash of air strike him, a breeze cutting through the smoke an instant before the ceiling fan whirled toward him.

Only a gaping chasm remained where the fan had separated from its mounts, swirling and swerving through the air. One of its whirling blades clipped Allison Dixon in the shoulder and spun her against the wall. The next spin smacked Sam's father in the head, dropping him back to the floor amid the shattered glass collected there.

Alex shoved Sam protectively behind him, backing up toward

a wall, as he fired the sprayer pistol upward, trying to catch the freed ceiling fan in its unleashed blast of water. The fan was still attached by dangling wires to its former post in the ceiling, and Alex righted his aim into the chasm, as the fan dive-bombed him again.

He ducked under its assault, pushing Sam down with him. Then he ducked again when it attacked from the opposite side. He kept aiming the sprayer pistol for the exposed wires and hole in the ceiling above them the whole time, soaking the plaster.

The fan's blades spun in an invisible blur, formed out of wood but with blades capped in decorative iron that could cut like a knife. Alex turned the hose on the fan itself, holding it at bay briefly. Long enough for the drenched ceiling plaster to give way, plunging the whole of the fan's housing and mounts downward.

The twirling blur stopped just short of Alex and Sam and clacked to the floor, allowing him to leave her with her mother and hoist her father off the floor. Sam and her mother reclaimed their feet too, and Alex led the way through the carnage of broken glass and charred appliances toward the door and escape.

He didn't discard the hose until they were all outside, greeted by the clouds of skunk-smelling smoke spiraling over the house and by the sound of sirens that seemed to be screaming from everywhere at once.

16

SAVIOR

SAM KNEW ALEX SAW that she was shivering. She was grateful he moved toward her, easing David Dixon toward his wife, before wrapping his arms around Sam and drawing her in. He held her against his body, which radiated the heat of a steam oven through his clothes.

"It's okay," he soothed, trying to reassure her. "It's going to be okay."

Sam felt so small in his grasp, engulfed more than swallowed, like they'd fused together, their bodies indistinguishable. It was like the motel room and the woods, when he'd needed her so badly. Only now she needed him; they needed each other.

Sam finally raised her hands to his chest and pushed herself away from him, holding him at arm's length. "I left my keys in the house," she said, clearing her throat before raising her voice over the symphony of car alarms that had turned the normal quiet of the day to a crescendo of chaos. "Mom?"

"Me too," Allison followed, feeling about her pockets.

"And me," David Dixon said, so wobbly on his feet he nearly lost his balance when he checked his pockets too. "And I don't think we want to risk going back inside," he added, gaze tilted back toward the house.

"No," Sam and her mother said in unison.

"Doesn't matter anyway," Alex told all three of them, his gaze fastened on the detached two-car garage.

The mechanical door was going up and down in a constant loop; it would be impossible to back either of the Dixon's cars out.

"We've got to go," Alex said, through the exhaustion threatening to overcome him. "Now, before they recharge, or whatever it is they do."

David Dixon's gaze brightened, as he grew more alert. "They're *machines*, for the love of God."

"Someone else is controlling them."

David's eyes seemed to acknowledge the boy for the first time. "Alex, what are you doing here?"

Then he gazed around, saw and smelled the smoke. He had taken a hard hit and now his mind was fighting back from whatever total blackout had seized him.

"What's happening?" he asked, confused, looking to Alex for answers.

"We need to go," Alex said, instead of answering him. "I'll explain, or try anyway, later."

"Go *on foot*?" Sam posed.

"We don't have a choice," Alex said, eyes flitting toward the garage door going up and down without pause.

But just then their eyes were drawn to the street by a clanking, sputtering, scraping sound, as Reverend Billy pulled his old van over the curb into the driveway, shedding the last of its hubcaps.

"Need a lift?" he asked, through the open passenger-side window.

17

RUST BUCKET

ALEX MANAGED TO GET the sliding door that had been caved in when the van was T-boned unstuck enough to open, so they could all pile inside. He and Sam helped her parents into the rear of the old van, before squeezing into the front seat just as they had the first time Reverend Billy had picked them up. The wheel looked wobbly on the side where the rear quarter panel had been mashed back at the intersection, and the whole back end seemed canted to the passenger side.

Alex slammed the door behind him and pressed up against Sam. "Go!" he said.

Reverend Billy worked the shift into motion, the gears grinding in protest.

"What happened back there?" Allison asked, her voice cracking, finally taking note of the madness that had swallowed the entire neighborhood as the van sputtered forward. "What's *happening*?"

"I told you we should have gone to the police!" her father blurted. "We've got to go back. The house, the fire! We've got to go back!"

"We can't," Alex said, trying to roll up the window to no avail. "It won't be safe. You're not safe."

"What do you mean?" Allison snapped at him, shock replaced by confusion. "We didn't do anything!"

"It's not you—it's me. My parents," Alex continued, trying not to choke up again.

The Dixons looked at each other, recalling the fate of the Chins from Sam's story the night before.

Alex felt Sam take his hand. "I knew Sam was in danger," he told Allison and David Dixon. "I knew they were coming."

"You knew *who* was coming?"

"Not who, what," Sam answered, so Alex wouldn't have to. "The ones who killed his parents."

"That doesn't make any sense," Allison said, her voice more of a whine. "None of this makes any sense. I don't care what we saw last night. This can't be happening."

"Never mind last night. The machines," David said, as if finally remembering where the big lump on his forehead had come from. "The machines went crazy *this morning*."

"They did it," Alex said.

"Who?" David asked.

"Whoever killed my parents. Reverend Billy told me."

"Who's Reverend Billy?" Allison asked.

"That would be me," Reverend Billy said from behind the wheel, lifting a hand from it and letting the van stray briefly across the road.

David kicked at the mattress to push it even farther from him. "And who are you?"

"The Resistance, at your service."

"Resistance," David repeated.

"To what?" Allison wondered.

Alex looked at Sam. Reverend Billy looked at Alex.

"What you just experienced," Reverend Billy said. "Taking over machines is child's play for them. I won't bore you with the specifics, but everything runs on chips and circuits these days that can be manipulated, controlled."

"We're talking about a *toaster*, for God's sake," David reminded him. "How does somebody take over a toaster, turn it into a weapon?"

"Right." Reverend Billy nodded, suddenly sounding professorial in a way that made Alex and Sam think it was somebody else speaking. "A simple machine, about as low on the mechanical food chain as it gets, only not really as simple as it seems. A circuit made up of transistors, resistors, and capacitors turns on and supplies power to the electromagnet. You charge a capacitor through a resistor when you push down the handle. Then, once a specific voltage is reached, the circuit cuts off and your toast pops out the top of the toaster."

"Sounds simple enough to me," David noted.

"Just like taking control of its workings is as simple as taking over the capacitors that regulate the voltage and electromagnetic discharge," Reverend Billy explained. "I'm guessing it was the same with all the machines that attacked you. They were taken over, manipulated."

"Manipulated by *who*, from *where*?" an exasperated David demanded.

"Pretty much anywhere remotely. It's not rocket science, but it's pretty close. It's what they do."

That left David shaking his head. "What *who* does? We should go to the police," he added staunchly, as Allison nodded. "That's what we should do."

"We can't," Sam said firmly.

"Why?" David and Allison said together.

"Because they can't be trusted. We can't be sure they'll be real cops. They could be..." Sam let her voice tail off, knowing she'd made her point from the expressions on her parents' faces.

"No time for stories or explanations right now," Reverend Billy said, doing his best to keep the vibrating van headed in a straight line. He looked toward Alex. "Too much else on the agenda."

"Like what?" Alex asked.

"What I didn't have time to tell you before, what Raiff told me to tell you. There's a way to stop them, to end this, Alex."

"I know all about that," Alex said, shaking his head. "It's right up here."

"No, that's just part of it."

"What's the other part?"

"I don't know."

"Who does?"

Reverend Billy swallowed hard, his attention lapsing from the road long enough to leave the van veering for a massive tree, until he twisted the wheel and the van righted itself again.

"Langston Marsh," he told them.

THREE

ENEMIES

The world as we have created it is a process of our thinking.
It cannot be changed without changing our thinking.

ALBERT EINSTEIN

18

HOSTAGE

"WE'RE ON THE SAME side," Raiff said from the heavy chair he'd been tied to, his hands fastened together by plastic flex-cuffs. "Can't you see that, after last night?"

Langston Marsh stepped back and let his gaze linger on Raiff's bound form. Neither of them had slept and the older Marsh looked the worse for wear. His hair was mussed, his clothes rumpled, his stiff-spined, authoritative posture slackened by a combination of exhaustion and uncertainty.

"You're one of them," Marsh said,

"One of *who*?"

"The Zarim, the outsiders, the monsters who want this planet for themselves."

"I'm not one of the monsters," Raiff told him calmly. "We killed the monsters last night at Alcatraz, and stopped plenty more from joining them. You've got this all wrong."

"Do I?" Marsh stepped back, surveying the sprawling, museum-like floor in which Raiff found himself as if seeing it for the first time. "I call this my Memory Room. Would you like to know why?"

"Tell me."

The floor before them, looking to be about half a football field in size and stretching up two stories, was lined with regularly spaced objects on display, one of which was instantly identifiable: the wreckage of what looked like an aircraft, a fighter of a kind Raiff had never seen before. Its reassembled remnants looked like a sleeker, much-scaled-down version of the old B-52 Stratofortress, the massive sentinels that had protected the United States against surprise attack for generations.

"You know planes, Zarim?" Marsh asked him.

"Well enough to know that that one never existed."

"That's because it's one of only three of the prototypes ever manufactured as part of Project Blue Book."

"Project Blue Book?"

"Goes back to 1947. My father was a World War II fighter pilot assigned to an experimental division in White Sands, New Mexico. Everything routine, until his division was scrambled. Three of these went up and one managed to shoot down the craft that destroyed my father's plane with a kind of pulse weapon that would still be cutting-edge today."

"You blame me for that?"

"I blame your kind," Langston Marsh spat at him hatefully.

"Except it wasn't us. We didn't come here through space. With all you've seen, you should understand that now."

"You did this because we were developing the means to stop you."

"No technology you possessed then, or have now, could stop those who want to claim your world for themselves."

Marsh ignored Raiff and returned his gaze to the aircraft. "This happened in July of 1947 not far from the site of what would become Area 51. The first shot fired in a war I've been fighting since I was old enough to make a difference, to save the world from the likes of you. I know you've been among us since the very dawn of civilization, laying the groundwork for an invasion. Call it a surprise attack, an intergalactic Pearl Harbor, but slowly, unfolding over a longer period of time as you solidify your strongholds."

"Alcatraz was one of those strongholds," Raiff told him. "And we destroyed it last night."

Marsh eyed him coldly. "Do you know the meaning of the term Zarim?"

"Vaguely."

"It's biblical. The general translation is 'outsiders' or 'strangers.' But another interpretation refers to the Zarim more like creditors or criminals known for seizing the possessions of others. Usurping their worlds, swallowing their identities. That's what will happen to us, to our world, if we don't act. So I hunt your kind down. I hunt the Zarim down and execute them before they can kill us."

"You mean like last night? When all your men were killed by the same *monsters* who would have killed you too?"

Marsh moved closer to him, into a wider swath of light, close enough for Raiff to grab the older man if his hands hadn't been laced behind him. "And who killed these monsters? You?"

Raiff shook his head. "No, not me."

"Not with this, you mean," Marsh said, taking Raiff's whip from a nearby table. Only it had retracted into the simple-looking smooth steel object that resembled a thickened hammer handle. "I watched the boy use it on my men last night. Quite impressive. I haven't been able to get it to work myself yet, though. Why don't you tell me how?"

"Why don't you ask one of the monsters?"

Raiff could almost *feel* Marsh's stare bore into him. "That's what I'm doing. And that's why you followed me here, all the way to the Klamath Mountains. To kill me so I wouldn't go after him. One monster protecting another."

Raiff didn't nod, didn't react, didn't respond. He just stared Marsh right in the eye. The truth was if he'd come here to kill Marsh in his fortress nestled in the hills and dwarfed by the band of mountains that dominated the horizon, Marsh would've been dead already. His mission, though, required infiltration instead. Raiff imagined the last thing Marsh expected was to be followed back here in the wake of the chaos on Alcatraz Island.

If Raiff had wanted Marsh dead, he would have planned his incursion in an entirely different manner. Considering the geological surroundings, he could have set enough explosives to trigger an avalanche in the Klamath Mountains that overlooked these hills. Do that, though, and what he'd really come here for—an object vital to mankind's survival—would be lost forever. How many of his kind had died throughout history to protect that object and its secrets, all so this opportunity might come at last? And now that Alex had come of age, now that Alex knew the truth, that moment and opportunity had arrived.

But only if Raiff could retrieve what he'd come here for.

Before him, Marsh held his ground in the silence that had settled between them.

"So, tell me," he said, breaking it, "is this boy Alex Chin your leader, the one brought here to command the assault that's coming? I lost a lot of men last night, but I still have plenty left, some particularly adept at torture."

Marsh crouched, even with Raiff's chair so they were eye to eye.

"How much you cooperate with me in the next few minutes will determine what happens when those men get here, Zarim. The choice is yours."

19

DR. DONATI

"WE'RE NOW MORE THAN twelve hours past the event's conclusion, Doctor," Donati heard the disembodied voice say and slid his chair closer to his computer. "And we still don't have an explanation for what transpired."

"And I'm not here to provide you with one, at least not yet."

"But you were there. You witnessed it all firsthand yourself."

"*Experienced* would be a better way of putting it, but your basic premise is correct. Being there doesn't facilitate a scientific explanation for the impossible."

After returning to NASA's Ames Research Center straight from Alcatraz the previous night, Donati had yet again assembled the Janus team, which was his conduit to the highest echelons of power in the country, if not the world, this time to discuss something far more than just theoretical. Not a warning so much as a report on events for which he could not provide a rational scientific explanation, because none existed. Not when the explanation lay in the fact that the technology responsible for what had transpired was a million years more advanced than anything Earth had to offer.

Janus had been established eighteen years before, in the wake of Laboratory Z's destruction, as an amorphous extension of the NEO, NASA's Near-Earth Object office, located at the agency's Jet Propulsion Laboratory in Pasadena. Its mission was to function as a kind of extraterrestrial NSA or CIA, responsible for dealing with threats posed to the planet from outer space. Unlike the NEO, however, Janus kept its focus to *hostile* threats, specifically from other life-forms.

Since its existence had been covertly circulated among the various departments responsible for monitoring space, primarily the Search for Extraterrestrial Intelligence, or SETI, three alerts had been called, all of them ultimately deemed to be false alarms.

Until the events of the past twenty-four hours.

Donati was all too aware that Janus owed its very existence to what had transpired at Laboratory Z when the spacebridge had been activated for the first time. He didn't know the names of the principles of the emergency response team with whom he was now speaking. To Donati, their identities were confined to four boxes on his computer with bar grids that danced in accordance with which of the participants were speaking.

"Doctor," the sharp voice of a woman started, from the top box on the right side of Donati's screen, "if you have nothing further to add to your original report, why have you bothered calling us together again, when we all have our own reporting to give, our own emergency teams to assemble?"

"I do have something further to add, just not to my original report," Donati told them.

Another of the quadrants on his screen began to dance, moments ahead of the voice becoming audible. "You're saying this latest information you need to share doesn't involve last night's incident at Alcatraz?"

"Not directly, no. Something else happened earlier today in a remote area of Texas, a town called Waxahachie."

Another bar grid began to fluctuate, one of the men this time. "Location of the unfinished project known as Desertron, which would have created the largest particle accelerator in the world, surpassing even the Large Hadron Collider in CERN, near Geneva in Switzerland. But the project was shelved due to cost overruns."

"Actually, sir, it wasn't."

"Wasn't what?"

"Wasn't shelved. It was completed in secret and has been online for seven years now."

"Why are we hearing about this for the first time?" the woman's voice demanded, her bar grid dancing up a storm. "What happened earlier today?"

"It's gone, ma'am. Just like the facility hidden beneath Alcatraz prison."

"Then you're suggesting . . ."

"Someone, or something, else must have come through."

20

TEXAS STRONG

"CAN I SHOW YOU something else, Doctor?" the boy asked Jack Finn.

"Another injury?" Finn said over the drone of voices rising from the emergency room waiting area, which was currently at standing room only.

"My cell phone."

"I look like Verizon to you?" Finn said, checking the teenager's ears for further signs of the bleeding that had led his mother to bring him here, along with symptoms of dizziness and nausea. "Or AT&T?"

Finn had spent his entire career in emergency medicine. He knew even in this setting that a good bedside manner could make a big difference. Science and medicine were great; but he never forgot the medicine he practiced was on people, and his rapport with them was sometimes more important than the drugs he dispensed.

But today was different. Today was taking every bit of patience he could manage, because of the sudden influx of patients.

"Where were you again when you first experienced the symptoms?"

"Riding my dirt bike in the flatlands, near that big complex they never finished," the boy told him.

"Desertron?" Finn posed, referring to the project that would've placed the largest superconducting supercollider in the world right here in Waxahachie, Texas, had the project not been abandoned years before.

Waxahachie, population just over thirty thousand, was the seat of Ellis County, Texas, United States, located just beyond the southern suburbs of Dallas. In Finn's mind, it offered all the advantages of small-town life with Dallas barely a stone's throw away. The town's main street was an assemblage of low-slung buildings, none over three stories, favoring the architecture from the middle of the last century. The parking spaces were all arranged in perpendicular fashion to the sidewalks, a tradition left over from the days where men parked their horses instead of their cars. Junction boxes had replaced horse troughs, though the wrought iron streetlights and traffic signals maintained a more down-home flavor. Waxahachie represented the final reaches of the urban sprawl spawned by Dallas, the last town before Ellis County dissolved into the emptiness of rolling flatlands, broken only by an occasional pumpjack and a slew of abandoned farms.

It was within those flatlands, ten miles from the Baylor Medical Center here on I-35, where construction of Desertron had been abandoned four billion dollars into the process. It was just a series of empty buildings now, pretty much part of the landscape, where it had been forgotten.

Until today.

"I don't know what it's called," the boy told Finn. "I try to stay as far away from it as possible, 'cause of, you know, the stories."

Finn had indeed heard tales of strange activity at the mothballed complex from time to time. Rumors persisted that construction had been restarted a while back, accounting for the occasional unexplained activity, but it was impossible to get a straight answer out of anyone even remotely associated with the project.

"So what's wrong with me, Doc?"

"You're suffering from a concussion. Let me see your cell phone."

The boy started to reach into his pocket. "How could I get a concussion if I didn't hit my head? It's not like I fell off my bike or anything."

"These symptoms could be connected to something that happened a week, or even a month ago," Finn explained, half lying because he suspected something else entirely was responsible for the symptoms the boy presented with. "Or the symptoms could be emblematic of blast overexposure."

"What's that?'

"When you're too close to something that blows up."

The boy shrugged as he produced his iPhone and worked its menu icons. "It was fine when I left the house. I don't know what happened, but it started right around the time I began feeling dizzy and I realized my ears were bleeding. Then the headache started."

The boy jogged his phone to the World Clock function, where he must've bookmarked his favorite cities to follow the time in hours, minutes, and seconds.

"See?" he said, handing it over.

The clocks, Finn realized, were all running backward.

None of the other patients Finn and his fellow emergency room physicians had seen had been anywhere close to the former Desertron facility, but all of them had crazy stories to tell in their own right, just like the teen with a cell phone clock running backward. Most of the injuries had occurred in a series of car accidents caused when the roadbed of a freeway that connected Waxahachie with Dallas appeared to collapse, leaving jagged gaps in the road that looked like fault lines ruptured by an earthquake. Some of the injured also told stories of windshields cracking in spiderweb patterns for no apparent reason and tires blowing out, similarly without explanation.

The driver of a bread truck claimed his vehicle was launched into the air and tipped onto its side, before crashing back to the pavement. A patrolling police officer, who'd arrived at the hospital in one of the dozens of ambulances and rescue wagons, said his police radio had exploded, forcing him to lose control of his cruiser. A woman Finn had treated already insisted a flock of birds had descended from the sky and crashed into her car en masse, forcing her into a telephone pole.

It got even stranger from there, too many stories to count or catalog.

"Has anyone contacted Washington?" a now haggard Finn asked the ER's chief receptionist.

"To tell who what exactly?" she shot back at him, never taking her eyes off the computer screen before her.

"I was thinking Homeland Security, since this involves—"

Finn was interrupted by a pair of paramedics shoving a gurney through the sliding glass doors, never breaking stride as they pressed, the milling crowd parting to create a clear avenue.

"You need to take a look at this one right away, Doc," one of the paramedics said.

Finn could tell the patient was a woman, but little else. He recognized this pair of paramedics from at least two other drop-offs earlier in the day, explaining why their expressions looked as drawn and anxious as his must have.

"She'll have to wait her turn," Finn said, leaving it there.

"I'm not sure she can do that," the other paramedic told him. "She's spiking a fever of a hundred and eleven degrees."

21

DROP-OFF

Reverend Billy had lapsed into silence after speaking his name, either to let the point sink in or because he had nothing else to say. But David Dixon was more than happy to fill the void, while the old van cluttered and clanked down the road, the damage it had suffered causing the vehicle to fall into a constant list to the right.

"Just drop us at the police, the FBI—anywhere," David said, his voice the most authoritative Sam had ever heard.

"Dad," she started.

"No, sweetie, let me handle this."

Sweetie, Alex mouthed to her, and Sam pushed against him with her shoulder, ending up hurting herself more than him.

"Ouch!"

"Oops." He smirked, before her father resumed again.

"Look, Billy—"

"That's Reverend Billy, sir."

"As a matter of fact, *Reverend* Billy, the next corner will do. Just pull over and let us out. We'll make our own way from here." David Dixon leaned forward, closer to the van's cab. "Does anyone have a cell phone? Can we please just dial nine-one-one?"

"And tell them what?" Sam asked, twisting awkwardly around to face her father.

"The truth."

"Like they're going to believe it. The news isn't even reporting what happened last night, at least not the truth."

"Never mind that," Alex chimed in, turning around too. "If you go to the cops, or anybody else, they'll know."

"*Who'll* know?"

He held his gaze on Sam as he replied. "The things that killed my parents yesterday and almost killed all of you this morning. They'll be watching and waiting for us, any of us, to surface again. They'll know the three of you managed to escape."

Allison's expression tightened; she was no longer able to contain the anxiety spilling over from last night's kidnapping, and now this. "So they're aliens. I get that now. I'm done arguing the point, but that still doesn't explain why you, Alex?"

"Because," Alex said, "I'm one of them. And they want me back."

"He's telling the truth, Mom," Sam said, when both her parents' mouths literally dropped in shock. "I was there. I saw, I heard. They murdered his parents. You need to listen to him, both of you."

Alex nodded slowly. "I've got the only thing that can stop them."

"What?" David managed. "Where is it?"

"It's a computer chip." Alex tapped his head again. "And it's up here. That's why I was brought here. But things didn't work exactly as planned and my mother saved my life. Eighteen years ago, when I was an infant. She and my dad have been protecting me ever since, hiding the truth from everyone, including me."

"All the more reason for us to go to the cops, the FBI," David Dixon persisted. "Somebody, *anybody* . . ."

Alex swung back toward Reverend Billy. "Tell me more about Langston Marsh. What's he got that can help us?"

Reverend Billy's answer was a shrug. "Raiff knows. He went to the man's mountain fortress last night after Alcatraz to retrieve whatever it is. I told him I'd pray for him. He was supposed to check in regularly. But he's gone dark, and that can't be good."

He twisted the wheel to the right and the van rattled around the curve.

"It's about time," David Dixon said. "This will do fine. We can get out right here."

But Reverend Billy ignored him, left his gaze fixed on Alex. "I was only supposed to tell you this if something went wrong. Now it has. If Raiff's been captured, the whole mission's compromised. My instructions are to get you somewhere safe to hide out."

"Good luck with that," Sam said under her breath, just loud enough to be heard.

"Where's this mountain fortress?" Alex asked Reverend Billy.

"That's not the plan, son. You're the key to everything. If Marsh gets you, it's game over. 'Then comes the end, when He hands over the kingdom to the God and Father, when He has abolished all rule and all authority and power.' From First Corinthians."

"If we can't figure out a way to get this chip out of my head, I'm dead anyway. From First Alex." He held Reverend Billy's stare. "Can you keep Sam's parents safe?"

"I can sure try, son."

"Then we've got a plan." Alex turned to look back toward David and Allison, rotating his gaze between them and Sam. "I'm sorry about this, all of it. You never should have been involved, none of you. Reverend Billy will have your back, won't you?"

"As God is my witness," he said.

"Not unless Sam comes with us," David Dixon insisted.

"No," Sam said, stiffening alongside Alex.

She had to be strong, and she had to hold her own. Even against the parents she loved, now more than ever.

"Alex needs me," she said to them. "I'm going with him."

"Sam—"

"She's right. I do need her." Alex swallowed hard. "See, I never learned how to drive. Never got my license."

Sam's parents looked at each other.

"Never got around to it," Alex continued.

"I'll be fine," Sam assured them.

Reverend Billy wrestled the sliding door open with a grating sound of metal against metal, a flood of sunlight pouring into the cab.

"No," David Dixon said, not budging. "You won't be fine, we won't be fine, none of this is fine."

"I'm going to call Dr. Donati," Sam said, as reassuringly as she could manage. "NASA's involved in this too. We're not alone."

David's features flared awkwardly, as all that had happened seemed to catch up to him at once. "No, Sam, we're most certainly not. Looks like the Earth should post a 'No Vacancy' sign, it's so damn crowded."

Allison squeezed his arm, focusing on Sam. "You really have to do this, don't you?"

Sam nodded. She almost smiled. Miraculously, her mother seemed to understand.

"Well, then."

"Allison!"

She turned to her husband. "Were we really any different? Remember?"

"That was a rock concert. This is about two eighteen-year-olds saving the world!"

Allison started to slide past him for the opening. "Come on."

"I, er . . ."

"David, come on."

She tugged at him gently this time, until he grudgingly stepped out onto the pavement.

Sam climbed out through the passenger door and came around the van, hugging her father tight, then her mother. She caught a glimpse of Alex through the open sliding door, imagining what he was feeling in that moment since he'd never be able to hug his parents again.

"You need to find a way to stay in touch," Allison said to her, choking back tears. "Let us know you're okay."

"I will. I promise."

Reverend Billy opened the driver's door for her, drawing a creaking, grinding squeal. Sam climbed up behind the wheel and watched him lay his hands on the window ledge, showcasing those ten letters:

T-H-E-N-D-C-O-M-E-S

He held his gaze on both of them, his eyes looking sad, but resigned. "The Book of Mark, chapter thirteen, verse seven: 'When you hear of wars and rumors of wars, do not be frightened; those things must take place; but that is not yet the end.'"

"Let's hope so," Alex said to him, from the passenger seat. "Now, Reverend Billy, tell us where we can find Langston Marsh."

22

LUCKY DAY

"LET'S TALK ABOUT TEXAS," Langston Marsh said, keeping his distance from Raiff's bound form.

"Large state. As big as all of Eastern Europe, I've heard. Never been there myself."

"An electromagnetic anomaly was registered in Texas earlier this morning, in the area of the former Desertron complex located in Waxahachie. You've heard of Desertron, I assume."

"Sorry," said Raiff, "I haven't."

"It was a project to build the earth's largest supercollider, supposedly shelved due to cost overruns."

"Supposedly," Raiff noted.

"Glad you picked up on that. It was completed in secret and has been operational for nearly a decade. Until this morning. Now it's gone. Just like Laboratory Z eighteen years ago and Alcatraz last night. Mean anything to you?"

"Coincidence maybe."

"I strongly doubt that. I won't pretend to understand the technology behind your use of wormholes, spacebridges, or whatever you call them, that enables you to manage the trip from your world to ours, but it does seem all these trips are one-way."

"Because of the heavy gravitational pull emanating from our side, once the bridge is opened. The side of the bridge in your world lacks the electromagnet integrity to withstand that kind of energy surge—that's how it was explained to me."

"Who came through at Desertron this morning, Raiff?"

"I don't know."

"More of you good aliens perhaps?"

"We both better hope so, Marsh," Raiff said, looking him square in the eye.

"You're going to have to do better than that."

"I can't."

Marsh crouched again, making sure to stay out of Raiff's reach, even though Raiff was still bound to a chair. "Do you know how I found you in that bar on Friday night, how I've tracked down so many of you?"

"I've got a few ideas."

"Then allow me to fill in the blanks. You know all humans give off radiation."

"You mean electricity."

"Same thing in this case. Call it electromagnetic radiation, also known as thermal, or infrared, radiation. Thermal radiation only transports heat and indicates the temperature of its source. Different people at different times give off differing amounts of radiation. Thermal images of a person captured using an infrared camera provide the temperature of the person's skin.

"What we've done," Marsh continued, getting to the point, "is take the principle of this infrared camera one step further. Zarim like yourself give off electromagnetic radiation within a higher bandwidth. Not very dramatic, but pronounced enough to be distinct and detectable to the sensors we've constructed that are programmed to alert our Tracker teams in the event the presence of one is identified in the immediate proximity."

"And you're telling me this because you don't think I'll ever be in position to use it against you."

Marsh took another step backward. "You're not the first of your kind we've managed to take prisoner. Autopsies, necropsy studies, and other scientific analysis have revealed much of your circulatory and other systems work in reverse of ours. I imagine this has something to do with you coming not so much from a parallel world across these spacebridges of yours, but from one that's a mirror image of ours."

"You're a fool, Marsh. Besides these anatomical anomalies you mentioned, we're identical because we're the same. You're here because my world seeded your planet millions of years ago, assuring life would flourish. Suffice it to say that my world's not the most pleasant place in the universe. That's why those like me, refugees, have crossed over space to get here. To hide and plan against our mutual enemies. And your efforts have screwed everything up, to the point where you may have assured the destruction of your own world."

"And where does the boy fit into all of this, Raiff? Is he your savior, your Christ? What's his part in the plan?"

Raiff lapsed back into silence, just stared at Marsh. He kept scanning the various objects on display, as unobtrusively as possible, in search of the one he'd come here for. Marsh called this his Memory Room, but the truth was it contained far more than just the fodder of his own memories. It was more a museum for the inexplicable, likely the world's greatest collection of oddities that defied rational explanation.

Among the products drawn from numerous myths, folklore, and misconceptions, there was the so-called Russian UFO "Tooth Wheel," which had been uncovered in the Primorsky Krai region, a tool made out of an aluminum-like substance carbon dating indicated was three hundred million years old. There was the Betz Mystery Sphere, a silvery object the size of a bowling ball, the energy of which was believed to have started a fire that consumed a hundred woodland acres, defied gravity, and couldn't be penetrated by X-rays. There were various renditions of aircraft dating back to ancient times, the infamous meteorite fossils recovered in Sri Lanka, and various artifacts and drawings attributed to the ancient Mayans, as well as the Egyptians. All of which Raiff knew to have no basis in either fact or science, which hadn't stopped Marsh from assembling the entire collection here.

And somewhere among it all was the single object that held actual validity. So far, though, Raiff hadn't spotted that object in sweeps of his surroundings under Marsh's watchful eye.

Good thing, in that sense, Marsh thought Raiff had come here to kill him, instead of to recover something that was supposed to provide a blueprint for defeating the forces of Raiff's world. He wondered how much time he had before the leaky chip in Alex's head ruptured, killing the boy and, with him, whatever hope this world had of survival.

"You've built an army," Raiff said to Marsh instead. "Your own personal Fifth Column."

"Which I've put to good use."

"Chasing the wrong enemy. If you really want to save your world, help me."

"Help you what?"

"Save your world, Marsh." Raiff swept his gaze about the room's sprawl, the items displayed under warm, ambient lighting in the style of a museum, his words meant to distract Marsh from paying attention to his continuing to catalog the contents. "You think all this means anything? You think anything you've got in here has anything to do with the future? It doesn't. It's all about the past. If you want to save your world's future, you'll listen to me."

Raiff froze his gaze briefly on an object at the edge of the light's reach, captured only dimly, but just enough for him to recognize it as the very item he'd come here to retrieve.

"You were saying," Marsh prompted.

Raiff swung back toward him, afraid for a moment he'd let his gaze linger on the object for too long. "Join me. Help me."

Marsh shook his head, half smiling. "You'd take me for a fool?"

"Only if you don't listen to what I'm telling you."

Suddenly emboldened, Marsh came right up to Raiff, close enough for Raiff to catch the scent of something stale rising off him. "I'm going to kill all of you, going to wipe your kind off the map." He turned to cast his gaze on the twisted wreckage of the old plane. "Starting with you, for my father."

Raiff heard a buzzing sound and watched Marsh jerk a cell phone from its holster clipped to his belt, all of his attention claimed by the contents of the small screen.

"The Tracker team I dispatched to Waxahachie, Texas, just reported a firm hit," Marsh said, already sliding toward the door as he regarded Raiff again. "Looks like you may be about to have some company."

23

LABORATORY Z

"THIS ALL GOES BACK to Laboratory Z, eighteen years ago," Donati told the fluctuating bar grids projected on the screen before him. "That was the first time they proved they could use our ability to generate high-intensity electromagnetic waves to open the door on the opposite side of a spacebridge."

"Spacebridge, Doctor?" the upper right-hand box asked him.

"A different application of a wormhole, which is normally associated with potential deep-space voyages, potential from our end anyway. Think of it this way: if a wormhole opens a highway, then a spacebridge opens a door. It's basically two extremely polarized fields of intense energy establishing a connection between time and space. This isn't space travel we're talking about. It's traveling between dimensions."

"Which sounds like scientific mumbo jumbo, because it is," chimed in the lone female voice among the four.

"No more mumbo jumbo than the ability to communicate from one corner of the world to another instantaneously would have been regarded a hundred years ago. And yet now we have the internet and, before that, long-distance phone dialing. In fact, I'd venture to say that the concept of a spacebridge is more rudimentary to the advanced civilization we find ourselves confronting than the internet, or even the telephone, was initially to us."

"With one notable exception," argued a raspy voice coming from the bottom left-hand square. "Communication via phone or computer requires two willing parties."

"Really, sir? What about hacking?"

"Are you saying in the case of Laboratory Z eighteen years ago, Alcatraz last night, and Desertron this morning, we were *hacked*?"

"I suppose I am, essentially. Hacking requires a single party able to penetrate the technology of an outside party to perpetrate an intrusion. So, yes, this was indeed hacking at a highly advanced technological level."

"So if we were to shut down all the supercolliders currently operational across the globe," the male voice occupying the top left-hand square started, "would we close off their access?"

"Not at all. I witnessed what they'd built beneath Alcatraz personally last night, sir, sir, sir, and ma'am. And I can tell you, in all certainty, that its construction was the product of a civilization far more advanced than ours. We have no idea, of course, how many other such facilities they've constructed across the millennia. Assume, well, dozens at the very least."

"Then how would you explain their initial visit here, Doctor?" the woman challenged. "If your theory is correct, and we are their offspring, so to speak, then how did they find their way to a world that lacked any technology of any kind, much less technology capable of producing a supercollider?"

"If we're going back to the first evidence of man's existence, say a million years ago, I'd say they came here via the same kind of spacebridge to seed the planet."

"We've already read and discussed your report about last night," the woman jumped in, before any of the other three participants could. "These descriptions of cyborgs produced via the principles of nanotechnology. Please tell me, if our enemies from the other side of this spacebridge, this other dimension, can build such advanced cybernetic organisms, why exactly would they need to enslave us, as the theory you advanced on their motivations would seem to suggest?"

"Because I believe that report is wrong, ma'am. I was elaborating on the claims of the refugee I encountered. In retrospect, I believe he was wrong. I believe their current intentions are rooted in something else entirely."

"Any idea what?"

"Not at this time, no. Not yet."

"I have a notion," said the speaker from the bottom right-hand square, with the vaguely European accent. "When the Nazis forced the Jews onto trains bound for Auschwitz and Dachau, they never revealed their true intentions. Right up until those last moments, the victims didn't realize what was in store for them."

"A dangerous analogy," noted the woman, "that should remain with us."

"Right now," picked up Donati, "my entire staff at NASA's Ames Research Center is focusing on answering all these questions."

In point of fact, that wasn't true because Samantha Dixon, his intern who was directly involved in this inexplicable war's onset, wasn't here, had yet to contact him, and wasn't returning his calls.

"But it's getting to the point where I believe we should focus on a more pressing priority," Donati resumed.

"What's that, Doctor?"

"How to stop them," Donati told them all.

24

THE WOMAN

"I WANT HER MOVED into isolation," Dr. Jack Finn told the head emergency nurse, after completing his initial examination of the woman recovered on the side of the freeway a half mile from the Desertron facility he was certain had been shut down twenty years before.

Until today.

"Use the containment ward," Finn continued. "Evacuate any other patients who may be housed there, to avoid potential infection. Glove and gowns for anyone who comes in close proximity to her. Is that clear?"

The head nurse nodded, leaving it there.

Finn's examination of the woman the paramedics had brought in had started with a simple check to confirm their reading of her body temperature as 111 degrees. Three checks in ten minutes revealed her temperature to be significantly lower, between 103 and 104.

"Check your equipment," Finn told the paramedics, recalling the boy he'd examined whose iPhone clocks were running backward. "I believe you'll find something off in their calibration."

"Everything checked out when we left the station," the senior man told him. "Everything checked out, until we picked her up."

"Meaning you were inside the zone at that time."

"Zone?"

"Cracked pavement, jagged, earthquake-like fissures in the road-bed and countryside."

The younger man nodded. "I had to steer around a whole bunch of them."

Finn weighed that against the other inexplicable reports from those who'd been filling the ER for hours. "But your windows remained intact, no damage to any of your vehicle's electronics?"

"No," said the younger man, "nothing like that."

Finn heard the crackle of a voice and watched the senior paramedic jerk a walkie-talkie from his belt to his ear.

"We're needed for another call, Doctor."

"If you think of anything else, anything at all . . ."

"We'll let you know."

The two men rushed away, disappearing from sight around the corner and leaving Finn alone to reflect on the examination of the woman he'd just completed. If he had to guess, he'd say she was in her late thirties, tall and built the way a skier or soccer player might be, with hard lines of banded muscle. Removing the sheet with which the paramedics had covered her revealed some low-grade burns across areas of her exposed flesh. Her clothes had been shredded and draped over her in tatters and were fused to her skin in several places. Finn had used a scalpel to remove the fabric, before bandaging the affected areas.

Finn's initial evaluation suggested the woman had been exposed to elements of extreme heat, the kind normally associated with a level of more intense burns no human could recover from.

Desertron . . .

He hadn't thought of that place in years. Why should he, given its vacant status? There had been rumors of any number of companies looking to purchase or rent the site from the federal government, which actually owned it. Nothing, though, had ever come to fruition; and the massive, unfinished facility had now been empty ever since construction had been abandoned more than twenty years before.

There were also rumors of varying degrees of activity taking place at the site. For this the government offered mundane explanations related to routine maintenance. All Finn could postulate with virtual certainty was that the Desertron facility was somehow responsible for the inexplicable occurrences currently riddling the Waxahachie area. He'd asked a receptionist to make some calls to Dallas-area hospitals to see if they were similarly besieged, but it appeared to be business as usual just thirty miles to the north.

The constant onslaught of patients into the emergency room kept Finn from digging deeper into the potential explanations for all this, leaving him able only to catalog what he knew in his mind. Whatever had transpired around the Desertron facility continued to play havoc with machines, anything that utilized microchip-driven technology. Regular analog watches, by all accounts, seemed unaffected, as were transistor radios and flashlights. As near as he could tell from the patients who'd been brought to his ER, the un-identified woman had been found closest to Desertron, meaning she may have witnessed whatever had taken place. There had been no reports of an explosion, anomalous seismic activity, or wide-scale power outages—nothing to suggest a more pervasive calamity or, God help them, a terrorist attack.

All Finn's imagination could conjure was that some piece of left-over equipment at the facility had gone bad. Damaged or degraded to the point where it had spewed a vast amount of electromagnetic radiation outward. The good news was that none of the patients he'd seen so far presented with anything even remotely suggesting exposure to dangerous levels of radiation. The effects of whatever had happened seemed wholly electrical in nature; and the injuries sustained by his patients, by all indications, were the result of ma-chines going haywire.

Except for the unidentified woman's.

She had presented with injuries consistent with exposure much closer to the source of whatever had transpired. Exposure to heat had clearly caused her burns and the fusing of her clothes to her skin in patches. But even those were not consistent with past burn victims he'd treated. They were more aligned with Finn's experience treating victims of contamination, like firefighters who'd encoun-tered toxic chemicals while battling blazes in manufacturing plants or storage facilities.

Finn checked his watch. Thirty minutes had passed since he'd had the woman placed upstairs in isolation. He'd left strict instruc-tions to contact him immediately in the event anything in her con-dition changed. He'd received a report at the twenty-minute mark that she seemed to be resting comfortably and that all her vitals were stable. He'd drawn blood and ordered up a battery of other tests, but the hospital was so backed up right now, there was no telling how long it would take before he knew any more about her condition than he did right now.

Finn checked his watch again and moved on to treat the next person on his list, a member of a bicycling club who had the misfortune of riding in one of the areas where portions of the pavement had ruptured. He'd just finished stitching up a forehead gash and was ordering up some X-rays on what he believed to be a broken collarbone, when the head nurse yanked back the cubicle's curtain.

"She's awake, Doctor!"

Upstairs, Finn found two nurses fighting to restrain the woman. Blood had leaked through her hospital gown where her bandages had peeled off.

"Can we give her something, Doctor?" one of the nurses yelled to him.

Finn didn't dare take the risk, not without a more thorough examination of the woman's condition.

"No!" the woman cried out herself. "No sedatives! Please! You need to understand what's happening here!"

Finn approached the bed. "Please calm down, ma'am," he said, in his best bedside voice, "and please, tell me your name."

She was a very attractive woman, if not beautiful, with long brown hair that was wild and matted, and blue eyes that were bright and luminescent as crystals. And she was more impressively fit than even his earlier examination indicated, as if she lived a physically active life—or spent a fair number of hours at a gym.

"My name doesn't matter," she said, settling back down as the nurses on either side of her looked on warily. "What matters is I'm not safe here. No one's safe here. *No one.* They'll be coming."

"Who'll be coming?" Finn asked her.

"They followed me across. I don't know how many, but they'll be armed. And, if they're armed, you won't be able to stop them."

Finn came right up to the bed rail, easing the nurse aside. "Followed you across from where?"

"You're not listening to me!"

"I will, but answer my question first."

"I told you, my name doesn't matter. If they followed me here, I'm not safe. You're not safe either, no one in this hospital is safe!" the woman raged, her voice picking up its cadence with every word.

The LED readouts showed her pulse and heart rate climbing dangerously fast.

"You need to remain calm," Finn said, his voice as restrained as he could make it. "No one followed you here. No one's coming. You're safe. But you need to tell us who you are, where you came from. Can we call someone?"

"I doubt where I came from is included in your calling plan, Doctor," she said flatly, her stare never wavering. "Unless it includes roaming to other worlds. Now, tell me where I am."

"Where you *are*?" Finn questioned, befuddled by this patient who seemed to be in more need of a psych evaluation than a physical one.

"Answer me!"

Was it best to play along? Was that the only way he'd ever get anything from her?

"Texas. You were found in the area of a mothballed scientific facility here in Waxahachie."

"Must be where I came through." The woman started to sit up, then thought better of it. "But I need to leave, before they get here. Believe me, it's for your own good, your own safety."

"Do you remember me examining and treating you?"

"No, I don't."

"You've got some nasty burns on your body. And the fact that parts of your clothes melted into your skin tells me you were exposed to extreme heat." Finn leaned over the rail, closer to the woman, trying to develop a least a modicum of trust. "Where were you when it happened?"

The woman lurched up to a sitting position, but held there. "Don't you hear what I'm telling you? They're coming!"

"Who's *they*?"

The woman's expression tightened in fear. "Imagine your worst nightmare. Imagine the monsters that kept you up at night as a child."

"What does that have to do with anything?"

"The monsters are real, and they're coming."

As if on cue, an alarm began to wail in a loud staccato squeal.

"Guess I was wrong," the woman told Finn. "They're already here."

25

POWERING THE FUTURE

"YOU WANT TO TAKE a turn behind the wheel?" Sam said to Alex, as Reverend Billy's van steamed north along I-5 toward the Klamath Mountains. "You know, let me give you a lesson."

"Hey, I've driven before."

"Where?"

Alex shrugged. "Parking lots, back and forth in the driveway."

"Not exactly the I-5."

They'd been on the road for an hour now, Sam settling into an uneasy rhythm of working the steering wheel to keep the van aimed straight ahead. According to the map Reverend Billy had drawn for them, they were halfway to Langston Marsh's fortress in the Klamath Mountains.

"What's so funny?" Alex asked her, when Sam couldn't contain her chuckle.

"I think you're scared."

"Of driving?"

"Uh-huh." Sam nodded.

"After the last two nights, you think anything could ever scare me?"

"Uh-huh." Sam nodded again.

Alex was biting his lip. "Okay, maybe a little," he conceded. "Well, a lot."

"I knew it!"

"I was going to learn how to drive. As soon as the season was over. Really."

"I'll teach you," Sam offered again.

"I think we've got more important things on our mind right now."

"I meant after."

"If there is an after, you mean," Alex reminded her.

Reverend Billy had scrawled out directions to Langston Marsh's fortress over a faded restaurant menu with a big black marker he'd found in the van's glove compartment, which had been held closed by duct tape. As a result, the directions were difficult to read in some places because the black print had soaked through from one side to the other. But they were headed in the right direction and could only hope Reverend Billy's hastily drawn, makeshift map would make more sense once they reached the Klamath Mountains and the landmarks became clearer. It was, in any event, easier to follow than the map conjured on the tiny screens of their throwaway flip phones.

"I thought we were in the same driver's ed class," Sam said.

"We were."

"What happened?"

"I didn't pass."

"Huh? Everybody passes driver's ed."

"You weren't my tutor yet."

"You didn't retake it?"

"Never got around to it."

"Want to tell me why?"

"Not particularly, no."

"Well, it is a little strange. You've got to admit that."

Alex shook his head, looking like he wanted to laugh but couldn't. "In the past couple days, I found out I was an alien, my parents were murdered, and I learned that the world is under attack. And you think me being afraid of failing out of driver's ed is strange?"

Sam jerked her gaze toward him. "You were afraid?"

"Forget I said that, okay?"

"I didn't think you were afraid of anything."

"That's because you bring out the best in me. And everyone's afraid of something."

"You mean, like driving?"

"Don't rub it in."

"I can't help it."

The van started bucking all of a sudden, Sam left squeezing the wheel to keep it straight. It clanked and it clunked, shook and shimmied, the whole time feeling as if it were going to come apart then and there.

"I think we're going to need to stop for gas," Alex said, canting his gaze to check the gauge.

"I'm afraid if we stop, I won't be able to get this thing going again."

"Then we'll get out and push. You heard what Reverend Billy said: Marsh has what we need. And maybe we'll find Raiff there too."

Sam started to look over at him, then thought better of it—the contours of the I-5 required her undivided attention. "But he didn't say what we needed is. You think it has something to do with..." She let her voice tail off, finally turning and letting her gaze linger on him briefly.

"You mean this?" Alex said, tapping his skull. "The fact that I've got a leaky organic computer chip up there that could rupture and kill me any minute?"

"Don't say that!"

"Why not? It's true, isn't it?"

"You're not going to die."

"And how can you be so sure?"

"Because you haven't learned how to drive yet," Sam said, focus back on the road. "You can't die without knowing how to drive."

She caught Alex rolling his eyes. "Sure, Sam, whatever you say."

"And I also say that Raiff is after the same thing we are, according to Reverend Billy."

"But, also according to Reverend Billy, Raiff has gone dark."

Sam thought for a moment. "Can you call Dr. Donati on your phone?"

Alex fished the old-fashioned flip from his pocket. "What's the number?" he asked, dialing the digits as she recited them and handing the phone to Sam as soon as it started to ring.

26

CRUISE CONTROL

IN THAT MOMENT, REVEREND Billy's van rumbled past a huge, spanking-new factory barely visible from the I-5 that, from the outside, could have been anything, especially with the familiar GOOGLE name and logo emblazoned on an art deco sign fronting the property.

Inside, floor foreman John Scotti watched the research and development team going through their checklist on the identical self-driving vehicles lined up in a neat row. Scotti marveled at the progress they were making, the latest test results having exceeded expectations in pretty much all ways, to the point where he dared to consider that mass production might be months ahead of schedule. The problem was the setbacks they continued to encounter every time one of the vehicles was tested in the field. Some of those setbacks were as minor as the vehicles' applying the brakes a bit late when approaching an intersection. Others were as major as their causing multiple-car pileups with serious injuries, and in one case, a death resulting.

That's when all six test vehicles switched on.

Scotti could tell from the perplexed look on the faces of the R & D personnel that they had no more of an idea what was happening than he did. And, like him, they were shocked when the test cars engaged their transmissions and steered straight toward a garage bay door.

"Who's doing this?" Scotti demanded, skirting one of the self-driving cars and darting out of the way of another. "Who's controlling the damn things?"

"No one," one of the R & D guys said, as if he didn't believe it himself. "They're controlling themselves."

27

LIFE IN THE FAST LANE

"WHO IS THIS?" DONATI'S tired, scratchy voice demanded. "How did you get this number?"

"It's Samantha Dixon, Doctor."

"Dixon!" He beamed excitedly. "Where are you? Why aren't you here? I need you here!"

"Something came up. I'm with Alex."

"Why isn't he here? At Ames, Dixon, Ames. You're both needed on the premises now. As in immediately."

"It's not over, Doctor, not even close."

"I'm well aware of that, Dixon. That's why your presence is required in the seat next to me. So we can put our heads together. Sort through all this. Plan our next step. You know, circle the wagons."

The metaphor was lost on Sam, but she didn't bother asking Dr. Donati to elaborate. It was hard to keep the van steady with only one hand on the wheel and she tried crimping her neck to hold the phone in place that way. When it started to slip, Alex grabbed the phone and held it against Sam's ear for her.

"We're headed to the Klamath Mountains," she told Donati, as firmly as she could manage. "Langston Marsh has something there we need."

"And this would be the same Langston Marsh who kidnapped your parents, would've killed you and Alex last night at the drop of a hat?"

"The very same."

"Not a wise move, Dixon, not a wise move at all," Donati scolded. "Think! You're not thinking like a scientist. Reason this out with me. What does Marsh have that you and the boy need?"

"We don't know. Raiff does."

"Raiff's there? With Marsh?"

"We don't know."

"So you don't know for certain if he's there and you also don't know for certain what it is you're looking for."

"That's right."

"Please, Dixon," Donati resumed after a pause, "please stop and listen to yourself."

"No, because if I did that I'd probably turn around and come back."

"Exactly! To Ames, where you can do some real good. We're prepared for this. We're responding."

Sam could tell Alex had heard what Donati said from the way he pressed the phone tighter against her ear.

"Ouch," she managed.

"Sorry."

"Are you okay, Dixon?" Donati said anxiously. "Is something wrong?"

"Nothing's wrong. I'm fine."

"At least let me drive up and meet you there. Let's do this together."

"We can't wait, Doctor, we can't—"

Suddenly she heard a series of clicks, then a repetitive beeping sound filled the line. Dr. Donati was gone, replaced by dead air.

"What happened?" Alex asked her.

"Something's wrong." She tilted her gaze toward the rickety side-view mirror. "Check behind us."

Alex shifted to check the mirror on his side, which looked ready to fall off. "For what?"

"I see some cars. All white, all the same."

"Anything else?" he asked, rolling the window down and starting to stick his head out.

Sam checked the driver's-side mirror again. "I don't think anybody's driving them."

FOUR

THE I-5

Only two things are infinite, the universe and human stupidity,
and I'm not sure about the former.

ALBERT EINSTEIN

28

VISITING HOURS

"WHO'S HERE?" FINN ASKED the woman.

He could hear the alarm screeching over the Baylor Medical Center sound system.

"I told you—they followed me through. You've got to let me out of here while there's still time. I've got to find him!"

"Who?" Finn asked through the still-screeching alarm.

The woman's gaze was hard and determined. "I'm the only one who can help. I'm the only one who knows what to do."

It took all of Finn's composure to remain calm and not raise his voice higher. "I'm going to see what's happening," he said to the woman. "I'll be right back." Then, to the nurses, "Stay with her."

"This is *your* world we're talking about!" Finn heard the woman scream as he closed the door behind him. "There's no time!"

In the hallway and at the nurses' station, Finn could tell people were as perplexed by whatever was happening as he was, and that added to the considerable tension already filling the hospital from the chaos of the morning.

"I can't raise the front desk," a nurse, holding a phone against her ear, told him.

Finn looked toward a pair of armed security guards standing stiffly against the counter. "The two of you, come with me."

They took the next elevator to the ground floor. The guards had their guns drawn by then, ready as soon as the cab's door slid open . . .

To the sight of a half dozen men dressed in commando gear, wearing neoprene masks and wielding automatic weapons.

The hospital guards raised their hands into the air, the guns stripped from their grasps as they were yanked from the elevator.

A pair of powerful hands jerked Finn out after them, a towering figure slamming him against the wall.

"Where's the woman?" a gravelly voice demanded from behind the mask.

He didn't want to answer, but knew he had no choice.

"Upstairs," Finn said, the assault rifle's tip now jammed under his chin. "Third floor."

"Is she armed?"

"What?"

"Did you check her for a weapon, something that looked like a club, maybe a whip?"

"What? No, she doesn't have a weapon."

The man pushed the tip of the assault rifle barrel in deeper. "Take us to her!"

Four of the masked commandos squeezed into the elevator with Finn. No words were exchanged, Finn conscious of his every breath.

They followed me across. I don't know how many, but they'll be armed. And if they're armed, you won't be able to stop them.

Were these the men the woman had been referring to?

If they followed me here, I'm not safe. You're not safe either; no one in this hospital is safe!

The woman's words echoed in Finn's head as the cab slid open on the hospital's third floor. Orderlies, nurses, and Finn's fellow physicians moved aside as the convoy of heavily armed, masked shapes moved purposely down the hallway. The gunmen advanced ahead of Finn, hands tightening on their assault rifles, the woman's room coming into view. Finn realized the guard he'd posted to shut the room off from the rest of the hall was gone.

Concern was already rearing up in him when the men reached the woman's room just ahead of him.

He followed close behind to find the gunmen frozen inside the doorway.

Then he saw why.

The two nurses and the security guard were bound by electrical cords on the floor, gagged with what looked like pillowcases.

And the woman was gone.

29

CARS

SAM TRIED TO COAX more speed from Reverend Billy's van, but the best she could muster with a damaged rear axle was barely forty miles per hour. Alex leaned his head further out the window, gaze aimed backward, when the I-5 dropped out of a curve into a straight-away. He could see the cars now, a half dozen of them, which looked vaguely like Toyota Priuses, all painted white. Enough of the sun pushed itself through the woods on both sides of the four-lane road for him to see clearly into the cars' front seats.

Where nobody was driving.

"You're right," he said to Sam. "No drivers."

Alex realized he could see the inside of the cars more clearly now, recorded the fact that they had no front license plates and a show-room gleam to them.

"We passed a Google factory a few miles back," Sam remembered. "They must've come from there, controlled by . . ."

Alex listened to Sam's voice tail off, no reason to complete her thought since he knew she was picturing everything electronic in her house becoming weaponized. He could only assume the oncom-ing cars were just another version of that. This as the self-driving cars picked up speed, two of them drawing up alongside the old van in synchronized motion.

Thunk!

Impact against the driver's side jarred him, forcing him further out the window to the point where he had to grab hold of the mir-ror on that side to keep from falling.

The mirror broke off in his hand, Alex left holding it when the self-driving car on his side sideswiped the van too.

Thunk!

Alex was angling himself to get his upper body back inside the van when the cars started banging the van across the road, from one side to the other.

Thunk! Thunk!

"You need to do something!" Sam cried out.

As he plopped back into the passenger seat, Alex watched her struggle to maintain her hold on a steering wheel that looked as if it had gone into some kind of writhing spasm.

"They're going to run us off the road!" Sam wailed.

"No, they're not," Alex said and pushed himself over the seat back into the van's cargo area, where Reverend Billy's ratty old mattress took up most of the space and his boxes of Bibles pretty much all of the rest.

Alex went for the Bibles, dragging one of the boxes with him toward the van's rear double doors. He pushed the doors open, just as the trailing three cars drew to within ten feet of the van, riding abreast of each other with a fourth bringing up the rear.

Thunk!

Impact jostled Alex to the right.

Thunk!

To the left this time.

"I thought I was the one who flunked driver's ed," he called to Sam.

"Very funny. Now, do something!"

Thunk! Thunk!

Alex braced himself for the next impact. He was reaching toward the open box of Bibles when the Prius centered among the self-driving cars sped up and rammed the van in the rear bumper, jostling Alex again before . . .

Thunk! Thunk!

The cars on either side of the van ping-ponged it once more, almost jettisoning Alex through the open double doors.

The center car surged forward a second time, directly in line with the van's bumper, Sam left powerless to do anything but fight to stay on the road. The car had just cracked into the van's mangled rear bumper again, when Alex hurled a Bible straight for its windshield. He threw it with the same force and speed with which he could throw a football through a moving tire. Three nights ago, his life was football; all he thought about was football.

Now, he might never play the game again.

Now, this might be as close as he ever came to throwing a pass.

The Bible slammed into the center of the car's windshield, and Alex watched the glass crack into a spiderweb pattern.

"Yeah, take that!"

But the car was still coming, undaunted by the fact that the windshield had been cracked by the King James Bible embedded there.

"Aim for the front grille!" Sam yelled to him from the driver's seat. "Somewhere between the two headlights! That's where the sensors are located!"

Alex took another Bible in his grasp, measured off his toss, and fired the book outward, as the self-driving car hung back, holding its ground while matching the van's speed. The book hit the car's front bumper dead center, bounced off, and dropped to the pavement.

"Damn!"

Alex took another Bible in his hand, adjusted his aim slightly, and then launched it, when the car suddenly surged forward once more. The book struck flush against a lightly flashing blue light, wedging in place there without doing any damage.

"Damn!" he said again, chalking up another failure, when the self-driving car suddenly dropped back, as if an invisible foot had come off the accelerator. It rode backward, canted on an angle that ultimately twisted it into a whirling, churning spin across the I-5. Straight into the path of a car carrier, loaded to the brim from top to bottom.

Alex heard the carrier's horn blare a moment before the truck smashed into the whirling dervish of a vehicle and hurtled the mangled mess of twisted steel, plastic, and rubber airborne. The car seemed to literally disintegrate on impact. The wrenching collision shook the carrier violently and sent it into an uncontrolled spin that coughed the cars it was carrying into the air in all directions. The freeway turned into a graveyard of twisted, broken steel, blocking any further vehicles from coming at them from the rear. But the car carrier remained upright, meaning the driver was safe.

"Oh, man," Alex managed, as the carnage shrank from sight.

At that, the trailing self-driving car sped forward out of the curtain of dust and sparks, roaring straight for the van's open rear.

Alex began pelting it with Bible after Bible, missing the sensor again and again, until a sizzling toss that obliterated a headlight also punctured the area of that dull flashing blue light he recalled from the first car he'd disabled. The car trailing them suddenly listed one way and then the other, trying to recover the bearings that had been torn from it. But it veered off the road into the woods and slammed into a massive tree head-on, folding up like an accordion.

"Got another!" he yelled to Sam, already reaching for the next Bible in the box.

"That's what I'm talking about!" Sam yelled back, having heard the crunching sound of impact.

Two down, four to go, thought Alex, as he tightened his hold on the Bible-turned-weapon.

"Er, Alex," he heard Sam start, and he swung back to look to the front of the van.

Through the windshield, he could see one of the self-driving cars that had been on the van's passenger side pull in front of it, its brake lights flaring just a few yards ahead.

"What should I do?" Sam called to him. "What should I do?"

"Ram it," Alex said.

"Ram it?"

"That's what I'd do."

"You can't even drive!"

"If I did drive, that's what I'd do. Like playing football. Plow it out of the way," Alex finished and then, just as fast, added, "Er, I mean plow *them* out of the way."

He'd spotted another of the self-driving cars, this one from the driver's side, join its twin in front of the van. Riding abreast of each other, the distance between them was razor thin. The two remaining cars at the van's rear, meanwhile, sped up to replace the ones that had surged forward to position themselves before it. Alex felt the grinding as they scraped up against the van's frame in the same moment the lead cars dropped back.

Thud!

In the next moment, their rear bumpers clacked against the van's front one.

"Plow, Sam, plow!" he called to her.

Alex could hear the engine rev, feel the torque rise when the van tried to surge forward. Its engine barked and skipped, pushed the van forward in a series of jolts and starts.

Thud!

And just as fast as he felt the van picking up speed, he felt it slow, its gears grinding, thanks to the driverless cars engaging their brakes, its engine racing and tires starting to squeal. The van bucked, disengaged momentarily from the rear bumpers of the self-driving cars until they drifted back again, holding their position in firmer fashion and further grinding the van's gears.

Impact jostled Alex backward, one foot finding only air when he tried to set it down. He grabbed a leather handhold at the last moment, just as his second foot joined the first kicking at the air. He swung, supported only by the leather strap he could feel tearing from its bonds under the strain of his weight.

Alex heaved his body forward, imagining this was some summer training camp football drill, pushing through the heavy air before him to reclaim the van with one foot, when a fresh jostling kicked him free again.

"Alex!" he heard Sam cry out.

"I'm okay!"

He joined his second hand to the strap, feeling the excess drag tearing it from the last of its bonds when he threw his whole body forward, leading with his feet. His sneakers planted on the van's tattered carpeting just as the strap gave way, leaving him teetering at the edge of the open doors, body canted backward and arms flailing wildly.

He somehow found the sense of mind to drive them forward, drive all of himself forward, latching on to the inside ledge above the open doors and finding enough purchase to hoist himself all the way through. He landed facedown against the mold-riddled and sodden carpet, strangely grateful for the awful smell and dank feel.

"Alex!" Sam cried again.

"I'm okay, I'm okay! I made it!"

"No!" he heard her call out to him. "Look!"

And Alex looked up through the windshield into the front grille of an eighteen-wheeler that had just crested a hill and was coming straight for them.

30

DEMOLITION DERBY

THE SELF-DRIVING CARS RIDING both their passenger and driver's sides had pinned the van in the middle of the freeway, no place to go with the eighteen-wheeler barreling straight for them.

There was a clothes rack, or something, that ran the length of the van's rear, and Alex grabbed hold of it, trying not to picture what the big, speeding eighteen-wheeler would do to the van on impact. He heard its horn blaring, the truck growing to monster size that filled the breadth of the windshield . . .

When he felt Sam jam on the brakes.

The van instantly dropped back from the self-driving cars engaged across its front bumper, as well as the twin vehicles riding it on both sides. Alex watched the big truck obliterate the front two in an ear-numbing collision of steel on steel. They were there and then they weren't, reduced to shards of iron and rubber fragmented and tossed about in all directions.

"Sam!" he cried out, spotting the blur of the tire coming an instant before her.

It smashed into the windshield, the integrity of the safety glass somehow preventing it from penetrating the cab. But Sam's hands were useless on the wheel now, even before the eighteen-wheeler screeched on across the I-5, keeling over onto its side. A shower of sparks kicked up when it spun across the freeway, its cab slamming into the van broadside.

Alex saw, actually *saw*, one of the remaining driverless cars launched airborne on impact. The second car projected into a churning roll across the freeway toward a drop where a delivery truck slammed into it in yet another ear-wrenching, metal-on-metal collision.

"Alexxxxxxxxxxxxx!"

He heard Sam's cry as he landed faceup on the van's floor, which felt suddenly soft and cushiony. He realized he was atop Reverend Billy's raggedy mattress just before the smell of it hit him. His head felt pumped full of air, ready to explode, a pain concentrated just behind his eyes from slamming against one of the sides or the van's carpeted floor, before ending up on the mattress.

Alex's gaze fastened above him, the van's roof seeming to melt away to reveal not the brightness of the day but darkness broken only by stars flashing in a sky he didn't recognize. Huge mechanical pincers, attached to some unseen mechanical monster, were peeling apart the sides as if the metal were no more than wrapping paper. Flaming red eyes loomed overhead, the pincers reaching down for him now, almost there when . . .

Alex came alert again when the van was jostled off the road in the whipsaw of the eighteen-wheeler's force. It lurched into an uncontrolled spin that launched it into a clamoring roll, the van thumping across the soft ground en route to the thick tree growth that swallowed the light and plunged his world back into darkness.

31

MISSION OBJECTIVE

MARSH WAS SURE TO have left guards outside the entrance to his Memory Room, Raiff alone inside it, still bound to the chair. Instead of futilely trying to free himself, he took advantage of the opportunity to measure the distance to the object that was the only thing that could save this world. He tried to gauge his chances of reaching it, if he was ultimately able to free himself. In that moment, the double doors burst open and Langston Marsh barged back into his Memory Room, slamming both doors behind him, with his guards again left on the other side.

"Who is she?" he demanded, his voice echoing through the high-ceilinged sprawl as he stormed toward Raiff. "The woman, who is she?"

"What woman?"

What exactly was Marsh talking about? Was he bluffing for some reason? Raiff knew the best way to cull more information out of him was to string the man along, so he waited for Marsh to continue.

"She escaped the hospital just ahead of my Tracker team. They were this close, *this close*!" He stopped near enough for Raiff to more clearly smell the stale sweat that had soaked into the stench-riddled clothes he'd been wearing last night as well. "You want to take me for a fool, go ahead, but don't play me for one. Tell me who this woman is!"

"I don't know what you're talking about."

"She came here the same way you must have. Don't bother denying it. I was there last night. I witnessed what happened with my own eyes, proof that everything I've believed all these years is true."

Raiff leaned as far forward as his bonds would allow. "You want to know what we found on Alcatraz last night, you want to know what we managed to destroy? An assembly plant, for soldiers and weapons, one of dozens likely scattered across the world. Machines building machines, the machines that will destroy the world, if you don't listen to me."

"*My* world," Marsh said, as if correcting him.

"What?" Raiff asked him.

"You said *the* world. I was correcting you. Because it's not your world. And it will never be your world. This woman came into *my* world this morning, then disappeared from the hospital where she was taken before my men could get to her."

"To kill her, Marsh?"

"That's what happens in war. Ask my father."

Raiff matched the intensity in Marsh's stare, along with the loathing. "I don't know what you think happened to your father or what actually did happen to him. But my world had nothing to do with it. We didn't come here in ships, we came across the space-bridge. I think the military sold you a bill of goods to protect the truth: your father was killed while flying an experimental aircraft subsequently abandoned or discontinued. You haven't been chasing aliens all these years, you've been chasing a cover-up totally unre-lated to the people from my world you've tracked down and killed. Know what that makes you, Marsh? A murderer."

The older man stiffened, his shoulders suddenly looking very small and slight. "The law is very specific when it comes to the defi-nition of murder. And I killed no men, no human beings, according to that definition."

"Really?"

Marsh leaned over, close enough for Raiff to feel the heat on his breath. "And I'm about to kill one more."

"I'd give that some more thought, if I were you," Raiff told him, still trying to make sense of Marsh's claim that a woman had crossed from his world into this one.

A woman . . .

"And why would I want to do that?"

"Because I might be the only chance you have to survive."

Marsh smirked. "Desperation would seem to be something both our civilizations have in common."

"Find the nearest airport to Waxahachie, Texas. See if a private plane took off from there this morning with a flight plan to Medford, twenty miles from here."

"You're stalling."

Raiff looked Marsh right in the eye. "What if this woman wasn't the only one who came through? What if she was followed, and whoever followed her is coming here, after you?"

Marsh stiffened, suddenly uncertain. "And if you're right?"

"Then you better untie me, so I can stop whatever's coming."

"*Whatever*?"

Raiff continued to hold his stare. "You don't want to know, Marsh, believe me."

32

INVASION PROTOCOL

THOMAS DONATI HAD COME to Bishop Ranch in search of Orson Wilder, his former boss at NASA. They had run Laboratory Z together on these very grounds. Today, Bishop Ranch was a sprawling office park that ranked among Northern California's most prestigious business locations. A massive interconnected complex of buildings that made it impossible for him to picture things as they were the day of the fire eighteen years ago when the facility housing Laboratory Z had burned to the ground.

Situated in a tree-laden valley dominated by rolling hills and the same oaks, elms, and spruce that grew like weeds over the entire Bay Area, the city of San Ramon sat in the shadow of Mount Diablo to the northeast. It was a curious mix of urban sprawl enclosed by untouched land that passed as wilderness ruled by grasslands and tree orchards. The dryness of fall had turned the vast plains of grasses a goldenrod shade that would've made for pleasant viewing on any day but today.

Donati walked about the sprawling grounds until he spotted a man seated on a cream-colored blanket splattered with grass stains. The man had long flowing white hair, gnarled and matted into ringlets in places, blue eyes the color of the sky, and a bushy beard that looked like cotton candy. The grounds he occupied alone had a parklike feel to them; likely they were still the civic property of San Ramon, which would explain why the man was allowed to stake his claim here undeterred. He held an unlit pipe in his mouth and a small pot hung from a swivel at his side beneath a sign that read:

DEPOSIT A DOLLAR AND ASK THE PROFESSOR A QUESTION.

But it was a series of larger signs staked in a semicircle around the bearded man's blanket that grabbed Donati's attention first, among them: THEY WALK AMONG US, TRUST NO ONE, THE WAR IS COMING, and, finally the largest: ALIENS GO HOME!

With the exclamation point formed into something that looked like a ray gun aimed downward.

The professor spotted Donati coming and pulled the unlit pipe from his mouth.

"Really, Orson?"

"I'm just making amends, Thomas, seeking redemption for all our transgressions in the past."

"Eighteen years ago?"

"We changed the world," his former cohead of Laboratory Z told him, "and not for the better. I should have listened to you, those cautionary words you spoke. But instead I became hostage to ambition and ego, no better than the lot that come to this place every day to run the rat race I always denied being a part of. How could I not, being a scientist and all? But I was just as bad as the rest of them and, as things turned out, even worse."

Donati sat down across from him and deposited a dollar in the pot.

"It's all our fault, Thomas," Orson Wilder continued, without prompting. "We did this. We opened the door that they came through."

"I didn't ask you a question."

"That's the answer you need to hear, all the same. If you're not satisfied, take your dollar back."

"Money-back guarantee, Orson?"

Wilder shook his head. "No such thing, not in this case, anyway."

"You've got things wrong."

"I've seen the boy, heard his story. And I know about Alcatraz, not everything but enough." Wilder gazed around him, comforted by the familiarity of his surroundings. "You should give up this useless fight and join me here. Educate the world."

"For a dollar per question?"

"A man's gotta eat, Thomas, even if it's to nibble at the corpse of our dying world, while seeking comfort for my sins that have brought these dark days upon us."

Donati glanced up at the sky. "Looks sunny out to me."

"I was speaking metaphorically."

"You were speaking like an idiot."

Wilder plucked the dollar bill from his pot. "Before you change your mind."

"I understand you met my intern."

"Did I?"

"Samantha. She was with the boy."

"You mean the alien we opened the passage for. We might as well have just blown up the world ourselves."

Donati dropped another dollar in the pot. Then he added a five. Wilder's eyes bulged gratefully at the sight.

"I suspect what we unleashed nearly did that, Orson. And it nearly happened again last night at Alcatraz. My intern as much as predicted it, she uncovered a pattern in electromagnetic spiking similar to what I did eighteen years ago. A lot has happened since then."

"And now the Doomsday Clock has finally struck midnight. You should have sought to make amends with me, Thomas, instead of continuing with your unholy crusade. You should have sought forgiveness and redemption, but instead you continued to pave the way for their coming, deluding yourself in the mistaken assumption that science knows no bounds. It's science that's destined to destroy us all, because people like us refused to renounce it when we had the chance. Laboratory Z was an unholy assemblage of misplaced knowledge man was never meant to possess. We opened the door for them, my friend, you and me! We have ourselves to blame for what's about to happen and trying to change it can only prolong the agony we so richly deserve."

Donati leaped to his feet, clapping. "Standing ovation, Orson, standing ovation. Because that performance deserves one." He started to pull another dollar from his pocket, then changed his mind and extracted a ten-dollar bill instead, dropping it into the pot. "No, that's not enough. How about a twenty? Take a twenty."

And he dropped a twenty to follow the same path as the ten.

"As a matter of fact, take it all," Donati continued, taking a cluttered clump of cash from his pocket and dropping the whole wad into the pot before Wilder's gleaming expression. "I can write you a check for more, leave you my credit cards. Your performance calls for it."

Wilder looked up at him from the blanket. "You've bought yourself a lot of answers, Thomas."

"I'm only looking for one."

"What's that?"

"Your specialty: wormholes, spacebridges, and the like."

"There is no *like*."

Donati crouched, his tired eyes meeting Wilder's haggard ones. "I need you to come back with me, Orson. I need you to help me stop this."

Wilder made no move to rise. "You still haven't asked me a question."

"How can you sit there and watch the world die?"

"That's not a fair question."

"I paid for it, all the same." Donati backed off to give Wilder space and so he wouldn't see the fear and consternation in his eyes. "You didn't see what I saw eighteen years ago."

"Your creature formed of pure energy, you mean?"

The tone of Wilder's question indicated it was meant to be cynical, but sounded foreboding instead.

"How many of our people at Laboratory Z did *my* creature kill?"

"It's been so long, I've forgotten."

"I haven't, Orson." Donati pictured those moments as if they had happened yesterday. "I witnessed it all and I haven't had a single good night's sleep ever since. The dreams, the nightmares . . ."

"And what would you have me do?" Wilder asked him.

"Help me save the world," Donati said, before his thoughts veered back to the CT scan he'd studied the previous night of Alex Chin's brain. "And there's a boy's life we need to save too. But first there's something I need to show you."

33

NEW WORLD

ELAINA TRIED TO GET her bearings, the world around her stark in its unfamiliarity. For eighteen years she'd waited for this day, fearing it would come before all the proper preparations could be laid.

And so it had.

She'd dressed in one of the nurse's uniforms, taking the cash and credit cards from the two of them and the security guard. The cards would be canceled soon, if they hadn't been already. The cash amounted, in total, to just over a hundred dollars, and she would have to figure out a way to make it last as long as possible.

Priority one, meanwhile, was finding Alex. He was the only priority, now that the secret of his existence was forfeit. The circumstances as to how all this had come to pass so fast remained sketchy, the little Elaina knew coming from spies placed within a circle familiar with the workings of the Overlords of her world, who were determined to bring him back.

Did they know, at least suspect, all of the truth? She knew they were aware of the chip implanted inside Alex's head and had a vague understanding of that chip's contents. But could they possibly have figured out the rest, the secret known to only a handful, as well?

Elaina could only hope not. The boy was the key, the boy was *everything*. There were ways to get messages between the two worlds, but they were complicated and took vast stores of energy and resources. So, communication over time with Raiff had been spotty at best and nonexistent since word had filtered down that Alex had been found and forces had been mobilized to retrieve him.

The main drag of Waxahachie looked as if it had been lifted from another era of this world. There were simple buildings along the street, mostly colored a mix of brick red and mauve, and they had a down-home comfort and familiarity about them—like Harry's Home Furnishings and the local diner. There was also an emporium of sorts, at which Elaina bought jeans and a shirt and light jacket from the "used" rack. Once they were paid for, she changed into them and stuffed the nurse's uniform she'd been wearing in the trash. Her new clothes felt snug but made for a decent enough fit under the circumstances.

Now she could turn her attention to finding Alex. All told, with everything that had gone wrong eighteen years ago, she counted herself fortunate that he had gone undetected for so long, though she was still uncertain of the precise circumstances which had changed that. Whatever those circumstances were, the clock was now ticking for Earth. If she failed in her mission, this world would die and hers, effectively, with it.

The Overlords wanted to use Earth for one thing. She and the others who'd been fighting them for generations wanted to use it for something else. But the risk posed had become too great for them, starting to outweigh the reward. She knew what was coming next and had only days to stop it.

Which is why she was here. To find Alex and set the plan into motion, to win this portion of an endless war Earth didn't even know it was a part of.

Her son. The beloved baby she had once held . . . and let go. Because he was the answer, because she had been so desperate that he live . . .

When she might not . . .

No, the people of this world had no idea of what was coming.

At least, they hadn't until last night.

Elaina's skin felt itchy, unused to clothing formed of the organic materials wrapped around her now. And the fit was tighter than she was used to. These things she could easily and quickly adapt to. She was well versed in this world's food supply and sources, remarkably similar to her own given the near-identical nature of her metabolism with the residents' of this world. The way food was grown and processed varied, and she expected taste to be something she'd need to grow accustomed to as well. She hadn't expected to be making the journey when she did, the necessity dictated by Alex's true identity having become forfeit. Elaina had no choice but to accept the meager preparations for what they were and self-acclimate to the best of her ability, as long as she freely could.

Because they had followed her across the spacebridge.

And they were coming.

Elaina walked to the outskirts of Waxahachie, attracted by the marquee for Pop's Burger Stand. This big town or small city—she couldn't decide which—certainly had its share of places to eat. But she found this one appealing because of its size, quaintness, and location apart from the population center. Drawing closer, she was also attracted to it by the pleasant cooking aromas sifting out on the smoke belching from what must've been the kitchen. Her stomach had finally settled enough to think about food, and made her realize how hungry she was.

She entered Pop's Burger Stand and took a seat at the counter to keep any of the patrons from getting a good look at her since sitting there allowed her to keep her back to them. A server had just wiped down the spot and set a menu down in front of her, smiling.

"Something to drink to get you started?"

Elaina realized how dry her mouth was. "Water, please. And I'll have whatever you recommend," she added, handing the waitress back the menu.

"Easiest order I've had all day," the woman said, jotting her choice down on an order pad.

She slid away to put the order in, then returned with a tall glass of water served in a rippled plastic cup that looked frosted over. Elaina gulped the water down as the server watched, the ice cubes clacking against each other when the cup was drained.

She wasn't just thirsty; she felt overheated, her bones, flesh, and blood simmering from the inside out. A typical reaction from the flood of electromagnetic radiation hitting her as she'd crossed over. If conditions weren't precise, if the measurements had been off in the slightest, she could have burned up en route; Elaina had seen that happen. And sometimes it took a very long time to cool down again, though there were occasions when those using the spacebridge never cooled off again.

But the water touched her insides like a bucket to flames and she set the glass back down, instantly thirsty again.

"Let me get you another," the server said, eyeing her a bit strangely. "And your burger will be right up."

The water made Elaina feel instantly better, helping to clear her head and sharpen her thinking. If the indications were correct, finding Raiff or the boy could prove very difficult indeed. But she knew Raiff was after the same thing she was, which meant he would be headed exactly where she needed to be. A start, anyway.

Elaina drained her second plastic glass of water more deliberately, the server setting a fresh one down with her hamburger and French fries. She'd never eaten either, but her exhaustive study of this world had familiarized her with the most popular foods so she could more easily fit in, for when this day ever came and because . . .

Because she wanted to know Alex's world better.

She's just taken her first bite, needing to wipe her mouth immediately with a napkin, when jangling bells announced the arrival of three men she spotted in the reflection of the pie case glass. All wearing black tactical gear, the pants tucked into their combat boots.

Elaina laid the burger back on the plate, realizing they were looking at her too.

34

CRASH COURSE

ALEX WAS BACK ON the football field, back where all this had begun on Friday night after the collision that had left him without feeling in his arms or legs and unable to move, fearing he'd been paralyzed.

The paramedics and ambulance were gone, the stands that had turned dead quiet were gone, even the field was gone. In their place were machines, vast tentacled steel monsters moving about with surprising agility. The field seemed to tremble under their weight, impressions that looked like miniature sinkholes left in their wake as their clanking steps kicked up swarms of the black rubber pellets lending the artificial turf its cushion. Alex looked up and saw one of the machines looming over him in place of the EMT, retractable arms extending from slots in what might have been shoulders and positioning themselves beneath him.

Don't touch me! Get away from me!

Alex tried to cry out, but couldn't find the breath he needed. The machines were everywhere, joined now by pilotless fighter drones that cruised the skies like hawks searching for their next meal.

The machines moved with purpose, circling around his still form and gazing down through eyes Alex couldn't discern in their shapeless steel skulls.

Who are you? What do you want from me?

And then he jerked upright, not on the St. Ignatius Prep football field, but the outer stand of woods rimming the I-5. The stench of spilled gasoline filled his nostrils and he spotted the mangled carcass of Reverend Billy's van straddling the shoulder, one stubborn tire clinging to a windswept spin.

"Sam!" Alex cried out, remembering. "Sam!"

He spotted her ten feet away, Sam having been thrown from the van too, and scrabbled toward her across the brush without trying to stand up.

"Sam!" he called again.

But she didn't stir. And when Alex reached her, he saw why:

A metal shard, a remnant of Reverend Billy's demolished van, was protruding from her neck.

35

TODAY'S SPECIAL

THEY WEREN'T WHO ELAINA had been expecting, not part of the force that had followed her across the spacebridge.

Because they were human.

Her relief was fleeting, momentary at best. The men wore pistols holstered to their belts, their eyes steely and emotionless. Soldiers, killers—take your pick.

She'd had a weapon when she came over, but it must've been shed and lost in the blast that had stolen her senses and left her staggering in the general direction of the nearest road. She remembered gazing back as much as forward, fearful the dozen things that had trailed her across the spacebridge were coming. There'd been no sign of them, though, and then the world had gone dark, not brightening again until she had awakened in the hospital.

Those things hadn't tracked her to this diner, but these men had. Langston Marsh's men. Langston Marsh, the man who had what she needed to save this world.

Elaina regarded them in the pie case glass again, their gazes indicating they still weren't quite certain it was her.

Which gave her the advantage. For now.

The server was refilling a cup of coffee for a man wearing blue overalls seated two stools down from her.

"Say, I'd love a cup too."

The server set a mug down before her and started pouring.

In the pie case glass, Elaina glimpsed the three men approaching, narrowing the distance between them. And now she spotted two more of them outside on either side of a big black vehicle.

Five in all. Two outside and three in. Those three drawing closer, hands on their holstered sidearms.

The server finished filling her mug.

"Thank you," said Elaina . . .

As she tore the glass pot from the server's grasp, swinging in a single swift motion and dousing the nearest man's face with the steaming coffee.

His screams drowned out the sound of the glass pot breaking on the skull of the second closest man, the one in the middle. The third was drawing his gun and the two men outside were now charging toward the door.

Elaina still held the smashed coffeepot's handle in her grasp and rammed a jagged shard of glass into the third man's eye before he could free his pistol all the way from its holster. She felt it mash flesh, his eyeball receding in its path, his screams instantly deafening as he twisted wildly, still with the presence of mind to remember his gun.

Except it was gone, held in Elaina's grasp now.

She'd never held such a weapon before, but knew exactly how to use it, intention and thought meshing as one instant unfolded into the next. Her finger found the trigger and fired toward the door, obliterating the glass and blowing a fourth man backward. Then she aimed at the fifth man and fired through the plate glass window, and the window blew outward under the force of the shell that knocked the final man off his feet, splaying him to the parking lot pavement.

Elaina held the gun low by her hip as she moved from the counter toward the ruined door, aware of her fellow diners clinging behind whatever cover they could find. In that moment, she remembered the uneaten hamburger the server had just set down on the counter.

She wanted so badly to go back and eat it.

But she'd reached the parking lot by then; the heavy boots she'd just purchased were crunching over the broken glass her bullet had sprayed over the pavement. That bullet hadn't found the fifth man, but plenty of the glass had; his face and arms were pierced everywhere with shards that drew matching blood lines down his skin. He was groping for the pistol that had fallen just beyond his grasp when Elaina pressed her right boot down on his wrist, raising her own pistol in line with his face.

"One chance," she said flatly, feeling very warm again. "Where can I find Langston Marsh?"

36

SURGERY

"I'M COMING BACK, SAM," Alex said, smoothing the hair from her scratched-up face. "I'm coming right back."

As long as she remained unconscious, he could do this, he knew he could.

Do what?

His thoughts carried him back to the demolished van lying on its side with that stubborn wheel still spinning. Alex had no idea where those thoughts came from, what was spawning them. Instinct was driving him, the same way it drove him to dodge a tackler or know which way a ball carrier was going to veer. But those were learned and well-practiced skills while this was . . .

This was *what*?

Whatever it was drove him to what remained of the van's front seat, looking toward the contents of the glove compartment scattered across the tilted floor. Alex reached in through the door that had broken off from the frame and snatched up a rusted and caved-in first-aid kit that was missing its latch.

Holding it, he rushed back toward Sam and dropped to his knees alongside her, conscious again of the thoughts that were coming one after the other and the pace at which they came.

How can I know all this stuff?

Without Sam's tutoring, he would have flunked out of biology, couldn't tell a heart valve from a car valve. Right now, though, he looked down at Sam with a medical student's knowledge of the anatomy. He could judge exactly where her carotid artery was strictly by feel, certain enough of its placement to be equally certain that the steel shard had just missed severing it. The shard had passed

through the subcutaneous fascia, stripping away a section of carti-
lage, but otherwise missing anything vital.

Huh?

Alex didn't even know the meaning of the words his thoughts
were forming. They came to him as pictures and images replete with
an understanding of tissue and arteries, blood vessels and veins.

An understanding of what he could not possibly understand.

What he *could* understand, though, was Sam was hurt and he could
help her. He pried open the jammed lid on the first-aid kit that might
have been even older than Reverend Billy's van itself. Inside, though,
it had been freshly packed with all manner of gauze and cotton
swabs, wrapped around bottles of peroxide and alcohol. There were
foil packets of over-the-counter pain medications, a roll of white adhesive tape, butterfly stitches, even the proper thread and needles for
suturing.

Alex spotted the traditional Band-Aids last, the kind you'd use
on a cut or a splinter, looking tiny and insignificant squeezed into
a corner of the kit. He took a wad of cotton in hand, before he con-
sciously recorded the action.

Going with the flow, just like on the football field, guided by instinct to the alcohol with which he promptly dampened the cotton
wad. Felt himself press it around the area where the shard of metal
had come precariously close to Sam's carotid artery without fatally
nicking it.

He used the alcohol-rich cotton to hold the metal shard on its
angle of entry, so it wouldn't come any nearer Sam's throbbing artery when he removed it.

Removed it? Did I really just think that?

Before Alex could process his next thought, he was *doing* it, a
spurt of blood followed the shard from the wound it had left. For an
instant, he feared he'd messed up and nicked Sam's carotid artery
anyway. Then he stopped thinking and went back to just doing.

He pressed the wad of cotton against the wound to stanch the
blood flow, as his other hand dipped back into the rusted and dented
first-aid kit for a fresh wad. He replaced the original wad, now sodden with Sam's blood, with the fresh one, realizing he'd also laid a
pair of scissors atop Sam's torso, next to a packet of silk sutures and
a just-the-right-sized stitching needle.

He stopped pondering how he knew these things and watched his hands go to work, guided by something beyond his conscious thoughts. The scene turned surreal, Alex viewing his motions as if they were someone else's. A third party to his own actions. The wound was still oozing blood and then tightly fitted stitches were tracing its jagged line. Some stubborn, stray blood oozed from the wound, so he swabbed it clean and held another fresh cotton wad in place until no more blood followed.

Alex added some antibacterial ointment the first-aid kit yielded, then applied a dressing using layered strips of gauze in a crisscrossing pattern, affixed to the skin with strips of the white adhesive tape. He canted his neck to inspect his own handiwork that felt like someone else's, still trying to fathom what had just happened. His headache had receded, but the pounding was back now.

The chip in my head, the leaking chip! It had to be the chip somehow!

Beneath him, Sam stirred. Her eyelids fluttered, then opened, her gaze out of focus, her eyes widening when they finally locked on Alex.

"What, what happened?"

"Shhhhhhhhhhhhh," Alex said, smoothing her hair.

"My neck hurts."

"That's because I stitched it."

"You . . ."

"After I removed the metal shard."

"You," Sam started again.

Then she tried to sit up. Alex restrained her.

"Easy there."

She seemed to get her bearings, as her gaze locked on to Reverend Billy's toppled van. The stubbornly spinning wheel was finally slowing to a halt.

"They attacked us," Sam said, remembering now. "Those cars attacked us."

A trio of vehicles tore to a halt on the rim of the forest amid the carnage of wrecked husks of steel, doors opening and closing with thuds and thumps. Sirens wailed in the narrowing distance.

Alex eased Sam up to a seated position. "They should have known better."

Then he scooped her up effortlessly, feeling her arms around his neck, as the first of the arriving bystanders rushed forward.

"Hey," said a middle-aged man wearing a shirt buttoned up to the neckline, "you're not supposed to move her!"

"Is that your SUV?" Alex asked him, eyeing the vehicle the man had emerged from.

"Yeah, but—"

"Open the back door for me, please."

The man complied. "I really think—"

"Thanks," Alex said, backing out after laying Sam across the rear seat and closing the door behind him.

Then, just as quick, he jerked open the driver's door and climbed behind the wheel.

"Hey!" the owner wailed, reaching for him.

Alex slammed the door and locked it, casting the man a wave as he drove off to begin the final stretch to Langston Marsh's fortress.

FIVE

COLLISION COURSE

There is only one good, knowledge,
and only one evil, ignorance.

SOCRATES

37

JOINING FORCES

"YOU MAY BE RIGHT," Marsh said, his tone and expression different as he hung up the phone. "A private jet just landed at the nearest airport to us."

"You need to untie me. They'll be coming."

"Why here, why now? What is it you're not telling me?" Marsh demanded, looking even more feeble than last night, when his forces had been wiped out on Alcatraz.

"There's no time for this. And I'll need my weapon back."

"No!" Marsh fumed. "Who are they? Who's coming?"

"You don't want to know. You want to hide. You want to get every man you've got ready to defend this place and get somewhere safe."

"From who, for God's sake!"

"For a mission like this, for them to take such a risk . . ."

"Make sense!"

"Plasteel," was all Raiff said. "Steel, metal in general, can't travel over a spacebridge, not with all those electromagnetic waves bouncing around. So the enemy we're fighting in my world developed a plastic polymer that's even stronger and more resilient. I call the compound plasteel. That's what's coming. That's what would've followed the woman across."

"As in suits, some kind of armor?" Marsh ventured.

"No. You saw what was left of the androids I destroyed at that FedEx store. Traditional buckets of bolts. Metal and steel androids, limited in their abilities by the technology available here. Not so with what's coming on that airplane. What's coming on that airplane will be plasteel, warriors who can withstand anything you can throw at them."

Marsh didn't look convinced. "And these warriors, if they're so indestructible and all-powerful, why hasn't there been evidence of them before? Why haven't I encountered them already?"

"Because their presence reveals the truth of another world with every intention of destroying this one. Their presence forfeits the element of surprise, the ability to hide that they're here. In this particular war, they're the equivalent of a nuclear bomb."

"You called it a war," Marsh said, curiosity piqued by Raiff's choice of words. "You must agree with me, then."

Raiff nodded. "It's the sides you've got wrong."

"Assuming you're right, assuming you're telling me the truth . . ."

"They'll be here soon enough to prove my point."

"After you or me?"

"After what I came here for," Raiff said.

"You came here to kill me."

"Killing you wouldn't be worth the risk."

Marsh came closer to Raiff's bound form again, his frame moving from a portion of his Memory Room bathed in shadows to a spill of light that hit him like a spotlight. "Then what was worth it?"

"A book."

"That book," Raiff indicated, certain a devastating attack was coming which left him no reason to hold anything back

Marsh's gaze drifted to another section of his Memory Room, following Raiff's. "Written in a language no one's ever been able to translate," Marsh said. "Called an elaborate hoax by plenty."

"It's not, believe me. That book contains this world's only hope for survival. For victory," Raiff added, because he thought the term would resonate more with Langston Marsh, something he could understand.

"I want to hear more."

"There's no time. You want to win, Marsh?"

"Win?"

"Stop the real enemy. You've actually been doing their bidding with your Tracker teams, by eliminating those like me who have even more reason to want them gone than you do."

Marsh stiffened, the book forgotten for the moment. "They killed my father."

"They had nothing to do with that, like I already told you. This isn't a science fiction movie. And you need to get somewhere safe."

"There's no place safer than this," Marsh scoffed. "You think I haven't prepared for such an attack? This fortress is impregnable."

In that moment, a screeching alarm began to ring.

"You better hope so," said Raiff.

38

SORCERER

GILLES DE RAIS HAD spent the flight in the private's jet front cabin, sectioned off from the rear by a heavy wall that blocked all electricity, electromagnetic waves, or even base amounts of radio-activity from passing through into the rear section. Nothing that could potentially disturb his soldiers' programming or upset their organic-based nervous systems, that could potentially set them off without command or provocation.

De Rais had never worked with soldiers like these before. In centuries past, he had used elements of his world's science to fashion his own soldiers. He would've preferred he'd be allowed to do that again, here and now, but his instructions dictated otherwise.

He called them the "Companions," after the faction of Alexander the Great's conquering army known as the Companion Cavalry, or Hetairoi. Back then, the Companions galloped into battle in virtually unstoppable wedge formations. Their legendary shock-and-awe-style assaults seemed to spring out of nowhere and typically targeted the undefended rear echelons of enemy phalanxes. A surprise attack unleashed by them was often enough to scatter entire Persian armies.

De Rais had long ago stopped measuring his age in the years of this world. He would live forever, or for however long it took for this world to no longer be considered a threat to his own. Resting for long periods in a kind of suspended animation when his services weren't required, and being awakened whenever they were.

After all these years, he still thought of himself as Gilles de Rais, the first name he had taken upon coming to this world to assume a mission that had now stretched on for seven centuries. That name was known to be associated with a legendary villain of history. As Gilles de Rais he'd been accused of killing hundreds of children through the province of Brittany in France, the vast bulk in the area of Côtes-d'Armor. In point of fact, at least one of these children had escaped his world, brought here to serve as the foundation for a force that would someday return to rise up against their perceived oppressors. De Rais's first mission was to kill them all, each and every one of the children who fit the profile of his intended victim, because it was the only way to accomplish his mission.

And he had succeeded brilliantly.

But not alone, no. He'd had help from an army he'd fashioned himself, using the science of his world to take advantage of what little this one had to offer. His success had earned de Rais historical infamy and a death at the end of the rope strung round an imposter's neck in 1440. Having another man die in his place hadn't bothered him—the man executed as de Rais had deserved the fate, having killed any woman who failed to satisfy him.

De Rais had gone by many names in the years since then. Many names, many countries, many battles.

But only one mission.

And that mission, no matter the name he'd gone by over the millennia, had led to him being branded a sorcerer, a black magician, a witch, an occultist, even a demon.

Which, de Rais supposed, was closest to fact, given that he was not from this world. His mission's purpose here was, and always had been, to serve as sentinel for his own race. Safeguarding it against the enemies who'd fled here to plot and plan for its destruction. They called themselves refugees, but de Rais had another word for them:

Traitors.

Traitors because they came here to hide secrets pilfered from their home world. De Rais's role was to uncover the depositories for those secrets and keep them from falling into the wrong hands, a mission for which his many successes vastly outweighed his few failures.

One of those failures, though, stood out, when his life's mission had brought him to the Admont Abbey in Austria in 1865 on the trail of one of those traitors who'd become caretaker of a book that had to be destroyed at all costs. The traitor had sought to protect that long-hidden book in the guise of a monk, until de Rais, roused from his resting phase, set out to find him. He'd succeeded in that much, succeeded in burning the abbey itself to the ground. But the monk had escaped de Rais's personally fashioned army long enough to hide the book he'd been protecting.

In a library, of all places. De Rais could look for an eternity and never find the book he sought among thousands of other volumes. The monk had killed himself to avoid capture, so de Rais had made sure to burn the section of the library in which the monk had been cornered, hoping that was the end of it.

It wasn't. Media reports chronicled a collector's discovery of the book, a book written in a language no one on this planet could read or translate. De Rais was awakened to take up the book's trail yet again, a journey that had brought him here, to Northern California in the company of his passengers.

The Companions.

Their odd scent permeated even the wall that closed their airless chamber off from any surges of energy or spikes in electricity. An aroma of an empty pot left on open heat for too long, a burnt odor explained by the high temperatures surging through the Companions to keep their inner workings properly engaged. Those temperatures superheated the impregnable plastic polymer that comprised their outer shell to the point where they smelled of corrosion and something like antifreeze at the same time, thanks to the cooling mechanism that coursed through them like blood.

De Rais wanted to be done with them, done with this, as quickly as possible. He would've much preferred working with the creatures formed by his own black magic and sorcery, as this world still called it, far more comfortable with his ability to control his own creations as opposed to the occupants of the jet's airless inner chamber. But he'd be rid of them once this mission was over, his enemies dead and the long-sought-after book in his possession at last.

Soon enough, he thought, as the jet thudded onto the runway.

A proper vehicle was waiting on the tarmac, so he could move the Companions from the jet straight inside the truck without anyone spotting them. That part of the plan went off without a hitch, and de Rais found himself behind the wheel, the directions to his destination in the Klamath Mountains already committed to memory.

39

DESIGNATED DRIVER

"YOU DON'T KNOW HOW to drive," Sam said, sitting up and alert now in the backseat of the SUV.

"I don't know how to stitch skin or remove foreign objects from people's necks either," Alex reminded her.

Her hand trembled against her bandaged wound. "You didn't do this, you *couldn't*."

But he had!

"Just like I couldn't drive."

Sam started to lean forward, then settled back again when she got woozy. Beyond the front windshield of the SUV Alex had "borrowed" she could see they were still headed north on the I-5, the Klamath Mountains towering over them ahead and sharpening in focus.

"I don't remember tutoring you in medicine," she told him. "Or in driving."

"How am I doing?"

"With which?"

Alex looked at her in the rearview mirror. "Either."

"Well, I'm not dead, either from your stitching or your driving."

He cast her that cocky gaze, the familiar glint back in his eyes for the first time since his parents had been murdered Saturday night. "Don't jinx me. We're not there yet."

She was so glad to see that look in his eyes again. And yet . . .

They were rushing toward danger.

Rushing toward death.

"Langston Marsh," Sam heard herself utter.

"Yup."

"But we don't know what we're supposed to find when we get there."

"Raiff will be there," Alex said, not sounding as sure as he meant to. "He'll know."

"But how do *you* know he'll even be there?"

"Reverend Billy told us. Remember?"

"No."

"Maybe you've got a leaky chip in your skull too."

Sam leaned all the way forward this time, battling back the wooziness that left her briefly feeling like the SUV was spinning. "The chip, it has to be the chip! All these new skills you've acquired . . ."

Alex cocked his gaze briefly toward Sam in the backseat. "I told you I'd driven before."

She grabbed the passenger headrest in front of her for support. "When was the last time you stitched someone's neck?"

"A half hour ago." Alex met her gaze in the rearview mirror again. "It was just like Alcatraz, Sam. I saw things there too, I *knew* things."

Sam sighed, squeezed her eyes closed for a moment in case they teared up. "I'm worried about my parents."

"Reverend Billy will take care of them."

She sighed again, deeper this time. "Things are never going to be normal again, are they?"

"They never were, Sam, we only thought they were. The joke was on us all along, especially me."

"Excuse me for not laughing."

Sam could see Alex's throat tense from the backseat, as if he were swallowing hard. "You heard what the Ash Man said back at Alcatraz," he reminded her suddenly, referring to the spectral astral projection shape imbibed with some form of granular mass. "That my parents were still alive, that he could take me to them."

"I think he meant your *real* parents."

She watched Alex stiffen now. "The Chins *are* my real parents." He went quiet and Sam watched him swallow hard before adding, "Were my real parents."

"I know. I'm sorry." Sam hesitated. "Were you tempted to go with him?"

"Not even for a minute. I didn't hear him invite you."

"You would have taken me?"

He twisted his shoulders enough for her to see him shrug. "I don't go anywhere without my tutor."

"You're not a bad driver, when you keep your eyes on the road."

"There's something else, Sam," Alex said, his tone growing somber again. "When I passed out after the accident, I saw the machines again."

"The ones you drew in your sketchbook."

He nodded, even though he wasn't facing her. "They were different this time. It didn't feel random. It felt like they acknowledged me. It felt like they were thinking. And . . . there was something else."

"What?"

"I don't know. Some kind of monster. It was there, but it wasn't."

"Okay," Sam said, leaving it there.

"This monster, it's different than the others."

"Like . . . bigger?"

"Like *everywhere.*"

Sam felt chilled but let it go. "How much longer to Marsh's complex?"

"Twenty minutes, a half hour maybe."

"You didn't program the address into the GPS."

"I've got Reverend Billy's directions."

"Where?"

"Up here," Alex said, tapping his head.

"Last Monday, you couldn't even remember your problem sets in math."

"Right. What a difference a week makes," he told her, driving on.

40

IMPREGNABLE

"THE ALARM HAS BEEN triggered from our perimeter post at the base of the mountain," Langston Marsh told Raiff, after speaking with the complex's command center. "That was the last contact we had."

"How far away?"

"Three miles. And all video surveillance between here and there just went out."

"Untie me," Raiff said.

Marsh held his ground, stiffening even more. "They could just as easily be coming to free you, and you want me to make that job easier?"

"You've had things wrong from the beginning, Marsh, and you've got them wrong now. You want to untie me because, if I'm right about what's coming, I'm the only one who can save you."

"How?"

"With that," Raiff said, gesturing with his eyes toward the object lying on the table against the front wall that looked like an old-fashioned policeman's nightstick.

"And what is it exactly again?"

"I call it my stick, but it's much more than that."

Speak softly and carry a big stick.

Teddy Roosevelt, one of Raiff's all-time-favorite characters lifted from this world's history, had said that. He read a lot, especially loved reading about men he considered heroes for one reason or another. Raiff's stick, meanwhile, was nothing like the one Teddy had been thinking of when he coined his famous phrase. It had been formed of subatomic, programmable particles based on nanotechnological principles. The particles responded to his thinking on command, first lengthening and then either hardening to the texture and weight of titanium steel or softening to be more like a whip. Raiff's mind could sharpen the stick to a razor's edge capable of cutting a man, or something else, in half.

"DNA-sensitive, you said, explaining why it feels like no more than a piece of steel to me."

"Also explains why you can't make it work. But I can and it's the only chance we have to defeat what's coming."

Marsh stopped just short of a grin. "I think you're underestimating our perimeter defenses, and I still have no reason to trust you."

"How about not having another choice?"

"So you say." Marsh's eyes sharpened. "Perhaps this was the plan all along. Weaken me, get me to trust you to facilitate our defenses being overrun. Facilitate you killing me. An assassin, that's all you are."

"I didn't come here to kill you. How many times do I have to say that?"

"As many as it takes to make me believe you, and I don't see that happening."

"They want the book. They've come for the book, just like I did."

Marsh's gaze drifted toward that thick, oversized book again. "Then that language no one's been able to translate . . ."

"Native to my world, but known only to a select few even there." Raiff nodded. "The book was brought here in the sixteenth century, safeguarded for generations by Resistance fighters like me posing as monks at an abbey in Admont, Austria, its existence and potential hidden at all costs."

"Potential to do what?"

"The book contains the means to defeat, even destroy our mutual enemies from my world. To save this world." Raiff hesitated long enough to meet Marsh's stare. "We're running out of time. You need to untie me, while there's still some left, while we still have a chance."

"Unless you're making all this up. Another ruse."

"Your father's death left you chasing aliens, Marsh; you were just chasing the wrong ones. That needs to change today, if you want to live."

The power died briefly, the emergency backup generators kicking on fast.

"Check in with your other security posts outside the complex. They'll be down by now too, Marsh."

Indecision painted Marsh's features as he touched a button on his cell phone Almost instantly, the double doors to his Memory Room burst open and four heavily armed guards stormed inside.

"Take off his cuffs," Marsh ordered.

41

THE LONG AND WINDING ROAD

DE RAIS HAD LET the location's logistics dictate his strategy. Google Earth maps, of all things, had revealed the locations of all the guard posts leading up to the fortress, identifying for him the first targets he needed the Companions to take out. He'd dispatched them to forward positions so they could strike all six posts simultaneously, while he handled the chore of disabling the video surveillance leading from the base of the mountain to Langston Marsh's fortress.

Where the book he had failed to recover over 150 years ago could be found.

All that lay between it and the Companions now was a three-mile private road that wound its way up the mountain like a snake. At that point, even Marsh's defenses, as formidable as de Rais fully expected them to be, would be no match for the force under his control.

It amazed de Rais no end that through all the centuries he had served his world here, how little such operations and warfare in general had changed. The principles remained the same, with only the logistics and weapons varying. So long as he had the Companions, though, none of that mattered.

And nothing could stop de Rais from recovering the book this time.

42

REINFORCEMENTS

"YOU THINK THIS IS it?" Alex asked Sam when they reached a private road off the I-5 North that snaked up the center of the mountain, virtually hidden from view.

"It must be," Sam said, trying to match their location to Reverend Billy's hastily scrawled directions Alex had committed to memory. "What time is it?"

She realized as she posed the question that Alex wasn't wearing a watch.

"Five twenty-five," he said anyway. "Five twenty-six now."

"How could you know that?"

Alex pointed to the SUV's dashboard. "It says so right there."

"Oh. Right."

"We left in Reverend Billy's van just past eleven. Puts us right on schedule."

Sam was seated up front now, still a bit dazed and woozy from their ordeal, but her mind having cleared enough to at least be helpful. She stared at Alex behind the driver's seat, trying to reconcile this version with the one she had known since grade school and had tutored for the past year.

"What?" Alex posed, catching her looking at him, before he started up the winding mountain road.

"It just feels strange."

"What? Me driving?"

"No, it's more than that."

"Like . . ."

"Like you knowing things I don't know."

"You mean, like I'm tutoring you?"

"Kind of, I guess."

"How's it feel?"

"Weird, like I said."

"You said *strange*. And if I could just pull things out of the air somehow, like I did today, I wouldn't have needed a tutor and we never would've met. Try that on for size."

"I'd rather not," Sam said, leaning back and massaging her temples. "Does your head still hurt?"

Alex kept his eyes on the road spiraling before him. "Off and on."

"More on or more off?"

"What's the difference?"

"Your life."

"Maybe I can perform brain surgery on myself to get the chip out."

"I'll stitch you up," Sam offered, trying for a smile. "You know, return the favor."

Alex suddenly jammed on the brakes and threw open the driver's door. "Stay here," he said, an order more than a request.

"What is it?"

He didn't respond, just moved on toward some kind of structure that had been camouflaged to blend in with the brush and foliage that rimmed the start of the road which spiraled up the mountain. He disappeared briefly and Sam was left alone with the chilly mountain air pushing its way into the SUV's cab through the door Alex had left open.

He reappeared moments later, his expression suddenly wary, eyes darting about this way and that.

"What is it?" Sam asked him, when he climbed back behind the wheel.

"Two dead guards. Looked like they got off a few shots, for all the good it did them."

"More drones?" she posed, using their term for the androids they'd battled for two days.

"I don't think so," Alex said, without saying why. "I think this is something different."

Then first explosions thundered through the brush cover farther up the Klamath Mountains.

43

THE BUNKER

THE BLASTS SENT RIPPLES through the complex, the walls themselves seeming to shudder.

"They're here," Raiff said flatly to Marsh.

"And I'm supposed to take you at your word?"

"Unless you want them to take your life."

"Then let's go."

Marsh managed to find a canvas case, wrapped in straps, that accommodated the oversized book and would keep its pages shielded from the elements. There were numerous drawings, averaging one for every other page, as well as that indecipherable language Raiff knew must have befuddled the top linguistic experts Marsh had hired from across the world. Raiff tucked the case under his arm, clinging tightly to it, as they moved to the elevator enclosed by the same four guards.

"Down," Marsh said, and the elevator immediately began its descent. "We're headed for the bunker. It's naturally fortified by tons of rock and shale, to which we've added layers of steel and concrete to make it impregnable."

"Maybe to the technology of your world," Raiff told him, "not mine."

"We'll see about that," Marsh said, his spine stiffening.

The cab door slid open in that moment before the cave-like confines, featuring exposed rock walls in an antechamber set before a sliding steel door guarded on either side by heavily armed men wearing black tactical gear. They snapped to attention as Marsh approached and laid his palm on an optical scanner. A light flashed green, and the door to the fortress's command center opened with a *whoooooshhhh*.

Raiff followed Marsh inside, feeling like he'd stepped into something designed and built by NASA. Huge screens with rotating pictures covered the walls, monitored by technicians working the most advanced computers Raiff had ever seen.

"I won't bore you with a recitation on what it cost to build this place. Instead, let me demonstrate our perimeter-based defenses."

They stopped near a row of technicians working from a slightly raised dais that faced a trio of screens occupying the command center's front wall.

"Show him the guns," Marsh ordered one of the techs.

A few clacks on his keyboard produced a screen dominated by one of the fiercest-looking weapons Raiff had ever seen. A thick-barreled, heavy machine gun he recognized as a prototype for the next generation model of the already fearsome fifty-caliber that hadn't come to market yet. As Raiff watched, the screen rotated among four of those guns, placed at strategic junctions at the building's front, spaced so they could cover the entire sprawl of the approach to Marsh's fortress. Raiff understood now why Marsh had chosen to base his compound here, constructed so that the mountain's footprint protected the rear and both sides, leaving it accessible only from the front.

"Activate the Sentinels," Marsh ordered, and the screen depictions showed the next-generation fifty-calibers rotating from one side to the other and back again. "Once operational, they key off motion and fire in totally independent fashion. The barrels have an automatic cooling mechanism to avoid overheating, and their ammo feeds are currently loaded with five hundred rounds."

"Two thousand in total," Raiff calculated.

"Enough to take out a small army."

"You're not going to be facing an army, Marsh. You're going to be facing something much worse."

"How many of them did you say there were?"

"Enough," Raiff said. "Just ask your men stationed at the guard posts who've already been taken out."

"The Sentinel guns are accurate up to a hundred yards, deadly accurate. They'll cut whatever's coming apart, tear your soldiers, or whatever you want to call them, to shreds where they stand."

"Your language doesn't have a word for what they are."

"Fitting, since they came from your world."

"And that's where the connection stops," Raiff said, continuing to follow the steady, ominous sweep of the big guns.

"You said you were the boy's guardian."

"For eighteen years." Raiff nodded. "Ever since I brought him here."

"*You* brought him here?"

"The mission of the Resistance was compromised. We'd been infiltrated, betrayed. I had no choice."

"And his parents?"

"Dead on both sides of the Universe."

"So you've been watching him all this time."

"Yes."

"But nothing happened until he was hospitalized after that football game."

"Right again," Raiff said, leaving it there, not bothering to elaborate on the CT scan that had set off a warning bell somewhere that Alex had been identified and located.

"You haven't told me what makes Alex Chin so important."

"And I'm not going to, not yet anyway."

"And this book," Marsh said, "you say it contains some kind of blueprint to defeat the forces you claimed to have escaped? How?"

"I don't know any more than what I told you. The book's the answer to winning the war against the world I came from—that's all I know. I don't know how, I don't have the specifics. We've run out of choices. It's all we've got left."

"Along with the boy. That's correct, isn't it?"

Raiff again stopped short of telling Marsh about the chip in Alex's head. One of the armed guards, not the biggest but definitely the most formidable, had wedged Raiff's stick through his belt. Raiff began measuring the distance between them, calculating his chances of getting to it before the other guards got to him:

Not good.

"We can't get the approach cameras back online," a lead technician informed Marsh, spinning around in his chair. "Just the ones offering a view of the—"

As if on cue, three different viewpoints of the fortress's front began flashing red ALERT signals. On the four screens labeled SENTINEL 1, 2, 3, and 4, the guns locked steady, their sensors having homed in on the motions of an approaching enemy.

"You still haven't told me how many of these things we'll be facing," Marsh said.

"We're about to find out," Raiff told him.

And, with that, the big guns started firing.

44

THE BATTLE OF KLAMATH

THEY REVERBERATED IN A constant roar, the sound filtering inside from exterior speakers broadcasting the guns' ratcheting roars. The Sentinels swept from side to side, freezing whenever their sensors locked on to motion or body heat. On the screen associated with each gun, a counter clicked off the rapid depletion of shells, counting down from five hundred.

The huge shells sliced through and chopped up all manner of trees and brush, launching clouds of debris into the air, their angle sparing nothing as the foliage visibly thinned before Raiff's eyes. The seasons changed from fall to winter right in front of him, time winding in fast-forward. Not a single square inch was spared the onslaught, making him think nothing that lived and breathed could survive such an onslaught.

At least nothing from this world.

The guns' primary firing angle was downhill, toward the thick swath of foliage that climbed the ridge, ending in the rocky expanse that dominated the clearing set between the ridge and the fortress itself. Raiff noted the big guns' angles shifting slightly straighter with each pass, realigning themselves as they recorded motion drawing closer to the plane on which Marsh's fortress was perched.

Which meant the army from a world entirely foreign from this one was still advancing.

"Oh my God," he heard Langston Marsh mutter.

Because that army had emerged from the cracked, broken, and thinned brush shredded by the big guns' incessant fire, while counters all dipped below the one-hundred-round mark. There were a dozen figures in all, dressed in form-fitting black suits beneath rounding, bald skulls that shined like wet plastic. Raiff thought of the action figures kids bought in toy stores blown up to the size of department store mannequins—that's what these creatures looked like. Hard to discern their precise size from this perspective, but they were big and identical, formed, it seemed, from the same mold.

The soldiers' features were uniformly bland and motionless. Their mouths didn't open. Their eyes didn't blink so much as flash into robotic motion, like someone else was controlling them, even though Raiff knew that their programmed actions were independent. There were dull patches amid the shine on their faces and exposed skulls, along with tears and slits, where the big guns' fifty-caliber shells had left their mark. But there should have been nothing left, gaping holes revealing their mechanical innards, their plastic-like skin pockmarked, drilled through, or at least dented. As things stood, two of the soldiers were missing one eye each. A third had lost a hand somehow, while the head of a fourth lopped to the side on almost a ninety-degree angle, which hadn't seemed to slow his approach in the slightest.

As Raiff and the others in the fortress's command center watched, the things raised submachine-sized rifles he knew fired concentrated plasma rounds the size of small marbles that expanded with exposure to air and exploded on contact, a seemingly endless supply packed into squat, rectangular magazines.

The fact that no metal could pass through the spacebridge meant those guns must have been manufactured on Earth. Or below it, within futuristic factories like the one they'd found beneath Alcatraz prison. His enemies had been preparing for this time for centuries, the stores of weapons and machines at their disposal incomprehensible and even infinite, like the streams of fire surging from the robotic soldiers' plasma rifles. There was no need for them to blend in, as other infiltration units were built to do. These were constructed with one purpose in mind and one purpose only, which did not require them to appear human.

Their fire blew the Sentinel guns apart before chewing into the fortress itself.

"Got them just where we want them," beamed Marsh, fitting a headset into place. "Fire at will," he ordered into it.

De Rais could hear the echoing ratchets of the constant fire stream from his position farther down the ridge, where he'd be safe until the battle was over. The programming of the Companions in his charge was deceptively simple: kill anything that moved, breathed, or possessed the thermal signature fitting a human being. No mercy and no exceptions, because the Companions' programming rendered them incapable of either.

Once their fire died down and ultimately petered out, de Rais would scale the remainder of the ridge to retrieve the book that had eluded him in Austria back in 1865. To him, 1865 felt like yesterday, his life measured only in those periods of activity once roused from his longer periods of hibernation when the need arose. Otherwise, his biogenetics weren't altogether different from those of this world. His particular biogenetics stopped all cellular degeneration and wasting in those periods when his physical mechanics shut down, essentially going into a period of stasis or suspended animation. In the six centuries he'd been on Earth, de Rais had banked barely twenty years of living. It felt somewhere between an eternity and no time at all, as if his life consisted of a series of disjointed moments in time.

He continued to listen to the sounds of the battle raging above, picturing his Companions advancing on the fortress now, the first breach coming at any moment.

Fire at will.

In the wake of Marsh's command, the perspective on the screens before Raiff changed to a front-on shot of the compound. Clear enough through the haze of muzzle smoke and debris clouds to show exterior panels sliding aside, so Marsh's men could slot their weapons through without exposing themselves.

Raiff recognized the short, squat barrels as belonging to the kind of grenade launchers affixed with a circular drum that pumped shell after shell into the barrel. Each jerk of the trigger fired an armor-piercing, fragmenting shell with an explosive force on impact equivalent to ten traditional fragmentary pineapple grenades. What looked like a trio of 7.62 mini-guns opened up as well, their barrels spinning in blinding fashion behind the constant stream of bullets bursting from them.

Between those and the roar of grenade after grenade showering dirt, rock fragments, and debris in all directions, the world before the fortress was mottled by a thick cloud that fluttered, thickened or thinned in waves that varied according to the level of fire. Raiff searched for motion within the cloud, finding it only in muzzle flares aimed upward for the defensive slots from which relentless streams of fire poured downward.

On the perimeter security screens, he watched the cloud slowly dissipate to reveal the humanoid machines chewed up in spots, smoking and charred, but all still plenty whole enough to continue their advance. Even one cut in half at the torso somehow edged on, its upper body pulling itself over the rocks and stray brush, while its lower half followed toward the entrance to the fortress.

Langston Marsh clearly didn't know what to say or do. He'd thought himself to be invincible here, especially from whatever effort the ragtag brand of refugees he was hunting might mount. Never, Raiff reasoned, had he expected anything of this magnitude, just like the bully who has no idea how to respond when someone fights back.

"We're safe down here," he said, groping for reassurance. "I'm sure of it."

On one of the screens, now displaying the fortress's interior, the steel-reinforced blast doors blew open behind a surge from the plasteel soldiers who'd come from Raiff's world. The camera caught glimpses of Marsh's mercenaries, members of his personal Fifth Column, rushing in to confront the enemy's much smaller number, only to be obliterated in waves, cut apart by the relentless fire from the plasma rifles. The force of the blasts obscured much of the picture in splotches, turned the misty sprays of blood and bone into nothing more than flickers of motion.

Raiff remembered he still had the book clutched under his arm in the protective, canvas case Marsh had provided and switched it from his left arm to his right. "Is there an emergency escape route?"

"Yes," Marsh affirmed, "but not from here. I told you this command center is impregnable. We'll wait them out until help arrives. We'll—"

Marsh stopped when the world itself seemed to shake, the heavy steel entry door that led inside the bunker bending inward with each impact.

"You better give me my stick back," Raiff told him.

45

WALK SOFTLY AND . . .

DE RAIS CLIMBED THE ridgeline. The once-incessant fire had already slowed, now sporadic at best, concentrated as opposed to wild. He pictured the Companions ferreting out the last of Marsh's men, and he wanted to reach the scene before the book could be somehow hidden from him again.

His life's mission was to retrieve it, so close to success now he was swept away by a euphoria that was easily the most powerful emotion he'd ever felt.

Because the book would soon be in his hands.

The heavy door continued to bend inward, starting to show separation at the seams both top and bottom before the sides started to buckle as well, giving way.

Stick in hand, Raiff watched Marsh's soldiers take up positions behind whatever cover they could find. The rest of the command center personnel huddled behind toppled desks and counters that stood no chance at all of withstanding plasma rounds.

The door was just about to give when Raiff handed the covered book to Marsh.

"You're trusting me with it?"

"Because it means I have to protect you and that will keep you from running."

Marsh shrugged and didn't argue the point. His features were bled of the cocksure certainty and abrasiveness that had character-ized his interrogation of Raiff in his Memory Room. He was just an

ordinary man now, stripped of his power and impotent in the face
of his fallen defenses.

The door finally gave, blew inward off its mounts behind a final,
relentless charge by the soldiers who'd come across the spacebridge
in Texas, just after the woman Marsh's Tracker team had traced.

The woman . . .

Raiff hadn't had the opportunity to ponder that further, but he
knew who she was, who she must be. Only one woman would risk
such a journey, knowing the trip was likely one-way.

Elaina . . .

But how could that be? When he'd seen her last, presumably for
the final time, she had been pushing him into the entrance to the
spacebridge after pressing her own baby into his arms. Willing to
sacrifice herself to assure her child's, and her world's, survival.

Could it be, might it be possible that—

Raiff's pondering was interrupted when a furious barrage of
gunfire from Marsh's guards greeted the entry of four plasteel soldiers into the command center through the breached security door.
It bent all four of them slightly over at the waists, held them still
for a time, before they straightened up again and returned the fire
in a dizzying wave, the plasma bullets dragging mini-vapor trails in
their wake. The plasma rifles generated combustion without a firing
pin or typical gunpowder charge, so the fire emerged in a smooth,
unbroken stream, flowing through the air like water.

Marsh's gunmen were standing and then weren't, the four soldiers
spinning in eerie unison, seeming to lock on to Langston Marsh.

That's when Raiff pounced.

He had remained at the edge of their vision, knowing Marsh
would be their primary target and they couldn't possibly be aware
of Raiff's presence yet. Raiff snapped his stick outward, extending it
into a whip snapping and biting at the air.

His first strike wrapped around the neck of the farthest soldier,
coiling like a snake in the moment before Raiff jerked and twisted
to slam him against the others. The plasteel soldiers ended up in
a tight cluster, clumped so close together they couldn't fire their
plasma rifles. That gave Marsh's remaining guards free rein to fire
on them at will. Raiff watched some of the bullets crackling off their

shiny skin. Others bullets fired from such close range that they tore off strips of fleshlike polymer from their polished faces. He pulled his whip off the initial soldier he'd targeted and lashed out in a wider motion just as quick. It unfurled and stretched out, looking like a massive tentacle as it wrapped itself around the entire clump of humanoid shapes.

Raiff twisted his hand so his closed palm was turned upright, picturing the whip wrapping itself firmer, its molecular particles forming and re-forming as it tightened and tightened around the torsos of the four soldiers. Compressing them as narrow as they could go, and then continuing to squeeze until . . .

Splat!

The soldiers burst apart at their waists, torsos tumbling to the floor, dragging sinews of thick rubbery wire amid a shower of sparks.

"You did it!" Marsh said in disbelief, eyes fastened on Raiff's whip as he retracted it back into a stick. "You really did it!"

"Not yet. There are still eight of them left."

"Press yourself against the cab's side," Raiff ordered Marsh as the elevator climbed back toward the surface. "All of you," he added to the three guards who'd accompanied them. "Out of sight when the door opens."

The guards and Marsh took positions as Raiff had instructed. The cab coasted to a halt, and the doors slid open to reveal three more of the big matching shapes. Their hands were ready on the triggers of their plasma rifles they never pulled, because Raiff worked his whip to strip them from their grasps.

He lurched from the cab in the next instant, whip lashing across the things' faces, a blur through the air as it snapped over and over again. Tiny orbs skittered across the floor, and Raiff counted them to make sure he'd gotten all the soldiers' eyes, blinding them and stealing the primary means of input into their chip-fueled brains. Robbing them of sight forced them off-kilter, causing them to stumble and stagger about. Raiff stooped to retrieve one of the weapons stripped from their grasp, only to have another in their number kick it away again.

"The exit!" Raiff yelled to Marsh. "You'll have to lead the way!"

And Raiff fell into stride alongside the man who'd been interrogating him just minutes before.

"The front's the closest," Marsh managed, heaving for breath.

"The front, then."

The gunfire still buffeting his ears from other areas of the complex told Raiff that the killing machines from his world were engaged with whatever was left of Marsh's mercenary force. The gunfire had dwindled to sporadic echoes coming from places Raiff couldn't identify, but the path was clear to the entrance toward which Marsh was leading the way.

"You need to blow this place up!" Raiff said as they tore toward the light beyond the breached doors. "You need to bury the rest of them in rubble, tons of it!" And when Marsh hesitated, his lips trembling, Raiff continued, "I know you can do it, I know you must have this place wired to self-destruct."

Marsh slowed, swallowing hard. The three guards from the command center surged outside ahead of them.

Straight into the twin halves of the plasteel soldier that was waiting.

46

ESCAPE

THE THING'S SEVERED TORSO spewed thick veins of rubber. Its lower half tripped one of the emerging mercenaries and began stamping at him, quickly crushing his throat with a heavy tactical boot. One of its hands still held fast to a plasma rifle, its bullets tearing Marsh's other two men apart.

Raiff shoved Marsh aside, making sure the man kept the canvas bag holding the book tight in his grasp. Outside, Raiff snapped his whip one way and tore the plasma rifle from the upper half's grasp, then whipped it around and sliced down the lower half's center. Its two legs fell in opposite directions, spitting sparks and flaming at the tips of its severed inner workings.

Raiff snapped the whip sideways next, slicing off the top portion of the upper half's skull starting halfway up its forehead. More sparks leaped from the thing's ruptured brain works, accompanied by a sizzling hiss Raiff felt as well as heard. The thing's eyes looked up at smoke now rising from the chasm where the top of its skull had been, then down toward the severed portion, before locking up and keeling over face-first.

Wasting no time, Raiff retracted his whip back into its stick form and darted back through the breached entrance to find Langston Marsh trembling on the floor behind a wall's cover, clutching the canvas bag to his chest as if it were an infant.

"What have I done?" he was muttering, in dazed fashion. "What have I done?"

Raiff hoisted him to his feet. "What matters is what you've got to do now!"

Shielding Marsh protectively, he burst back into the light in the same moment a new figure he didn't recognize emerged from the foliage at the head of the ridge spared the onslaught of the Sentinel guns. The stranger's eyes bulged in shock.

"*You!*" he rasped, eyes meeting Raiff's. "After all these years... You're dead! *You're dead!*"

Raiff yanked out his stick, turning it into a whip again, as the stranger twisted away, disappearing back into the cover of the brush, something square and shiny flashing in his hand.

"Who was that? How did he know you?"

"I have no idea, Marsh. Get ready to bring this place down," Raiff added, the sounds of gunfire now over.

"I'll never make it down the mountain on foot," Marsh gasped, doubling over.

Raiff took the canvas sack containing the book from his grasp and looped his arms through the straps. "I'm not giving you a choice. Let's go."

An SUV tore over the last of the ridge and screeched to a spinning halt on the flat stretch of ground between the fortress and the ridgeline. The driver's window was already down, revealing Alex Chin behind the wheel and Samantha Dixon seated next to him.

"You've gotta be kidding me," Raiff managed.

"Ha-ha," Alex said, pretending to laugh. "Now, get in."

How could it be? de Rais thought, racing down the mountain along the same trail he'd followed the Companions, the remainder of which continued to lay waste to Marsh's complex.

Over a hundred and fifty years ago, on the trail of the long-sought book, he'd traced it to that refugee who'd hidden in the guise of a monk at Admont Abbey, a monk whom de Rais recalled as if that had been yesterday.

That's how he was sure of what was plainly impossible. Because the man he'd just laid eyes on, the man wielding a weapon from his world as opposed to this one, was...

How could it possibly be?

... that monk!

De Rais was still searching his mind and memory for an answer when a rumbling explosion shook the ground, a huge burst of flames sprouting from the ridge above.

The blast shook the SUV, its tires seeming to leave the ground briefly before thudding back to the uneven surface of the mountain road that snaked from the base to Marsh's now destroyed fortress.

Marsh was still holding the cell phone he'd used to activate the destruct mechanism, as if wondering what he'd just done.

Next to him in the backseat, Raiff leaned over and scooped the canvas bag containing the book from the floor by Marsh's feet.

"You're driving," he said to Alex.

"I am."

"But you don't know how."

"He knows how to do this too now," Sam said, from the front seat, showing Raiff the neat bandage stretched across her throat.

"What happened?"

Alex cast a quick glance toward Sam before responding. "Let's just say Reverend Billy won't be getting his van back."

"Pull over," Raiff said. "I'll drive."

"Whatever you say." Alex frowned, as if his feelings had been hurt.

He jammed the brakes hard and threw their stolen SUV into park. Then he climbed out and exchanged places with Raiff, who tore off before he'd even gotten the driver's door closed again.

Sam's eyes locked hatefully on Langston Marsh. "Bet you didn't think you'd be seeing us again."

Marsh didn't acknowledge her, staring blankly at his phone's screen as if he'd slipped into some kind of trance.

"Is this . . ." Alex started, sliding the book out from the canvas bag he'd noticed Raiff holding. "This is it, isn't it?"

"Is what?" Raiff asked him.

"What Reverend Billy told us Marsh had: an object that's the only thing that can help us win."

"Close enough, yes."

"An old book?"

"It's a lot more than that, believe me."

"Why?"

"Because nobody's ever been able to read the language," Raiff said.

"I can," Alex told him.

47

RESIDUE

DE RAIS MOVED AS close to the blast zone as the heat, flames, and soot-rich air would allow. The implosion of the structure, the way the layered explosives had collapsed it in upon itself, gave him little hope that any of the Companions had survived. Still, he had to be sure before slinking off himself.

The man he'd glimpsed, the man who might've been a twin of the monk he'd chased down in 1865 . . . How could it be?

De Rais hadn't managed to snap a picture of that man before he'd fled in a black SUV that had torn onto the flat patch of ground in front of the compound out of nowhere. But he had managed to hold down the button of his phone's camera and get dozens of shots of the vehicle itself. Those shots would be uploaded to a program powered by software designed by the National Security Agency, capable of tracking any vehicle from its point of origin. It utilized all manner of satellite and security camera footage, in conjunction with complex algorithms that filled in the travel gaps, to pin down a precise location.

The Companions were invincible on this planet, used only for the most extreme purposes where the risk and residue were deemed worth it. But they had failed in their mission thanks to this man, this stranger who was a twin of the monk.

Could it be the same man? No, the monk was dead, having perished in the fire that had consumed much of the abbey. Someone else, then, who must have been an ancestor of some kind.

One of the pictures he'd taken revealed Langston Marsh himself clutching a canvas bag bearing the approximate dimensions of the book de Rais had been pursuing for centuries. Scrolling through the rest of the shots he'd snapped off on his cell phone yielded a pleasant surprise, a positive among a day that had not gone at all as planned. The driver could only be Alex Chin, another escapee from his planet who'd been brought to Earth as a key cog in the Resistance's ultimate plot. De Rais was not privy to the details beyond that, knew only that capturing the boy had been placed at the top of all priorities, once he'd surfaced after eighteen years on Friday night.

That meant it was still possible to salvage this mission by recovering the book and the boy. De Rais, of course, would not have the Companions to serve him toward that end anymore. That meant he would have to summon another force, a force as deadly and efficient as the Companions, though more difficult to control and at times unpredictable. It was the collateral damage they wrought that made them an option of last resort. That collateral damage was a harmless liability in more ancient times, but an unacceptable one today.

Until now.

SIX

SAVIOR

When injustice becomes law, resistance becomes duty.

THOMAS JEFFERSON

48

DIAGNOSIS

"I LOVE WHAT YOU'VE done with the place," Orson Wilder said to Thomas Donati, an Ames visitor's badge flapping against his chest thanks to the lanyard looped over his head.

"We've come a long way since Laboratory Z," Donati told him, the spiraling corridor before him seeming to have no end and the arched roof giving it the feel of a vast tunnel.

"Apparently not, Thomas. In fact, I'd venture to say quite the opposite is true. Laboratory Z was just the beginning of what we set into motion and what you've dragged me back into."

"The beginning you speak of actually dates back millions of years before that, but no sense in quibbling."

They reached one of the center's astrobiology labs, accessible once Donati fit his access card into the appropriate slot and waited until the door clicked open before removing it.

"Is this where you perform all those terrible experiments on alien beings you've managed to capture?" Wilder smirked.

"No, that's the next door down."

"Very funny."

Donati kept his expression flat and deadpan. "You asked."

"Sorry I bothered. Don't make me sorry I agreed to come back and help you save this boy's life."

"What happened to saving the world?"

"One step at a time."

"In this case, Orson, they might be one and the same thing."

Donati led Wilder inside the lab and closed the door behind them. They were alone in the spacious confines, Donati having arranged the lab to be cleared since none of the technicians were in a position to help them.

"I've never seen electron microscopes like this," Wilder said, moving toward one of the three with which the lab was equipped and running his hand along its casing almost lovingly.

"They were developed specifically for analysis of what astronauts dragged back with them from space. Where most see a rock—"

"We see a world," Wilder completed the thought.

"Nice saying. I've used it often. Apologies for not crediting you."

Wilder left his hand atop the nearest microscope. "And did your efforts ever produce anything, prior to this past weekend? I feel like I should be charging you a dollar for the answer."

"My credit's good. And the answer's no, Thomas. Nothing organic or biological, not even a microbe or germ."

"Space remains an unforgiving place."

"If it wasn't, Orson, I suspect our civilization would've been wiped out many times over from exposure to some germ or microbe harmless in its own environment, but deadly in ours."

"Germs and microbes aren't the issue here, though, are they?"

Wilder swung toward Donati from the microscope, which was hardwired to a computer rigged to one of the most powerful servers in the world. Among the other contents of the lab that drew his keenest attention were the incubators, benchtop homogenizers, centrifuges, spectrophotometers, tube rotators, and vacuum-sealed containers outfitted with robotic pincers of varying sizes that could do everything the human hand could do. Wilder's gaze lingered last in amazement on the molecular biology equipment to manage hybridization and electrophoresis. The lab was also outfitted with wall-mounted, flat-screen monitors, so findings could be projected for all to see.

"I want you to tell me all of this, what the world's experiencing now, isn't our fault," Wilder said suddenly, his attention back on his former cohead of Laboratory Z.

Donati was all too happy to do just that. "The wheels were set in motion long before the day in question eighteen years ago. And actually, quite the opposite is true. The day we lost Laboratory Z, we gained hope for the world. Because that was the day this boy came across from his world to ours via the rudimentary spacebridge we constructed—with a chip in his head, like nothing you've ever seen before. A million years and untold technological generations beyond anything you'll find here, or in any division of NASA. A mix of organic materials with subatomic particles keyed to his DNA, so as not to be recognized as a foreign body by his immune system. My guess is the chip contains nothing we consider to be hardware whatsoever."

"You *guess*?"

"I was only able to review the boy's CT scan in the few moments before our tour boat was sunk by your friend Langston Marsh."

"I honestly believed he was the world's friend, Thomas, cleaning up the mess we made eighteen years ago."

"Nothing could be further from the truth," Donati said. "You should understand that yourself now, after meeting the boy."

"And your intern. Brilliant young woman, from what I could tell. She must have a good teacher."

Donati nodded. "Last week, Samantha Dixon uncovered a pattern of electromagnetic anomalies it took a supercomputer for me to find."

"I still remember you chasing me into the elevator eighteen years ago," Wilder reflected. "Maybe if I'd listened . . ."

"It was already too late, Orson."

"I meant listened to your earlier warnings about slowing the pace of our experiments."

"Neither of us could ever have imagined someone coming through the doorway we opened. And if you'd listened to me, Alex never would've come across and our world would have no hope now."

Wilder looked at Donati, his expression growing first somber, then fearful. "The boy wasn't the only thing that came across that day, though, was he?"

Donati stuffed his hands in his pockets so Wilder wouldn't see them trembling.

"What if that thing comes back, Thomas?"

"Then we'll destroy it again."

"We didn't destroy it the first time. You know that as well as I do. It can't be destroyed. And what if there's more than one of them this time? What if there's an army of those things?"

Donati started to look away, then fastened his gaze on Wilder.

"I've been preparing for this, or something like it, ever since you dropped off the grid."

"And what's become of your intern?"

"I heard from Dixon this morning," Donati said. "Sounded as if she'd encountered more inexplicable phenomena. Sounded like they were still after her."

"Who?"

"The ones after the boy, because of that chip in his head, whatever it contains."

"You've seen it?"

Donati nodded. "I told you: from multiple angles in the CT scan done when he was first rushed to the hospital after being concussed on the football field. I was proceeding on the notion that the force of the impact dislodged it somehow and caused the leakage that showed up on the scan."

"Leakage?"

"The chip's degraded organic material leeching into the tissues of his brain."

"It's possible," Wilder agreed. "But where's this scan? I can hardly wait to see it."

"It's gone."

"You don't have the actual CT scan results?"

"My laptop was lost when the tour boat was sunk and the thumb drive I'd backed the scan up on, well, let's just say what we encountered on Alcatraz wiped it clean."

"Then use one of these computers of yours and draw it for me, Thomas."

"Not a bad idea," Donati agreed, moving to the nearest terminal.

49

SYMPTOMS

THE DRIVING DISTANCE FROM Waxahatchie, Texas, to the Klamath Mountains was nearly two thousand miles, and Elaina had started out her journey in the big SUV that had delivered the men she'd neutralized at the diner.

Elaina figured she could make it in thirty hours or slightly less.

That changed after only six had passed. Traversing interdimensional worlds over the spacebridge was not without side effects, but the intensity of them surprised her. Her first symptom was the color washing out of the world, everything turning to black and white. Then her hearing became hypersensitive, recording every tick and clack of the big engine as it hummed away. She switched off the radio, but could still hear the sound of the talk radio voices, as if her own body's electrical receptors had received the signal on their own. Finally, a numbness spread over her hands and feet, turning the mere act of steering or working the accelerator pedal into an arduous and then an impossible task.

She'd already researched the drugs available here she needed to relieve the symptoms, at least for a time. For motivation to keep going, she need only conjure a picture of Alex in the clutches of Langston Marsh. For added motivation, she need only think of the book that only Alex could translate in the madman's possession.

Find the book.

Find Alex.

Save this world, so she could save her own.

But her body temperature had spiked to a point where she wondered how much longer she could go on. Even turning the air-conditioning up as high as it would go did little to cool her. Both her adrenal gland and hypothalamus were running hopelessly out of whack.

She was still in Texas, on the outskirts of Amarillo, when she pulled into the parking lot of a big chain drugstore likely to have a well-stocked pharmacy.

Elaina entered through an automatic door, headed to the pharmacy, and handed her list to a clerk, the whole time boiling inside the new clothes she'd purchased after escaping from the hospital.

"Do you have your prescriptions?" the young woman asked her, looking up from the list.

"Prescriptions," Elaina repeated.

"From your doctors, for all these drugs."

"Oh, yes," Elaina said, forcing a smile. "I left them in the car."

She retraced her steps back to the SUV and reached under the backseat for a pistol belonging to one of Marsh's soldiers she'd taken out at the restaurant. Then she pulled her arms through the jacket she'd purchased, so she could tuck the weapon beneath it.

"Did you find them?" the clerk asked her when she returned to the rear counter.

"Right here," Elaina said, laying the barrel of the pistol atop the counter between them. "I'll wait, if you don't mind. And don't let me see anyone back there pick up a phone, even if it rings."

Nine minutes later, Elaina left the drugstore with seven prescriptions and a bottle of water tucked into a bag. She lit out into a dash back for the SUV across the parking lot, knowing she'd have to swap it for another vehicle as soon as possible.

She parked around the side of a gas station a few miles up from the store, out of sight from the road, and waited for the next driver who opted to pay inside. The first two took their keys with them, but a third left them in the ignition.

Elaina passed him halfway to the building, the man too busy looking down at his phone to acknowledge her. He was standing in line inside, still looking down at his phone, when she screeched out of the parking lot, back on the road for the Klamath Mountains in Northern California.

Less than an hour later, though, she knew she'd never make it, not without rest, the last thing possible right now. There was just too much road to cover and she lacked the strength and stamina to manage the trek. So if not by road . . .

Elaina turned around and steered back east to the next exit, a new plan in mind. But exhaustion claimed her again before she got very far, and she pulled into a truck stop that featured a shabby motel and free-standing diner by the same name that slipped from her mind as soon as she read it.

She needed to rest, just for an hour or so. But not at the motel, not anywhere there might be cameras or prying eyes. So she pulled the vehicle she'd stolen up to the motel, away from the rest of the cars, and closed her eyes.

Just an hour, she told herself, *I'll rest for an hour and then continue with Plan B.* She reached for the radio tuner to find a station that played soft, soothing music, but drifted off before she found one.

50

THE BOOK

RAIFF HAD CONTINUED DRIVING while Alex, in the passenger seat now, perused the pages of the book from beside him. Sam watched him from the backseat, alternately glaring at the still-cowering Langston Marsh, remembering how he'd kidnapped her parents the night before and might have even killed them if things hadn't finished the way they had.

The pages looked to her to be in surprisingly smooth condition, not brittle or fragile the way she knew many ancient volumes were. That was hardly a surprise, given that the book had been produced in another world altogether and manufactured to survive the ages. The cover itself looked to be made of now washed-out, tattered animal hide, likely in order to blend in with other, comparable tomes. Hard to believe this book had been the source of so much consternation and death over the years, although that shouldn't have been too much of a surprise given the purpose behind its creation.

"You can actually read the words?" Raiff asked Alex, glancing at him quickly as he drove.

"I think so, the letters anyway. I look at the letters and it's like they're translated for me into their English equivalents. But that's all it looks like—a bunch of letters. No sentences or paragraphs. Letters strung together that don't really say anything. Gibberish."

"Maybe it's written in some kind of code," Sam suggested.

Raiff shook his head. "No, if there was a code, he'd be able to decipher it. Otherwise, his being able to discern the letters makes no sense."

"Unless..." Sam started, leaning further forward, so her upper body was canted over the console, as much in the front seat as the back.

"Unless what?" Raiff prodded.

"Hold the book closer, so I can see it," she said to Alex.

"This is starting to feel like one of our tutoring sessions," Alex said, and held the first pages of the book open before her. "Let me know when you want me to turn the page."

"You don't have to turn the page at all," Sam said. "I think I just figured something out."

51

TENTACLES

"FASCINATING," SAID ORSON WILDER, studying the drawing Donati had fashioned, to the best of his recollection, of what Alex Chin's CT scan had revealed.

Donati followed his gaze to its projection on the screen constructed as part of the wall. "I didn't need the world's foremost expert on astrobiology to tell me that."

"No, you needed me to tell you how to extract this organic chip intact, given the importance of its contents."

"And?"

"You can't, I'm afraid."

"You're making me afraid too, Orson."

"Understand something, Thomas," Wilder said, moving closer to the screen, tracing a finger between the organic chip and the boy's brain. "These 'tentacles,' as you call them, that connect the chip to these two nodes, here and here, have effectively fused the chip to his brain to the point where the chip is now an extension of it. That means removing it could, likely would, compromise his nervous system, speech, motor functions, breathing."

"You're saying removing it surgically would kill the boy."

"Or severely incapacitate him, yes." Wilder nodded.

"Sounds like I'm talking to the man begging for dollars in Bishop Ranch right now," Donati said, his voice ringing with disappointment and dismay. "Not the man who knows more about molecular biology and its relationship to planetary science than anyone else I've ever met."

"Even in the past eighteen years?"

"I wouldn't have come to you otherwise. Now I'm wondering if I made a mistake. Should I give you a dollar for your trouble?"

Wilder turned his gaze back to the depiction of a vaguely oblong organic chip and its proximity to Alex Chin's brain, as if seeing it for the first time. "The boy was brought here as an infant."

"That's right. Primarily to hide the chip's existence."

"It's more than that," Wilder said, still studying the screen. "Given that this other world, although similar or even virtually identical to ours atmospherically, is substantially more advanced, I'd wager that the operation was performed when Alex was still a developing fetus. We're not even sure he gestated in a real womb or an artificial one. Either way, though, first creating the chip from the basis of the fetus's DNA and then implanting it in utero in a much less developed form would allow it to grow in conjunction with the rest of the brain. Let's call that biochemical molecular engineering, shall we? The process utilized would be one that involves selecting molecules that interact in a way that achieves the desired result through the process of DNA self-assembly, where disordered collections of molecules would spontaneously interact to form the desired arrangement of strands of DNA."

"Makes sense," Donati agreed.

"Of course, brain surgery performed on a fetus is extremely rare in our world and seldom effective. But give me a thousand, ten thousand years and I could tell you a dozen ways it could be done noninvasively. The simplest way would be to inject the chip in its own early form into an area adjacent to the brain."

"Nanotechnology," Donati said, recalling the scene in the underground factory from Sunday night when he'd witnessed intelligent machines building other machines.

"I suppose, but far advanced from the principles we hold for it today."

"And what about the surgical principles of removing the chip from the boy's brain?"

"I already told you that's likely far beyond our capabilities, Thomas. It's now anatomically impossible to detach the chip from the brain. It can't be removed."

"It's killing him, Orson."

"Removing it would almost surely kill the boy even faster. But . . ."

"But," Donati repeated, detecting hope in Wilder's voice.

"You said the contents of the chip were vital. So perhaps we should focus on a means to copy the chip's contents instead of risking an impossible surgery to remove it. Of course, that might very well entail wiping his entire brain."

"Meaning the boy would still die."

"I'm afraid so," Wilder said grimly. "Or worse, depending on your perspective."

"I can't accept that."

"You don't have another choice I can see. If we remove the chip, Alex dies. If we leave the chip in place, it kills him. There isn't a third option."

"What exactly is it that's leaking from the chip?" Donati asked, as if the answer to that question might yet yield a solution.

Wilder studied the drawing intently once more, tracing the line of leakage Donati had recalled from the scan. "Looks like a trail of fluid, doesn't it?"

"That was my assumption."

"Simplest and wrong. You disappoint me, Thomas. Looks like you've grown lazy without me around to push you."

"I don't encounter alien anatomies every day."

"Then try this," Wilder resumed, sticking a finger in the center of the pool that had formed between the boy's brain and the organic chip on the drawing. "I don't believe the chip is leaking at all."

Donati regarded his finger pointing out the apparent contradiction to his own thinking and started to reach into his pocket. "Let me get you that dollar, so you can be on your way . . ."

"What happens when a silicon-based computer's memory fills up?"

"It discards memory to free up more data, oldest to newest."

Wilder tapped the screen with his finger. "I believe that's exactly what we're looking at here, only in what is effectively a carbon-based molecular computer. Discarded rather than leaked, and I sincerely doubt the injury he suffered had much to do with that at all. More likely, he'd already been experiencing symptoms that would've worsened on their own anyway, because of excess pressure on the brain, but not all of these symptoms will appear as warning signs initially."

"What do you mean?"

"I suspect the boy will find himself able to do things he never learned or was taught to do, thanks to the chip's initial programming. It's like an encyclopedia the boy's subconscious couldn't access until it began to dump the excess memory—that's the leakage you're referring to. The problem is that same leakage, as you call it, will continue until the pressure on the brain puts him in a coma he'll never wake up from."

"There's got to be some recourse here," Donati said, groping.

"The best we can do is try to drain the discarded organic materials to relieve the pressure enough to at least prolong the boy's life."

"Is that a prognosis or a possibility?"

"It's a theory. It's a hope. Meaningless, of course, if we can't locate him in time."

"Wherever he is, we've got to find him. Saving our world means saving him first."

"Saving the world from what exactly, Thomas?"

"Glad you asked, Orson, glad you asked . . ."

52

TRANSLATION

"**WHAT DO YOU KNOW** about your people in their ancient times?" Sam asked Raiff, looking from the book toward him.

"Not much. That would've been several million of your years ago. That's how old our civilization actually is."

"So when you read a book back in your world, do you do that from left to right, as in our world, or right to left, as with Hebrew and other languages?"

Raiff shrugged. "We don't have books anymore, but when we read on screens or projections, it's left to right."

"Maybe not through your entire history, though, right?"

"I'm not sure."

"Instead of reading across, try reading from the top down, like the vertical boxes on a crossword puzzle," Sam suggested.

Alex swung the book back toward him, squinting slightly. "Oh man, you're right. Top to bottom. I can make sense of the words now, the sentences . . ."

"What's it say?"

"You're right, Raiff, it's a history, a history of your movement from the very beginning. 'The Resistance,' it says here." Alex looked up from the book. "Who sent you over here with me? Who came up with the plan in the first place?"

Raiff looked like he wasn't going to answer, but then he began to speak softly, gaze remaining fixed straight ahead. "A brave and brilliant woman who had that chip implanted in your head, one of the leaders of our resistance against the Overlords."

"Overlords?"

"Those mechanical monsters you've been seeing in your visions and drew in that sketchbook of yours. Call them phantom memories or, more likely, phantom images your brain is pulling from the chip residing near it. They rule our world, in conjunction with a cadre of humans who control them. And a good chunk of the 'everybody else' makes up the Resistance."

"Like that woman," Alex picked up from there.

"She sacrificed herself to keep you safe," Raiff said, still clinging to the hope that the woman who'd come across the spacebridge in Texas was Elaina. "It hurt her so much to hand you over, but someone had to stay behind to destroy the mechanism, or we would've been followed."

Alex thought back to how An Chin had described finding him as an infant just before Laboratory Z was destroyed. Everything made sense now, at least that part of it. One mystery solved.

"This woman sounds like something special."

Raiff turned to him again, eyes motionless and drained of emotion. "In more ways than one. Because she was your mother, Alex."

53

PILLS

ELAINA WAS AWAKENED WITH a start by a big man wearing a Stetson rapping his knuckles on the window she'd kept lowered halfway.

"You okay, ma'am?" he asked in a thick Texas drawl, the concern plain in his voice.

She realized night had fallen some time ago, hours maybe. She cleared her throat.

"I wasn't feeling well," Elaina told the man, managing to force a smile. "But I'm fine now."

"You sure?"

"Yes, but thank you."

The big man seemed reluctant to take his leave. "There somebody I can call for you?"

"No, but thanks again," she said, gunning the engine. "I'll just be on my way."

And she drove off, leaving the man standing there, his shape shrinking in her rearview mirror.

He had awoken Elaina in the midst of a nightmare. A big, awful nightmare from which she couldn't rouse herself, no matter how hard she tried.

In the dream, she was pregnant with the boy who was now called Alex, ready to give birth. But she wouldn't let herself. The baby wanted to come out, and she willed the contractions to stop. And when he started to emerge anyway, the crown of his head beginning to show, she pushed him back inside her as far as she could. Breathing heavily, holding tight.

Let him out. You know his fate, you know his destiny. Let him out.

The speaker was a hideously elongated grayish form, shaped like a shadow more than a man. Fitting, since it was not a man at all, but a projection, an apparition, cast by Overlords so that they might communicate with the humans with whom they shared power on the one hand, but sought to dominate on the other.

In the dream, the baby kept coming and she kept forcing him back until his will grew too strong. He spewed out in a long dark wisp, not a newborn at all, but an elongated projection of one, shadow more than person.

And you thought he was going to be the answer, the savior. You thought the chip inside his head was the final piece of a puzzle you believed would defeat us. And now you've lost. And now it's over.

The grayish shape loomed over her when he'd spoken those words. He reached out, taking her in his grasp. Elaina could feel herself dissolving under his touch, melting away piece by piece, until soon she wouldn't exist at all.

That had only been a dream, but this was real, and the book was the key, the book was everything. Its contents held the means, the plan her predecessors with the Resistance had set into motion centuries and centuries before. She would make herself live as long as she was needed, gulp down as many of the pills as it took to keep her deteriorating system functioning.

Elaina wondered if she'd know Alex when she saw him, wondered if he might somehow know her, wondered where he was right now.

Those thoughts sent pangs of angst through her that felt like someone taking a wire brush to her insides and scraping them raw. She returned her focus to her destination in the Klamath Mountains of Northern California, to Langston Marsh, and the book that had fallen into his possession.

Elaina drove on, taking the fastest route to Tradewind Airport in Amarillo.

54

SPACEBRIDGES

"WE NEED TO FIND all these particle accelerators they're building to create multiple doorways, spacebridges, on this side," Donati
continued to Wilder, after explaining in more detail what they'd
encountered beneath the remains of Alcatraz prison the night before. "There could be dozens, even hundreds of them out there, just
like the one we found beneath Alcatraz last night."

"Hundreds, Thomas? Really?"

"Why not? While the world looked to the sky for contact with an
alien race, you and I looked toward wormholes, spacebridges, and
the like, because we knew that was how they'd come, either as enemies or friends."

Wilder weighed Donati's words. "You always suspected, feared,
they'd be the former."

"Because there could be no good reason for a race advanced that
far beyond us to come. It would be like us visiting a planet of cock-
roaches. I suspected they'd only come if they needed to take something we had. Turned out that it's *us* they want. To enslave, to turn
us into their drones, to replace another of their planets they'd finally exhausted."

"Do you have any idea how crazy this all sounds?"

"Crazy was our business, Orson! We were in the business of
crazy when we built Laboratory Z as the first step in the process to
make contact with foreign worlds ourselves."

"But we were thinking of other planets, not dimensions. Inter-
dimensional travel wasn't covered under the principles of quantum
mechanics."

"We considered the possibility," Donati reminded him, "but we didn't plan for it. That's how we were caught so ill prepared, why we didn't see the signs earlier and understand their meaning."

Wilder glanced at the screen again, gazing at Donati's hand-scrawled rendition of what he recalled from Alex Chin's CT scan. "So if they're building their own particle accelerators, what did they need Laboratory Z for eighteen years ago? What did they need Desertron for last night?"

"I'm not sure," Donati said, from alongside Wilder. "Most likely because they don't want to give away the locations of their own facilities in the resulting energy spikes. The resources it would take to build so many supercolliders, never mind the necessity of hiding their existence from the world, are incalculable."

"Not to our friends from this other dimension, apparently," Wilder noted.

"We need to destroy every single one of these facilities, Orson," Donati said, "but first we have to find them. And that's where you come in. If anyone can figure out where they're located, it's you. But there's something I need to show you before you get started."

55

MOTHER'S DAY

"HER NAME WAS ELAINA," Raiff resumed. "You look just like her."

Alex remained silent. He'd closed the book resting in his lap, his arms laid across its withered binding. He almost spoke a few times, but ended up losing the words as quickly as he found them, choking up.

Raiff was driving east into the night with no particular destination in mind yet. They needed to get someplace where Alex could study the book more closely. He needed to find whatever information and clues it held by which they could defeat the civilization from which he came and that his mother had died fighting. As if on cue, he felt Sam's hand on his shoulder and cupped it with his own, so she'd know he wanted it there, the only thing that made him feel even remotely better.

"And you're just as brave as she was too," Raiff continued. "She'd have been so proud of you. I know that doesn't mean much to you right now, but you need to hear it anyway."

"So both my mothers were murdered. That's what you're saying."

Raiff nodded, eyes back on the road ahead. "Focus on the book, Alex," he said.

"Why bother?"

"Because, one way or another, both your mothers died for what's inside it. The words only you can read, the message only you can decipher. You want to get back at those who killed An Chin and Elaina? The way to do it is in that book."

"Elaina," Alex echoed, trying to picture his birth mother.

Alex blew the hair from his face with his breath. He felt so young and alone, a little boy again. Just like he had that day at the fairgrounds when he'd attacked the cops who were arresting his Chinese parents for kidnapping a Caucasian child. His mother had stumbled and fallen when one of the cops tried to drag her away. Alex saw her lying on the ground, looking so weak and helpless, even frail. Her eyes meeting his with so much sadness and fear filling them.

Everything had gotten worked out but the impact of that experience had never left him. No matter what frustrations he might've felt about his parents, as all teenagers do, there was always that moment to recall how much An and Li Chin loved him and how much he loved them. And since Saturday evening, when they were killed, that was the moment his mind kept reverting to for comfort.

Like Sam's hand on his shoulder. Her touch was what he needed, her friendship. He thought about Reverend Billy's question before he'd reached Sam's house.

Do you love her?

The answer was yes. And in all this, maybe it was something even deeper than love.

She was all that kept his pain at bay.

An Chin had been murdered on this side of the spacebridge, his birth mother on the other side. And he was stuck in the middle, suspended between them, two pieces of his past that had left him with nothing to cling to now.

He wished he could turn and hug Sam to him, hug her close and never let go.

His tutor.

Thinking of her that way drew a smile to his lips. Had he always felt this way about her and denied it, or had he just not realized his feelings? He'd dated Cara, head of the cheerleading Cat Pack, the homecoming queen to his king, because it was easy and expected. He didn't have to work at it, any more than he had to work hard at anything.

Except school. Alex couldn't admit, even to himself, how he felt about Sam because she made him feel so small. Every time she corrected him in their studies, he thought she was judging him. Just as Sam had felt she wasn't in his league for one reason, Alex didn't believe he was in hers for quite another. The thought they could be together had been the most distant thought in both their minds, even though that's what each of them wanted, no matter how much they denied it.

He regularly showed up late for their sessions, always pretended they were nothing but an effort in drudgery, because it made him feel safe from his own feelings. But the deaths of his parents had turned his feelings all out of whack. He couldn't, didn't want to hide them anymore. How he never could have gotten through the last few days without Sam.

"Let me off," Langston Marsh said, startling the three of them by rousing from his trance out of the blue. "Let me off here."

"So you can turn us in?" Raiff asked him. "Call in your Tracker teams?"

Marsh's voice was distant. "I'm recalling them all. You're right. We're on the same side. I see that now. I see we're fighting the same enemy and I still believe that enemy killed my father." Marsh looked uncertain, fearful, eyes darting this way and that as if unsure of what they were seeing. "I'm going to give you a phone number. Call it if you need me for anything. My resources, my wealth, my power—they're yours now, along with my army, my Fifth Column, as you call it."

Raiff veered to the side of a road in the direction of a truck stop. "We just might need them, Marsh."

SEVEN

RITUALS

Whoever fights monsters should see to it that in the process
he does not become a monster. And if you gaze long enough
into an abyss, the abyss will gaze back into you.

FRIEDRICH NIETZSCHE

56

MEDICINE LAKE

"I HAVE A CONFESSION to make," Alex said to Sam, the big book opened to a random page on the table before him.

Sam took a seat on the opposite side of what was little more than a folding card table they both figured was among the standard furnishings for the Cabins at Medicine Lake. The cabins were advertised as rustic, another word in this case for run-down. They were located far along Medicine Lake Road in woods that were close to the lake's northern spur. Raiff had chosen these cabins for refuge precisely because they were off the path normally traveled by tourists. He thought they'd have the place pretty much to themselves, and as far as they could tell from the few other cars parked before the line of cabins, they pretty much did.

They'd driven east from the Klamath Mountains along a road oddly named the Volcanic Legacy Scenic Byway, also to avoid scrutiny. They'd watched the sun sink the rest of the way down the sky during the three-hour drive, darkness bringing a storm with it that intensified the farther they drew east. The cabins were equipped with neither telephones nor televisions, which suited them just fine given that they'd had their fill of electronics for the day. And here they could have their own dedicated cabin, which was much easier to keep secure, from Raiff's perspective, than individual rooms in an ordinary motel.

Upon arriving, he'd instructed Sam and Alex to check in on their own.

"Three's a crowd," he explained, "an adult traveling with two teenagers certain to draw attention. But a young couple traveling together? That's something else again."

"Couple?" Alex and Sam had offered in unison, looking stiffly away from each other.

"A disguise," Raiff elaborated.

The cabin itself was roomy enough and plenty rustic, offering a view of the forestlands that extended a half mile to Medicine Lake itself. It smelled of a combination of rich pine, fabric softener from the bed linens, along with whatever shampoo and conditioner Sam had doused her hair with when she'd taken a shower. With no change of clothes, she'd climbed back into the same ones she'd been wearing through the day that felt more like a week.

Raiff was out in the woods somewhere, keeping watch. Sam figured he feared—perhaps expected—the return of the forces that had laid siege to Langston Marsh's mountain fortress.

It was all too much, Sam thought, taking the chair across from Alex, and then positioning herself so she could follow his progress with the book.

"I'm listening," she told him.

"My confession is that..." Alex said, stopping as quickly as he'd started, and then resuming, "that I've never read a book before, not a whole one anyway."

"Wait a minute..."

"I skimmed them, okay? I read the important parts."

"How can you know what's important or not, if you didn't read the whole thing?"

"They're just books. Fiction. It's not like they're real. What am I supposed to learn from them anyway?"

"They're called novels, Alex. And a novel idea in your case would be to learn how to appreciate good writing, since it looks like my efforts failed."

"Don't blame yourself."

"Who am I supposed to blame? We talked about those books, discussed them. How'd you fool me?"

A familiar glint flashed in Alex's eyes. "I just let you do most of the talking..."

"Thanks."

"And then I agreed with you," Alex finished. "Once in a while I threw in my own two cents."

"Which wasn't worth even a penny."

He tapped his finger on the page the big book was opened to atop the table. "Those books didn't have pictures, like this one does."

Sam shuffled her chair closer to him. "And what do those pictures tell you?"

57

MEMORIES

RAIFF STOOD AT THE rim of the woods, shielded by the trees. The storm had dissipated, but he could still hear the rumble of thunder, and flashes of lightning continued to pierce the night sky, telling him the quiet interlude wouldn't last.

The cabin Alex and Sam had rented lay directly before him across a ruddy gravel plain, around which the cabins nested in a semicircle. They'd drawn the shades and blinds, as he'd instructed, and Raiff could see the faintest hint of light burning through a sliver-sized gap where those shades hadn't closed all the way.

Eventually, he'd join them, and supposed he could have accomplished this very task just as well from the warmth and comfort inside. But he was plagued by those final moments outside Marsh's mountain fortress, the gaunt stranger whose eyes had bulged in recognition when they met his.

You! . . . You're dead!

It brought Raiff back to a distant, unsettling memory that had slipped from his consciousness. He couldn't remember his parents, orphaned as he and so many others were by their parents having fallen as Resistance fighters, battling an enemy they couldn't possibly defeat. One day, not long before he carried Alex across the spacebridge to this world, he'd met an older, grizzled fighter. Raiff caught the fighter staring at a picture of his own parents he carried everywhere with him.

"So I'll never forget why we do this," he said to Raiff, showing him the picture.

The lighting was bad and Raiff had been exhausted at the time, elements that helped explain the fact that the picture seemed identical to one of the digital shots he had of the mother and father he had no memory of. Same pose, same background.

Same couple, it seemed.

That was impossible, of course, and Raiff had dismissed it as such. But it remained an unsettling moment he was glad to forget.

Until today. Until the man outside Marsh's fortress had seemed to recognize him.

You! . . . You're dead!

Who did he resemble? Could it have been a relative, his own father even?

Questions without answers that continued to plague him.

It started to drizzle, quickly turning to a driving rain, forcing Raiff to pull up the hood on his jacket and retreat slightly into the lee of a sprawling maple tree. Still, though, he preferred being outside to in. He could still see the faint light filtering through the cabin's blinds and pictured Alex inside.

How much he looked like his mother . . . Raiff had been little more than a boy that day Elaina had pressed her infant into his arms and sent him on his way across to this world, sacrificing herself for both of them. Their parting gaze had been so sad, Elaina looking at him after her child, as if there was something she wanted to say but had run out of time.

Or maybe not, Raiff thought, holding on to the hope that the woman who had come over the spacebridge that morning was somehow Elaina. That she had managed to survive eighteen years ago and—

Raiff's thoughts froze right there. He wasn't a believer in precognitive or paranormal feelings, but had developed over the years a keen reliance on his instincts, which had alerted him time and time again when trouble was about. Standing at the rim of the woods in that moment, the rain beginning to pelt him through the receding leaves above, Raiff felt trouble was coming.

No, not just coming.

It was already here, he thought, as the storm returned in all its ferocity.

58

ELIXIR

THE WOODED SETTING SUITED Gilles de Rais's needs perfectly. He simply couldn't have asked for more favorable logistics to fashion the army he needed to complete his centuries-long mission.

The tracking software, into which he'd uploaded photos of his quarry's vehicle, worked even better than expected. They swapped vehicles twice in their drive here from the Klamath Mountains. And both times the switches had been recorded by parking lot security cameras. That helped him trail his quarries, but the process was facilitated far more by something else he was tracking with a handheld device no bigger than a cell phone: the boy himself.

But finding his quarries was only the first part of his plan. His mission to retrieve the book, which had begun almost six hundred years ago, would require soldiers, a loyal army capable of withstanding time and the ages just as he had. The process to create that army worked only with organic matter, not inanimate objects. Something that lived and breathed, or had once lived, in its own right. Expose such organisms to the elixir he'd kept these many years and, after a brief time, he'd have his soldiers, his army.

The first time he'd "summoned" them had been in Prague in 1580, also the first time he came close to the manuscript that held secrets this world could never see. Betrayed and besieged by those he'd enlisted in his charge, being branded a Jew and marked for death, had forced de Rais into woods like these, where he'd molded the soft ground, roots and brush into the vague shapes of men, six in all.

Then as now, he had sprinkled his elixir over the figures he'd formed out of the earth itself. Soil may have contained no DNA in its own right, but it was formed of life-bearing nutrients collected in the ground. That included plant life, which maintained rudimentary levels of DNA in chromosomes located in the nucleus, as well as the mitochondria and chloroplasts. Its ability to sustain life, as a vital ingredient of the food chain, made soil the perfect receptor for the age-old elixir to push the strands of cohesion and structural integrity through its chemical composition.

That night in 1580, a stormy one much like this, his Christian pursuers had caught up to him, just as his creations were coming to life.

Call it magic, call it sorcery.

De Rais called it science, just not of this Earth.

He recalled growing breathless with delight over his enemies being torn limb from limb by creatures who hadn't even existed a few minutes before. They had no hearts that beat, or brains that thought, or blood that had flowed through the ropy plant roots which served as their veins and arteries. And when their task was complete they would return to the ground from which they'd come.

It turned out his pursuers had rounded up another target before venturing into the woods on de Rais's trail, a rabbi and leader of Prague's Jewish community, who'd witnessed the entire ordeal. De Rais never quite understood why the creatures he had fashioned left the man alive, although he suspected it must have been due to the fact that his hands and feet were chained, leading the creatures to somehow not view him as a target or foe.

The man was a rabbi named Yehudah Loew and in subsequent years de Rais would learn that his survival in the woods that night had given birth to the legend of the "golem," culled from religion instead of science, and for which Loew claimed credit. The legend, and improper credit, persisted to this day, which pleased de Rais no end. It helped quicken dismissal of any witness reports to the actions of the creatures he had not unleashed since that night in 1865 at Austria's Admont Abbey . . .

Where he'd encountered the monk who bore an uncanny resemblance to the man who'd escaped the Klamath Mountains with Langston Marsh, and the book, in tow.

Who was he? What was de Rais missing here?

Just as he had done in 1580 and then again in 1865, de Rais sprinkled his elixir on the mounds of earth laden with plant life that provided enough structural integrity to keep the darkening mud from washing away in the storm. The man-shaped mounds remained intact, seeming to lighten and dry, as the elixir formed of life-bearing chemicals coursed through plant roots and vines, creating life at its most basic level.

The mounds of plant-infused soil, mud now, straightened, thickened, and hardened. Crude features like eyes and ears and fingers and toes began to take shape. Then they seemed to move, just a twitch at first but quickly becoming more pronounced, the eyes glowing a soft red before brightening to a piercing blood color.

He watched as his golem continued to solidify, flexing their fingers and toes, seeing the world for the first time through brightening sockets dug out of the dirt that formed them, red eyes bright enough to light the night.

Moving, shifting, starting to sit up.

Ready.

59

THE VAULT

"WE CALL THIS THE Vault," Donati told Orson Wilder, entering the proper code into a keypad and then placing his palm against a scanner.

"Redundant security measures," Wilder said, clearly curious, "and yet no guard. Or guards."

"Because we don't want stories getting out that there's something in here that needs to be guarded. The fewer people who know, the better."

The door slid open, Wilder waiting for Donati to lead him inside, freezing at what he saw.

The chamber was ten by ten feet and contained only what looked like a museum-style glass display case. In point of fact, Wilder knew, the glass was an offshoot of a space-age polymer used by NASA. Completely shatterproof and impervious to all elements.

"The case is actually a prototype," Donati explained, as if reading his mind, "designed specifically to contain what's inside."

The object floating inside was the crystalline sphere with a symmetrical outgrowth of viruslike spikes that had landed at his feet eighteen years before when Laboratory Z had been destroyed by a creature Donati had concluded was formed of pure energy.

"I've spent the last eighteen years studying it." Donati continued, "unable to attain any rationales for its existence because its presence in our world remains utterly unprecedented."

"But the quantum physics applications and rules must apply for it to exist in our world, within our gravity."

"Because it could only have come from a world with comparable, if not identical, gravity, Orson."

"From that other dimension we discovered the day Laboratory Z was destroyed," Wilder said reflectively, unable to take his eyes off the sphere.

"We didn't discover it," Donati corrected him. "It discovered us. But your theory, based on all my studies, is correct. Where regular electrons have a negative charge, antimatter 'electrons' have a positive charge that are also called positrons."

"Spare me the doctoral lesson, Thomas. How when a particle and an antiparticle meet, they *annihilate* each other and their whole mass is converted to pure energy."

"And the thing that attacked us eighteen years ago, that came through from the other side, was formed of pure energy," Donati reminded him. "I should have surmised that as soon as I realized the black ooze it was sucking up was melted electrical wiring from the walls that it consumed to sustain itself. Somehow able to convert that electricity into the antimatter electrons it needed to constantly recharge itself at the subatomic level from microsecond to microsecond."

Wilder was visibly shaken by Donati's assertion. "You're describing a force unknown and unprecedented in our universe."

"Because it's not from our universe, Orson, it's from theirs, whoever *they* are. And whoever they are, they figured out how to create a creature that literally feeds off destruction by swallowing everything it comes into contact with."

"How many of our people did it kill that day, Thomas?"

"Twenty-one. But the word isn't *kill*, it's *absorb,* specifically electromagnetic energy, a vast amount of which is processed in through food and sensory impressions that blend together like a chord blends notes to make harmony, and then radiates the excess. In other words, every human being is a living, breathing convergence and divergence point, a veritable walking, talking fountain of cosmic energy."

Wilder had still not taken his eyes off the sphere. "Food for that thing, in other words." He finally swung toward Donati. "Has it ever..."

"Transformed back into its deadlier form? The reason it appears to be floating is what you're looking at is a zero-gravity tank, containing no electromagnetic conductivity whatsoever."

"You're talking about a vacuum chamber."

"That's a rudimentary way of describing it. This is more of a void akin to a black hole in space. Nothingness, so there is literally nothing the sphere can do to morph back into pure energy."

"Einstein's conservation of energy and matter theory," Wilder expounded.

"Postulating that energy and matter cannot be destroyed—"

"—but merely transformed. How am I doing, Thomas?"

"Put it on my tab."

"I'll erase your tab, if you explain to me how it transformed from pure energy into matter. This boy you think you glimpsed . . ."

"A man now," Donati said, nodding, "because he was there. He charged into the cloud."

"And never came out."

"I never saw him emerge but I was dazed. All I remember is feeling like I was turning inside out. I don't know another way of describing it. I'm now convinced it was the boy's protector, Raiff, only a boy himself all those years ago."

Wilder's gaze darted back to the sphere for a moment, before returning to Donati. "He must have had some kind of weapon capable of interrupting, or halting, the collision of particles that would have otherwise continued to reconstitute the creature's existence as pure energy. But what, Thomas, *what*?"

"The answer to that question lies in that world on the other side of the spacebridge, Orson."

Wilder stood by Donati's side, looking into the void as well. "Good thing you came and got me, Thomas. You're going to need my services."

60

KEYS

"SEE," ALEX SAID, "I told you there's something to be said for skimming."

She yawned and stretched her arms. "Only when the process calls for it."

"The pictures are nice, you've got to admit that."

The book itself consisted of hundreds of unnumbered pages with almost no empty space, save for the separations between picture and text. Reading each page from the top line down, by column, proved impossible to get used to, especially given the lack of paragraphs or even spaces. The story the manuscript told just went on and on and on, supplemented by drawings, some of which were as crude as cave wall depictions and others drawn to museum-quality art.

"How old do you think it is?" Alex asked, looking up from his skimming of the pages and trying to stretch the kinks out of his neck.

"Impossible to tell without carbon-dating machines." Sam reached out and ran her fingers across the page to which the book was open. "This feels like vellum; people wrote books on vellum during the Middle Ages and the Renaissance. But even the best-preserved books written on vellum age, yellow and grow brittle over the centuries. Plenty degrade and deteriorate altogether. This one, though, is remarkably well-preserved."

"So it was made to look like vellum," Alex surmised, "but it's not really vellum."

Sam leaned back in her chair and smiled. "Look's who's teaching who now."

"How's your neck, by the way?"

"Hurts like a bastard."

"It was my first stitching job."

"I'm only kidding. It doesn't hurt at all."

Alex went back to skimming the pages, pushing past the histori-cal parts and slowing only when he came to the section about the forbears of Raiff and Alex's birth mother, Elaina, discovering the existence of Earth and marshaling their forces to begin sending refugees to settle there in preparation for what the book called the Great War.

Alex traced a finger from the top of the page to the bottom as he read silently, finally paraphrasing a section that drew his eyes closer to the page. "It says their coming here was also part of their plan to defeat their oppressors. It says they knew they couldn't possibly lay the groundwork for that in their world, so they laid it here."

"How?"

Alex flipped the page, Sam noticing they were two-thirds of the way through the book. "Three keys were to be brought here over time."

"Keys?"

"That's what it says, the exact word. It also says these keys would be kept separate until the time came to join them up with a fourth."

"I thought you said there were only three."

"Because that's what it says, meaning the fourth key hadn't been brought here before the book arrived. It must have come later."

That struck a chord in Sam she hid in her expression. "Anything else that can help us?"

Alex shook his head. "Not yet. That's just a kind of introduction. I haven't gotten to the details yet. But, if I'm reading this right, these keys, whatever they are, are just what we need to defeat the aliens. You know—my people."

"They're not your people."

"They are by birth."

Sam looked at him closer, hesitating, not sure of her words until she spoke them. "Your mother died over there for what this book contains."

"You don't have to tell me that."

"I think maybe I do, Alex, to remind you you're not one of them, any more than she was."

He leaned forward, and then out of his chair, to kiss her lightly on the lips.

"What was that for?" Sam asked him wide-eyed, pleasantly shocked, watching Alex settle back in his chair.

"I just wanted to do it."

And with that, Sam came out of her chair and kissed him.

"Now we're even," she said, sitting back down.

"I hate when games end in a tie."

"I guess you'll have to do something about that, then."

"I guess I will." Alex turned away from her gaze, back to the book, and started reading again, as if nothing had happened. "It says the fourth key is needed to complete the square, that it alone breathes life."

"Oh my God," Sam said, pushing her chair backward and standing up.

"What, Sam?"

"Don't you get it? Oh my God . . ."

"Get *what*?"

But before Sam could answer, the cabin door blew inward off its hinges.

61

THE STORM

RAIFF RESISTED THE URGE to finally head toward the cabin and the respite from the storm that it promised. Thinking of Elaina made him realize how much Alex resembled her, and that made it hurt for Raiff to regard the boy. They were mother and son, so the resemblance wasn't surprising. What stood out to Raiff more was the fact that Alex resembled Elaina in other ways. They were both purposeful, for one thing, relentless in their chosen fields: Alex on the football field and Elaina when it came to spearheading the forefront of the Resistance. The more he was around Alex, the more the boy morphed into his mother.

Which made it difficult to be around Alex.

Which explained why he was standing out here in the driving rain, feeling it soak through his clothes.

Raiff had moved away from the cover of the tree and closer to the edge of the actual forest, the dark background of the trees shifting in the storm now his only cover. His new positioning gave him a total view of the parking lot and area around the cabin. Nothing could get anywhere close to it without Raiff seeing, but that comforted him not in the slightest.

Could it be that some of the plasteel soldiers might have survived the implosion of Langston Marsh's fortress? Were they coming or already in the area? Was that what he was feeling?

No, this was something else. A different kind of threat, but a threat all the same.

Because something was out there.

I won't let you down, Elaina.

Had he said that or only thought it?

The rain picked up, pelting him, joined by harsh winds that swept waves of it against his skin and clothes. Raiff backpedaled, flush against a tree for cover, which diminished his view of the cabin across the parking lot. He thought he spotted something blowing across the pavement, big bags of trash, it looked like, before one of the objects passed briefly beneath the spill of a floodlight, heading straight for the cabin door.

Not a bag of a trash, not an object at all.

A dark figure was silhouetted by the pole lamps swaying in the wind over the parking area, a pair of red eyes piercing the darkness. Its arms long enough to appear vaguely simian, the light revealing it as more shadow than shape.

Raiff threw himself into motion, bursting into the height of the storm raging around him, stick in hand as the cabin door blew inward and the first of the dark shapes burst inside.

62

GOLEM

ALEX SHOVED SAM BEHIND him as two more of the figures followed a first inside, dragging the storm with them. They looked like men camouflaged by mud and earth. Alex quickly realized they weren't men at all, rather creatures that seemed to be fashioned from the ground itself. Mud and earth limbs with glowing red spheres for eyes.

They shed clumps of it to the floor as they sloshed forward, making a sucking sound with each step, which left a muddy footprint on the floor. The narrow spacing of the three figures made it impossible for Alex to take Sam in tow and barrel past or through them. And they were big, really big, the clumps they were shedding refastening themselves, even if not to the creature they'd been part of originally.

Creature, Alex thought, noting his word choice.

Because that's what these things were. Not even vaguely men, except for their general humanoid shapes.

They kept coming in deliberate fashion, clumps of mud continuing to slide off them. Focusing on Alex and Sam and never once acknowledging the presence of the other two in their party. Each seemed to be individually focused and intent. The color of the mud made it look like animal hide, the shape it had formed seeming to alter slightly with each step.

Alex grabbed a floor-standing lamp and yanked its cord from the wall. He tore the shade off and twisted the base behind him, held parallel to the ground. Then he swung it like a baseball bat toward the nearest creature.

He expected to feel a thud on impact, but, instead, felt the metal cut straight through the creature's torso, spilling watery mud to the cheap carpet. As quick as the opening had appeared, though, it closed up again, the creature missing nary a step in its advance.

"Stay behind me!" Alex ordered Sam, lashing the floor lamp outward again.

This time it passed straight through another of the creature's narrow, squat necks. And, again, the wound, or gap, closed up as quickly as it had appeared, that creature too slowed not at all in its approach.

Alex felt his mind working fast, searching for a way to get past the creatures and out the door or . . .

"The window," he said to Sam.

He'd started to sidestep toward it when the glass exploded inward behind the force of two massive dark arms, spraying flecks of mud and grime into the air. The creature attached to them hoisted itself through in the same moment Raiff appeared in the doorway.

Raiff extended his stick into a whip and lashed it through the air, slicing right through the creature closest to him, while moving to position himself between Alex and Sam. His whip obliterated the nearest thing's midsection, hurling curtains of dripping mud against the wall to ooze downward in an impressionistic design. Then it seemed to coagulate, gathering and congealing to make the creature whole again without missing a beat.

One of five—no, six—now in the room with three more having entered through a shattered window, one of which positioned to close it off as a route of escape.

"Alex!" Raiff yelled.

"I'm okay!" Alex cried back, keeping Sam shielded behind him.

He watched Raiff snap his whip out again, this time cutting right through another of the creature's necks. Then he brought the whip back again, reversing the motion before the slice could close up, and the creature's head lopped to the side and then pitched to the ground. Landing with a *splat!* that flattened the oozing mud into a puddle.

Raiff thought he could count that one out, at the very least, only to watch the puddle sucked back up to rejoin the mud, out of which the creature must've been formed. And, just as fast, a fresh headlike

extremity poked out of the thing's neck and began to retake its original form, red eyes gaining brightness with each passing moment.

He knew of the tales drawn from the mystical golem of lore, and
he'd always suspected something more nefarious had lurked as that
legend's origins.

Now he knew that for sure.

"I've got an idea!" Sam said into Alex's ear, not giving him a chance
to stop her when she darted past him, then under the grasp of one
of the creatures.

The thing swung, storming toward her as she reached the bed,
where she flung off the cover and took the bedspread in hand, holding it like a matador's red cape. The thing lurched at her and Sam
tossed the bedspread over it. Disoriented, the creature wheeled
wildly about, grit and gravel filling the air as its arms flailed to pull
the bedspread off. Buying Sam enough time to steer a clear path
toward the still-open door.

Another of the things blocked her path, hand closing around her
throat, shedding flecks of mud. She tried to scream Raiff's name, but
three more of the creatures had him trapped against the wall.

He held them back with his whip, but each time it lashed through
them, the parts congealed again as quickly as they'd come apart.

Sam felt her toes dangling off the floor, her breath choked off and
the pressure in her head building when a blur flashed to her side.
Then the blur turned into the sight of the creature being slammed into
a wall, giving Sam her breath back as she sank to her knees, gasping.

Alex!

The thing managed to clamp its hands onto Alex's shoulders and
fling him through the air. He hit the table on which the book rested
and spilled it over to the floor.

Sam seized the moment to surge through the open front door
into the rain-swept night, steering toward something she remembered seeing bolted to the side of an adjacent building.

Raiff watched the creature lurch off the wall against which Alex
had slammed it, a pattern of filth and grime tracing its outline. He

couldn't see Alex behind the toppled table and could do nothing about the three golem advancing toward the boy, because of the three that had him pinned in place.

Edging closer, the creatures were wearing him down. He was only able to hold them at bay with his whip. He wondered how they'd been brought to life and thought immediately of the gaunt figure who'd seemed to recognize him earlier in the day. He'd been guardian of the plasteel army now entombed at Langston Marsh's imploded mountain fortress and was almost surely guardian of this army too, as well as its maker.

Alex was back on his feet now. Sweeping and sliding, dipping and darting. Raiff wondered if these things had been slowed somewhat by the rain, but the mud from which they'd been formed was hardening, their features sharpening with each passing moment. Getting faster, stronger, as Sam charged back into the room holding what could only be a . . .

Fire hose, Alex realized.

The end Sam held of the fire hose thickened and stretched with the surge of water coursing through it. Sam was almost knocked off her feet when it spooled out and locked, before she twisted the nozzle and a powerful surge of water blew outward. The hose opening was about two inches in diameter, and water burst from it with enough force to peel paint off a wall.

Sam turned the nozzle to tighten the stream, increasing the force of the flow surging from the hose. She balanced her feet wide and hit the first creature with the spray, washing parts of it away until it was no more than a headless torso that keeled over and puddled after hitting the ruined rug.

Sam wielded the hose like a machine gun, blasting golem after golem into mud that sprayed in all directions, ultimately painting the walls and puddling on the rug. Three down, the last still converging on Raiff.

She watched him dive to the floor when she opened up on the remaining golem with the hose, blasting them, literally, in all directions to keep them from solidifying again, buying time at the very least. Raiff was picking himself up off the mud-soaked floor, and Alex was coming toward her with his gaze aimed over her shoulder.

"Sam!"

She swung in that direction and saw the first three golem that had burst apart under the powerful spray of water re-forming. Puddles and pools of mud sliding across the floor and down the walls to coagulate into three distinct shapes of the initial golem she had washed away.

"How can we stop these things?" she cried out, ready to hit them with the hose again.

"You don't," Raiff said, clambering up to her side. "You run."

63

ESCAPE

SAM CONTINUED PELTING THE golem with water to keep them from re-forming all the way, freeing Alex to scoop up the book. She watched as he brushed the still-oozing mud from the page it had been opened to before wrapping the canvas sack around it while surging toward the door.

"Get to the car!" Raiff called to both Sam and Alex.

Sam stubbornly held her ground, refusing to budge, as she continued to hold the creatures at bay. As crazy as the last two nights had been, battling androids dressed as cops and armored endoskeletons, this seemed even crazier. The way the mud splashed all over the walls and floor under the water's fierce spray, only to pool together and re-form into something vaguely humanoid again. The creatures pulling the mud toward them from all angles, seeming to suck it out of the very air.

She heard both Alex and Raiff shouting her name, firing away with the nozzle until the stream slowed and then faded to a trickle.

"Sam!"

Alex this time. She dropped the hose and rushed for the extended-cab pickup truck they'd grabbed from a parking garage at the halfway point of their drive. She reached the vehicle and piled into the backseat, as she glimpsed the creatures continuing to regain form inside the cabin.

A pair emerged, paths of mud trailing them from the cabin as they approached the truck from the front, seeming to glide more than walk. Raiff gunned the engine and tore off. The big truck slammed into both golem, obliterating them on impact, at least for the moment. The other four creatures were moving from the cabin by then, but Raiff gathered too much speed for them to catch it.

Sam was just beginning to believe they were in the clear when a dark passenger van slammed into the driver's side of the truck, crinkling the steel and forcing all ten airbags to engage.

Although she was shaken and dazed, Sam's vision cleared to find Alex trying to unbuckle his shoulder harness with one hand, the book having slipped from its canvas wrapping to the floor. Raiff was fighting to clear the flattened casings of the airbags from him.

The van had ended up partially in front of the now stalled truck, its windshield wipers frozen in place against the glass, and the pelting rain hiding much of the world beyond. Sam glimpsed the van's bashed-in front end and a figure slumped behind the wheel.

The driver's-side mirror was a memory, and the passenger-side one gave up nothing of the golem tracing their brief flight through the storm.

"Get out!" Raiff called to them. "Run!"

"Not this time," Alex said back to him, his harness finally snapping free. "We tried that already."

"No choice!" Raiff yelled back at him, unable to free his own seatbelt. Alex tried to help him, but Raiff pushed him off. "You know what to do! Go! *Go!*"

Still regarding him, Alex threw open his door, reaching down to grasp the book.

Sam let out a scream of warning.

Two dark arms were reaching in.

64

DEAD ZONE

"ALEX!" SAM SCREAMED, ANOTHER of the creatures at her door now.

It was pressing on the glass, not trying to break it so much as push the pane out altogether. She lurched toward the front seat, squeezing over the console and feeling the stormwaters pelt her thanks to the wind.

Sam saw Alex fighting back against the golem, mud caking his clothes and skin. Then she realized the thing reaching inside the truck was actually going for the canvas sack holding the book that had slipped to the floor, and Alex was struggling to stop it.

Think!

Something she'd always been good at it, her specialty. But there was nothing Sam could think of now, with their truck stalled, Raiff trapped, and Alex engaged with one golem and the rest of them coming at the truck.

"Duck!" Raiff yelled to Alex.

Sam saw he was holding his stick. She watched as it extended not into a whip but a sharp-edged lance. Alex ducked as ordered, and the weapon crossed right over him and speared the thing straight through one eye, then pulled back and speared it through the other.

That golem reeled wildly, slamming into the creature that had just popped the entire window glass free and dropped it inside the cab. More of the storm washed inside, showering Sam with sheets of rain. But Alex had already dived outside the truck past the golem, with the book held inside the canvas sack clutched tightly to him.

Summoning all the strength she could muster, Sam shouldered

the door on the driver's side open and spilled out into the rain, which seemed to have swallowed all of the air.

She landed facedown on the parking lot. The pooling water was so deep her entire face was buried in it. She rolled onto her back, holding to her bearings and needing to reclaim her feet.

Thump!

Thud!

Sam looked up to see a third creature atop the truck's roof and a fourth in its bed, the final two, reconstituted, seeming to glide the rest of the way across the parking lot. She scrabbled to her feet and sloshed around the truck, met there by Alex, who grabbed her arm in his free hand, the book clutched in his other one.

"Come on!" he cried into the night.

And then they were running.

Sam's lungs felt like they were on fire, her legs heavy and her steps feeling weighed down by the ground squishing underfoot. Alex continued to drag her along, making her keep to his pace, Sam unable to find the breath needed to protest.

They rushed through the woods that rimmed this section of Medicine Lake, sodden tree branches scratching at their faces and the ground feeling like quicksand beneath their feet. Sam's mind conjured an image of the entire mud-rich forest floor coming to life, closing in on them shapelessly to entomb them forever. She wanted to ask Alex where they were going, but couldn't find the breath to manage that either, not that it mattered.

Because where *could* they be going?

"This way!" Alex signaled, dragging her to the left.

He obviously had a destination in mind, more of an idea than she did, leaving Sam wondering what it was Alex had figured out.

He moved without slowing, seeming to know exactly where he was going through the storm-ravaged night. They could hear the squishing sounds of pursuit as the creatures gave chase, closing fast.

"Any ideas how to kill these things?" he managed, breathing hard himself now.

"No," Sam said.

He sniffed the air, his nose wrinkling at a scent he detected. "Plan B, then," Alex said.

He was holding Sam by the hand now, pulling her on with one hand while the other clung to the canvas sack containing the book to keep it as dry as he could. The brush thinned slightly, and still Sam could hear the sloshing steps of the golem burning her ears through the pounding of the storm, joined by the pattering sounds of the pelting raindrops hitting . . .

Water! Sam realized.

They emerged from the tree line before Medicine Lake itself, a dark reflective black pool dappled by the driving rain. Sam felt Alex yanking her on into the water, felt it deepening around her. The odor she had faintly detected in the woods but ignored had thickened into a stench that intensified the farther they drew into the water. And amid the stubborn, wind-driven rain, Sam noticed a thick film riding the surface.

"An algae bloom," she realized.

"That's right," Alex acknowledged. "Trust me. I've got an idea— the new me, that is."

Sam felt him stiffen and followed his gaze to the edge of the shoreline. The six golem stood there, huge shapes silhouetted against the rain-splattered night, the glowing red orbs of their eyes illuminating the motionless mud that formed their bodies.

"You want to dissolve mud, drop it in water, right?" Alex said, as they continued to wade out from the shoreline. "Just like you did back at the cabin."

"You mean, what I *tried* to do. It didn't work," Sam reminded him.

"This is different."

"Why?"

Before Alex could answer, she realized it herself: the algae, a type called Cyanobacteria, which was especially rich in nitrogen and phosphorus. Sam glanced down at the blue-green sheen stubbornly clinging to the lake's surface amid the storm pounding it.

"The bloom consumes oxygen," Alex elaborated, as if reading her mind.

Sam thought of how soil was oxygenated, another word for aeration, to create the richest environment for plant life.

"Suck all the oxygen from soil . . ." Alex started, leaving his thought there.

"And you destroy the golem," Sam completed for him.

They watched four of the creatures wade into Medicine Lake in a neat line, as if moving as one. Alex and Sam retreated until the water was up to their chests, the golem heading straight for them.

"Alex . . ." Sam started, too frightened to complete her thought.

"Trust me."

And, sure enough, the progress of the things slowed quickly and then stopped altogether when the golem were waist-deep in the water. Sam and Alex watched as they seemed to tremble, shaking off patches of the soil that composed them. Only this time they were unable to reconstitute themselves, the deoxygenated soil spilling off the golem lost to the black waters until the four shapes vanished altogether.

"I told you!" Alex said, as Sam realized the final two golem had vanished from the shoreline.

EIGHT

QUEST

The journey of a thousand miles begins with one step.

LAO TZU

65

TWINS

RAIFF REACHED INTO THE van's front seat through a jagged hole in the driver's-side window and drew the gaunt figure's head through the remainder of the glass. The man's eyes fluttered, looking dazed, sharpening only when Raiff slapped him twice in the face.

"Who are you?"

The man looked at him, recognition flashing in his eyes, as it had the last time their paths had crossed outside Langston Marsh's fortress.

"A loyalist," the man said, through the rain dividing them, "as opposed to a traitor."

Raiff yanked his head farther into the storm, the downpour washing the man's blood from the glass. "You think you know me. Who do you think I am?"

"It's not what I think, it's what I *know*, because it *is* who you *are*. But you're dead."

"When? When, goddamnit!"

"Eighteen sixty-five. At least that's what I thought. Which means you survived. Which means you're like me, monk."

"The truth, or I'll cut your throat with this glass!"

The man seemed unperturbed. "Don't let me stop you. Six hundred years is enough for any man to live."

"They sent you over here."

"As the other side must've sent you."

"I'm not the man you think I am."

"Yes, you are; you just don't know it."

"Make sense!"

"I found you back in Austria. Who you think you are doesn't matter, because you're still that man, the same man."

"The book!" Raiff realized. "You came for the book!"

"But the boy would've made a nice bonus. We'll still get him, if not me, then someone else. I'm expendable, replaceable." The man looked him over again, hatefully. "Just like you, monk."

"I already told you, I'm not this—"

"That's what you told me, because you don't even know who you are yourself. You only think you do. That's the problem with ideals; they harm a man's judgment and his ability to see the world for what it is."

"Who are *you*?" Raiff demanded again.

"Gilles de Rais is the name I took when I came here."

Raiff felt the hand holding the man by the neck tremble. "You're a murderer," he said, recalling the awful, sordid tales he'd heard of this man, crimes for which he'd supposedly been executed.

Obviously, that story needed some tweaking, because here he was, still alive and on the trail of the very book with which Alex and Sam had managed to flee. The creatures he'd somehow fashioned out of flecks of organic material had similarly given birth to the legend of the golem. That reminded Raiff just how much of human history, especially its lore, originated with the presence here of refugees like himself, along with those from his native world determined to destroy them.

"You'd better run before my children come back," de Rais was saying.

"They won't get the boy."

"The boy is likely dead by now, the girl too. And when the golem return, they'll have the book."

"You underestimate this boy and this girl."

"They bleed, they die—that's all I need to know, monk."

"I should kill you," Raiff said, holding de Rais tighter.

"Go ahead, kill me. Without me to return them to the ground, the golem will kill and kill and kill, and all those deaths will be on your conscience." De Rais hesitated, Raiff was sure, in order to milk the moment and enjoy the upper hand he wielded for now. "Make your choice, monk!"

"We're going to win," Raiff insisted, but not sounding as certain as he'd hoped. "We're going to destroy you."

De Rais looked as if he almost found that funny, the storm's pelting rain forming a curtain between them and pooling off de Rais's face into a puddle on the ground below. "With a boy and a girl as your only allies? You're as mad today as the last time I killed you. Or maybe you think the woman will—"

He stopped, eyes suddenly jerking away, as if he knew he'd said too much.

Raiff felt a chill. De Rais must have been referring to the woman who'd come across the spacebridge ahead of those plasteel soldiers, the one who could only be Elaina, which was impossible.

Because Elaina was dead.

"What woman?" he screeched at de Rais anyway.

De Rais said nothing, still avoiding Raiff's gaze.

"What woman?" Raiff demanded again, drawing the man's head farther out the window, sharing the storm with him now. "I'll kill you if you don't talk!"

"Go ahead. I told you, I've lived long enough anyway."

Raiff spotted something on the rubber mat, just short of the van's brake pedal. He leaned in and snatched it up with his free hand: a large vial that must've been shaken loose by the impact of the collision.

"Your magic elixir, right? The chemical compound that brings your golem to life."

De Rais's eyes widened, feeling for his coat pocket as if expecting the vial to still be there. "There's no magic involved. You want to kill me, go ahead. And if you think you can figure out how to use my elixir..."

"It doesn't interest me at all, and I'm not going to kill you," Raiff said, shifting his grip on the vial. "What would happen if I sprinkled this on you or made you drink it?"

The bravado slipped entirely from de Rais's expression.

"Tell me about the woman," Raiff demanded

"She went across the bridge ahead of the Companions."

"Keep talking," Raiff ordered, making sure de Rais could see the vial.

"That's all. There's nothing else to say."

"Describe her."

"I didn't get a good look."

"Do the best you can, then."

De Rais's eyes were locked on the vial as he replied, "She looked like the boy—that's the best I can do."

Raiff released his hold on him and backed up. He held de Rais's stare briefly, wondering if it was possible, wondering if this truly could be.

Elaina . . . Could she really be the woman de Rais was describing?

The brush rustled at the rim of the woods, something big and dark shifting at the tree line.

"I'd run if I were you, monk," de Rais taunted him. "You're already dead, you and this world you love so much. You're dead and you just don't know it."

Raiff saw a pair of golem approaching in a neat line, neither Alex nor the ancient book anywhere to be seen. He could practically smell the stench of rot and death pouring off them. Kill de Rais and they'd be free to wreak havoc, a vast killing spree that might never stop.

"Go, then," de Rais taunted him again, snickering. "Go see what my other children have done to your precious boy. We've both wasted our lives, monk, but it will be worth it for me in the end."

Raiff hurled de Rais's vial into the air as far he could. "Before this is over, I'll be burying you," he told him, after the sound of breaking glass pierced the night.

Then Raiff disappeared into the storm, into the darkness.

66

MATERNAL INSTINCTS

TRADEWIND AIRPORT IN AMARILLO was closed when Elaina got there, just as she'd expected.

And planned.

Once it became clear she was in no condition to spend upward of another full day behind the wheel when time was of the absolute essence, flying to the nearest airport to the Klamath Mountains where Langston Marsh would be hiding became easily her best strategy. Tradewind Airport was the closest facility to what she needed, accessing its tarmac as simple as picking a single lock on a chain-link gate.

The pictures she'd looked at on the phone she'd grabbed from the same drugstore where she'd forcibly obtained the drugs she so desperately needed made it appear perfect for her needs, a reality reinforced when she got there. The premises consisted of little more than a single departure lounge building and a few hangars erected on the opposite side of the single runway. A dozen single-engine planes were parked on the tarmac, and it took Elaina only a few minutes to settle on a Cessna 182 Skylane for its thousand mile–plus flying range. That meant reaching Klamath Falls airport would require only a single refueling stop.

Elaina had been a master when it came to electronics for as long as she could remember, able to grasp instantly how to make the controls of even something as complex as an airplane work as well as if she were a pilot with hundreds of hours in the air. Though she'd never flown a plane, she knew her way around comparable machines from her world. Helping matters further, the

Skylane's controls were simple and intuitive and plenty similar to far more intricate machines she'd learned to operate back in her world.

It took her several minutes to grow familiar enough with the controls of the plane she was stealing to first start the engine, then begin her taxi down the runway. Her stomach fluttered at the moment the Cessna lifted off into the night sky, and she remained light-headed enough throughout her climb to eight thousand feet to make Elaina fear she was going to lose consciousness again.

But she didn't and quickly settled into an easy rhythm flying the plane through the clear night sky with no potentially disruptive storms in the offing. She plotted a course for Van Nuys Airport outside of Los Angeles with an estimated flying time of just under five hours. Van Nuys was open for business twenty-four hours a day, though only a skeletal staff would be on station when she landed to refuel by whatever means might be necessary.

She was making great time, until she hit unexpected headwinds there was no way to steer clear of. The air became choppy and rough, forcing Elaina to burn through fuel at a much faster rate, which necessitated her looking for an alternative landing spot to Van Nuys. The Cessna's onboard computer identified an airport comparable to Tradewind at the edge of her revised flying range: North Las Vegas Airport, which was located three miles northwest of downtown Las Vegas and operated by the Clark County Department of Aviation. Like Tradewind it would be closed when she arrived, leaving Elaina the challenge of coming up with a means to refuel prior to setting off again for Klamath Falls Airport.

She flew the final stretch of miles with a LOW FUEL warning light flashing and a buzzer sounding in unison. Elaina thought she actually heard the engine sputter as she taxied off the runway toward a fuel truck parked on the tarmac near the airport's single building, which might have been a twin of the one she'd left in Amarillo.

She had just coasted the Cessna 182 to a stop when bright headlights flashed on, blinding her. When she was able to see once more, she realized these were revolving red lights perched atop what looked to be an armada of Nevada Highway Patrol vehicles,

SUVs all. They converged upon her from all angles, leaving Elaina no possible means of escape either on foot or by retaking the air with only fumes to fly on. No choice but to remain in the cockpit with her hands in the air, as the doors of the SUVs seemed to open in unison, allowing a flood of armed, uniformed figures to sweep toward her.

Apparently, the Cessna had been reported stolen to the Department of Homeland Security, which tracked it all the way into Nevada airspace as a potential terrorist threat to Las Vegas. When Elaina overflew the city proper, the highway patrol had scrambled to intercept her here at the North Las Vegas Airport.

After Elaina could produce neither identification nor an explanation for her presence, she was handcuffed and tossed into the caged rear seat of one of the highway patrol cruisers. No further conversation was exchanged with anyone in authority, until she was ushered into the Nevada Highway Patrol Southern Command substation in Las Vegas on West Sunset Road.

She was fingerprinted and booked there, and her mug shot was taken from a variety of angles. Beyond that, the officers on duty had no interest in questioning her, since Homeland Security agents would be taking her into custody tomorrow. But Elaina did witness the officers who booked her entering all the information they'd gathered into a computer, leaving her chilled.

"Don't do that," she said to them. "Please."

The two men looked as if they found that funny. "Sure," one of them said, "whatever you say."

"You don't understand. This is for your own good, not just mine. I'm not safe here. *You're* not safe here. Nobody's safe here now!"

Both officers approached her chair warily. "Why don't we get you settled in a cell? You'll be safe enough there."

"No, I won't," Elaina pleaded. "They'll come for me. That means they'll be coming for you too!"

The officers exchanged a glance. Then three more appeared to serve as Elaina's escorts down a flight of stairs toward a trio of cells contained in the basement.

The sound of the cell door rattling closed set Elaina's head pounding again and she plopped down atop a cement platform, surrendering to unconsciousness.

67

COLLISION

"SO THIS IS WHAT the destruction of Laboratory Z wrought," Orson Wilder said, surveying the small, cramped room from which Donati communicated with the Janus team. "Janus."

"Everyone thought I was a fool for recommending it," Donati said from behind the computer where he had just initiated the contact. "Including me, most of the time."

"But not anymore."

"No, Orson, not anymore. Not all of us had the luxury of spending the last eighteen years as an eccentric answering questions for a dollar."

Wilder looked toward the computer screen coming to life. "I suspect I should charge this group considerably more than that."

"They'll need to hear our conclusions first."

"But will they listen this time?"

"Oh, they'll listen, all right," Donati said.

The bar grids took shape on the oversized monitor screen, divided into quadrants.

"We have someone else joining us today," Donati began, once they were all assembled. "Gentlemen and lady, may I present the former head of Laboratory Z, Orson Wilder."

Silence.

"I believe Dr. Wilder lacks the security clearance to be on this call, to even know of Janus's existence," the lone woman snapped, her voice bouncing in the bottom right this time.

"I sought his help because he's the foremost expert in the world on what we're facing here. You should all be familiar with him from the unredacted report I circulated on the destruction of Laboratory Z."

"We're familiar with the fact that he left NASA almost immediately after that event and hasn't been heard from since." From the woman again.

"I believe," started the male voice that occupied the top right this time around, "Dr. Wilder wouldn't be here if he didn't have something of vital interest to us to share."

"I do, indeed," Wilder said, looking from the screen at Donati.

"As you'll recall," Donati picked up, "in our last call, I mentioned the necessity of finding the other supercolliders our enemy has constructed in secret over the years, like the one we uncovered beneath Alcatraz more than twenty-four hours ago now, as my report indicates. Orson?"

"What I did," Wilder picked up, "was seek out patterns of extreme power disruption. Science, as my associate Dr. Donati has no doubt told you, is all about patterns. Patterns are like a road map, directing you which way to go. Now, as Dr. Donati has also surely informed you, supercolliders require immeasurable power to operate, of a level that would be impossible to self-generate. So I confined my search for patterns to civilized areas where such levels of energy were readily and steadily available, and the drain of which wouldn't raise the kind of flags our determined enemy would seek to avoid at all costs.

"This was no easy task," he continued, "given that these facilities would've been built with subterfuge in mind, to disguise any means we might use to identify their locations. And they did a magnificent job."

"Magnificent enough to make your efforts futile?" a male voice asked.

"Not at all, thanks to weather satellites."

"Weather satellites?" the lone woman raised.

Wilder nodded, even though they couldn't see him. "I went back over many years—decades—studying patterns of atmospheric disruption that had changed, and then sought to identify the sources of that change. Not power disruptions in the grid so much as inexplicable ripples in barometric pressure consistent with the effects of large amounts of electromagnetic radiation forming what is essentially a heat grid."

"Tell them how many you found," Donati urged.

"I'm getting to that."

"Tell them."

Wilder cleared his throat. "I can say, with reasonable scientific certainty, that I've located twenty-seven colliders operating right under our collective noses. My preliminary findings indicate all of them were constructed underground, within areas of existing fortification like salt mines, limestone caves, caverns, and even among the ruins of a few lost cities that would have otherwise been an archeologist's dream."

"These are the beachheads for their coming attack," Donati interjected.

"Do the two of you truly believe that this alien race expects to conquer an entire planet from only twenty-seven locations?" challenged the man in the top right corner. "After all, we aren't without our defenses. And, from your own reporting, Dr. Donati, it's virtually inconceivable that these travelers could bring anything metallic through the wormhole with them. Since that is likely to include weapons, how exactly do you believe they're going to defeat us?"

"Oh," said Orson Wilder, "we no longer believe they want to defeat us. We believe they want to destroy us."

"And they brought the means to do so across the spacebridge, twenty-seven spacebridges, one for each of the supercolliders Dr. Wilder has identified," Donati picked up.

"Wait," a male voice crackled over the speaker, "we just established they couldn't bring weapons, anything metallic across these spacebridges."

"What's here now isn't metallic," Donati told him, told them all. "But it can destroy our world, obliterate every living thing."

"Only organic matter can cross the spacebridge," from the woman again.

"Not just matter," Wilder said.

"What else is there?"

"Energy, pure energy. That's what the creature that destroyed Laboratory Z eighteen years ago was comprised of."

"Creature?" one of the male voices raised.

"Figure of speech."

"All the same," rang out another digitally processed voice, "one *creature,* or whatever you want to call it, could hardly destroy the entire world."

Donati shuddered at the memory of the thing he had faced eighteen years ago. "Maybe not, but what about twenty-seven of them?"

68

INTO THE WOODS

THE GOLEM VANQUISHED, ALEX had led Sam from the water, checking the condition of the book as soon as they reached the shoreline.

"You're not going to believe this," he said, easing its bulk from the sack.

He felt Sam peering over his shoulder. "What?"

Alex moved the book where she could see it. "It's dry, undamaged. Don't ask me how or why."

"Neither of those matter, so long as you can still read it. What happens now?"

"It's not safe to go back to Raiff. So we spend the night here."

Alex fished some discarded camping gear out of a recycling bin set in a clearing near the shore of Medicine Lake. The clearing also featured picnic tables and concrete posts upon which barbecue grills had once rested. No more, because of the increased fire danger.

He handed the shredded remains of a tent, the posts too bent and broken to use, back to Sam and returned to sorting through the refuse.

"What are we supposed to do with this?" she asked, balling up the canvas material to make it easier to tote.

"You were never a Girl Scout?"

"No, and don't tell me you were a Boy Scout either."

Alex smiled. "Not my thing, but I know how to make a lean-to."

"What's that?"

"Smart girl like you? You're kidding, right?"

"I'm a scientist, not an outdoorsman."

Alex tossed some reasonably stable tent posts from the bin. "You mean outdoors*woman*."

"I'm not one of those either."

The wind had suddenly diminished, but sheets of rain continued to dominate the air. Once Alex had salvaged everything he could, he fastened the remains of the tent to a tree and then looped its cord ends around the still-usable posts Sam had wedged into the ground. He tied them as tight as he could while leaving sufficient slack to allow the tent to act like a sail, turned slightly against the slowing winds so that the return of a gust wouldn't uproot the meager shelter.

Moving about had spared them from the effects of the night's chill but now, with their clothes soaking wet, both were shaking from the cold rawness of the air.

"Too bad you didn't find some clothes in that bin," Sam said, after pushing herself under the makeshift lean-to.

"Actually, I did, but nothing you'd want to wear, believe me."

"Don't be so sure about that."

She looked up at the tent remnants strung over them, which had already begun to sag from the weight of the water. Raindrops were leaking through narrow slits in the fabric and the sound of the drops hitting the canvas reminded her of the noise of someone clacking away on an old-fashioned typewriter.

"I'm worried about my parents," she blurted out suddenly. "If something happens to them . . ."

"They're not targets."

"Meaning I am."

"Thanks to me."

Sam pressed closer to him. "I didn't mean it that way."

"It's true, all the same."

"I wish I had a pillow."

Alex lifted his head from the canvas sack he had placed under him to keep the book safe. "You do," he said, and eased a hand beneath her hair to settle Sam's head on his chest.

"I can feel your heart."

"Only one I've got—at least I think it's the only one."

"It's beating fast."

"That's what fighting golem will do to you."

"Explains why mine's beating so fast too."

"Could be the cold," Alex told her.

Sam shifted her frame forward in order to kiss Alex lightly on the lips. "Now we're even."

He kissed her back. "Not anymore."

"Yeah? Okay."

She kissed him again and this time it lingered, lengthened, ended with them wrapped firmly together.

"Let's call it a tie," Sam suggested, her voice soft, her body still cradled against his.

He felt his arms tighten around her. He tried to speak lightly. "Only for now."

He felt her smile.

And he was glad they were there together despite the hazards of the day.

Despite the near-death of the day.

But there was something amazing she'd given him. Hope.

Belief that they could save the world.

And each other.

"What happens tomorrow?" Sam asked.

Alex stroked her hair, unfurling the patches gnarled by the rain when he came to them. "We make a phone call."

69

VISITOR

ELAINA COULD FEEL HERSELF deteriorating. The most recent dose of pills she'd gulped down had achieved only a negligible effect and, under the circumstances, no more would be coming.

I had no choice. What other choice did I have?

She lay on her side on the stiff bunk, shivering and passing in and out of consciousness. It didn't really feel like sleep, just dream-like episodes, conjured by her mind, of Alex at various stages of development. But the visions of him weren't chronological. Piecemeal instead, splotches of his life in random order, pleasant for moments but also disconcerting, because she had to recognize him all over again each time.

Elaina believed the chaotic order in which these images of Alex's life unfolded was the product of her own guilt and, probably, longing. Back home, she could hide her pain and angst behind the fabric of duty and mission. But here, the closest she'd been to Alex physically in eighteen years, that cushion was removed, forcing her to confront the feelings she'd long hidden or denied.

So this was her punishment, Elaina reflected, seeing her own son as the stranger that he was.

It wasn't a sound that stirred her alert, so much as a feeling. The sense of someone watching her, pushing coldness out on his breath, chilling her to the bone through the fever that was racking her.

Elaina jerked awake and struggled to sit up despite the heaviness that had settled in her head, the world conspiring against the effort. Gazed outside her cell at something that wasn't there, then was.

"You disappoint me, Elaina," said the thing that was more shape and shadow than physical being.

He was tall and gaunt to the point of being almost skeletal, his clothes hanging on his body like an ill-fitting curtain. At first glance the figure's skin seemed albino white, almost translucent. But on second glance, in the flickering light from the weak fixtures strung overhead, it looked grayer, as if the man had rubbed ash all over his skin. He seemed almost spectral in form, more liquid than solid the way he stood there as if the air moved through instead of around him. His head came to a peak at the top, where hair shaded with the same grayish tint rode his scalp, so even and still that it seemed painted in place.

"What exactly did you expect to accomplish by coming here?" the shape continued.

His voice had an odd twang to it, almost a harmonic echo. It sounded like it was coming from somewhere else, as if it were a broadcast of sorts, and the shape was just mouthing the words.

"To keep you away from him," Elaina said, pressing her shoulders back against the wall to keep as much distance as she could from the figure.

"You're a bad liar. You always were. And now you've thrown your life away for nothing. I can see you're dying. Such a waste for that to happen before Alex learns the truth."

"What did you tell him?"

"That I could take him back with me. That he could be reunited with his true family and take his rightful place in our world, his *world."*

"You're a bad liar too."

"Tell me what in my words wasn't true."

"You're not his family."

"I never said I was. I'll leave that to you, now that you're here."

"I'll never find him now."

"You forget how well I know you, Elaina. Your strength and determination. It's why I chose you."

"Stop it!" Elaina cried out, hoping this was the product of another vision, not happening any more than the fever dream that had produced Alex growing up in random order.

"You don't think he deserves to know the truth?" the shape continued, the motion of his mouth and emerging words out of sync suddenly. *"You don't think he deserves to know who he really is?"*

"You killed his parents, destroyed his world."

"They were not his parents, and this is not his world. You're the one who endangered him by sending him here, making him part of a plot that was doomed to fail from the moment it was conceived."

"I came here to save him!"

"He can only be saved in our world, not this one. You sealed his fate without knowing it. You made his return not just inevitable but also a necessity. You made him a sacrifice to your hopeless cause, and now this is what we're left with. You may never go home, but he will."

"He'll destroy you," Elaina insisted, the threat sounding lame even to her.

"He's tried that twice already," the shape said, the slightest of smiles spreading over the projection of his long, thin face. *"And yet here I am."*

"Before this is over—"

"It already is over, Elaina. That's why I came to visit you here. To say goodbye."

"No, I'm going to save him," Elaina insisted again, placing her feet on the floor of the cell and making herself stand. She approached the bars, stopping just short of them. "I'm going to save him so he can destroy you."

"Without knowing the truth, without knowing who I really am?" The shape shook its head, spreading what looked like a flood of tiny gnats through the dim air. *"Do you really want him to die with the rest of them?"*

"Rest of who?" Elaina asked, something quivering inside her.

"This world is becoming more of a burden than it's worth, too much of a way station for your foolish plans and ambitions. How long has it been? Hundreds of years, thousands? Enough."

"What does that mean?"

"That Alex is going to come with me because there isn't going to be a world for him here much longer, and . . ."

"What?"

"There are things about our world you don't know, enemies beyond your Resistance that could destroy us all."

Elaina felt suddenly cold, nothing to do with the fever that had curled her up on the hard cot's surface and filled her mind with dreams that didn't feel like dreams at all.

"You look surprised, Elaina. Why? What did you think was going to happen when you escalated this war? What did you think was going to happen now that Alex knows the truth of his being?"

"You're scared of him."

"I'm scared of what he can do, unless he realizes the folly of his pursuit. I'm scared for our world. You think me a monster? I'm not the one who sent him here, am I? I'm not the one who was willing to sacrifice him to a worthless cause."

"You're going to destroy this world, aren't you?"

"You've left me no choice, Elaina. But you can take comfort in the fact that you'll be dead already. Look at you, you're dying even now."

Footsteps pounded down the stairs. Before Elaina could respond, a highway patrolman rounded the corner and walked straight through the apparition as it thinned and then dissipated, leaving a grayish residue in the air that looked like wisps of smoke from burning leaves.

"Security cameras went out," the officer told her, looking around as if to see if anyone else was there. "Were you talking to some-body?"

"No one," Elaina told him, still shivering. "No one at all."

70

FLIGHT

"I THINK HE THOUGHT I was a hooker," Sam said, handing Alex the cell phone she'd borrowed from a trucker in the Medicine Lake Diner parking lot, where another driver had dropped them off.

Alex shifted the book, now tucked into a paper shopping bag, from his left arm to his right and waved his thanks to the man perched high in the nearby cab.

"She's not a hooker!" Alex shouted to the driver, lost between whatever was playing through his booming radio.

Sam punched him in the shoulder. "How do you know I'm not? Maybe I wasn't interning at NASA all those nights. Maybe that was just a front to fool my parents."

"All those brains you've got make for a great disguise."

She felt around the pockets of her still-moist jeans for the number Langston Marsh had provided before they'd dropped him off. "I can't find it, the piece of paper."

"Don't bother. I memorized the number," Alex said, already dialing it.

"You couldn't even remember a simple algebra formula last week."

"I know. Miracle after miracle, right?"

They had emerged from the woods safely away from the rental cabins, which were certain to be teeming with activity in the wake of last night's chaos. Raiff had their throwaway cell phones' numbers, but those cell phones had been ruined by their plunge into Medicine Lake. And Raiff had never given them whatever number he was using now, either an oversight or a precaution.

Unfortunately, their disheveled appearance had made passing

cars loath to pick them up. But the truck driver had disregarded that and brought them this far.

The book, thankfully, had suffered no damage at all, its pages and binding unaffected because whatever they were composed of was impervious to the elements. The storm had ended just before dawn, and the sun rose with the promise of drying the two of them out at least a little.

"Make the call, Alex, so I can give that guy his phone back."

Alex winked at her. "Wonder what he's going to expect in return."

"I'm glad you called," Langston Marsh said, not bothering with a greeting.

"How'd you know it was us?" Alex asked, holding the phone close enough to Sam for her to hear.

"Someone calling from a number I've never seen before—who else could it be? I'm relieved to see you're still alive."

"Not by much," Alex told him. "We need a plane."

"Where to?"

"Europe. Or the Middle East. Maybe some place in Asia. I haven't figured out the specifics yet. I found some clues in that book, but got interrupted before I could nail down the exact locations. There were these maps, enough to tell me where we need to go to finish this."

"Where are you now?"

"Near Medicine Lake in California."

"You're less than two hours from Rogue Valley International-Medford Airport. Can you get there?"

"We'll find a way," Alex told Marsh.

"I'll have a private jet waiting."

"Sounds like a plan."

"And what exactly are you looking for?" Marsh asked, trying not to sound as eager to know as he clearly was.

"Four ancient keys," Alex told him.

"Keys?"

"I'm not sure if the book meant that literally or otherwise."

"A Gulfstream will be en route in minutes. I'll have the pilot file a flight plan to New York for refueling, so you can use that leg of the trip to figure out where you can find these keys."

"Thanks."

"It's the least I can do. I'm sorry, Alex, sorry for everything but mostly for being a fool."

"There's a lot of that going around lately, sir."

"Anything else I can do for you?"

Alex realized his socks were still sloshing about in his ruined sneakers, and Sam's shirt was still dappled with soaked patches of fabric that refused to dry. "As a matter of fact . . ."

After finishing his call with Langston Marsh, Alex approached a woman just about to get into her car.

"I got us a ride," he told Sam, trotting back toward her, "from that woman over there."

"That was fast," she said gratefully. "What'd you tell her?"

"That you were pregnant."

71

BY THE HOUR

THE NEAREST LIBRARY TO Medicine Lake that suited Raiff's purpose was the Tulelake Public Library in a town of the same name. It boasted computers with internet access for use, but only for one hour at a time. They were all available when he arrived at the library's 6:00 A.M. opening time, and Raiff settled into a chair behind one of the machines, a clock starting to tick down in his head as soon as he'd logged on.

He had no idea where Alex and Sam were, but knew the golem had failed in their mission. Raiff had the sense that if something happened to Alex he'd know it, as if they were intrinsically bonded. He'd spent eighteen years watching and protecting the boy from afar, knowing him better than he knew himself. Was it that far-fetched to believe they were connected on a whole other level that defied reason?

All of this defied reason.

As casually as he could manage, Raiff gazed about to make sure no one was watching him. Satisfied that was the case, his fingers began flying across the keyboard, activating a dark underbelly of the Web. Known exclusively to government operatives of the highest security clearance, the powerful and proprietary software program he'd accessed had been designed to predict terrorist attacks by tracing the trails of their potential perpetrators. The software keyed on large, bulk purchases of the elements likely to be used in building a homemade bomb, as in the fertilizer variety. It keyed on murders, deaths, and unexplained disappearances of any known terrorist operative or enabler. It keyed on flight patterns across the world in the wake of such occurrences, as well as weapons thefts or large-scale purchases on the secondary markets.

As such, the software, known as Cerberus, wasn't very good at predicting attacks carried out by lone wolves. And although it had been tweaked to account for that, little progress had been made since the same patterns weren't present to lead the software anyplace. Raiff didn't particularly care, because he wasn't after a terrorist.

He was after the woman who'd crossed the spacebridge into the Desertron facility in Texas. She had come across the bridge ahead of what Gilles de Rais had called the Companions, Raiff's name for the plasteel soldiers who'd attacked Langston Marsh's fortress.

So, once Cerberus was up and running, Raiff started his search the morning before in the area of Waxahachie, Texas, site of the nearest particle collider. Sure enough, a violent incident had been reported there at a local restaurant. Apparently, a woman seriously injured four would-be attackers and killed one. Marsh's men, no doubt, the Trackers he'd sent after the woman Raiff was more convinced than ever could only be Elaina.

Next, Raiff postulated where the woman would be headed from Texas. Alex was in Northern California, as was Langston Marsh's former fortress in the Klamath Mountains. That meant a drive initially west out of Texas, before doglegging to the north.

Farther west in Texas, almost to the border with New Mexico, a pharmacy had been robbed by a lone suspect, a woman brandishing a pistol that matched the description of one taken from a man in Waxahachie. The software allowed Raiff to access security camera footage from the robbery and he clicked on the link, waiting for the footage to unspool.

And there it was, grainy and slightly out of focus, but with a reasonably clear view of the woman in the moments prior to her drawing a pistol from beneath her coat:

Elaina!

Raiff felt a rush of excitement, elation, exuberance. Emotions he was hardly familiar with but that the opportunity to see Elaina again had stoked in him. Then he remembered something and backtracked through the Cerberus software, finding the inventory of drugs stolen in the robbery. He wasn't intimately acquainted with any of them, but was familiar enough to know they were serious and powerful and didn't bode well for the state of Elaina's health, lending his search a new level of urgency.

In his mind, Raiff traced the quickest route west from the area of the pharmacy to California, specifically Marsh's fortress, and focused the Cerberus software on towns along that route. While that search drew a blank, an associated one flagged an item about a Homeland Security operation conducted at an airport north of Las Vegas where a stolen plane was recovered and a woman taken into custody.

A woman.

And, according to the report, the plane had come in from the Amarillo, Texas, area, not all that far from the pharmacy the same woman had robbed at gunpoint.

Cerberus allowed him to view the entire police report, including the mug shots that had been inputted into the system.

Elaina . . .

It would take him upward of ten hours to get to the Las Vegas Highway Patrol barracks where she was being held, Raiff figured, after calculating the route.

Which meant he had no time to waste.

NINE

THE JET STREAM

Somehow, we'll find it. The balance between whom we wish to be and whom we need to be. But for now, we simply have to be satisfied with who we are.

BRANDON SANDERSON, *THE HERO OF AGES*

72

SHAPE-SHIFTER

THE POSTED SECURITY GUARDS made no effort to approach or stop Gilles de Rais as he entered the Canfranc International Railway Station, tucked away amid the Pyrenees mountains between France and Spain. Neither did they even acknowledge him, nor he them. Had de Rais not been in possession of an access card read by hidden scanners at all remaining functional entrances, alarms would've been set off, at which point his presence would have indeed been acknowledged.

The station's at times glorious history bore the historical stain of having been commandeered by the Nazis during World War II and used as a primary way station for German troops. As punishment for that, perhaps, it slipped into an extreme state of disrepair after the war's end and today stood as little more than a crumbling shell of art nouveau construction of gothic proportions.

At least on the surface.

Deep below that surface, the old tunnels had been retrofitted by Spanish officials into mobile astro-particle laboratories where some of the world's greatest scientific minds toiled at unlocking the mysteries of dark matter. De Rais found this ironic, given that his destination was not those tunnels themselves but, rather, a second installation buried in the shale and rock deep below, accessible via an ancient elevator everyone else believed to have been shuttered generations before. The facility had been constructed years prior to the renovations on the upper portions of Canfranc Station, begun in earnest back in 1985, and its presence now afforded the far-larger facility ideal cover for its power drains and any otherwise inexplicable activity that may have occurred.

The elevator descended a full eighth of a mile beneath the ground, opening into the automated factory, where assembler machines manufactured android soldiers constructed for either infiltration or combat. It wasn't a factory so much as an assembly plant responsible for building cyborgs nonstop for who knew how long. But there wasn't a person, at least of the flesh and blood version, in sight anywhere. The entire assembly process looked completely automated, with various stations manned only by drones sized and shaped to tasks specific to them.

The farthest section of the plant was churning out finished limbs and steel body parts. The next sequence along the line was responsible for assembling the pieces in a manner akin to automated car factories, with robotic arms swaying about soldering, screwing, affixing, and clamping.

The pale surface flesh was draped over the fully assembled cyborgs in thick sheaths at a final station before they dropped down a conveyor through the floor, likely toward another assembly line where their unfinished chips would be programmed to enable them to spring to life. Looking, talking, and acting almost entirely human. Equipped with learning chips capable of cross-converting one language instantly into another to the point where they would always "think" in their native language but speak in the language of whomever they found themselves among.

Continuing on brought de Rais into clearer view of the next stage of the process, where the unfinished cyborgs were sprayed with various flesh-colored tints and had glass eyes fitted over their swirling orbs. It looked also like the assembling mechanism fit them with distinguishing features, like various hairstyles and lines, scars, and flesh tones.

From this vantage point, de Rais had no view of the storage facility located on another sublevel where the cyborgs were kept in anticipation of being needed someday, a day when order would have to be kept over whatever remained of this world. There would be tens and tens of thousands stockpiled there by now, more space created in the vast cavernous factory by massive excavating machines when that space was needed.

But they wouldn't be needed anymore because the plan had

changed, this world not worth the bother it was causing. Although de Rais sensed it was more than that, that the Overlords of his world felt genuinely threatened by what was transpiring and could no longer take any chances. Why else would the thing contained in a vacuum-sealed chamber have been sent here?

There were twenty-six other identical chambers scattered across the world, all constructed as part of a doomsday scenario. Doomsday for this world, that is, and having witnessed the work of things like the one currently residing in the vacuum-sealed chamber, de Rais knew the only question was how long it would take that scenario to unfold.

He ventured as close as he dared to the entrance to that chamber, conspicuously lacking a view plate he wouldn't have dared peer through anyway. He could hear a slight hum and felt a buzzing in his ears. De Rais pictured the thing forming and re-forming inside the demagnetized, yard-thick steel, never assuming the same shape twice and holding to its integrity for only a millisecond at a time before shifting again.

The ultimate power . . . A creature that didn't think or reason. Felt no compassion, sympathy, or pity, felt nothing at all. It existed only to swallow and absorb anything it came into contact with, recharging and strengthening itself from moment to moment. Once set loose on the world, it and all the others wouldn't stop until they had sucked all the life, all the energy from this planet. Sucking it dry.

The new plan.

His phone beeped, signaling he was right on time for the rendezvous as he moved forward, steering along a catwalk that overlooked the sprawling, clanking, hissing confines of the factory below. De Rais wondered how long exactly it had been in operation, how long ago the seeds of this war had been planted in relation to his own journey here in the fifteenth century.

"You failed us twice," he heard a voice say. *"First with the soldiers and then with your golem."*

The voice echoed dully inside his skull, reverberating in a dry monotone. De Rais turned to his right to find a spectral shape standing there. Translucent at first glance, but on second seeming to swallow the light more than block it. The shape's gaze turned back to the assembly line below.

"The responsibility for those failures is mine and mine alone," de Rais told the shape. "In both cases, the opposition was better than I expected, especially this boy. A clever one he is, and a warrior to boot."

"The boy calls me the Ash Man."

The projection of the elongated spectral shape, long and thin like a stick figure drawn onto the scene, was indeed monotone. Somewhere between black and white amid the color around him. *Ash* seemed as apt a description as any, de Rais thought.

"Fitting, don't you think, given that we may have no choice other than to reduce this world to ash," the projection continued. *"I believe the phrase is 'cutting our losses.' This world has become more trouble than it's worth. There's only one thing that can stop us, two, actually, in point of fact."*

"I'll get the boy for you. And the book as well."

"You're running out of chances."

"I won't fail you again."

"And how will you find him?"

De Rais hedged. "I'm working on that."

"Perhaps I can help."

"You know where the boy is?"

"I will. The time for subtlety is over. The boy will remain your responsibility. Everything else, as we approach the end-time for this world, rests with us."

Us echoed in de Rais's mind, making him wonder about the extent of the projection that remained unchanged from six hundred years ago. Did he inhabit the entire consciousness of the machine race that enabled the Overlords to rule the world from which de Rais had come?

"The boy must be taken alive. You understand that?"

"I do."

"He is crucial to our plans. We must bring him home before this world deconstructs at the hands of the beings we've dispatched for that purpose. Time is of the absolute essence," the shape continued, seeming to drift in and out of focus, alternating between gaseous and solid. *"The boy*

doesn't fully understand the nature of his importance, what he's capable of doing. And he must be captured before that comes to pass."

"I understand."

"Don't fail me again."

73

NONSTOP

"THESE JEANS ARE TOO tight," Alex said, flexing his legs aboard Langston Marsh's Gulfstream G650 as it streaked across the country.

Sam looked at him while continuing to dry her hair with a towel within the confines of a thick, plush bathrobe that had been hanging along with several others on hooks inside the bathroom. "I don't know, they look pretty good to me."

Alex continued trying to find comfort, stretching this way and that. "Yeah, well, I don't know how anybody can wear these things. No wonder they went out of style."

As Marsh had promised, the jet was waiting for them at Rogue Valley International-Medford airport when they arrived. Sam slipped back into the bathroom, where she'd just finished the most welcome shower in her life, after Alex had done the same. There, she'd slipped into the change of clothes that had been waiting for them on board. She and Alex had met the pilots only briefly, their brief encounter both curt and tense, lasting only long enough for the pilots to provide them with the passports Langston Marsh had arranged for them. How he came upon their likenesses, turned them into passport photos, she had no idea and didn't ponder the question any further. The pilots, a man and a woman, neither introduced themselves nor asked them their names. And once the cockpit was sealed again, she fully expected they wouldn't be seeing either of them again until they reached New York, when it would be necessary to tell them exactly where she and Alex were going from there.

Toward that end, when she emerged from the bathroom in her fresh change of clothes, she discovered Alex had tucked himself into one of the jet's leather seats with the book spread out over a folding desk set between his seat and a matching one. Sam took the seat across from him, aware Alex was looking at her, a different look than she was accustomed to from him. She played dumb about catching his eyes lingering when she squeezed into the chair and fastened her seatbelt.

"You really think that's necessary?"

"Habit. I always wear my seatbelt."

"I didn't know you flew so often."

"I don't. But I drive a lot."

"I wonder what happened to your car," Alex said, referring to the old Volkswagen Beetle they'd abandoned Saturday night, after their first meeting with Raiff.

"It's probably still in that parking lot, just where we left it. It's not like anybody's going to steal the old thing." Sam settled back in her seat, the book centered between them. "I wish I could call my parents," she said, instantly regretting mentioning anything that could raise unpleasant memories in Alex.

"Go ahead. There are phones on the plane. I counted three of them."

"We told my parents to get rid of their cell phones. I have no idea how to reach them."

"Reverend Billy?"

"Do you have a number for him?"

Alex shook his head, frowning as if he were disappointed in himself as a result. "We'll figure out something. He'll keep them safe, the same way he's kept himself safe for God knows how long."

"Wonder if he knows we totaled his van."

"Maybe you could lend him your Bug."

"I lost the keys."

"When?"

"I have no idea."

Alex eased the book closer to him, then turned his gaze on her again. "Those clothes look good on you."

"Thanks."

"Marsh would make a pretty good personal shopper. For you, anyway."

Sam grinned at that and then aimed her eyes back at the book. "Figure anything out while I was changing?"

A familiar playful glint flashed in Alex's eyes. "I was too busy peeking through the crack in the door."

"Very funny."

"How do you know I'm not serious?"

Sam rolled her eyes, shook her head, and sighed—but couldn't hide her smile. It was good to see him acting like his old self again, however short-lived it might be. This plane, this trip, was just what they needed. The world buzzing by thirty thousand or so feet below, with nothing that could hurt them way up here for the first time in what felt like forever.

Though it had only been since Saturday night.

What was today?

Sam had to remind herself it was Tuesday, more hours bleeding away as they winged their way eastward, first to New York.

"Are you?" she asked him.

"Serious? You bet, especially about the book," he said, tapping the page it was open to. "Like what you realized about the fourth key back in the cabin, what you didn't get a chance to tell me then."

74

JAILBIRD

"YOU HAVE A VISITOR, ma'am," the California Highway Patrol officer said, from outside her cell.

Elaina pushed herself up from the cement cot against the side of the cell in which she'd spent the night, fighting back a wave of dizziness. "Visitor?"

"Your lawyer."

"Oh."

"Please approach the door with your hands extended before you."

Elaina did as she was told, no idea exactly what this meant or who was upstairs waiting for her. She could envision no way this could be good, since she hadn't called a lawyer, or anyone else for that matter. The clock in her head told her it was late in the day; Tuesday now, if she had her bearings right. She guessed around four o'clock in the afternoon, though she had no way to be sure.

The officer reached through the bars and fastened a pair of handcuffs to her wrists, the old-fashioned metal kind, the tumblers clicking into place on each side when they locked. Then he unlocked the cell and stepped back as he opened the door.

Elaina emerged and he led her forward by the arm. She contemplated trying to overpower the man, maybe catch him by surprise. Even if she succeeded, though, what could she do next with no exit visible on this level and the stairs promising only an ascent to more police upstairs? Besides, she was still woozy, the symptoms she feared worsening doing just that without the drugs she'd stolen to calm them. Her motions felt slow and laggard. She'd be lucky if she could make it up the stairs without a railing to clutch, much less overcome an entire barracks' worth of police in trying to escape.

And who was this lawyer anyway? It made no sense she'd be provided with one in advance of being taken into custody by the Department of Homeland Security.

Upstairs, the same officer escorted her to a windowless room and knocked on the door. He opened it without waiting for a reply and led Elaina in.

There was a man standing by a metal table, fading in and out of her vision. He'd still been a boy the last time she'd seen him, but his features, strong and vulnerable at the same time, had remained remarkably similar after eighteen years.

Raiff.

The highway patrolman led her to a chair at the table, pulling it back so she could ease into it, and then started back for the door.

"Please take the handcuffs off my client," Raiff requested.

He stopped and swung back, retracing his steps reluctantly to Elaina, where he removed her handcuffs and returned them to his belt.

"Thank you," Raiff said, and sat down in the chair directly across from hers.

He had managed the ten-hour drive from Tulelake, California, to North Las Vegas in just under nine hours, driving two different cars, stolen for their speed and handling, along US-95 South. He'd grabbed water from a vending machine at a motel just before exchanging the first stolen car for the second, which got him here just after four in the afternoon.

Neither he nor Elaina spoke until the officer had left the room and closed the door behind him. Then their eyes met, each conjuring images of the other from the last time they'd seen each other eighteen years before, after she'd pressed her son into Raiff's arms.

"Take him!"

"But—"

"No buts! We've been betrayed! They knew we were coming!"

"You're the one who should go."

"You're the warrior, Raiff, far better suited to protect him once you get there. And he'll need protection—both of us know that. It's only a matter of time."

That time had come Friday night. The last time they'd been to-gether, Elaina had pushed Alex into his arms. Now Raiff had to fight the urge to take her in his. He could feel his heart thudding against his chest, the woman he never expected to see again seated directly across from him.

The woman he'd first looked up to and then fallen in love with, a love that had persisted for the eighteen years of Alex's life.

Raiff laced his fingers together so she wouldn't see his hands trembling. Elaina's eyes hadn't left him once since she'd been es-corted into the room, her shock and relief making her look vulner-able in a way he couldn't recall from all those years before. But there was something else he glimpsed in her eyes, something at once both unsettling and disturbing. They'd always been so sure, so strong. Now they looked distant, uncertain, and something else.

Frail.

That was the word he'd been looking for upon her being escorted into the room. Elaina looked more like someone else pretending to be her. The passage of time might have accounted for her being so lean, as well as for her cheekbones having grown more pronounced. But all that, combined with the dullness of her eyes, increased the trepidation Raiff had first felt when he'd uncovered the footage of her robbing a pharmacy at gunpoint.

Her voice, weaker than he remembered and crackling dryly, put a halt to his thinking. "How did you find me?"

"Long story."

"Alex," she said. "Tell me about Alex. That he's okay, please," Elaina implored, as if Raiff could change the boy's fate simply by his will.

And in that moment, he fully grasped that her love for Alex had endured for eighteen years, just as Raiff's love for her had. She was still the same woman. The same spark persisted within her, the will to save those who needed saving—to fight their oppressors.

"We were together last night."

"What happened?"

"Long story."

"That's twice you've said that. It's not like I'm going anywhere."

"We found the book," Raiff said.

Elaina leaned forward, as if to make sure no one was watching. "He was able to read it, right? The only one who can."

"You should have told me."

"There was no time. And how did he find the book?"

"He didn't. I did. He was on his way to get it at the time. With Sam," Raiff added.

"Who's Sam?"

"Long—"

"Story," Elaina completed for him. "I get that."

"Well, it is. Eighteen years crammed into the past five days."

"Can we trust him, this Sam?"

"Sam's a girl."

Elaina eyes narrowed, unsure how to take that. "Like you said, long—"

"Story," Raiff completed this time.

"You still haven't said how you found me."

"I traced your movements. Not a hard trail to follow."

"The pharmacy?"

Raiff held his gaze on her. "And the North Las Vegas Airport, where you landed that stolen jet."

"I'll explain everything, once you get me out of here."

"Easier said than done. And you need to tell me something. You need to answer a question."

"Anything. I owe you that much. Anything."

Raiff swallowed hard, his mouth so dry he had trouble managing to get the air down. "Who am I?"

75

OPENING SALVO

"WE NEED TO PIN the locations of these facilities down," Thomas Donati told Orson Wilder.

Wilder was working on a wall-sized, three-dimensional map of the world that required him to wear a pair of thick goggles similar to the kind used to simulate virtual reality. This map was comparable to a much smaller, Google Map variety on a home computer the operator could manipulate with a mouse. The VR wall map was similarly interactive, allowing Wilder to use his fingers to enlarge and focus on any part of the planet, down almost to the square foot if he homed in close enough. The computer-assembled depictions worked off direct feeds from NASA's own bank of satellites in constant orbit over the Earth. They were capable of detecting any subsurface changes or disruptions almost instantaneously, keying off a combination of weather patterns and seismic activity used to provide advance warnings of sub-sea earthquakes and potential tsunamis.

"We could have used this eighteen years ago," Wilder said as data generated by computers of the areas on which he was homing in seemed to float in the air over his head.

Donati stared at his phone, as if willing it to ring. "I need my intern."

"The high school student?"

"I don't think of her that way."

Strange to find himself longing for the assistance of Samantha Dixon, but after Sunday night, what they'd both seen and experienced, who better to rely on? Even before the world had turned upside down, it had been Dixon who'd isolated the pattern of

geothermal disturbances characterized by sharp spikes in electromagnetic radiation, just as he had eighteen years before.

When Raiff had brought Alex across the spacebridge, using Laboratory Z as a doorway from their world.

Amazing, Donati thought, *truly amazing.*

An understatement, obviously, even coming from someone who
had spent his career waiting, preparing, and studying for what had
transpired on Sunday. But those events had proven to be nothing
like what either he, or any planetary scientist or astrobiologist,
could ever have foreseen or anticipated.

"What happens once we've pinned down all these underground
bases?" Wilder asked him.

"I suspect Janus will move to destroy them."

"You suspect?"

"They don't share their intentions or their plans with me."

Wilder lifted the goggles to his forehead and turned to face Donati. "I never took you for a company man, Thomas."

"You mean, like you were?"

"It's what kept me from listening to your warnings eighteen years
ago."

Donati noticed the impressions the goggles had left around Wilder's eyes were already fading. "I suppose it's also what kept me from
discovering the electromagnetic patterns my young intern did last
week. I wish I was still just a scientist."

"There's no such thing," Wilder told him. "We used to be charged
with preparing for the future. Now we're charged with building it,
forming it, making it. That's why I got out. I realize that now. After
Laboratory Z, it was too much of a responsibility, too much of a burden, to bear."

"We both ran away, Orson, but in different directions. And, I
suppose, we were both hiding."

"You weren't answering questions for a dollar."

"No, I buried myself in the theoretical, where I was safe, where
the world couldn't hurt me again. Just like you, only different," Donati
added.

"So what would you call the task before us now, Thomas? Redemption?"

"Duty."

"And that duty is to mark twenty-seven targets for your friends in Janus."

"Apparently it's not twenty-seven, it's twenty-eight," Donati added, after performing his own count.

"That's odd," Wilder said, stepping back from the wall-mounted virtual world before him. "I'm certain I only mapped out twenty-seven, the most recent dug out of the bedrock beneath the abandoned train station in Berlin."

Donati moved to another section of the three-dimensional depiction before him. "I don't recall this one generating electromagnetic waves around Mexico."

Wilder sidestepped toward it. "That's because it wasn't there before. It wasn't there until now. As if it just came online."

"Impossible, of course."

"Not if they were hiding it, Thomas."

Wilder fit his goggles back in place and pinched his fingers together over the general area of the flashing light, somewhere in the vicinity of Guatemala. Instantly, readouts began flying, projected onto the air just above his head.

"My Lord," Wilder muttered, "look at the levels of subsurface electromagnetic discharge. How do we quantify this in comparison to the others? What do we call it?"

Donati watched Guatemala's Petén jungle, seventy-five miles south of Mexico at the base of the Yucatan Peninsula, take shape before him.

"Headquarters," he told Wilder.

76

KEYS

"I WANT TO HEAR about the three keys that are covered in the book first," Sam said, instead of telling Alex what she'd realized about the fourth, which was covered only cryptically in the book.

She caught him looking at her again, the same way he would've caught her countless times in the school cafeteria, library, or during one of their tutoring sessions if he'd bothered to notice.

"Whatever you can tell me about what you've figured out so far," Sam finished.

Alex turned the book so she could follow along with him, even though the words looked like gibberish to her. "Near as I can tell, each of these three keys has a story associated with it, going back a whole lot of years. Each of them was brought here by a refugee from my world."

"But it doesn't say how they're supposed to save this world?"

"Not yet, no."

"And it doesn't say how to find the keys."

"Let's take a look at the section about the first key."

Alex spun the book around so it was facing Sam. The color pictures were elegantly drawn, to the point where she had to remind herself that this book had been fashioned entirely by hand, a true one-of-a-kind. The pictures connected with the first key centered on a figure who could only be an Egyptian pharaoh, charting his reign and achievements. More a history lesson, it seemed, than clues to the location of some mystical, ancient key.

But the clues had to be there.

"Wait," Sam said, studying the pictures closer, "it's a woman!"

"I thought it was just a dude with long hair."

"Men of ancient Egypt didn't wear their hair long."

"Whatever you say. But they had female pharaohs? That's a surprise."

Sam traced the pictures with her finger. "I think it's Hatshepsut, the first female ruler of Egypt with the full powers of a pharaoh. She was the only child of Thutmose the First and enjoyed one of the longest and most successful reigns of any pharaoh, male or female. These pictures are a visual depiction of her life, rule, and accomplishments."

"What did she do that was so important exactly?" Alex wondered.

"Opened trade routes and was known as a great builder. She's reputed to have built a series of obelisks that should have been an impossible task for the time, along with other projects that rivaled the construction of the Pyramids themselves."

"Hold on," Alex said. "How could this Hatshepsut be an alien, and have one of these keys, if her father was a king himself?"

Sam's eyes widened, gazing at him knowingly. "What else?"

"What else what?"

"What else strikes you as important about her?"

"Well," Alex started, thinking, "you said she was an only child."

"Remind you of anyone else?"

"Holy shit."

"I think maybe Hatshepsut came here the same way you did. Then she was raised by a couple that saw her as a gift from the gods, when the king was unable to sire a child to be his heir."

Sam watched Alex's features pale. "Just like my parents, minus the heir stuff . . ." He swallowed hard, revisited by the pain that had been racking him since his parents had been murdered Saturday night.

"Alex . . ."

"I'm fine. Let's stay on point—that's what you always say, isn't it?" He cleared his throat. "So the key holders were all brought here as infants, just like me."

"Maybe being a king is in your future," she said, hoping to snap Alex from the funk into which he seemed to be slipping.

"Right now, I'd settle for any future."

"It's what I was going to tell you, Alex, but didn't know how. The book says four keys are required to complete the square and save the world."

"Right," he nodded, "but there's nothing about the fourth key, only the first three. It's like pages are missing."

"I don't think any pages are missing," Sam said, her eyes boring into Alex's, moistened now with the rekindled thoughts of his parents. She tried to give him a gentle and encouraging smile. "I think they were never included, because they tell a story that wasn't written yet when the book was brought here to be hidden for safekeeping."

Sam stopped there to let her point sink in.

"Wait! You think I'm . . ."

"Yes, the fourth key."

"Except I don't have it."

Sam reached out across the table between them and took his hand. "Yes, Alex, you do."

77

LOCKS

SAM TAPPED HER TEMPLE with a finger on her free hand. "It's up here. Maybe Hatshepsut's was concealed the same way. Whatever the case, like you, it's a safe bet she was no more aware of her true identity than you were before Saturday."

"So these keys, all four of them, are some kind of *computer chips*. Like the one in my head—that's what you're saying."

"Yes, that's what I'm saying. And remember what the book did say about the fourth key?"

"That 'the bearer of the fourth key alone shall have the knowledge to complete the square,'" Alex recited from memory. "But I don't have that knowledge."

"I think you do; you just haven't figured it out yet."

"The chip in my head, or should I say the key in my head, will probably kill me before I get the chance."

Sam grabbed his other hand in hers and squeezed both as tight as she could. "You're not going to die."

"You heard what Dr. Donati said."

"He doesn't know you. He doesn't know about the book, about Hatshepsut and the other two infants who were brought to Earth just like the two of you."

"And all of them grew up with a chip like mine inside their heads."

"Or hidden somewhere else inside them."

"And, according to the book, we need to recover all four, which means getting the one that's in my head out, to defeat the aliens whose world I came from."

Sam let go of his hands and grasped his arms just above the

elbows, feeling his muscles grow taut under her grip. "You're not an alien."

"Where have you been the last five days?"

"I don't care. You're not like that. You're not one of them. The Chins raised you to be who you are. You came here with the same heart as everyone else, only bigger. That's what matters."

"Wow, Sam."

She pulled her hands from his arms to wipe the tears that had welled up in her eyes.

"Now, that was a mouthful," Alex continued.

Sam wiped again. "You buy any of it?"

"Let's start with the facts. These keys are locked up either inside the heads, or somewhere else, in the remains of Hatshepsut and the other two people the book depicts. That's what you're saying."

"It's what the book says, or at least suggests."

"And I'm the one who's supposed to join the keys, the chips, together, because I'm the one who was supposed to find the book that nobody else can read."

Sam nodded. "Starting in Egypt."

"Hatshepsut?"

"Her sarcophagus is on display at the Egyptian Museum in Cairo."

Alex settled back in his seat and sighed deeply. "Well, at least we know where we're going now."

78

DE RAIS

RAIFF'S MIND FLASHED BACK to last night at Medicine Lake, interrogating the man who called himself Gilles de Rais above the sound of the pounding rainstorm.

"I'm not the man you think I am," Raiff had told him.

"Yes, you are; you just don't know it."

"Make sense!"

"Who you think you are doesn't matter, because you're still that man, the same man."

He could feel Elaina watching him, her eyes having recaptured their strength, their majesty. And in that moment Raiff realized she was at her strongest when she was fighting for others, thinking of others. Her eyes always on the bigger picture, the greater good, that explained why she had given up her own son for a higher cause.

Because that cause was worth fighting for.

"I crossed paths with someone from our world, commanding the aberrations who came across the same spacebridge you did," Raiff said to her, still trying to fit the pieces together for himself. "He called me 'monk,' claimed he knew me from Austria."

"Who was this man?"

"Gilles de Rais."

Elaina just looked at him, her expression flat.

"You're not surprised," Raiff resumed.

"He was sent here a long time ago."

"To recover the book, the book only Alex can read. The book you must've been after too. Am I missing anything?"

"Yes and no, Raiff."

"Which?"

"Both, like I said. Because retrieving the book was only part of de Rais's mission. What do you know about him?"

"He was a monster. Found guilty for murdering hundreds of children. They must have executed another man in his place."

Elaina tried to settle herself with a deep breath, but failed to finish it. "Alex wasn't the first child to come here, holding the secret to our survival. The Overlords knew about the plan. They sent de Rais to stop it. Except they didn't know exactly who to target, any more than they knew about Alex. All they had initially was a location: the province of Brittany in northwestern France, specifically Côtes-d'Armor."

"You're saying de Rais killed all of these children just to get the single one the Overlords had targeted?"

Raiff watched tears well up in Elaina's eyes. "The rest died horribly for nothing."

Raiff visibly shuddered at Elaina's mention of that. "I should have killed him last night when I had the chance."

"It wouldn't have mattered. The only way to save Alex is to finish what we started eighteen years ago, once and for all."

"And that's possible?" Raiff said, so softly he wondered if she could hear him. "You still believe that?" Sounding like a boy again.

Elaina nodded. "It's why I'm here, Raiff. To finish this, to win."

79

PURSUIT

HIS CONVERSATION WITH THE Overlord from his world completed, de Rais entered his laboratory, glad to close the door behind himself and shut out the powerful, corrosive smells of molten steel and hot rubber, the residue of constructing a cyborg army.

He had no particular use for the cyborgs, having come to this world long before construction of such facilities had begun. He favored the more traditional means and methods long practiced. Now, though, his time, and the time of this entire world, was coming to an end. De Rais didn't fear death; in fact he welcomed it, but not before he completed his final mission of retrieving and delivering both the boy and the book.

The laboratory also held reserves of the various ingredients that comprised the elixirs which had led to him being branded a witch and a sorcerer, including the one that had given birth to the legend of the golem. But that wasn't the one he'd come here to retrieve. No. This particular potion was something else entirely, the most dangerous and powerful compound he had ever worked with, beyond even the golem, which left him capable of fashioning an entire army if necessary.

The boy had to be stopped.

The book had to be recovered.

And the army he could now create held the surest means for de Rais to accomplish both.

The boy was the only thing standing in the way of the destruction of this world. De Rais already knew the boy's second destination and he would be waiting for him there.

He was going home, at least as close to one as he had in this world.

80

NIGHTMARE AT
THIRTY THOUSAND FEET

ALEX TRIED NOT TO sleep, as if he knew what awaited him, but exhaustion won out, and he drifted off just after Sam did, awaking almost immediately.

But he wasn't on the plane anymore.

Not even close.

At first, he thought he was back on the football field, standing at midfield of an empty stadium. Then Alex realized he wasn't back at St. Ignatius at all but standing amid a formless black void. There was no turf beneath his feet, just a black emptiness with no bottom, and yet when he moved it felt as if it were solid ground.

"This isn't a dream, Alex," said a now familiar voice that sounded scratched out of the air.

Alex turned and found himself facing the elongated shape of the Ash Man, the distance between them seeming to vary, the shape going in and out of sharp focus.

"It's time to come home, to where you belong, to your own world."

"This is my world!"

"What do you see when you look at me?"

"I . . . don't know."

"Yes, boy, you do. You just can't admit it. Search your heart and don't be frightened by what you find. I'm offering you the future. The only alternative is to die here, squander everything for a world that was never yours. Join me and return to where you belong."

Alex felt as if he were floating now, fighting to remind himself this wasn't real, that he was still aboard Langston Marsh's jet heading for Egypt in search of the first key the book had described.

"There is no future for you here because there is no future for this world," the Ash Man continued. *"These people you care about so much are about to be destroyed by an unstoppable force beyond their comprehension."*

"Not if I can help it."

With that, the shadow extended a hand that pulsed with ever-changing degrees of composition, alternating between sharp and vague. *"Come with me, or die with them."*

"I'm going to stop you."

But when he tried to clench his hands into fists, he couldn't make his fingers move, the physical laws skewed as they were in a dream.

Wake me up, Sam! he willed. *Wake me up!*

"You will see," the Ash Man continued, as if Alex had not just said anything at all, *"the folly of your mother's pursuits, how wrong she was to oppose me and hide the truth from you."*

"You killed my mother."

The Ash Man's eyes, at least what passed for them, bore into him. *"No, Alex, I didn't."*

"An Chin, Li Chin!" Alex tried to shout. "I want you to hear their names so you understand I'll never forget what you did, and that someday I'll make you pay."

Wake me up, Sam! Wake me up!

He didn't want to hear any more, didn't want to be here.

Please, Sam, please!

"Don't listen to her, Alex," the Ash Man said, his voice sounding prerecorded now.

"Who?"

An invisible hand squeezed his shoulder.

"She'll lead you down a path to your ruin."

Alex could feel the same invisible hand shaking his shoulder now.

"I don't believe you."

"You will."

"I won't! I'll find the other three keys and win this war before it starts."

Then the Ash Man's other hand was reaching out for him. One hand jostled Alex's shoulder while the other split his flesh and stretched through his skull toward the chip inside, the fourth key. He heard himself scream.

Then his eyes snapped open and he found himself staring into Sam's, her hand on his shoulder instead of the Ash Man's.

"That must've been some nightmare," she said.

And Alex lost herself in her arms, as the jet began its descent into Cairo.

81

OLD HOME WEEK

"YOU STILL HAVEN'T ANSWERED my question," Raiff said to Elaina, on the other side of the steel table in the cramped interrogation room. "De Rais told me I didn't know who I really was. What did he mean?"

"Raiff—"

"Tell me!"

She looked at him with a stern gaze. "You're not eighteen anymore."

"No, I'm not. I've been here for half my life protecting your son, because I . . ."

"What?" Elaina prodded, when Raiff's voice tailed off.

"Never mind. Answer me: How could de Rais have recognized me? Why did he think I was somebody else?"

"We need to get out of here," Elaina told him, looking toward the door, toward anything but him. "We need to find Alex."

"Who am I, Elaina?"

She barely met his gaze. "Our world is dying, Raiff."

"It's been dying for a long time."

"Something had to be done. The Overlords needed workers for their factories, workers to keep our planet functioning."

"What does that have to do with me, with who I really am?"

Raiff watched Elaina's lips quiver. "You're not listening to me."

"I heard you say our world was dying."

"I meant *literally*. You heard the stories of what they did to forestall resistance, rebellion."

Raiff nodded once. "Forced sterilization."

"And in dealing with one problem, they created another, even greater one by robbing themselves of the workforce they desperately needed to survive themselves. There was only one alternative, until they were ready to enslave this planet,"

"Cloning," Raiff realized, feeling cold.

"A race entirely dominated by machines," she picked up, "needed flesh and blood to sustain itself. They all thought they were going to live forever, believed they had discovered the secret to immortality. Then they started dying, had no choice but to rely more and more on the machines they'd created to do their bidding. But that wasn't enough. All the worlds they seeded and harvested weren't enough."

"Something went wrong." Raiff heard his own voice as if he were detached from his body, someone else speaking the words.

"The Resistance grew in number as theirs declined. They became the desperate ones, their only weapon being destruction, annihilation. It's all they had left because we turned the tide, sapped their resources . . . and raided their farms."

"Farms?"

"Where their workers were raised."

"You mean grown, like plants."

"We turned them into soldiers, an army."

"You mean, turned *me*. That's why de Rais thought I was that monk he encountered centuries ago. Because I am, close enough anyway."

Raiff felt Elaina grasp his hands from across the table, trying to still the trembling that had increased. "No! We raised you, not them. Made you think you'd been orphaned in a battle that had taken your parents."

"Because I never had parents," Raiff said, Elaina's hands squeezing his tighter.

"You had me."

"No. *Alex* had you, not me."

"And I lost him, because I had no choice, just like I lost you. Never thought I'd ever see either of you again."

"Your hands are cold," Raiff said, squeezing back.

Elaina pulled them away.

"What's wrong? Why did you need those drugs from that pharmacy you robbed?"

"It doesn't matter," she said, looking away from him again.

"It does."

"Not compared to so much more." Her eyes teared up and she swabbed them with a sleeve, only to start tearing up again. "Our world's not the only thing that's dying, Raiff."

He wanted to say something, so many words and feelings cluttering his head in that moment, but nothing emerged.

"It doesn't matter," he heard Elaina continue. "Only Alex matters, Alex and nothing else. That's why I came, to—"

A knock fell on the room's door an instant ahead of its opening,

"Your client's transport is here," a cop said to Raiff, sticking his head in.

"Transport?" Raiff asked him.

"Homeland Security just arrived." The cop focused his next words toward Elaina. "You must be pretty important. They sent four guys outfitted like Rambo. And, strangest thing, they look like twins."

82

EVENING THE ODDS

RAIFF WAS WAITING WHEN they came through the door, seizing upon the advantage that they weren't expecting him. A patrolman had confiscated his stick prior to admitting him inside the highway patrol barracks, leaving him weaponless except for the chair in his grasp, angled so he could nail the first two to enter with a single blow.

Thud!

It was like hitting a wall, no give at all. A shock wave spread numbness through his body. The first drone thing, as Alex had called them, turned his way, then the second. The first had a divot pressed into its forehead and the second had an even bigger depression in its cheek, like a dent. Their eyes recorded his presence with a single, emotionless blink, Raiff detecting that their DHS tactical uniforms fit all wrong, one too tight and one too loose, indication that they had ambushed the real Homeland Security team and replaced it.

Elaina had bounded over the table by then, leaping atop the nearest one of the drone things.

"Hey!" cried the highway patrol escort who'd followed the things wearing Homeland Security uniforms into the room. "Hey!"

He went for his gun, when one of the drone things lashed a hand backward, sending him reeling against the wall. His gun went flying.

Raiff scrambled for it as Elaina rode the other drone thing's shoulders, holding firm with her fingers clawing over its scalp for its eyes. She began to rake at them mercilessly. They went wheeling about the room as the thing sought to shed her, banging into one wall, then another, before pitching backward over the table that left the drone thing pinning Elaina against it. Raiff watched her still raking at the thing's eyes, fingers digging deep.

Raiff dove and slid across the floor, recovering the cop's pistol in a single motion and opening fire on the other drone. It was a Glock 19 and he emptied as many bullets as he could into the creature made to look like a man.

Each impact drew a hollow thumping sound, causing the drone's head to whiplash to the side and back, showing more dents and divots where the bullets struck home. But the thing had its own gun drawn by then, angling it to fire on Raiff, when a trio of cops rushed the room with their Glocks out.

The drone swung stiffly in their direction, already firing.

Raiff watched the cops knocked off their feet by the bullets, training his own fire on the drone thing's wrist as he reclaimed his feet. The impact of the first two bullets locked its wrist solid, and his final two severed the connective wiring that joined its hand to its wrist. That hand flopped downward, bullets chewing into the floor as it fired repeatedly.

Click.

The slide on Raiff's pistol locked open and he half dove, half slid across the floor toward a Glock still grasped in the hand of another of the downed highway patrolmen. Catching a glimpse of thick, viscous fluid soaking past Elaina's thumbs as . . .

Pop!

One marble-like eyeball of the drone thing she was battling came free and clattered across the floor, joined quickly by . . .

Pop!

The other. The thing finally shed her and flailed about blindly, arms twirling in a bizarre pirouette, its equilibrium compromised, slamming into one wall, then ricocheting off it into another.

The drone thing with its hand flopping from its wrist took the pistol in its other hand, sighting it again on Raiff, ready to shoot, when Elaina slammed the table against its torso and jammed its gun hand against the wall.

That bought Raiff the seconds he needed to collect another pistol shed by one of the downed cops. He leaped atop the table, firing straight into the drone thing's mouth until the back of its head exploded in a sizzling burst of plastic, fake hair, wire, and diodes.

The blinded drone thing clipped Elaina with one of its flailing hands, staggering her, then groped wildly, managing to latch onto her hair and reel her in. Raiff took the chair in which he'd been seated in his grasp again and brought it down in line with the thing's shoulder joint. He felt something crunch on impact and the shoulder came free where the ball met the socket. Two more strikes and the arm broke off altogether, hand still clinging to Elaina's hair, leaving her twirling about as she fought to pull it off.

The arm came free and thudded to the floor, just as Raiff grabbed Elaina and yanked her toward the door.

"Stay behind me!" he yelled, scooping up a final Glock halfway there.

He burst into the squad room with Elaina tucked protectively behind him, the air rich with the coppery scent of blood, loosed papers fluttering through the air. Raiff's eyes locked on the second pair of drone things, which had just killed the rest of the highway patrolmen, their faces pockmarked with the futile return fire the officers had managed to get off.

Raiff spotted his stick in a collection box atop the reception counter. He pushed Elaina down behind a filing cabinet that had toppled over and then launched himself into a headlong slide across the shiny tile. That path took him beneath the drone things in a single fluid motion that left him close enough to snatch his stick from the box.

With the highway patrolmen vanquished, the last two drone things turned their fire on the filing cabinet behind which Elaina was pinned. One of them broke off that line of fire and turned toward Raiff in the moment he snapped the stick into its whiplike form and slashed it outward.

The first impact cut through the first drone thing's neck, spewing sparking wires. His next snap wrapped the whip around the second drone thing's legs. He then proceeded to yank the legs out from beneath it.

Turning his attention back to the thing with wires dangling from its neck, he snapped the edge of the whip so it closed around the thing's throat, tightened his hold, and pulled. The thing's head came free of its neck in a shower of sparks and fizzling flames. Its body toppled over, and its skull slammed against the wall.

The remaining drone thing he'd toppled was steadying a pistol in his direction when Elaina brought a filing cabinet drawer down atop its head. Loose pages spewed into the air, like giant flakes of snow fluttering down toward the drone's head, which was now flattened out on the top.

The drone deflected Elaina's next strike and rammed her with the drawer instead, reclaiming its feet, as Raiff dropped to the ground and rolled, his whip in motion. Low first toward the one on the right, slicing off both its legs at the ankles. Then he snapped the whip with a violent jerk of his wrist, sending it on an upward trajectory from floor level directly between the second android's legs.

Wires, electrodes, and capacitors popped, frizzled, and flamed as the whip made a neat slice upward all the way through the android's metallic skull. The motion left both halves of it sputtering on either foot. Somehow the halves managed to retain their balance while the matching eyes on the perfectly symmetrical husks popped out in a final flame burst.

Raiff reeled his whip back in, starting to push himself to his feet when a boot clamped down on his hand, the disembodied foot of the android he'd upended. The rest of the thing hopped along on ankles spewing smoke and wire, the burnt smell noxious enough to turn Raiff's stomach.

He felt the severed boot trying to crush his hand, the pain starting to shoot up his arm, when he swept it off into the air by whipsawing his own foot across his body. Launched airborne, the booted, disembodied foot struck the android it had belonged to in the face, toppling the thing over as it continued hopping after Elaina.

Raiff got one leg up in front of him, balanced on his other knee, and lashed his whip out from there. The blow obliterated the thing's face, left it a mass of severed, spaghetti-like wiring with the eyes still attached by clear strands.

Elaina!

He spun to find her lying on the floor, blood leaking from her forehead where the drone thing's blow had struck home.

"Come on," Raiff said, lifting her gently to her feet, "lean against me."

He held his whip in one hand and Elaina with the other as he led her toward the door and the black van parked outside, the logo for the Department of Homeland Security stenciled on its rear quarter panel.

TEN

THE FIRST KEY

One in two hundred stars has habitable Earth-like planets
surrounding it—in the galaxy, half a billion stars have Earth-
like planets going around them.
So when we look at the night sky, it makes sense that someone is looking back at us.

MICHIO KAKU

83

LIVING HISTORY

"I ALWAYS WANTED TO come here," Alex heard Sam say, as she started to sip her tea, then stopped. "Egypt. The Pyramids, the Sphinx . . . you know."

"Only because we covered it in our tutoring sessions," he told her. "World History, right?"

"Seems less important now," Sam reflected, "like, smaller."

"The world or history?"

"I think maybe both."

They sat at an outdoor café just down the street from the Museum of Egyptian Antiquities, known more commonly as the Egyptian Museum. Located in a sprawling two-story building in the heart of Tahir Square, the museum served as a repository for the most important artifacts of Egyptian history, especially those lifted from the tombs of the pharaohs. Those finds had been relocated here, along with the mummified remains of several of those pharaohs themselves, including Hatshepsut.

The first key.

"I wonder what else you may have in common with Hatshepsut," Sam said, managing a smile.

"Well, I don't think we have to worry about me becoming a pharaoh."

"You know what I mean."

"The only king I've ever been is homecoming."

"You don't count being captain of the football team, a superstar athlete? Like maybe the ones from your world who've taken refuge in ours are all leaders, bound for great things?"

"I think you look like her."

"Who?"

"Hatshepsut. Don't you remember her picture?"

"I don't look anything like her!"

"Come on, picture her wearing glasses."

"I can't."

"Okay," Alex said, taking off Sam's glasses, which had somehow managed to endure everything the last few days had thrown at them. "Yup, just like I thought. You could be twins."

His hand grazed her cheek and he hadn't meant it to linger there, but it did, cupping Sam's cheek. Then he felt Sam press a hand atop it, pinning it in place, the warmth of her grasp relieving his chill and chasing off the throb in his head, at least for the moment.

"We should get over to the museum," Sam said, finishing her tea and checking her phone for the time. "Stick to the plan."

"Four keys to save the world, Sam—that's the plan," Alex said, standing up slowly so the pain in his head wouldn't feel like a giant bell were clanging around inside his skull. "But what's going to save me?"

84

TRUTH BE TOLD

"YOU STILL HAVEN'T TOLD me where we're going," Elaina said to Raiff after they'd screeched away from the Nevada Highway Patrol barracks.

"To change vehicles. Both of us will be all over the security footage, this vehicle too. It's only a matter of time before our pictures are circulated through every security apparatus in the country, maybe the world."

"You must have a plan."

"Right now, head to Fannette Island in Lake Tahoe," Raiff confirmed for Elaina, from behind the wheel of the black van with the Department of Homeland Security logo stenciled across the side, "where Langston Marsh is holed up."

Elaina leaned forward, testing the bonds of her shoulder harness. "You're serious," she said, after studying Raiff briefly, incredulous over his speaking of Langston Marsh the way one might an ally instead of a mortal enemy.

"He had a change of heart, I'd say around the same time you were stealing cars and knocking off drugstores." Raiff glanced over to meet her gaze, ready to explain further when something else claimed his mind. "How bad is it?"

"How bad is what?"

They went over a bump that left her grimacing from a fresh wave of pain, gritting her teeth to avoid uttering even a sigh of pain.

Raiff tapped the steering wheel with one hand while holding it fast to the road with the other. "You played me for a fool once before. Please don't do it again."

"I don't know what you—"

"Yes, you do. Eighteen years ago, when you handed your son to me and sent me here in your place. Only you never had any intention from the beginning of going at all. It was a ruse, a plot. I was no different than those androids we killed back at the highway patrol barracks, unless you count the fact I was born, but they were made."

"An important distinction, don't you think?"

"Given that I was spawned in a test tube, not really."

Raiff stopped tapping the steering wheel with his free hand and clenched it.

"Birth doesn't matter," Elaina said quietly. "Character does." Before he could reply to that, Elaina continued, "Tell me more about this Sam, Samantha, or whatever she calls herself."

"A mother's curiosity?"

"More like suspicions. It's been a long time since I trusted anyone."

"You trusted me," Raiff reminded her. "With your son's life. I guess I should feel honored, given that you could have sent anyone. So I'm going to ask you again: Why me?"

Elaina started to say something, then stopped just as quickly, sighing deeply as she focused outside the van's windshield. "You'd only been with us for a short time."

"Exactly my point."

"But you're missing mine, Raiff. You think your being recruited into our circle was an accident? I'd been watching you, studying you, for some time. That group of lost boys you were leading."

Which drew a smile from Raiff. "Is that what you called us?"

"Isn't that what you were?"

"Minus Peter Pan, I suppose we were."

"Peter Pan?" Elaina raised.

"I forgot that you're not up on the culture of this world."

"I know what I need to."

"I knew practically nothing when I came over. Was that another reason why you chose me?"

"Your age, as much as anything. I needed someone young to be my son's protector, given how long the assignment might last. And you weren't just a leader, you were a loner, and that was something else I knew would be important."

"Because I'd be alone, right?"

Elaina nodded. "I couldn't make it an assignment and it wasn't just a matter of trust. I was never sure what the Overlords knew and when they knew it. I couldn't risk planning the mission out in advance, where they could've caught wind of my true intentions. It had to appear random. It had to appear as if I always intended to go myself until the very last moment."

Raiff's eyes cheated toward her. "What is it you're not telling me?"

"What you don't need to know."

"About Alex, right? Something beyond the chip he's carrying in his head that makes him special."

Raiff swayed into the adjoining travel lane, chased back with a jolt by the blare of a horn.

"Maybe you should just keep your eyes on the road," Elaina said, hands pressed against the dashboard.

"You owe me the truth this time. I'm not a boy anymore."

"Don't go there, Raiff."

"Why? It's where I've been for eighteen years. Alone for eighteen years, watching over Alex and nothing more. You think that was easy?"

"Do you really need to ask me that? *Me?* We've all made sacrifices in order to survive and we needed to make sacrifices so this world could survive too."

"We were talking about Alex."

"We still are."

"And you're holding something back, Elaina."

"Because you don't need to hear it, you wouldn't want to hear it."

"Let me be the judge of that."

"Tell me more about Langston Marsh first."

"He had a change of heart."

"You said that already. But that doesn't fit his profile; why should we trust our lives to a man committed to eradicating our race?"

"What Sunday night beneath Alcatraz didn't change in his mind, yesterday did. He never realized he was hunting down the good guys, whoever got swept up in his technological net. Once he saw the bad guys at work, it wasn't hard to draw the right conclusion, which led to that change of heart."

"And if you're wrong about him?"

"I'm not."

"But if you are?"

"Then this is going to be a one-way trip."

85

TARGETS

THERE WAS A LONG pause on the part of the Janus team members after Thomas Donati and Orson Wilder had reviewed and reiterated all of their findings, conclusions, and, ultimately, their recommendations, which had left all four bar grids on the big computer monitor still.

"You say you've identified twenty-eight of these sites," the lone woman, occupying the top left-hand quadrant of the screen, weighed in finally.

"Twenty-seven positively," Wilder nodded, even though the voices on the other end couldn't see him, "with a twenty-eighth we haven't been able to pin down yet because it seems to be far deeper underground than the others. We've discovered these through a combination of electromagnetic discharge and subsurface activity."

"In English, please, Doctor," one of the voices requested.

"Disturbances and ripples indicative of a massive convergence of energy levels."

"You're talking about this . . . what did you call it?" the same voice asked Donati.

"Creature, although I might have said *monster* because that's truly what it is. An utter aberration of nature—in this case, twenty-seven aberrations."

"Twenty-seven of these things with the potential to destroy the world," said the woman.

"More than the potential," Donati corrected, "the clear and overwhelming capacity."

"So what do we do?" another voice posed, after a pause. "What's your recommendation?"

"We believe this twenty-eighth site, located just outside of Mexico, functions as a kind of command center. Theoretically, if we can find and disable it, the remaining twenty-seven sites will be neutralized."

"Theoretically," a voice said, a caustic edge to his voice.

"We are operating in unchartered territory here."

"But, *theoretically* speaking, we need something more concrete than that to take to the president."

"Beyond the president," the woman interjected. "This is a global problem and must be treated as such with a global response."

Something in her tone disturbed Donati, something he couldn't quite put his finger on. "We just need a little more time to complete our analysis and pin down that site outside Mexico to recommend a protocol, ma'am."

"Time we may not have, Doctor. Janus was created in case just such an eventuality came to pass. We have our protocols too."

Donati felt chilled. He looked toward Orson Wilder, who was shaking his head, just as disturbed.

"Perhaps, ma'am, if you could be more specific . . ."

"I've already stated that this is a global crisis, a global threat, and must be treated as such. You're a hero, you're both heroes for calling an alert and establishing the parameters of what we're facing. You'll hear from us soon on the course of action the powers we report to have decided upon."

"I really think we should—"

"Just wait for our call, Doctor."

86

THE MUMMY'S TOMB

"HEY," ALEX SAID, SAM feeling him nudge her in the shoulder, "you think we could get extra credit for this? . . . Sorry, that was lame."

"I think we should get extra credit for saving the world," she said, drawing a smile from him.

And we're going to save you too.

Sam formed those words in her mind, but stopped short of uttering them. That was the last thing Alex needed to hear right now, given this quest they'd found themselves on.

They approached the Egyptian Museum an hour before its scheduled closing, enough time to familiarize themselves with the layout and enact their plan for the mummified remains of Hatshepsut without appearing to linger too long. The building reminded Sam of a school. Its rectangular structure was finished with a light stucco design and had painted red bricks. School structures, of course, lacked a reflecting pool laden with fallen palm leaves set directly before the ornate entrance, as well as a small version of the Sphinx serving as greeter just past the sidewalk.

The interior was just as she'd pictured it. Two columned floors featuring a great hall of displays on the first floor and various individual exhibit chambers off both sides. The first thing Sam saw after clearing the security check in the building was a sprawling atrium lined with sarcophagi, small boats, and enormous statues drawn from various periods of Egyptian history.

That same checkpoint left her relieved over the fact that they'd opted to leave the book behind on the jet. While that presented its own series of risks, they paled by comparison with lugging an apparent relic around a foreign city, its appearance certain to draw unwelcome scrutiny if it happened to be noticed. Neither of them had even considered the ramifications of trying to get the book past a security checkpoint.

According to the pamphlet Sam had taken from a pile at the entrance, the ground floor also featured an extensive collection of papyrus and coins used in the ancient world. The numerous pieces of papyrus were generally small fragments, due to their decay over the past two millennia. The coins were not only Egyptian but also Greek, Roman, and Islamic. The many different coins had helped historians research the history of ancient Egyptian trade.

In spite of everything, Sam found herself fascinated by the displays, especially another section featuring artifacts from the New Kingdom, the time period between 1550 and 1069 B.C. Artifacts including statues, tables, and coffins. But it was a pair of so-called special exhibits housed in two rooms near the far end of the atrium that drew the bulk of her attention, as well as the largest crowds.

Because the mummified remains of Hatshepsut were on display, among more items lifted from her tomb, in one of those rooms.

"You look bored," Sam noted to Alex, as they took their place in line to enter that room.

"I'm pretending to be myself from last week. Figured that's the best way to avoid drawing attention."

"I grabbed a pamphlet for you," she said, stopping short of plucking it from her pocket.

"Nah, that would ruin my disguise."

Sam caught Alex's gaze drifting, as the line continued to move slowly. She wondered what he was thinking, feeling. As much as they'd been through these five days, as close as they'd drawn, there was a surreal quality to it all. Life viewed through a window blocked by a sheer curtain, precluding a clear view of what lay beyond.

"What do you say we go meet Egypt's actual first female pharaoh?"

Hatshepsut's ornate sarcophagus was carved with a likeness of her on the lid, with an inlaid, turquoise-shaded jewel grasped in wooden hands directly over her heart.

"It's a scarab amulet," Sam said softly. "Common among Egyptian royalty."

Around the closed coffin, pictures were displayed chronicling the discovery of her mummified remains and what those remains looked like from different angles and in detail, since the sarcophagus itself was contained in a thick glass case and surrounded by rope lines to discourage approach. There were three other sarcophagi on display as well, along with ornate materials lifted from the Valley of the Kings, where the remains had been discovered.

"So she's inside there," Alex said, nodding toward Hatshepsut's sarcophagus. "Which means to get the key we have to . . ."

"What else were you expecting?"

"I don't know. Not that. Having to, geez, unwrap her and remove the chip from her head."

But Sam's eyes had strayed elsewhere and so did her mind. "Maybe we won't have to."

"Remember what the book said?" Sam asked Alex, when they were back in the main exhibit hall.

"That the key 'would always be kept close to her heart,'" he said, recalling the exact quote. "Figure of speech, I thought."

"I think it was a clue, like a riddle. So 'close to her heart' could mean that amulet. Just about the right size, assuming its hollow."

"A riddle," Alex repeated.

"More like a clue."

"Which means we don't have to mess with the mummy itself."

"If I'm right."

A bell chimed, signaling the museum would be closing in ten minutes.

"We need to find a place to hide," Alex told her.

87

FANNETTE ISLAND

"SOMETHING'S WRONG," RAIFF SAID, stiffening behind the wheel of the launch they'd rented. It was now approaching the island Langston Marsh had purchased from the state of Nevada to use as a secure refuge.

Raiff knew Marsh had built a stone fortress on the island, which had once been open to the public, constructed it to both mirror and preserve the rebuilt ruins of a stone building known as the Tea House. The fortress was built up against the rocky shoreline on three sides to form a defensive perimeter. The front of the fortress was two hundred feet from the west-facing shore, accessible only by a single dock Raiff fully expected to be under guard.

Except it wasn't.

"Even at night, there should be patrol boats," Raiff said to Elaina, as he slid the launch toward the single dock. "They should be approaching to ward us away now."

"And since they're not?"

"We keep going until there's a reason not to."

Raiff saw what was left of the bodies just after they tied up amid several sleek patrol boats and climbed the ladder to reach a plank walkway leading onto Fannette Island. The remains were strewn everywhere, nothing recognizable as even vaguely human. It looked as if Marsh's formidable force of security guards had been dropped into a giant blender, Raiff viewing the upshot of what had been poured out.

"Only one thing could have done this," Elaina noted.

Raiff recalled crossing the spacebridge with her baby in his arms, having the sense that something had preceded them to the other side. Elaina had prepared him for even that, providing him the weapon he needed not to destroy so much as alter its form and render it harmless.

"Can you tell how long ago, Raiff?" she asked him now.

"Not long."

Raiff glimpsed a ghostlike figure gliding toward them through the night, its shape silhouetted by the moonlight, the pole-mounted security floods having all blown and shattered.

"It's Langston Marsh," he said to her.

Raiff sprinted toward Marsh.

"Marsh!" he cried out, when Marsh still didn't seem to notice him.

Marsh was wearing what looked to be shapeless pajamas beneath a bathrobe, the bottoms worn backward, dragging on the ground, darkened by dirt and moisture. His hair was wildly askew, making him look as if he'd just climbed out of bed. He was viewing the familiar surroundings as if seeing them for the first time. The darkness kept him from noticing the remains of his guards scattered everywhere.

"You," Marsh managed, finally acknowledging Raiff.

Raiff took him by the arm. "We need to go. Keep moving, Marsh."

"I don't want to see him again. Please tell me he isn't here."

"Who?" Raiff asked him, wondering why Marsh's life had been spared.

"He didn't have a name, but it looked like he was made of ash."

Marsh didn't speak again until they were whizzing through the waters of Lake Tahoe, their launch bouncing atop the waves with Raiff getting all the speed from it he could as Fannette Island shrank behind them.

"He looked like a cigarette," Marsh said, his gaze still fixed on the dwindling shape of the island.

Raiff and Elaina exchanged a glance.

"He said he knew my father," Marsh continued, gaze and voice still drifting, there and yet not there at the same time. "He said I was right all along. That aliens like him had shot down my father's plane, but that he would take me to him if I cooperated."

"He was lying," Raiff said, but Marsh didn't acknowledge his words or even his presence.

"I was seven years old again—that's what it felt like," Marsh continued. "Seven years old, scared and lonely. I knew he wasn't really there, but I couldn't wish him away. I closed my eyes but I could still see him. I had to tell him. It was the only way to make him go away, to wake myself up. It was a dream, wasn't it? What else could it have been?"

Raiff looked back at him from behind the controls. "What did you tell him, Marsh?"

Marsh pulled away in terror, for that one brief moment. "Where Alex was going."

88

BRAIN SURGERY

ALEX AND SAM'S INITIAL reconnoiter of the museum's expanse had revealed several options as potential hiding places, but none sure to withstand a security check or maybe even the rounds by guards who remained on duty after closing. The bathrooms were the most obvious choice and were quickly ruled out. Alex had considered the two of them squeezing together into one of the sarcophagi on display, but that would mean likely triggering an alarm when they opened the case.

Upon entering the museum, both Sam and Alex had noticed several areas that had been cordoned off due to water damage. One of these leaks had necessitated a large tarpaulin be placed over a massive, gold-inlaid statue of two standing sarcophagi facing outward, side by side. Sam recognized them from the pamphlet she had grabbed after getting through security.

But how could they create a distraction to provide the opening they needed?

"I think I've got an idea," Sam said.

She'd stuffed a bottled water into the backpack Langston Marsh had left for her on the private jet. She eased that water out at the end of the museum opposite the twin-sarcophagi statue and subtly spilled a portion of it out onto the tile floor. Then, as Alex watched from a safe distance, she pretended to slip and nearly fall right in front of one of the armed soldiers serving as a guard. He came to her aid and Sam aimed her gaze upward as if she'd spotted another leaky section of the roof.

The incident drew the attention of more guards, then in the process of ushering patrons toward the main exit. All of them were left gazing upward toward the apparent leak, while Sam slipped away.

She found Alex already standing beneath the tarpaulin, pressed tight against the statue, and joined him atop the pedestal, which offered scant room for their feet and leaving them pressed tightly to each other.

"Now," he whispered, "all we have to do is wait."

89

THE AMULET

THEY COULD TELL FROM the echo of footsteps that two guards were on duty. It was impossible to know whether the pair were responsible for just this floor or both, although the cadence of their steps made it easy to discern how far away they were.

Alex and Sam made themselves wait for a full hour, shifting beneath the tarpaulin's confines just enough to avoid cramping. Once when trying to stretch her arms, Sam nearly toppled from the pedestal, but she was caught by Alex, who pressed her even more tightly against him. She remained there until she stopped shaking and then for a few moments afterward to let her heart slow down.

Except it didn't, not when she was tucked this close to him.

Finally, Alex sifted the tarp through his fingers and peered out to check the position of the guards, taking Sam's hand and easing her from beneath it with him. One guard was all the way across the floor, at the other end of the hall, facing away from them in the thin light shed by recessed ceiling floods dimmed to post-closing mode. The other, at this point, was nowhere to be seen.

Alex and Sam scrabbled silently together the brief distance to the special exhibit room that contained Hatshepsut's sarcophagus. Inside, only a single emergency-exit light was burning, plenty for them to work their way to the glass case constructed around it.

Their eyes adjusted to the darkness enough for Sam to trace a fingertip along the glass.

"What are you doing?" Alex whispered.

"Feeling for the alarm sensor. Last thing we need is the Egyptian police converging on the museum."

"That's for sure. But what happens when you find it?"

"First things first," Sam said, feeling about the side of the glass where it joined with the display case in which the sarcophagus rested. "Here we go," she added, holding the end of a small, virtually invisible wire that ran from a rear corner of the case before disappearing in the floor.

"That's not good," he said.

"You have any gum?"

"One piece left. You want it?"

"I want you to chew it."

Alex peeled off the wrapper and popped the gum into his mouth. "For how long?"

"Just keep chewing," Sam told him, and went back to feeling about the glass.

"Should I ask?"

"I'm trying to find the seams, where the glass sections fit into place. There," she said softly, her finger finding the narrow groove she'd been feeling for.

It was the section closest to the head of the sarcophagus, with the glass panel perpendicular to the floor. Sam continued working her nail about, until the panel separated from its slot ever so slightly.

"Can you work your fingers in where mine are?"

Alex positioned himself next to her. "My fingers are bigger than yours."

"Start with the nails, then, but not until I tell you. First, let me have your gum."

"Really?"

Sam stuck out her hand, and Alex took the gum from his mouth and placed the wad in her palm. She retraced her path back to the alarm wire and readied the gum in line with it.

"When I give you the word, lift the glass up slowly. Ready?"

"Ready."

Sam got herself into position, knowing she'd only get one shot at this. "Okay," she said, taking a deep breath. "Now."

Alex bent at the knees, worked his nails into position, and began lifting the glass from its perch. The moment it separated from the seam through which the wire was threaded, Sam wedged the gum against the wire to keep it in place. Then she lifted the glass from her side as well, mirroring Alex's efforts.

It was heavier than she'd been expecting, and took all of her strength to budge. Together, she and Alex lifted the glass panel off and laid it down on the floor, the wire remaining held in place by the piece of gum.

Next, Alex trailed Sam to one side of the sarcophagus, which opened like a traditional coffin. Working carefully so as not to disturb the piece of chewed gum holding the alarm wire in place, they lifted the lid in unison to reveal the mummified remains of Egypt's first actual female pharaoh.

Alex started to reach in toward the scarab amulet fitted into place over the chest of Hatshepsut's mummified remains. "You mind taking things from here?"

"Worried you'll drop it?" Sam asked him, positioning herself.

"I don't want to touch that thing, the body."

"You mean Hatshepsut."

"Yeah, the body," he said, backing away.

Sam took his place. "Chicken."

She eased her hand inside the case, canting her body at an awkward angle to get a firm grip of the amulet. For a few moments, her efforts seemed for naught when she couldn't budge it from the tailored slot to which it had been affixed for centuries. But it loosened, and then wobbled, before ultimately coming free in her grasp.

She handed the amulet to Alex, then backed off to catch her breath. He held it up to the meager spill of the emergency light, squinting to better peer into its translucent turquoise sheen.

"There's something inside it, all right. Looks like a marble, small and dark."

"That doesn't sound like the chip you're carrying," Sam said, tapping the side of her head.

"Maybe it's dormant," Alex whispered.

"Dormant," Sam repeated.

"Why are you smiling?"

"You—using that word."

"I only used to be stupid." He tucked the amulet into his pocket. "One key down, just two more to go, not counting . . ."

He let his thought tail off, as they reached the door to plot their flight through the nearest museum exit. Then he froze, holding Sam behind him.

Because all the lights in the exhibit hall beyond were now off.

90

ESCAPE

THE MEAGER SPILL OF the few emergency exit lamps provided the only light on the first floor of the museum, enough to reveal what was left of the armed guards scattered across the floor. Blood, shards of bone, and spewed remnants of the two men plastered the walls as well.

Alex felt something lurking about, a burnt odor filling the air.

Sam fell against him, pressed against his chest, too horrified to look further. Alex eased her away.

"We need to go. It's still here."

"What?"

"Whatever did this?"

"It?"

Whatever it was, this thing was different from the mechanical monsters that had ruled his nightmares and filled a sketchbook he never remembered drawing in. He held fast to Sam's hand, guiding her through the darkness, the air feeling thick and gritty, as if supercharged by some foreign particles spilled from the sky.

"Alex," he heard Sam mutter and turned to see her wobbly on her feet, looking off-balance, as if the world had turned suddenly onto its side and she was struggling not to slip off into some endless black void. "Alex," she repeated, more of a rasp now, and he scooped her up in his arms before she fell.

The world hummed with something that seemed to split the air like a knife, and Alex felt a stirring deep inside him, like a surge of static electricity mixing with his blood. He felt a strength, a power, different from anything he'd felt before. It was like breaking the huddle in a football game, the feverish collision of thoughts and feelings that came with the snap, as bodies flew in all directions and there was only instinct to rely on. Only this was more intense, more concentrated, more powerful. He felt as if he were floating, detached from his own body and gliding through the air instead of feeling his way over the ground.

The supercharged particles of air felt like grains of sand peppering his face and clothes. He could feel himself slogging on, Sam held tight in his arms, struggling to peer through the darkness, toward the nearest exit before them.

It's not real, Alex told himself. It had to be a projection, just like the Ash Man himself.

But this wasn't the Ash Man. It was more like something electrical, giving Alex a series of small shocks that pricked the gooseflesh risen on his arms.

It's not going to kill me. It wants me alive.

Alex wasn't sure what the source of that certainty was. Just a feeling, he supposed, but if this thing had wanted to kill him, his and Sam's remains would be strewn amid that of the guards right now.

He recalled Raiff's explanation of the Ash Man being more granular than simply an astral projection, a strange image with substance. It was as though those granules were what filled the air, making Alex feel like he was trapped in a sandstorm. He could feel individual grains were meshing together behind him, taking a shapeshifting form he glimpsed in the window glass on his left.

Sam felt weightless in his arms, and the world soft and cushiony underfoot, as he surged through the exit door into the warm Cairo night, like he was charging for the end zone. Ready to stiff-arm anyone or anything that got in the way—granular, astral, physical, or otherwise—the first key tucked in the pocket of his too-tight jeans.

ELEVEN

ALLIES

We make war that we may live in peace.

ARISTOTLE

91

NUCLEAR OPTION

"WE'VE DETERMINED OUR RESPONSE," the woman said, reporting back so quickly that it shocked Donati. "Plans are currently being laid for twenty-seven simultaneous thermonuclear strikes on the sites in question."

"You can't be serious," Donati said, after the woman had laid out the plan approved by global leaders.

"Twenty-eight strikes, Doctor, if you are able to pin down that location in Mexico for us."

"Lunatics!" Orson Wilder blared. "You're all lunatics!"

"The matter has been settled. All that remains to be decided are the timing and coordination, as our nuclear subs and missile carriers are moved into position."

"You're playing right into their hands," Wilder snapped.

The woman started to object, but Donati cut her off. "I believe Dr. Wilder's concern lies in your apparent dismissal of our report earlier today."

"That report was the basis for this action. I thought you'd be pleased."

"I am—with your commitment. But I'd respectfully remind you about the portion of our report dealing with the energy creature we encountered eighteen years ago."

"Yes, a monster, you called it."

"Twenty-seven of them this time."

"You're making my point for me, Doctor. The employment of twenty-seven targets was not random."

"And you're missing our point," Wilder broke in, before Donati could respond, "specifically the one about how these creatures are formed of pure energy, reconstituting themselves nanosecond to nanosecond at the subatomic level."

"I recall the point, but don't understand it any better now than I did a few hours ago."

Donati let Orson Wilder keep the floor.

"Then allow me to clarify. These creatures feed on energy and that includes *nuclear* energy. These bombs of yours wouldn't stop the destruction of our world, they'd only hasten it by increasing the power of these creatures a millionfold."

"We've taken that under advisement."

"If you'd taken it under advisement, you wouldn't be proposing feeding these things the electromagnetic equivalent of steroids."

"It's not a proposal, Dr. Wilder, it's now a plan accepted at the highest levels globally. We've been able to corroborate your assertions about these twenty-seven sites, but have not been able to confirm the presence of these energy forms you claim exist."

Donati watched Wilder grow red-faced with rage, backing away from the monitor in a huff.

"See if you can talk some sense into them, Thomas."

Donati cleared his throat. "You're forgetting something, ma'am. You're forgetting that I witnessed firsthand eighteen years ago what one of these creatures can do, the destruction it has the capacity to wreak. What twenty-seven of them could do was impossible to comprehend even for me *without* being supercharged by thermonuclear explosions."

"Can you offer any definitive proof of all this?" the woman asked him, after another pause. "The existence of these creatures?"

Donati thought of the spherical object contained in the vacuum-sealed void. "Given time—"

"There is no time—you made that claim yourself, Doctor. According to you, this alien race is committed to the virtual enslavement of our civilization, if not our outright destruction. Our planet has been a haven for their refugees for too long and all indications are their world is committed to eradicating that problem, one way or another. That's correct, isn't it?"

"Yes, but—"

One of the male voices cut Donati off. "There are no buts in this case, Doctor. Unless you have proof of these energy creatures' existence, we have no choice but to proceed with the plan."

"It's already in motion," the woman added. "I'm not sure we could stop it now even if we wanted to."

"Then you've just killed us!" Wilder yelled at the screen. "You've killed us all!"

"We'll keep you both updated," the woman said.

The screen went dark, leaving Donati and Wilder looking at each other.

"It's our fault," Wilder muttered, as much to himself as Donati. "We should have realized the intellectual limits of those we were speaking to."

"It's our fault because they listened to us, Orson. We ended up making things worse than they were already. Now we need to fix it, fix what we broke."

"And how do you suggest we do that, Thomas?"

"By finding that site outside of Mexico. By shutting this all down there."

"Headquarters," Wilder remembered, nodding.

92

HEADING SOUTH

"DONATI'S THE ONLY ONE we can turn to," Raiff told Elaina, while Langston Marsh gazed blankly out the Lake Tahoe hotel window.

"A NASA scientist?"

"Whose specialty is astrobiology, who's spent his entire career believing aliens are real."

"As in us."

"The girl, Samantha, was his intern," Raiff reminded her. "That makes Donati our best chance to find Alex as well."

"And you trust him?"

Raiff turned toward the barely lucid Langston Marsh, still clothed in his pajamas and bathrobe. "I don't see another alternative."

Elaina started to respond, but seemed to lose her train of thought mid-sentence. Her knees wobbled and she just managed to sink into a chair before her legs gave out altogether.

"You need more pills," Raiff said. "I could—"

"Forget it. I'm way past them working. I just need to hold out until we find Alex."

"You'll be proud, Elaina."

"Thanks to you," she said, watching him head to the bathroom to get her a glass of water. "You're the one who's kept him safe all these years."

"Until Friday night."

"You can't blame yourself for that," Elaina said.

Raiff looked away, then back again. "What exactly was your plan, if Friday night never happened, if that CT scan didn't broadcast Alex's location to the very forces determined to destroy him?"

Elaina almost laughed. By the window, the still-dazed Langston Marsh was pawing at the glass, as if looking for a way to open it, maybe jump out. His actions surprised neither Elaina nor Raiff, given his encounter with the shadow Alex and Sam called the Ash Man, not to mention witnessing the creature formed of pure energy tear his security guards apart.

"He's not always like this, is he?" she wondered.

"Not when he was threatening to kill me, no." Raiff glanced over at Marsh continuing to scratch at the glass, like a cat trying to find a way out. "Let's get back to Alex, Elaina."

"What about him?"

"What I asked you before. He has this chip in his head that's the secret to saving this world, and maybe our own, when it's combined with three others. Have I got that much right?"

Elaina nodded. "You do."

"You never told me, because I wasn't supposed to know. Because you always knew you'd be coming when the time came, when Alex needed you the most. You sent me over here to protect him, and what he's carrying in his head, knowing ultimately you'd have to come here to save him yourself."

Elaina swallowed hard. "You want to know what the plan was? The plan was to wait."

Raiff positioned himself closer to Langston Marsh, a billionaire wearing rumpled grimy pajamas, still scratching at the window, in case Marsh tried to break the glass.

"For what?"

"Until we were ready, until our forces were properly marshaled and prepared. That all went to hell on Friday night when they found Alex. But we got lucky, because of what's coming tomorrow night."

By the window, Marsh had discovered the chain cord operating the blackout shade. Started alternately raising and lowering it, much to his suddenly infantile delight. His efforts turned Elaina's face into a patchwork of grids shifting between light and dark, the effect oddly becoming and appropriate to her.

"And what's coming tomorrow night?"

"A rare occurrence that will create the atmospheric conditions we need to join the four keys together. We knew it was coming up, but we weren't ready yet and needed to push back our plan. Now there's no choice. Now we've got to take our shot because it might be the only one we ever get."

"This occurrence, Elaina, what is it exactly?"

"A blood moon, Raiff, just over twenty-four hours from now."

93

THE FORTY-FIRST VICTIM

"LOOK FAMILIAR TO YOU?" Alex said, spinning the book so Sam could regard the portrait occupying the page he just reached.

Sam moved closer, squinting through her glasses. "Wait, hold on. It looks like the guy Raiff told us about from the Klamath Mountains, outside Marsh's fortress."

"According to the book, his name is Gilles de Rais," Alex said, reading on.

"He was a child killer in fifteenth-century France, who was hanged for his crimes," Sam recalled.

"Or not."

"What does the book say about him?"

"How he believed his victims to be refugees from my world, that he did it because one of them might've had the second key. Turned out he was right about one of them, anyway." Alex pointed to the portion of the book in question, which Sam couldn't read. "His forty-first victim, according to this, a boy whose remains are entombed in a graveyard in Brittany along with most of de Rais's other victims. That's in France."

Sam rolled her eyes. "I'm the one who taught you where it is. Remember?"

Alex read on. "Apparently, the victim's family was well acquainted with de Rais . . ." He paused. "I don't think you want to hear the rest," he said, pulling the book back, even though Sam couldn't decipher its contents. "Including how many children he killed."

"No, I don't."

Alex closed the book over his hand to mark the page. "Find this graveyard and we find the second key."

Sam leaned closer, practically pressed against Alex from the seat next to him, when he went back to studying the book. "The book must have been smuggled here for safekeeping after de Rais was sent after the holder of the second key. You see a name for him?"

"Not yet, but the number forty-one keeps coming up. That's why I'm guessing it was de Rais's forty-first victim. Where's Brittany exactly?"

"So you don't know everything after all," Sam chided. "When this book was created, Brittany was a province in northwestern France that was divided in a bunch of subareas called departments in the wake of the French Revolution. Remember the approximate period that took place?"

"Is this a tutoring session?"

"Guess I can't help myself. Come on, World History again."

"Around 1789."

Sam nodded, clearly impressed. "Brittany was divided up in 1790, March specifically, so that's a solid answer."

Alex opened the book again and flipped to the next page. "But where in Brittany are we supposed to look? Which of these, what did you call them, departments?"

Sam spotted a drawing or a small rectangle embossed over what had once been the province of Brittany that looked innocuous at first glance, but on second looked like something else altogether. "I think that's a gravestone," she said. "That's our destination."

94

RETURN TO AMES

DONATI MET THE CAR carrying Raiff, Elaina, and Langston Marsh at the secured main entrance to Ames and drove with them onto the sprawling grounds toward his offices in the Ames Research Center. The short flight from Lake Tahoe to San Francisco had taken hours to arrange, because Marsh couldn't remember the names or phone numbers of the people he needed to make the arrangements. Raiff had finally coaxed them out of him by playing word games to jar Marsh's memory. He was still wearing the same bathrobe and pajamas he'd been wearing when they'd found him wandering about Fannette Island the night before.

That morning back in Lake Tahoe, Marsh had first refused to leave the hotel room and then locked himself in with a chair braced against the door, after Raiff and Elaina had exited ahead of them. When all attempts to get him to open the door failed, Raiff got security to open the door, finding Marsh again trying to open a sealed window to escape. That had cost them more time they could ill afford to lose. Fighting exhaustion after spending the night awake and on guard, Raiff had managed to sleep on the flight from Tahoe to San Francisco, dreaming he was a boy again with Elaina before the years had so badly worn her down.

"I never thought I'd see you again," Donati told Raiff.

"We're fighting the same war now," Raiff told him. "And you're our only hope to win it."

Donati kept peering into the backseat at Langston Marsh, who was sitting next to the woman Raiff had introduced as Elaina. She bore an uncanny resemblance to Alex Chin, and Donati saw no reason to inquire about that when the reason was obvious.

They could only be mother and son, and now something had brought the mother here on the trail of her son. Again, Donati stopped short of inquiring further. He knew where she must have come from and how she had gotten here.

He noticed Langston Marsh staring vacantly out the window as if there was something beyond the glass only he could see. Donati recognized him from Sunday night, when Marsh's forces had sunk a ferry and followed Donati and the others onto Alcatraz, where those forces were summarily wiped out by alien fighters made of metal instead of flesh. To Donati, Marsh had been the personification of evil, who would have killed all of them, Alex and Sam included. He was now reduced to a driveling, empty shell wearing pajamas with a bathrobe that hung open for want of its matching rope tie.

"Let's go," Donati said, after parking his car. "My former partner's waiting for us upstairs."

Raiff couldn't hide his discomfort at being confined inside such a sprawling, cluttered complex. He watched recognition flash across Orson Wilder's expression when he first glimpsed Langston Marsh, followed by what looked like a combination of shame and guilt. Clearly, Wilder thought he must have had common purpose with this man committed to wiping out the aliens that Wilder believed his efforts had unleashed upon the world. Now, Wilder clearly understood the folly of that pursuit, just as Marsh had even before his encounter with the Ash Man on Fannette Island.

Donati closed the door to the conference room into which he'd shepherded them. "You're saying Marsh was helping Sam and Alex," he said, "that he can tell us where we can find them."

"He doesn't remember the number they called him from and wasn't carrying his phone when we picked him up," Raiff explained. "They left the country in his private jet, but he's in no condition to help us track its whereabouts."

Donati moved to the side of the table opposite where Marsh had taken a seat. "Where was the plane going, Mr. Marsh? Where can we find Alex and Sam?"

"I had a cat named Sam once," he said, digging his thumbnail through the finish of the table. "And a dog named Alex."

"A dog and a cat."

"What?"

"You said you had a dog and a cat."

"I did?"

Donati laid his palms atop the table and leaned across it. "Where are they, Mr. Marsh?"

"My dog and cat?"

"Sam and Alex."

"That's what I said. I haven't seen them in a long time, since I was a boy. Sam and Alex, cat and dog. They got along very well. Magnificently."

"That's not what I'm talking about."

"What are you talking about?"

"Sam and Alex the *people*, the kids."

"They're not people," Marsh said, not looking up from whatever he was drawing into the table's finish. "I told you that. A cat and a dog."

"Where'd they go in your plane?"

Marsh looked up. "I have a plane?"

"We need to find them, Mr. Marsh."

"Who?"

"Sam and Alex."

"My cat and dog?" Marsh asked, without looking up.

Donati gave up and looked back at Raiff. "Which brings us to another subject . . ."

Donati laid it out all for him. The twenty-seven sites, the theory that one of the energy creatures was currently contained at each one, and soon to be released upon the world; and the twenty-eighth site, over the border with Mexico and Guatemala, that he believed was some kind of command center.

"It was you eighteen years ago who saved my life, Raiff, when you were a boy," Donati picked up from there. "I only caught a glimpse of you, but the resemblance is striking."

"No thanks necessary," Raiff told him.

"Not thanks, a question."

"How can we kill it?" Elaina interjected, before Donati could continue.

"You can't kill it," Raiff told them. "It's impossible."

"Because of Einstein's conservation of energy law," Donati picked up. "But you stopped the creature eighteen years ago. How did you do it, change the creature from energy to matter?"

"An ion fusion charge that interrupted the process of the creature's molecules from regenerating," Raiff explained. "Breaking the cycle of its perpetual reconstituting and expanding itself. It transformed in order to survive."

"A great plan, except you'd need fissionable material to build this charge and we don't keep any stored at Ames."

"Yes, you do," Raiff told him.

Raiff could extract the fissionable material he needed to build his fusion charge only from the sphere in a zero-gravity chamber free of all electromagnetic waves. The chamber in question was essentially an airless void that required him to don a breathing apparatus and heavily weighted, astronaut-style boots.

Donati watched the process through a view plate, since no cameras were permitted in the chamber. The charge Raiff was building required only minute shavings of the sphere to create the necessary reaction; Raiff scraped them off with a scalpel from the spiky extensions from the sphere's exterior. Donati had collected the remaining ingredients Raiff needed, which were all fortunately on hand at Ames, although the assembly process required some jerry-rigging and retrofitting of the capacitors responsible for igniting the blast.

"You're sure that thing is going to work?" Donati asked, after Raiff emerged from the chamber cautiously toting in his gloved hands a chrome, baseball-sized object with several ports spaced at equidistant points.

"I'm sure enough," Raiff said, removing his breathing gear.

"There's something else," said Elaina.

"Alex wasn't the first to cross over from our world with a chip like the one in his head," she continued. "There were three others. And joining those four chips together can end this once and for all."

"How?" Donati and Wilder asked together.

"You wouldn't believe me if I told you."

Donati and Wilder exchanged a glance, Wilder speaking for both of them. "At this point, we'd believe anything."

"Why don't you start with what brought you here?" Donati added.

Elaina swallowed hard. "Alex is my son. I came here to find a way to save him and your world at the same time."

"Except," said Donati, "removing the chip would kill him, as would leaving the chip in his head."

"That's why I'm here. There's a third option."

"Seems impossible."

"It isn't, Doctor," Elaina told Donati. "Believe me."

"Only we don't know where to find him," Wilder interjected. "We don't know where he's gone in search of these other three keys. And what if he fails?"

"In that case . . ." Raiff started, but didn't finish.

"In that case," Donati picked up, "we have to move fast. Finish this before Janus launches."

"Launches?"

Donati exchanged a glance with Wilder before responding to Raiff. "Twenty-seven nuclear missiles targeting the underground bases your friends have constructed on Earth over the centuries."

"They're not my friends . . ."

"Figure of speech."

Raiff approached the screen and pressed a finger against the flashing dot in Guatemala. "We need to get to this site you call the command center."

"Except we haven't found its precise location yet," Wilder noted.

"Does NASA have access to a military jet, something that can get us to the general area fast?" Elaina asked.

"No," said Donati, "but Janus does."

95

CÔTES-D'ARMOR

ALEX READ ON, IN search of more information about the grave and the cemetery containing it.

"Here's another drawing that looks like a map," he said, pointing it out to Sam.

"It didn't exist at the time," she told him, "but today this would be the location of Côtes-d'Armor."

"Tell me more."

"There's not much more to tell," Sam resumed. "It's a coastal town known to be a great destination for tourists. Prior to that it was home to the child killer who fashioned the golem. But it's also got its share of historical landmarks, including Les Ramparts de Dinan, a medieval fortress that weathered attacks for centuries. I think there's a medieval cemetery just outside the walls and..." Something changed in her expression. "Wait a minute..."

"What?" Alex prodded.

Sam had the look of someone who'd just found what they were looking for. "Morbihan," she said softly.

"What's that?"

"A coastal town near Côtes-d'Armor. Morbihan is filled with fascinating megalithic sites, unique stone structures that are the most ancient found anywhere in the world, including Le Grand Menhir, the largest stone monument ever erected in prehistoric Europe. It's huge, weighs about two hundred and eighty tons, and was built around forty-five hundred B.C. That and the other monuments are evidence of a prehistoric culture about which, get this, almost nothing is known. Can you guess what I'm going to say next?"

"That there are theories the monuments are connected to an alien race."

"With good reason," Sam affirmed, "not the least of which is a neolithic stone burial chamber that was built around thirty-five hundred B.C. in the shape of a pyramid."

"And given that we just came from Egypt..."

"It's not a coincidence, Alex, it couldn't be. I'm thinking the people coming here from your world all those centuries ago had their reasons for choosing this region as a base. And I'm thinking the process started thousands of years before Gilles de Rais showed up on the scene, around the same period as it did in Egypt."

Alex flipped back to the preceding page, made of what felt like heavy parchment but he knew to be an imitation capable of enduring the centuries, as well as the elements. "We need to find the grave of de Rais's forty-first victim."

He extracted the turquoise scarab amulet and held it up to the light to better view the marble-sized, black oblong shape contained inside. It seemed to shift, as if scurrying to avoid the light. *An illusion*, Alex thought.

Maybe.

He tried to picture what would happen when all four of the chips, or keys, as the book called them, were joined together. How that action would save mankind. But his head started throbbing once more, as if so full to the brim with input that it could accept no more. *Then again ...*

"Stop thinking that," Sam said suddenly.

"Thinking what?"

"That you're going to die. You're not. That's not going to happen."

"How did you know I was thinking about that?"

"The look in your eyes, I guess. Drifting, sort of far away."

"How long have you been watching my eyes?"

"Just a few seconds."

Alex wanted to laugh. "I mean, generally."

"I don't know. It's something I picked up from my parents, hearing them since I was a little girl talking about the eyes being the window to the soul. I look at someone, the eyes are the first thing I notice."

"Window to the soul, like you said."

"I did."

Alex squared his gaze up with hers. "And what do you see in them now?"

"Tomorrow, which I couldn't see yesterday."

"Then let's go find the second key."

96

GRAVEYARD SHIFT

"WHAT DAY IS THIS?" Alex asked Sam, as the train rumbled north through the descending night.

"Wednesday, I think—no, Thursday. It's Thursday. I think."

They'd landed at Brest Bretagne Airport and then took a cab to the train station, where they began a circuitous journey north toward Côtes-d'Armor, requiring several changes. At one point, they'd actually boarded a train headed back south, losing an hour in the process and then watching the sun bleed from the sky when they were finally headed in the right direction.

The ride got them to the station in Dinan just after midnight French time. After sitting in the stale air for so long, they welcomed the walk to Les Ramparts de Dinan and the cemetery dating back to medieval times. While the French government and local authorities went through great pains to keep the sprawling seaside fortress itself in prime condition, the cemetery, well off the beaten path taken by most tourists, had fallen into a state of disrepair. The tightly congested gravestones and hulking tombstones looked as if they were under siege from an overgrowth of weeds and dead brush. The gothic, wrought iron fence that enclosed the cemetery was missing posts in some places, with entire sections bent backward and on the verge of collapse, and it was so rusty it was hard to tell whether the fence was black or copper colored. The trees that once provided ample shade during the hottest of days had turned frail and skeletal, as if the ground had gone sour and was slowly killing them.

The only thing whole seemed to be the main entry gate, which was chained shut, forcing Alex and Sam to backtrack until they found a severed portion in the fencing they were able to slip through. The weeds clawed at their feet as they moved amid the clutter of grave markers and massive memorials, most of which finished in a cross, hand carved out of stone. The dates on the graves, which had no apparent rhyme or reason to how they were laid out, went all the way back to the early 1300s. De Rais had claimed his victims more than a century later, but there was no way to identify which of those buried were those children, never mind the order in which they'd been killed.

"Okay, what do we do now?" Alex asked Sam. "How do we find de Rais's forty-first victim?"

"I'm thinking."

"I'm scared."

"Of a little ole graveyard?"

"It's spooky."

"I didn't think anything could scare you anymore."

"Roller coasters," Alex said, as they continued tracing a zigzagging path past the graves. "I can't ride roller coasters. Never could. They make me sick."

"Me too."

"Really?"

"Yup." Sam nodded. "I threw up on the new Harry Potter ride at Universal."

"When?"

"Last year."

"Hope you weren't wearing that sweater," Alex said, noticing several shuttered, aged stone buildings off to the side. "What are those?"

"Holding chambers," Sam told him. "For when people died during the winter and the ground was too frozen to bury them. The bodies were left to freeze in those holding chambers until the ground thawed enough so they could be buried."

They continued walking toward a sprawling array of mausoleums that were very likely family crypts reserved for noblemen.

"How are we supposed to find de Rais's forty-first victim? There are no numbers and, if there's some clue, it's written in French."

"I speak French," Sam offered.

"For all of the good it's doing us."

They drew closer to the arrangement of stone crypts that backed up against another section of fencing, dominating that side of the cemetery. Sam noticed something on the side of one of the heavy wooden doors and crouched to better regard it.

"It's a number," she told Alex, able to read it thanks to the light shed by a strange moon that looked nearly full but not quite. "Twenty-three."

"So?"

Sam moved on to the next crypt, having to dig through some weeds and ground brush to reveal another number in a comparable spot.

"Twenty-four," she said. "So maybe . . ."

"We're not looking for de Rais's forty-first victim," Alex picked up.

"We're looking for a crypt marked forty-one where the boy was buried," Sam finished.

"So forty-one," Alex started, casting his gaze down the long row that curved to the right to follow the shape of the cemetery, "should be right over there."

The crypt marked "41" came after an empty patch of earth where number forty should have been. It was one of the larger structures, featuring thick windows blacked out to the night and a massive stone door, the ages having left their share of chips, cracks, and fissures in it. Ornamental swords angled toward each other hung on either side of the door. The latch wouldn't give; it was either locked or warped from age and exposure to so many elements after so long. Alex kept jiggling it no effect and then pounded his shoulder against it three times in frustration.

"Ouch," he said, holding his shoulder. "Guess that wasn't too bright."

Sam slipped past him and put both her hands on the iron latch, which was caked with rust. Then she pressed down on the latch, instead of up, as Alex had done. They both heard a click, the door grinding open behind a subtler thrust of Alex's shoulder.

Gilles de Rais was having trouble catching his breath. He hadn't been back here in a very, very long time, even the memories having faded after so long.

Except for the murders. He'd never forget the murders.

The air smelled sweet to him and, also familiar. It smelled like . . .

Home.

Because that's where he was. The place he'd come to in the fifteenth century to begin his mission. Right in these parts.

The vast majority of his victims were buried in the cemetery outside Les Ramparts de Dinan. At his trial, it was claimed he drank the blood of his young victims. The authorities had no idea of his true motives, that his victims all had to die to make sure he killed the one who was his actual target.

De Rais had glimpsed the boy and girl entering the crypt numbered 41 and assumed the book had directed them there, meaning the crypt must have contained the body of the actual young refugee de Rais had slain among the hundreds of other victims. He did not regard the others as anything more than collateral damage. De Rais had been beyond anything passing for guilt or remorse for centuries. He lived only for his mission, which might be drawing to an end at long last here tonight.

Thanks to the boy and girl being inside the crypt, with no idea what would be awaiting them when they emerged.

With his targets out of sight, de Rais eased the dark apothecary bottle from his pocket and moved about the gravestones, sprinkling its contents atop the overgrowth beneath which bodies buried for half a millennium lay.

Listened to the world hiss. Felt the ground seem to shift.

Then a sliver appeared in the ground, widening as a hand comprised only of bones poked itself through.

97

MAUSOLEUM

AS THEIR EYES ADJUSTED to the breaks in the darkness made by the moonlight, Alex and Sam spotted twin rows of stone tombs, each with its own ornate marker, affixed with a crucifix. Several of the windows that had looked to be covered or blacked out from the outside were actually cracked or missing, allowing more of the virtual day-glow spray of the moon to filter in.

Sam took one side of the tombs, Alex the other. Without the victim's name, they were looking for children who'd died around 1432 or 1433, the period during which Gilles de Rais had embarked on a reign of murderous terror that now made all too much sense.

"Over here!" Sam cried out suddenly.

Alex hurried toward her, peering into the slivery band of moonlight that illuminated the gravestone marker. A boy, born in 1420 and died in 1433.

"Only child in here who died in the right time frame," Sam reported. "He's got to be the one."

The stone tomb's dust-encased sliding top refused to budge, sealed thanks to the many years of collected moisture in the poorly maintained conditions. Sam lent her efforts to Alex's, the two of them finally succeeding in nudging the coffin top from its hold and then, recharged by the progress, managing to move it further aside in fits and starts.

An odor emerged, not of death so much as stone rot and mold. There was a sudden expulsion of the odor, rancid air released after centuries, and then no scent at all save for something spoiled and old.

Alex found himself wondering how the condition of Hatshepsut's mummified remains would've compared to the thin bones revealed from the waist up. Broken slivers of moonlight shone on the skeleton of this victim of Gilles de Rais. It didn't look male, female, or even even human; more like the plastic version of high school biology-class skeletons that dangled from a post and clacked when the wind blew through the windows.

What looked like moldy, rotted clothing fabric had affixed itself to the bones in several places and Alex noticed that the skeleton had broken off at the torso.

"I was hoping the chip would have slipped from the body after it decomposed," he said, feeling about the stone coffin. "But there's nothing here."

"Did the book say anything about where to find it?"

"It said to look the victim in the eye and what we seek would look back."

Alex managed to find an angle where his frame didn't block the swatch of moonlight he needed to steer his hands by. He worked them about the corpse's ridged neck bone and twisted. The skeleton's head snapped off its neck at little more than Alex's touch, allowing him to hold the skull up to the moonlight as he peered into its empty eye sockets.

"I think I can see something."

But his fingers—great for gripping footballs, but not so much this—were too big to work even two of them through the socket to grasp whatever he had spotted in the moonlight.

"Sam," he called.

"Ew," she said, moving in alongside him and easing two fingers through the right eye socket, which was slightly bigger than the left.

"I think I've got something."

She didn't rush, and he watched patiently as she took her time, finding and then pinching the marble-sized object Alex had spotted.

"Cold and smooth," she murmured. "I think . . . it might have adhered to the top of the skull. It's not letting me . . . but I'll get it. Eventually. It comes free, then slips back."

A bit more pressure finally dislodged it, and Sam drew it out in her grasp.

"Looks like whatever's inside the amulet," Alex said, recalling the oblong object of comparable size receding from inside the jewel scarab when he'd held it up to the light.

"We need to find something to put it in."

"Looks like you're in pain."

"Feels like it's pinching me."

They looked at each other. Alex knew that they were both picturing the CT scan's depiction of the chip riding Alex's brain, the tentacle-like growths affixed to various tissue.

Alex had pocketed a small ziplock bag he'd found on board Marsh's jet. He drew it from his pocket and held it open for Sam to drop the second chip into. It took her a few moments to pry it from the skin of her finger, but it finally popped free, dark and shiny, and dropped into the bag.

Alex sealed the bag and stuffed it into the same pocket of his jeans that held the amulet.

"Two down, one to go," he said, as they followed a shaft of moonlight toward the crypt's single door and emerged back into the night.

Alex felt the cool, clean air hit him with the wind carrying a distant cry that sounded like an animal's plaintive wail. He heard Sam gasp an instant ahead of glimpsing the skeletons still clawing their way from their graves, rising on feet formed only of bones and their eyeless skulls trained straight at the two of them.

98

BONES

ALEX SAW THE SHAPE of a man standing just beyond the moon-light's reach at the far edge of the cemetery: Gilles de Rais, looking unchanged from the drawings of him in the book. Alex knew he was grinning, even though he couldn't see the smile from this far away.

The skeletons that had already emerged began to approach the crypt awkwardly, as if learning how to walk, a flood of them consuming the night. Bones clacking and grinding together, as more pulled free of their centuries-long resting places. An army of the dead dozens strong approaching to claim two more of its own.

His own victims, many of them anyway, enlisted as soldiers in his grand cause. . . .

De Rais gleefully watched his army of the dead moving as one to swallow their targets en masse. He knew the grand mission that had brought him to this world was fast coming to a close, just as he knew he'd never be able to return home. After so long, there would be nothing left for him there, as there had been little to start with when he was dispatched on this centuries-long mission.

Here he had wielded power, he'd had meaning, he'd had the screams of his victims, which had assured him he was fulfilling his duty. He never tired of the sense of satisfaction, of completion, that yielded. And soon there would be two more sets of screams to add to the considerable collection in his mind, lending what passed for purpose to his life. His orders were to capture the boy

alive, but those orders said nothing of the condition in which he'd
be left.

The screams would be worth it. They always were.

The skeletons converged on the crypt from all angles. Several were
missing parts of themselves and others shed limbs as they moved,
continuing by crawling if they'd lost one leg or both.

"What are we—"

Sam was in the middle of that question when Alex yanked one
ornamental sword from its slot by the door and then the other,
handing the second to her.

Age and disrepair had dulled the edges, weakened the hilts, and
left the blades slightly bent. They were big, with a slight curve,
and weighed a lot more than it appeared at first glance.

Alex clamped two hands, one over the other, on the handle, and
stepped down from the single step, just as the first wave of skeletons
drew within range. He tried to keep Sam just to his side, slightly
behind him. But his initial sweep of the blade drew him into a narrowing circle of the advancing skeleton army, even as he positioned
himself protectively between Sam and the horde.

He whipped the sword one way, then the other, the dull blade
still deadly enough to lop off heads and limbs, or shatter rib cages.
He fought, careful to keep moving, not to let this army of the dead
encircle and close in on them to the point where proximity would
render his sword useless.

Sam had moved off to his right and was doing her best to mimic
his motions, but she was boxed in against the front of the crypt,
her means of flight cut off with a wave of flailing bones converging upon her. So she slid sideways, away from the crypt and closer
to the rows of grave markers featuring shredded ground through
which the dead had risen. She realized too late she was surrounded,
skeletons that stank of spoiled earth nearly upon her.

"Alex!"

Alex leaped atop a tombstone, jumped from it to another, and
then a third. He was close enough to Sam to lay siege from the rear
of the wave attacking her. Felling them like dominoes, he cleared a

path toward her. He could see she was already breathing hard, the heavy sword moving slower in her grasp with each motion. There were still plenty of the skeletons closing on her, when Alex moved the sword to his right hand and grabbed Sam by the shoulder with his left.

He dragged her along a clear path from the skeletons, back toward the center of the cemetery, where more of the things continued to claw their way from the ground. Gilles de Rais, for his part, hadn't budged. He was still taking it all in, seeming to revel in watching the army he had unleashed to do battle, Alex now close enough to see the grin stretched across his face.

Alex stayed as protectively close to Sam as he could. The clutter and number of graves in the ancient plots accounted for the endless, seemingly unbroken wave of the remains of the dead advancing through the night. Too many to fight on their own terms.

So he needed to change those terms to *his* own, focusing on the refuge promised by the ramparts themselves.

Alex kept wielding the sword with a single hand, feeling his muscles wrench and start to seize, while still keeping the other one close to Sam until she broke away from him.

Sam clung to the glorious history of this fortress, taking solace in how the walls around them had fought back sieges for thousands of years . . .

How countless lives had been saved by the protection they afforded . . .

How they allowed the good guys to win . . .

Especially that.

With more and more of the skeletons converging, Sam began lashing out at them to divide their numbers so the entire wave wouldn't be able to descend on Alex. Wielding the heavy sword, though, quickly took its toll on her arms and she deftly dodged the creatures and their clacking bones to steer back toward Alex.

He had just reached the foot of a siege ladder, which led to the top of the ramparts, and had been put in place to simulate the tools of battle for tourists. Sam fought against her own muscles, slicing the air again with the dark weathered blade to keep the things off her long enough to join Alex. She angled for the bottom of the ramparts that had withstood attacks from invading armies for millennia.

Amid the whirl of heavy, weathered steel and the collapse of spilled bones at her feet, Sam felt her shoulders bang up against the ladder.

"Go!" Alex shouted, when she reached him. "Climb!"

Skeletal hands groped for her as Sam reached for the highest rung of the ladder she could grab, discarding the sword. She felt the skeletons flailing for her heels and then felt nothing but the rungs closing in her grasp. She peered down toward Alex to see him clearing a semicircle around the ladder's bottom with wicked, sidelong lashes, his blade a blur. Then he mounted the ladder with an agile leap that skipped the initial rungs and left him scrabbling upward in Sam's wake, still clutching his sword in case he needed it when he reached the top.

De Rais saw his target climbing away from the army of his making, saw his skeleton soldiers dissolving into a single clump as hands of bone struggled to close on rungs that denied them purchase.

"Get them!" he shouted through the night. "Get them!"

His command seemed to renew the skeletons' efforts but none found a firm enough grasp with their skeletal hands on the rungs of the ladder.

"Get them!" he cried out again in frustration. "Get them now!"

Alex caught up with Sam near the top of the ramparts and helped her the last of the way, before handing her his sword to finish the climb himself. They stood together upon the wall, the cluster of skeletons so tight beneath them that it had become impossible to distinguish one from the other. Just a mass of shifting and crackling bones, a great portion of which were de Rais's victims.

Thinking of that made Alex think of something else. *Worth a shot, anyway.*

"De Rais!" he cried out, but not really calling out to him.

More to the skeletons.

"De Rais!"

Alex watched de Rais advance toward the throng of the dead he'd unleashed that had massed at the foot of the ladder, incensed that Alex and Sam had managed to claim the high ground.

"De Rais!" Alex screamed again, at which point de Rais froze, clearly realizing his intent.

A huge grouping of the smallest skeletons in the mass swung toward de Rais, rattling, their feet kicking up the top layer of ground. They began moving toward de Rais as one. Somehow recognizing him, somehow realizing that the killer responsible for their deaths was in their midst. The other skeletons kept clawing at the ladder, having no more luck in negotiating the rungs.

"De Rais!" Alex screamed again, to further drive home the point.

The first wave of smaller skeletons converged on de Rais, engulfing him from all sides before he could flee. He froze in the face of their advance and by the time he swung to flee, they were on him. And then the monster who'd claimed their lives was gone, lost to the swarm beneath the dull moonlight, his own screaming swallowed swiftly by the wind as their skeletal hands flailed away at him, ripping and tearing at anything they grasped.

"Take that, asshole!" Alex yelled down.

He had just turned back toward Sam, when he felt the world start to spin around him, his legs turning to jelly, as his knees wobbled and he felt himself falling.

TWELVE

THE LOST CITY

Victory belongs to the most persevering.
NAPOLEON BONAPARTE

99

EL MIRADOR

JANUS HAD ARRANGED FOR a private jet to take Donati and Wilder, along with Elaina and Raiff, secretly to Guatemala City, where a helicopter was waiting to bring them the rest of the way to the lost Mayan city of El Mirador. The principals of Janus had also agreed to delay the missile strikes for as long as possible, hopefully buying the group enough time to find a way to destroy the facility, the command center, that awaited them.

The highest concentrations of electromagnetic discharge and subsurface disruption had been detected from this area, but the specific location of its source had proven difficult to pin down thanks to increased volcanic and seismic activity playing hell with the satellite readings. For that reason, El Mirador hadn't been included in the initial target package: twenty-seven thermonuclear bombs to be dropped in eight hours, instead of six.

Which they had to make enough. That gave them until 5:00 A.M. in this part of the world, just short of the crack of dawn.

"I didn't realize there were any active volcanoes left in Guatemala," Wilder had commented, when the full analysis of the site came in.

"There aren't," Donati acknowledged. "At least not until very recently."

Langston Marsh had accompanied them, busying himself through the duration of the flight with crayons and a children's coloring book, still clad in his pajamas and bathrobe. They'd opted to leave him with the jet under the watchful eye of the pilots before setting off themselves in the chopper.

"Say hello to Sam and Alex for me," he called after them from the foot of the jet's steps. "Good dog, good cat."

They piled into a blue-striped Bell helicopter for the one-hour flight to the Mirador Basin, a nearly twenty-five-hundred-square-mile swath of jungle straddling northern Guatemala and Campeche, Mexico, where the famed Lost City could be found. They knew they were close when the chopper soared over the peaks of the Mayan pyramids, nearly as sprawling as and remarkably similar in design to their Egyptian cousins. Based on what they knew now, that was clearly far more than a coincidence.

After the pyramids, clearings could be spotted in the forest below, smoke rising from cooking fires through the canopy. An occasional road sliced through the wilderness for several more miles until all trace of human habitation vanished. All that interrupted the endless ribbon of the jungle were swampy open patches called *civales,* breaking the great green quilt formed by the canopies of the ramón and sapodilla trees, which produced the sap used to make chewing gum. Next came their first glimpse of the ruins of the lost cities of Tintal and Nakbe, beneath which ran part of what had been the first freeway system in the world.

"Where are we going exactly?" Raiff asked, gazing out the window on his side of the chopper.

"Filtering through the disruptions as best we can," Donati explained to him, "it appears the extreme power spike is being generated in an area between and beneath three volcanoes that were dormant until two days ago."

"How is that possible?" Elaina wondered, her voice strained with fatigue.

"It's not," Wilder said, "at least not by prevailing geothermal principles. One showing signs, glimpses of increased activity—sure. But three coming back to life at once?" He shook his head. "Utterly unprecedented and inexplicable."

"Not inexplicable," Elaina said. "It's the blood moon."

The increased seismic activity had led the Guatemalan government and military to close off all of the sprawling jungle surrounding El Mirador, making the group feel as if they had the prehistoric world below all to themselves. The chopper set down in a clearing right in the center of the triangle of stirring volcanoes. Raiff felt the air rumble, the Earth's surface seeming to kick up gravel at their feet, upon climbing out of the chopper.

Seeing the others' faces, he knew they were feeling the same sensation of the entire planet seeming to shift on the tectonic plates on which it was formed.

Raiff helped Donati and Wilder with their equipment, recognizing some but not all of it.

"Heat sensors," he realized.

"Simplistic, but effective in pinpointing the precise origins of the subsurface electromagnetic discharge from this area," Donati explained.

"I don't need any of that to tell we're close, Doctor, very close."

"And how is that exactly?" Donati asked him.

"The tree monkeys, birds, reptile and snake life told me," Raiff explained.

Wilder looked about dramatically. "I see none of those about anywhere, young man."

"That's exactly my point," said Raiff.

100

FUTURE HISTORY

SAM HAD CAUGHT HIM just in time, an instant before Alex would have slipped from the ramparts and fallen to his death. He seemed to be having trouble focusing when she clutched him in her grasp, mumbling incoherently as if the words formed in his mind got no further.

Still trying to shut the final awful screams of Gilles de Rais from her mind, Sam managed to get both of them back to the airport and, thankfully, the private jet was still parked on the tarmac, waiting for them. She remembered that when scanning ahead in the book, Alex had mentioned something about the Mayans. That would mean this plot conceived by the refugees involved not only Egyptian pharaohs, but also those among the oldest of Western civilizations as well. Then again, given all the legends about the Mayan and ancient Egyptian cultures, perhaps it wasn't so far-fetched at all. Perhaps both those cultures had been inundated with an alien populace laying the groundwork for what was to come by quickening the development of this world.

Considering that possibility reminded Sam of how much she loved interpreting history from the angle of space exploration. Not just Earth venturing to foreign worlds, but also foreign worlds coming to Earth. Of all the scenarios she had considered and studied, not a single one resembled what she'd ended up embroiled in for real. But there was an undeniable, even logical rationale to the first alien race Earth had encountered to any degree coming from a parallel, yet far more advanced civilization located in another dimension, as opposed to a galaxy. As a NASA intern, she thought dryly, this was akin to the ultimate field trip. Living the future of history, instead of merely recording or theorizing about it.

The future of history . . .

It was a phrase coined by her mentor, Dr. Donati, in one of his flightier moments of thought, though it pretty much summed up everything the Ames Research Center, particularly the parts dedicated to astrobiology, was all about. Sam wished she were still just an intern serving under Donati, preparing for college and taking her big dreams home every night.

She helped Alex up the stairs into the jet and got him settled in his seat with the seatbelt fastened, before knocking on the cockpit door to inform the pilots they were heading somewhere in Latin America. More details to follow, once Alex regained enough of his senses to decipher the portion of the book pertaining to the third key, which must have held a distinct Mayan connection.

He stirred a few times but didn't come alert through the first leg of the flight back west. Sam tried rousing him gently to no avail, beginning to fear that the inevitable damage caused by the degradation of the chip had reached a tipping point.

What if he never fully regained consciousness? What if he only declined further from here?

Fear gripped Sam, coiling around her insides and forging a lump in her throat she couldn't force down. She'd been scared plenty these past seven days, starting on Friday night, when Alex lay broken and battered on the football field before a hushed stadium. There was a great difference, though, between fear stoked by something sudden and fear stoked by an inevitability turned real in its grim finality.

What if . . .

She tried not to finish the thought.

What if . . .

Sam felt herself sniffling, then sobbing, taking Alex in her arms to comfort herself more than him.

"Hey," she heard him rasp dryly, "not so tight."

She eased herself away from him, her voice still barely air, and said, "I thought you were dead."

He almost smiled.

"Read my will," he said, adding gravely, "I left you these jeans."

"Thanks."

"Hey, they'll fit you better than they fit me." He noticed the big book, opened on the table before their seats. "Catching up on your reading?"

"Yep."

He picked up the book, reading the page she'd had it open to, then suddenly started turning pages.

"El Mirador," Alex said, after flipping through several of the pages connected to the third key.

"Center of Mayan society." Sam nodded. "Located just south of the border between Mexico and Guatemala. Also known as the Lost City."

"Is there anything you don't know?"

"How to read that book, for one thing." Then, softer, "How to get that thing out of your head, for another."

"Yeah," he nodded, "there is that."

"What else does the book say about El Mirador? What body do we have to dig up next?"

Alex flipped back through the sequence of pages he just read. "No mention of a person, a body, or a grave this time. Nothing I can make any real sense of yet."

"No hints?"

"Just this," Alex said, turning his attention back to the book. "'The third key can be found where the light shines through.'"

"What's that mean?" Sam asked him.

"I have no idea."

"Okay," he said, an hour later into the flight, after Sam had left him to quietly read, nodding off a few times herself. "I think I may have something." He flipped the book's big, parchment pages back to whatever he must have been referring to. He looked at her and asked, "Does this drawing mean anything to you?"

It did indeed.

"Holy shit . . ."

Alex laughed.

"What's so funny?"

"I never heard you swear before," he chided.

"Maybe you haven't been listening."

"Oh, I've been listening."

"I'm talking about our tutoring sessions, when you stop paying attention to me."

He slid the book closer to her. "So?"

"You really don't know what that is?"

"Do I sound like I know what it is?"

"It's a drawing of a crystal skull."

"I'm still listening, Sam."

"We're going to El Mirador, the Mayan lost city, right? Well, according to Mayan legend, there will come a time when thirteen ancient crystal skulls are reunited that can change the course of humanity."

"As in save it?"

"The legend doesn't say."

"I thought we were supposed to be looking for three *keys,* not thirteen *crystal skulls.*"

"You're missing the point."

Alex tapped his cheek. "This is my listening face."

"At least a few, maybe lots more, from your world must have helped the Mayan culture rise to become the most advanced of its age. We still have no explanation for how they came up with a lot of the things they did, like building roads, sewer systems, water storage, even primitive medical treatments that seem more modern the closer you study them."

"Was that the point I was missing?"

"Part of it," Sam told him. "It stands to reason that some of these Mayan legends were drawn from what your race was really up to. So maybe twelve of those skulls don't matter, just one. A crystal skull that contains the third key we need to save the world. 'The third key can be found where the light shines through,'" Sam repeated. "Makes perfect sense, doesn't it?"

"There's more," Alex said, flipping the pages forward again. "The book talks about the dawn of a new world, the rising of a sun that will shine forever against a war with eternal darkness."

"According to the Mayan calendar, the world was supposed to end in 2012."

"Everybody makes mistakes, Sam."

"No, I think the whole interpretation was wrong. They weren't predicting the end of the world, so much as the dawning of a new one."

"Holy shit," Alex said, this time.

"My thoughts exactly."

"But 2012 has come and gone."

"Again, we can't take Mayan legend literally," Sam told him. "It must have grown out of plans hatched by those who'd fled your world and joined their culture. Open to interpretation at best. So it wasn't December 21, 2012 the Mayans were talking about at all."

"So when was it?"

Sam shrugged, trying not to let her eyes give away her thoughts. "Maybe never. Maybe just a figure of speech."

Alex met her stare, his gaze tightening in a way that told Sam he'd caught on. "Or?"

"Or," Sam conceded, "maybe tomorrow."

"Listen to this," Alex picked up from there, tracing a line on the page the book was open to. "'Victory lies in the light of the blood moon.'"

101

CRYSTAL SKULL

THE SENSORS DONATI AND Wilder had brought along pinpointed the highest levels of heat to a fissure that had opened in the ground at a point almost perfectly centered among the three long-dormant volcanoes that had sprung back to life. It looked jagged at first, but upon closer inspection appeared to be spherical, a passage into the depths of the Earth.

"I need to go down there," Raiff said.

"No," Elaina replied, "I do. If you survive the descent, you won't know what you're looking at, what you need to bring back up."

"Which of us stands a better chance of surviving in the first place?" he shot back at her, leading Donati and Wilder to glance at each other uneasily. "How much rope did we bring with us?" he asked the scientists.

"A thousand feet," Donati answered. "Five two-hundred-foot sections. They're back at the vehicle with those guides Janus arranged for us."

"Get the rope, Doctor, and the guides. We're going to need them."

Their Guatemalan guides, ex-military with a background in special operations, pounded a series of stakes through the ground and into the layers of rock and shale below. Then heavy-duty climbing rope was strung around the stakes for maximum support. Seven-sixteenths-diameter rope coming to a thousand feet in total.

"So what's the record for an underground descent?" Donati wondered.

Raiff was testing the array of carabiners clipped to his belt.

"Two thousand feet into the Sistema Huautla cave north of here in Mexico."

Orson Wilder peered down the shaft into the empty blackness. "The record's safe, then."

Raiff might've been no stranger to physical challenges, but in this case he would be descending blind with no idea whatsoever what awaited him at the bottom of the shaft. A thousand feet might not have been a relatively great distance outside with his eyes to guide him, but underground, amid utter darkness, Raiff knew he was facing what might be an impossible challenge. He wasn't a spelunker or a speleologist, underground caves pretty much a total mystery to him until today.

First time for everything, he supposed.

"Let's get started," he said, threading the rope through his carabiners.

The first stretch came easy, Raiff holding the rope with both gloved hands as it slowly lowered him through the expanse that resembled the width of a submarine corridor, barely big enough for two. He reached the end of the first of the five ropes with nary an issue, starting in on the second in identical.

He plucked the walkie-talkie from his belt and pressed the talk button. "How's the weather up there, Doctor?"

"Hot," Donati reported.

"Then you'd love it down here. Thirty degrees cooler and sinking. How far down am I?"

"Looks like you've gone through maybe three-quarters of the second rope. See anything yet, because—"

Donati's voice drifted out in a burst of static.

"Say again, Doctor . . . Doctor?"

Nothing. Just static again, making Raiff think wherever he was headed was coming up soon.

Raiff fell into an easy rhythm not unlike the sensation of rappelling down a sheer mountain face. The darkness complicated matters, utter blackness with nothing to break it other than the dome light built into his helmet, which shone weakly in whatever direction he turned, barely making a dent in the nothingness beneath him.

The rope continued to spiral out as he followed the shaft's downward slope, which angled slightly to the right. He was into the final rope now, past the eight-hundred-foot mark, closing in on eighty stories belowground.

No wonder they couldn't get a firm reading from this site . . .

Finally, a light he first took to be an illusion poked up at him through the darkness. It brightened more with each foot he dropped, growing to a glisten, then radiating out in a day-bright glow.

Plop!

Raiff's feet touched down on rocky, gravel-strewn ground that formed a narrow path with the light emanating from the other end. It thickened the closer he came, becoming so bright that Raiff had no need for the flashlight tucked in the backpack strapped to his shoulders. The path widened and then opened into what looked like a sprawling underground cave.

But Raiff realized it was something else altogether.

It was the bottom of a volcano, a fourth one centered among the other three. Emerging from the path into the jagged, steaming, lava-coated chamber brought Raiff face-to-face with the source of the light. It was a massive spinning orb that might have been a miniature version of the Earth itself, except for the fact it looked to be translucent. More a projection, like the Ash Man, except for the dull harmonic whine that told Raiff it was every bit as real as he was. He heard that whine reverberating in the deepest part of his skull, felt its humming vibration in the pit of his stomach.

The closer he drew to the massive orb, the deeper the effects grew to the point where he felt dizzy, then nauseous, and had to force himself to continue forward. Something made Raiff stop suddenly and he realized the spinning orb seemed to be hanging in the air, suspended over a vast jagged chasm that might have descended to the very center of the Earth.

Then something else caught his eye amid the radiating light, something swirling around inside the orb, seemingly caught in its miniature gravitational flow. Raiff moved his feet as close to the edge of the chasm as he dared, stretched a hand out toward the orb, tensing just on the verge of touching it and reflexively closing his eyes.

He felt nothing and opened them to find his hand had passed straight through the orb, something that looked like connected strands of gas swirling both past and through his fingers, re-forming as quickly as it came apart. He realized his hand felt cold and was quickly getting colder, as if he'd stuck it in ice water, his fingers starting to go numb.

That made Raiff think of cold fusion or some other vast undiscovered power source. But this was no factory or manufacturing plant like the one beneath Alcatraz. There were no robotic soldiers or the plasma pulse rifles they wielded anywhere about. There was nothing.

Just the orb.

Raiff knew his hand could stand only a few more seconds of the cold. He spotted something else swirling about through the strands of mist-like gas, unnoticed until now because it was translucent as well. He stretched his hand in farther, flirting with the chasm's edge as much as he dared and finally snaring the object in his grasp. Then withdrawing it to the realization that, instead of frigid, his hand had grown pleasantly warm.

An hour later, the Guatemalan soldiers-turned-guides yanked Raiff up the final stretch to the surface. He dropped to a seated position on the ground, heaving for breath, sweat having darkened his shirt in thick splotches.

"Well?" Donati prodded, as the others looked on.

"What I found down there isn't what we thought, not even close," Raiff managed.

"Then what was it?"

"There's something you need to see," he said, words aimed at Elaina, as he unslung his backpack and removed the object he'd snatched from inside the spinning orb:

A crystal skull.

102

A WALK IN THE WOODS

"THERE'S GOT TO BE something," Alex said, reviewing the pages yet again.

But this review produced the same result the others had, offering no further instructions on how the four organic computer chips, including the one fused to his brain, were supposed to fit together. More drawings and more language that ran in endless sentences down the page in vertical fashion.

A number of the drawings featured the moon, big beyond scale, full, and colored bright red.

"That's a blood moon, all right," Sam said.

"'Under the light of a blood moon,'" Alex repeated from earlier. "But what's a blood moon?"

"An illusion, mostly. It happens during a total lunar eclipse when the full moon glows red thanks to the Earth casting its darkest shadow."

"According to the book, the keys can only be fit together beneath the spill of a blood moon," Alex told her.

"You're not going to believe this," Sam said.

"What?"

"A lunar eclipse is happening tonight—well, morning, depending on what part of the world you live in."

"So what's the significance?"

"For centuries, primitive cultures, and some not so primitive, have viewed the disappearance of the moon during a lunar eclipse as a portent of danger. Some sources even equate the blood moon as a sign of the apocalypse."

"Reputable sources?"

"Try the Bible," Sam told him.

"You're kidding."

"Not unless the prophet Joel was," she said, and proceeded to quote the passage in question. "'And I will show wonders in the heavens and in the earth: Blood and fire and pillars of smoke. The sun shall be turned into darkness. And the moon into blood, before the coming of the great and awesome day of the Lord.'"

"So we need to get to El Mirador fast, that's what you're saying."

"Before the blood moon rises, anyway.'"

Alex tilted his gaze out the window, as the jet settled into its final descent. "It's getting dark now, Sam. Let's hope wherever we're going, we get there in time."

They'd landed in Guatemala City, taxiing to a halt next to a second private jet. A man wearing pajamas and a bathrobe looked to be chasing imaginary butterflies on the tarmac.

Langston Marsh.

"Alex and Sam," he said, when he spotted them approaching. "Have you seen my dog and cat?"

It took considerable coaxing, but they managed to get Marsh to arrange for a helicopter to take them to the same place another one had brought the team that had flown in on the other private jet. One of the pilots made the arrangements on his instructions and ten minutes later they were soaring toward the Mirador Basin, over trees so thick they seemed to swallow the ground.

Clearings started dotting the scenery after they flew over the pyramids, followed by the first of the lost cities, before Sam and Alex landed in turbulent air that might have toppled the chopper if it had attempted to fly any farther. A vehicle, also arranged by one of Marsh's pilots, arrived minutes later and took Sam and Alex deep into the jungle until a military roadblock forced them to set off on foot.

"How do you feel?" Sam asked Alex, as they followed a route laid out in a map found in the book, currently tucked into a backpack stretched at the seams to accommodate its bulk.

"Ready to finish this," Alex said, gritting his teeth. "Once and for all."

They traipsed through the jungle, their path lit by powerful flashlights provided by the driver, who'd gotten them as far into the jungle as he could. It wasn't a terribly long walk but arduous, given the heat and the terrain, which was rough in some places, soggy with mud in others, and almost impassable in still more. Those would have been formidable challenges, even before the element of darkness was added, a darkness barely penetrated by the full moon thanks to the thick tree canopy overhead. Glimpses of that moon revealed an aura of something colored orange capping its top like a halo thanks to the coming eclipse.

The plan was to follow the map from the book to the location of the crystal skull and the third key. At that point, they could only hope the skull would also yield more clues as to the rest of the process, most notably how they were supposed to get the chip, the fourth key, out of Alex's head to join it up with the other three.

"You're the scientist," Alex said to Sam. "So how exactly do you think it's going to happen if we can pull this off, fit the four chips together?"

"I have absolutely no idea," Sam said, staring at him and trying not to think about what came next.

El Mirador was located within the farthest reaches of Guatemala's Petén jungle, seventy-five miles south of the Mexican border. Sam passed the time and tried to distract from the rigors of the journey by playing tour guide, highlighting the primary technical features of El Mirador from the time of its flourishing in the sixth century B.C. to its heights of power over the next six hundred years. She described how the scale of architectural planning and construction at El Mirador indicated the presence of a powerful elite.

There were hundreds of structures at El Mirador, but a major ongoing excavation has never been undertaken, so almost everything was still hidden beneath the jungle floor. Just glimpses of those impressive and vast structures peeked up over the surface, with not much evidence of them at all showing in the night. And perhaps most important, virtually nothing was known about what had led to the fall of one of early civilization's most advanced societies.

"Seems pretty obvious to me," Alex said. "I mean, if so many of my kind had taken up with the Mayans and these Overlords back in my world found out . . . Do the math. We're witnessing firsthand how they deal with rebellion."

"You're saying El Mirador could be a microcosm for whatever the entire world is going to face."

"Why tonight?" Alex challenged her instead of responding. "Why a blood moon?"

"I guess we're about to find out," Sam said, as a loud crack of branches snapping sounded not far ahead of them in the jungle, followed almost immediately by another.

103

THE FOUR KEYS

"IT'S NO USE," ORSON Wilder said, holding the satellite phone, "I can't get a signal."

Raiff recalled losing contact suddenly on his walkie-talkie, wondered if some atmospheric interference associated with the looming eclipse was to blame. Whatever the case, the lack of communication had effectively isolated them out here, with no way to contact the outside world.

"Meaning we can't reach Janus to update them, get word to call off the strikes, if we're successful."

Raiff looked from one scientist to the other. "How much more time do we have?"

"One hour. That's it."

"Just after the peak of the eclipse," Raiff noted.

Elaina was examining the crystal skull again, closer now, under the focused beam of a flashlight.

"You're wasting your time," Raiff told her. "I told you, it's empty."

Her eyes followed the beam, gaze tightening. "You need to see this, all of you."

All three men slid toward her in the base camp they'd set up amid a nesting of what looked like tables carved out of chiseled logs laid side by side, but with nothing apparently holding them together.

Elaina held the flashlight in a trembling hand. "Follow the beam of light and tell me what you see."

"Nothing," Raiff said, as the scientists looked on.

Elaina changed the angle of the light so it reflected differently off the skull's glimmering surface. "What about now?"

Suddenly, a dark, translucent object was revealed floating inside the skull, just as the skull had been floating inside the orb.

"It's a computer chip," Dr. Donati said, having come up behind Raiff's shoulder. "Organic and virtually identical to Alex's without the extra extensions for additional memory. It's crystalline, Raiff, just like the skull itself. That's why you couldn't see it before."

The bright moon was already haloed by a red hue with the full lunar eclipse coming fast. Raiff noticed the light spilling from the sky made Elaina's face look shiny, while cloaking her deep-set eyes in a murky haze that made them look even more worn and haggard. He was thinking about a lot of things in that moment but mostly about her, that last glimpse of her eighteen years ago before he'd slipped into the tunnel forming the spacebridge to this world with Alex in his arms. How that glimpse had sustained him all this time, freezing her in his mind with the certainty he'd never see her again.

What might have he done differently had he known she'd survived? How might these eighteen years been different? Why hadn't she tried some means to contact him?

The answers didn't matter. Elaina had wanted him to think she was dead, so his focus would be entirely on the mission before him in the new world at the other end of the spacebridge. Keeping Alex safe was all that had mattered.

But the rising of the blood moon allowed him to see Elaina as he remembered her from all those years ago, instead of in the frail condition that had befallen her. Her life ebbing seemingly by the moment, no matter how brave a face she put on.

"There are three more of these chips, according to the book," Raiff reminded her, gaze locked on the glistening crystal skull. "One of those being the one in Alex's head. But even if he and Sam managed to track down the other two . . ."

"What?" Elaina prodded, when Raiff's voice tailed off.

"We can't get the fourth chip out of Alex's skull without killing him. He has to die in order to save the world."

"I can save him," Elaina insisted, her voice cracking.

"He's not even here."

"He's coming," she said, her voice strong again in that moment.

"You can't know that."

"I do. Alex is coming, and he'll be here before the eclipse, in time for the chips to be joined." She rose and angled closer to him, supporting herself by resting a hand atop the log table. "That's why I'm here, Raiff. That's why I came. So Alex doesn't have to die. This was the plan all along."

And that's when a pair of thunderous cracks sounded, ahead of a loudening mechanical whir and hum.

"Looks like we've got company," said Raiff.

104

BLOOD MOON

ALEX SAW THE MASSIVE, tentacled machines gliding through the jungle and obliterating everything in their path as vague shadows projected against the night. The monsters of his dreams coming to life, no longer the product of a vision.

They seemed to float, hovering several feet over the ground, comprised of something that looked like steel but boasted the supple flexibility of flesh. But there were blips, intervals between instants, where the monstrous machines seemed to vanish from the scene, only to reappear in the precise moment and motion where he'd seen them last. He wondered if they were, in fact, a kind of projection, but one imbued with some form of physicality, similar to the Ash Man but clearly possessing more substance.

Alex eased Sam reflexively behind him, even though the machines seemed uninterested in his presence.

So who, or what, are they after?

The angle of their approach made it seem like they were headed for the same clearing in the jungle indicated on the map torn carefully from the book, so he could follow it more easily. The clearing that was still well ahead of them beneath the brightening spill of the blood moon as the eclipse drew closer.

Alex continued to watch the machines' armlike tentacles sweeping aside everything in their path, still several hundred yards off when he parted a thicket of brush to emerge into a clearing.

To find Raiff standing there, whip extended in his hand, ready to take on the monsters.

"Alex!" Raiff cried out, not believing his eyes, as Alex dragged Sam with him into the clearing. "The other two keys . . ."

"Right here."

Alex extracted the oblong-shaped chip contained in a ziplock bag and the amulet containing the other from his pocket.

Raiff extended a hand, pointing to the west as the machines drew closer. "That way, maybe an eighth of a mile."

"We know," said Sam "Thanks to the book."

Raiff's expression remained flat, his gaze only on Alex. "There's someone waiting for you there. Now go!"

The machines continued closing in on them.

"Trust her, Alex," Raiff continued, instead of moving to face them.

"Her?"

"You'll see when you get there."

If the machines had been physical instead of an astral projection with only minimal form flitting in and out of substance, Raiff never would have stood a chance against them. He centered himself among the three of them, waiting until they were close enough to regard him, waiting until the tentacles of the middle one began to sweep his way in a blur.

Raiff rolled under the sweep, lashing out with his whip as he reclaimed his feet and slicing through the tentacle. It was like cutting through nothing because, in a physical sense, that's what it was. The severed portion of the tentacle didn't drop, but hung in the air briefly before disappearing.

He'd claimed the attention of the machines now, dipping and darting to avoid the reach of their deadly tentacles, which obliterated trees and brush instead. They were converging on him, just as he'd hoped, to buy Elaina the time she needed.

Alex and Sam emerged from the rim of the jungle together, side by side. The clearing before them had been turned into what looked like a command center. Sam saw Dr. Donati, not bothering to ponder what had brought him down here. He met her gaze, eyes bulging in what looked like relief when they fixed on Alex. A familiar figure with long gray hair dangling past his shoulders stood along-side him.

The man who called himself a professor at Bishop Ranch business park, providing an answer to any question for a dollar!

Sam wondered if he'd be able to answer the questions she had on her mind now, starting with whether they would be alive tomorrow. Then she spotted the woman.

Trust her, Alex, Raiff had said.

And Sam understood immediately why they could, noting the crystal skull atop a table formed of logs.

It can be found where the light shines through.

The clue to this final key, the day-glow-bright moonlight shining straight through the crystal.

Alex moved to the table stiffly, never taking his eyes off the woman.

"Who are you?" he asked, when he got there.

The woman didn't look like she was going to respond, Alex about to prod her again when she finally spoke.

"Elaina. And you know who I am, Alex," she said, unable to keep the sadness from her voice.

His mouth dropped. His knees buckled. His insides felt numb.

"You're my . . ."

"Yes," she said, sparing him the need to finish his thought, "I am."

Raiff twisted and turned, dove and rolled, his whip a constant blur of motion. He could see the sky changing, as the eclipse drew to within mere moments, the moon looking like a bloody orb in the sky.

He continued to sever parts of the machines, vanquishing pieces of them into the ether and holding a measure of his ground. Slowing their approach to the clearing enough for Elaina to finish her work.

One of them tripped him up, and Raiff went down hard, banging his head on a rock or the edge of an exposed ancient Mayan structure. Stars exploded before his eyes, and he shifted to the side just in time to avoid a slash by one of the tentacles that ended

up piercing the ground instead, kicking up dirt and brush where
he'd just been. He brought his whip around and severed the pincer
extremity, which remained in the ground for a moment before it
disappeared.

Back on his feet, trying to keep his breathing settled, Raiff continued to wield his weapon, the start of the eclipse drawing ever
closer.

Sam wondered if she'd heard the woman right, literally replayed her
words in her mind.

Yes, I am.

Alex's mother.

"No, my mother's dead," she heard Alex say to the woman named
Elaina, sounding like a little boy. "Just like I'm going to be soon."

The woman moved closer to Alex but stopped short of touching
him, needing to force herself not to. "No, you're not. That's why I'm
here. To save you and this world at the same time."

"It's too late," Alex said, as she drew up alongside him.

"No, it's not. Not for you or this world. There's a way. Trust me."

"I don't even know you. I, I don't believe you're my mother."

Sam watched Alex stiffen as Elaina reached out and took his
hands in hers. "Look into my eyes and tell me you still don't believe."

Alex did, swallowed hard, said nothing.

"They feared you from the beginning, Alex," she continued. "Realized they'd made a mistake."

"Who?"

"The Overlords. They thought they were creating the means
to defeat those who resisted them but they ended up creating the
means of their own fall. You, Alex, you."

"This doesn't make any sense."

"They're organic machines," Elaina told him. "They don't have
DNA as we understand it but they do have a genetic sequence capable of breeding life, at least imprinting a preprogrammed genetic
code. That was their plan."

"What are you saying? That you're *not* my mother?"

"Oh, I'm your mother, all right. I let them do this to me, I let them do it, because if it worked I knew I'd have the means to defeat them and at least save this world."

"Wait, then you're saying . . ."

"One of the Overlords is your father, Alex. The one you call the Ash Man."

105

SACRIFICE

IT SHOULDN'T HAVE SURPRISED Alex, given how things had gone this past week. Just another impossibility added to the mix. He felt numb everywhere, staring at a woman who was a total stranger but felt akin to looking in the mirror.

"The other two chips, did you manage to recover them?" the woman asked him.

"I, er, I . . ."

Sam drew even with Alex, unable to take her eyes off Elaina either. "Yes, we have them."

"You must be Sam. I'm Elaina, Alex's . . ."

"I know," Sam said, when Elaina couldn't finish her thought.

"The chips," Elaina prompted. "Quickly. While there's still time."

Alex eased them from his pocket and handed them across the log table in a trembling hand. He could see the final chip inside the crystal skull, gleaming red in the spill of the blood moon, and could feel its presence somehow in his head.

"We're still missing one," he told his mother. "But you know where it is."

"I had it put there, Alex. And, for what it's worth, I'm sorry."

"For what?"

"Using you, endangering you, abandoning you. I could go on. There's a lot to be sorry for."

"If it saves this world," he told her, "then it was all worth it."

At the table, Elaina cracked the scarab jewel, pulled the pieces aside and removed the marble-sized organic chip. She then eased a nearly identical one from the ziplock bag Alex had placed it in, as a shocked Donati and Wilder looked on. Brilliant scientists reduced to spectators with their mouths dropping in unison.

Alex moved alongside Elaina, his mother, and watched her ease the first chip he'd recovered toward the forehead of the crystal skull. The crystalline structure receded, looking like gelatin, and seemed to suck it in. Elaina repeated the process with the chip Alex had removed from the corpse of a victim claimed by Gilles de Rais. Those two joined the near-matching one already inside the skull, seeming to float behind its eye sockets.

Three of the chips they needed to somehow save the world had been joined together.

Leaving only one to go.

"What now?" he asked Elaina.

"You let me save you, Alex," Elaina told him. "Lie down on the table."

Raiff was heaving for breath, the projected forms of the machines seeming to gain more substance with the coming of the eclipse, the sun arranging itself between the Earth and the moon. Suddenly the parts of their tentacles he managed to lop off with his whip stopped dissipating into the formless ether. Flitting in and out of substance, they were attacking him like mad snakes as soon as they hit the ground.

If he could claim the high ground, find some way to attack their more vulnerable areas . . .

But the deadly machines were almost to the clearing, and any new strategy Raiff embarked on would cost vital seconds, seconds Alex and Elaina could ill afford to lose. The best thing he could do to assure their success, he had the sense to think, was to hold the mechanical monsters at bay for a few more minutes.

Alex tried to move, couldn't. Every bit of his being seemed to have seized up. He couldn't move, couldn't think, couldn't speak.

"Everything I did, I did because I believed it would help us win," Elaina told him. "And there's so much of it I regret. I'm sorry I made you a victim of that. But we have no choice now, either of us. See, I have a chip in my head too. Control me and they could control you, use you for whatever ends they desired. That's why I had to send you away. And that's why I had to find you now, to save you and this world from the destruction that will come in minutes if we don't do this. Please, let me save you, Alex. Let me do that much for you and this world."

A long breath blew out of Alex's mouth as he pulled himself up upon the log table.

"Sam," Elaina said softly, sitting atop the table next to him. "That's short for Samantha, isn't it?"

Sam nodded.

"Take the skull. Take the skull and, when I tell you, hold it over our foreheads, hold it upside down. Close your eyes and don't open them no matter what."

Sam hesitated. Elaina gestured toward the blood moon, the eclipse reaching its peak.

"No," Alex said, shaking his head. "I won't do it."

"Yes, you will, you must! We're running out of time. We have to do this while the eclipse is happening." Elaina stopped and sucked in some air dryly. "I always loved you. And I promise, I will always be with you!"

"Please!" Alex said. "Please, tell me what—"

"There's no time now. No time. You have to trust—"

"*Tell me!*"

Elaina swallowed hard, sapping her dwindling strength further. "The atmospheric convergence caused by the blood moon will power the chips into an unstoppable force, drawn to our enemy's radiating energy fields like magnets, destroying them."

"How? If I'm going to die for this, I deserve to know how!"

"You're not going to die," Elaina found the strength to insist firmly. "And the answer is black holes, swallowing everything when they reach their destinations, just like what you witnessed in Alcatraz Sunday night. Now, please, we have to do this."

They laid down on their backs, head to head, their feet pointing in opposite directions. Elaina positioned herself so the top of her skull was pressed flush against the top of Alex's.

"Now, Sam," she said, her voice cracking. "It's time."

Sam took the crystal skull in her grasp and centered it over their foreheads, closing her eyes as instructed. Immediately the skull turned warm, then hot. So hot she wanted to let it go. But she couldn't. It was almost like it had attached itself to her flesh. Her eyes snapped open briefly, long enough to see both Alex and Elaina caught in the throes of violent spasms, their bodies literally lifting off the table.

Alex's eyes rolled back.

Elaina's eyes rolled back.

And in both pairs Sam thought she caught a glimpse of something moving about, seeking a way out.

She couldn't close her eyes, no matter how much she tried, and watched Alex's mouth gape as if he were screaming, but no sound emerged. She saw, literally *saw*, his scalp quiver, as if something beneath it was pressing up against his skull. She watched what could only be the organic chip moving toward the top of his skull where it was aligned with his mother's. The same thing was happening to Elaina, she noted. The chip she was carrying was actually pushing her hair about as it shifted position, pressing against flesh and bone.

Then the two chips seemed to come together, meeting at an equidistant point at the tops of Elaina's and Alex's skulls where they were pressed together.

Then Alex was screaming. Screaming and screaming and screaming and screaming.

"Dixon!" Donati cried out. "Dixon!"

She swung toward him and saw the giant mechanical monsters burst into the clearing ahead of Raiff's desperate efforts to keep them back.

Raiff backpedaled into the clearing, lashing out higher with his whip in the hope of disabling a whole leg of one of the things. But the machine wrapped a tentacle around the weapon and tore it from his grasp, sending the whip flying.

That left Raiff lobbing nothing more than rocks. Impact either rattled off the machine's iron skin or passed straight through it in one of those momentary losses of structural integrity.

Then, suddenly, the monstrous machines looming over Raiff froze in place, dimming in and out of focus. The electricity faded from the air.

What had happened? Had he won? Was it over?

Raiff had just begun to feel hope when a shrill breeze spun debris in a circle. It seemed the air was being sucked up, his breathing turning labored, when he caught a glimpse of something blazing a trail of destruction through the jungle, toppling trees and kicking up brush in its wake. Raiff saw what looked like a cloud rolling toward him, then discerned the dark, ink-like blotches contained within the cloud that formed a quasi-humanoid appearance which shifted in and out of clarity.

An energy creature, as Dr. Donati had called it, just like the one that had preceded him across the spacebridge eighteen years ago into the facility known as Laboratory Z.

He pulled from his pocket the crude ion fusion weapon he'd fashioned in the Ames lab, holding on to the hope it would work.

Sam couldn't believe what she was seeing and feeling. The air had turned to static, prickling her skin, hitting her with tiny jolts of electricity that felt like frigid pinpricks.

In the reddish hue of light shed by the eclipse, now at its fullest point, the bulge beneath Elaina's scalp had swelled to twice the size it had been just moments before, while Sam could detect no trace of the chip beneath Alex's skin.

As if, as if . . .

As if the chip in Alex's head had somehow fused with his mother's without piercing his skull. She realized his proximity to his mother must have allowed the contents of Alex's chip to be absorbed into his mother's, the way information can be shared between smart phones by bringing them close.

How was this possible, how was *any* of this possible?

It must have been the plan all along, his mother's chip useless without Alex's. Sam felt the air pressure tightening, the world seeming to constrict around her. She wanted so badly to drop the crystal skull, discard it into oblivion. The three chips, three of the four keys, swirled about faster and faster inside it, like a turboprop pro-peller spinning so rapidly that to the naked eye they didn't seem to be spinning at all.

The three chips inside the skull still hadn't joined up.

They were waiting for the fourth.

Sam didn't think it was going to happen, until a red mist sprayed up against her. She retrained her focus downward to see a gash in Elaina's skull beginning to spit globs of blood and bone matter into the air an instant ahead of a sound like a powerful wave smashing against rocks that accompanied the fourth chip hurtling upward.

To be absorbed inside the crystal skull

Raiff drew as close to the creature as his breathing allowed, stop-ping when there was no more air to suck in.

Eighteen years ago, he had activated his fusion device and rushed inside the cloud that contained the creature formed of pure energy. He remembered the feeling of being utterly weightless, the sense of having his insides sucked out, before the darkness swept in and then receded. He'd shook horribly from a cold that permeated him to the core, not unlike being submerged in icy, frigid waters. But then, the thing was gone, turned into harmless matter.

Raiff had no way of knowing if the crude device he had fash-ioned at Ames would work in the same manner or even if it would work at all. If he failed, it was over: for the group behind him in the clearing, as well as this entire planet. His only chance for success lay in repeating exactly what he'd done eighteen years ago.

Under the spill of the blood moon's light, the creature grew in shape and definition. The air gone, Raiff's world in that moment no more than a void. For some reason, he still held his breath as he charged toward the creature, passing through the frigid reaches of the cloud into a center shifting mass that made him think of an eye of a hurricane.

Then he detonated his fusion bomb.

Sam watched it all unfold in a sudden wash of light emanating from inside the crystal skull as the chips formed together, attached by the sinewy, tentacle-like extensions that reminded her of the ones wielded by the machines controlled by the Overlords of Alex's native world.

She understood how these chips had originated now, the physical model on which they'd been based. She looked back down to see the wash of Elaina's blood coating her face, having splattered Alex's with scarlet droplets as well. Elaina writhed in one final, violent motion.

Her body stilled.

The crystal skull continued to glow, then lit up in blinding fashion, sending a host of energy pulses upward in a near-constant stream. Those pulses seemed headed for the blood moon, which was blazing down at the height of the eclipse. The energy pulses shooting out of the skull broke into dozens of beams that flashed in all directions like a Fourth of July fireworks starburst, heading to the twenty-seven sites at light-speed to suck them out of the universe.

The chips inside the crystal skull, the four keys, stopped spinning, stopped hovering, and dropped to the skull's solid bottom as no more than oblong, marble-sized objects.

Raiff regained consciousness, still standing. Exactly where he was standing when he'd detonated the makeshift fusion bomb, which made him realize that the creature was . . .

Gone.

Well, not quite.

The rays of the blood moon illuminated a crystal sphere with spiky extensions rising from it, identical to the one from eighteen years ago, only bigger.

Reluctant to expose his bare skin to it, Raiff removed his jacket and wrapped the sphere inside it and headed back for the clearing.

"I've got a signal!" Donati yelled, satellite phone pressed against his ear. "I've got a signal!"

He had just watched the starbursts shooting into the air, almost certain there were twenty-seven of them. Speeding in blinding fashion toward the underground lairs containing the energy-absorbing monsters that would have ravaged the world. He tried not to again picture how the nuclear weapons just moments away from launching would supercharge those creatures, rendering them indestructible to even the kind of fusion bomb Raiff had used eighteen years ago and again tonight.

The Janus line rang once. A click sounded.

"This is Thomas Donati!" he shouted into the satellite phone. "The alert is over. Repeat, the alert is over. The twenty-seven targets have been destroyed. Abort the launch. Repeat, abort the launch. Mission accomplished."

Another click sounded and then Donati heard a woman's voice he knew only as a bar grid dancing across his computer screen.

"Dr. Donati?"

Alex stirred, his eyes back to normal, slowly regaining his senses.

"Sam," he managed.

She took his hand.

"Sam," he repeated, gaze jittery as if trying to ensure where he was, seeming to fix on Raiff as he limped into the clearing and stopped short at the sight before him, dropping to his knees.

Alex sat up from the table, then tentatively eased himself from it. He started to angle himself to better see Elaina, then stopped. Because there was no need to any further. He'd seen enough to know her final fate and felt as if he had lost her a second time.

But how could you lose something you never had?

Alex felt the tears coming, helpless to ward off the heavy sobs that followed, Sam taking him in her arms like she'd never let him go.

"*Alex . . .*"

A muffled voice in his head.

"*Alex . . .*"

He broke away from Sam and wandered awkwardly to the edge of the jungle, drawn to the voice.

"Alex?" Sam called softly after him.

"Stay with her," Alex said, turning to regard the mother he had never known who had just sacrificed her life for him. "Stay with my mother."

Just inside the tree line, his feet seemed to sink into the ground, the rest of his frame ready to follow, when the voice returned.

"I'm here, Alex, I've come for you."

106

VOICE IN HIS HEAD

"IT'S NOT TOO LATE," Alex heard the voice say to him. *"We can still make this right."*

"Where are you?" Alex cried out in his mind.

"Inside you, where I've always been."

"You're not my father!"

"That's your head talking. Search your heart."

"No!"

"You fear me . . ."

"I hate you!"

"For giving you life?"

Alex looked back toward Elaina's body. "For killing my mother!"

"She killed herself. She knew she was dying, knew she'd grown weak. The same fate that awaits you if you don't come home."

"Where you come from isn't my home—"

"It's where you were born, boy."

"And you're not my father."

"Then how did you defeat me? Why did you not shrink away in fear? Because you knew we were one, parts of the same whole. This world is dying. I can give you a hundred more of them, all the same, all interchangeable."

"My friends, my family, are not interchangeable."

"Then die with them or come with me, boy. The choice is yours."

"Call off the strikes!" Donati blared breathlessly. "We stopped them, do you hear me? We shut all the sites down! *Call off the strikes! Abort!"*

"It's too late," the woman told him. "The missiles have already reached their targets."

"Oh my God . . ."

"Wait, Doctor, they never detonated. They just, well, they just disappeared."

"You think you've won?" Alex heard in his head. *"You think your feeble attempt at resistance will stop us from claiming this world as our own?"*

"I know it's over."

"Only for now, boy. What of the next century, or the century after that? If you truly want to save this world, you'll return with me and stand by my side. Do that and I promise you it will be over. I'll spare the weak-minded you were raised among. I'll teach you how to be strong. I'll teach you how to rule."

"Promise me," Alex said in his head.

"Promise you what?"

"What you just said. That you'll spare this world forever. If I come with you."

"This world is not the only one that's endangered. A force like none the universe has ever seen is coming. And it will destroy us all, if it's not stopped."

"Why should I care?"

"Because both our worlds are facing extinction. And if you want them to survive, you need to come with me."

Her thoughts jumbled and feet heavy, Sam trudged to the edge of the jungle where Alex had wandered. It felt like she was walking in thick mud. The air felt prickly with static, the last glow of the blood moon making the world look red around her.

"Alex?" Sam called out, first tentatively, then shouting. "Alex! . . . Alex!"

Listening to her voice echo in the supercharged air.

"Alex!"

It was no use.

He was gone.

FROM SAMANTHA DIXON'S JOURNAL

WE BURIED ELAINA'S BODY in the dawn light, leaving her remains in the very spot where she had sacrificed herself to save this world and to save Alex. Alex had never known his real mother while she was alive and his disappearance kept him from saying goodbye to her in death.

You want to know what happened next, but I can't tell you; I'm not ready to yet. Just thinking about that moment brings a heaviness to my mind that makes me want to forget.

Even as I know I have to remember, remember it all. Get it all down, so somebody will know the whole of the story and, believe me, there's a lot more to tell.

We thought saving the world, saving him, would be the end of it, but it wasn't. We knew the nightmare was far from over. We were all part of a new reality, embroiled in a war we now knew had been waged for centuries. Having prevented the end of the world under the blood moon had proven we could win, that we need not cower in the face of an all-powerful and determined enemy. Just as we would never quit, though, neither would our enemy and we had to face the undeniable reality that only one of us could survive.

I don't know who you are, or where and when you're reading this. I only know that if it all comes as a shock, you need to beware. You need to be ready. You need to be prepared to see the world differently, since it's nothing like you thought it was.

Above everything else, though, I want you to know there's hope. It lies not just in our minds and our wills, but also in our hearts. Beyond everything else, never forget what it feels like to love, because that love is what will guide you, even as it lends you purpose. Out of everything that happened, I had Alex, and that made it all worthwhile, in spite of all that I had lost.

There's more to this story, lots more. But it hurts too much to put it all down now because of what happened next, where life took us after El Mirador, the rising that followed that of the blood moon.

Us . . .

Alex and me.

As for him, what happened next, well, that's another story . . .

ACKNOWLEDGMENTS

We'd both like to thank our team at Tor, led by Tom Doherty, Linda Quinton, Bob Gleason, and Robert Davis, for their faith, dedication, and patience in bringing this book to fruition. We also had great help from others outside the family, including Natalia Aponte and especially Jeff Ayers, who helped make sense of our ramblings. Finally, we were blessed to have a terrific copy editor in Karen Richardson and a fantastic senior production editor in Jessica Katz. Folks on that side of the business don't often get the credit they deserve, but *Blood Moon* is so much the better because of their input, diligence, and passion.

Quite a bit of time passed between the publication of *The Rising* and *Blood Moon,* and we promise you won't have to wait nearly as long for the next installment in the series. We'd love to tell you more about it, but to repeat this book's final line: That's another story.